QUANTUM LEAP

OBSESSIONS

A NOVEL BY
CAROL DAVIS
BASED ON THE UNIVERSAL TELEVISION SERIES *QUANTUM LEAP*
CREATED BY DONALD P. BELLISARIO

BOULEVARD BOOKS, NEW YORK

Quantum Leap: Obsessions, a novel by Carol Davis, based on the Universal television series QUANTUM LEAP, created by Donald P. Bellisario.

QUANTUM LEAP: OBSESSIONS

A Boulevard Book/published by arrangement with
MCA Publishing Rights, a Division of MCA, Inc.

PRINTING HISTORY
Boulevard edition/March 1997

The Putnam Berkley World Wide Web site address is
http://www.berkley.com/berkley

Make sure to check out *PB Plug*, the science fiction/fantasy newsletter, at
http://www.pbplug.com

ISBN: 1-57297-241-6

BOULEVARD
Boulevard Books are published by The Berkley Publishing Group,
200 Madison Avenue, New York, New York 10016.
BOULEVARD and its logo are trademarks
belonging to Berkley Publishing Corporation.

PRINTED IN THE UNITED STATES OF AMERICA

10 9 8 7 6 5 4 3 2 1

For my dad

QUANTUM LEAP

OBSESSIONS

CHAPTER
ONE

Adrenaline poured through his body.

At that moment, it didn't matter that Samuel John Beckett had a measured IQ of 267, or that he had managed to collect six doctoral degrees in subjects as varied as ancient languages and quantum physics. It didn't matter because the parts of his brain that had helped him earn those degrees, the parts that boosted Sam Beckett light years above the norm, had shut themselves off. The only parts that were working now were primal.

And they were insisting, in a numbing mezzo soprano, *Get your ass out of heeeeeeeeeere!!!*

Unfortunately, Sam Beckett was flat on his back and could move his ass pretty much no place.

He tried to scream, but the only sound that got past his lips was a raw, whispered rasp. The odor of raw meat (*of death,* his mind insisted) surrounded him. He gagged, then coughed, forcing himself not to vomit, trying to find a moment of calm, to stop the thundering of his heart just long enough to *think,* but the primitive part of him would not allow that. The monster was on top of him, had him pinned to the ground, and in less time than he normally took to put on his shoes, it was going to tear his throat open and kill him.

"Help me," he murmured. "Please . . ."

The monster's head dipped toward his. All he could see of it was fangs. Huge, pointed, yellowed fangs. A trail of slime oozed out past them and dripped onto his chin.

Helllllppp m . . .

But help wasn't coming. He knew that. Not from Al, not from God, Time, or Whoever, and not from any sudden burst of his own ingenuity. The only thing that would save his life was the same thing that had saved it dozens of times before: listening to his gut. To the voice that was still shrieking *Move your asssssssss!!!!*

So he listened. He forced his chilled, limp arms and legs to move. Somehow, he scrambled out from underneath the monster and scuttled away.

Go!!! Go!!! There . . . more . . . keep going . . .

It would follow him, he was sure. Those thick yellow fangs would sink deep into his flesh and tear him to pieces. A long-buried memory hinted at what the pain would feel like, and he gasped.

But maybe, *maybe,* he could fight it off long enough to . . .

The solid ground underneath his hands and knees was suddenly not there any longer. His body finally let go of the scream that had been trapped inside him, and the sound echoed through his head as he plunged down, still scrambling, into ice-cold water. Taken completely by surprise, he had no time to close his mouth before he began to sink. His lungs protested receiving water instead of air and spewed it back out. Each time he coughed he sucked in more liquid.

I'm going to die. I'm going to drown. But I'm here to do something! What's this going to put right? Who . . .

When he broke the surface, he screamed one more time, then dissolved into a fit of choking. His arms and legs wanted to flail, to search out something for him to grab; the rest of him was more than willing to simply go on panicking. But years ago, in between doctorates, he

2

had studied a series of Oriental mental disciplines that reminded him now how to relax and tread water.

Just calm down. Calm down! Then you can swim back to . . . whatever you fell off of.

But what if it's still there?

What if it can swim???

He ignored that idea and concentrated on moving his arms and legs, slowly, rhythmically—which was really all he could have done, because they were rapidly growing numb with cold. When he was finally close to breathing normally, he flipped his head backward to toss his dripping hair out of his eyes. Now he could look back. See the thing that intended to kill him. See if it was waiting for him.

It was.

The beast watched him, its eyes never leaving his face. As he paddled toward it, fighting the rubbery lack of control that the fight-or-flight instinct had inflicted on him, he stopped being terrified and began to feel incredibly, award-winningly stupid.

The monster was an enormous, furry black dog, standing sentinel at the end of a small, private boat dock.

"Dog food," Sam cursed. "Raw meat? You smelled *dog* food. For crying out loud."

Muttering under his breath, he hauled himself up the three-step ladder onto the dock and stood frozen and soaked, streaming water onto its weather-beaten planks, a couple of yards from the thing that had threatened his life. The canine continued to study him. Its jaws *were* huge (matching the rest of it), but it no longer seemed dangerous. In fact, right now it just seemed . . . confused.

"Wurf?" it inquired.

"What are *you* staring at?" Sam demanded.

The dog blinked at him.

"I suppose you think this is pretty funny," Sam said. "Well, it's not. Whoever it is that drops me into these things? Their timing stinks."

3

A breeze that under other circumstances would have felt crisp and pleasant drifted over the dock, making him shudder. Renewing his mumbled complaints, he stuffed his hands into his armpits and began to look around, hoping his host had left behind a jacket he could use to warm himself. There wasn't any clothing nearby, but the single boat tied to the side of the dock was tightly covered with a canvas tarp. He could pull the tarp free in a minute or two, he decided. But then what? Stand here wrapped up in bright green canvas when his host undoubtedly lived nearby and had a closet full of warm, dry clothes?

A glance down told him that the dog had started to circle him, sniffing curiously at his ankles. "Yeah, yeah," he complained. "You could make yourself useful, you know, and tell me where I live."

The dog raised an eyebrow but said nothing.

"You owe me one, Fido," Sam told it. "You're the reason I'm freezing my butt off out here. How about it? Which one of those houses is—"

"I know, I know!" a voice bellowed behind him.

Sam spun toward the sound, lost his footing on the slippery surface of the dock, and began to pinwheel his arms frantically. He and the dog howled in chorus. An instant before he would have flopped into the icy water a second time, he flung his arms around one of the pilings that supported the dock, crunching his left knee and right shoulder into the wood. The pain brought his voice to a crescendo, forming a single word: "Shiiiiiiiiiittttt!"

He clung to the piling until his heart stopped banging inside his chest. As he slumped into a soggy, bone-chilled heap, Al Calavicci inquired mildly, "No 'oh boy'?"

"This is *not* funny," Sam snapped.

"Didn't say it was," Al replied. "Are you okay?"

"No," Sam said. "I'm not. Do I look okay to you?"

"You look kinda wet. It's November, Sam. What're you doing swimming in November? And in your clothes? You oughta go get changed before you get pneumonia.

4

Right, boy? See, the poochie here agrees with me.''

Still furious, Sam pulled himself to his feet. '' 'The poochie here' is the reason I fell in.''

''Playing around?''

''I thought . . . Never mind.''

The terse tone in Sam's voice might or might not have bothered his partner. Either way, Al broke into a ridiculously broad smile, crouched down and extended a holographic hand to the dog. ''Hi there, boy,'' he greeted the animal. ''Don't mind him. He's not grouchy like this all the time.''

''I am not . . . ,'' Sam sputtered.

''His name's Rufus,'' Al said.

''You know that? What else do you know? Ziggy's figured out why I'm here? That would be a first.''

Al's hand moved toward Sam, cutting off the scientist's rapid-fire commentary. ''We don't know anything yet. It says 'Rufus' on his tag.'' Ignoring Sam's scowl, he pointed to the ID plate attached to the dog's collar, then straightened up. ''But relax. We've got your name and address. The guy you Leaped into settled down pretty fast—he's talking to Beeks right now. Your house is Twelve Maple Lane.'' He tipped his head to indicate something behind Sam. ''One of those, I guess.''

Sam didn't linger to hear anything more Al might have wanted to say; he was already striding up the dirt path that led away from the dock, leaving a trail of sneaker-shaped puddles in his wake. With Al and Rufus bringing up the rear, after a couple of minutes of searching he located a cottage with an embossed brass sign alongside the front door announcing that it was Twelve Maple Lane. His hands dipped into the pockets of his sodden jeans and came up empty. ''No keys?'' he fussed.

''Try the door,'' Al suggested.

He expected it to be locked, and was prepared to issue another gripe. Instead, the knob turned easily in his grasp and the door swung open. This seemed to thrill Rufus,

5

who let out a yelp that sounded uncannily like "Hi!" Frowning at him, Sam moved inside the house, peeling off his host's sweatshirt as he walked.

"Hey," Al called after him. "Who'd you want to close the door, me or the dog?"

With the dripping sweatshirt dangling from one hand, Sam reluctantly returned to the door, paused long enough for Rufus and the Observer to enter, then pushed it closed and locked it. Hologram and canine followed him into the cottage's only bedroom and stood waiting as he changed into dry clothes. The wet ones—sweatshirt, T-shirt, jeans, underwear, socks and sneakers—were dumped into the bathtub.

"Now," he told Al as the three of them paraded out of the bedroom, "tell me something that's really going to impress me."

"Your name is Clarence," Al replied readily.

"Clarence."

"Yup."

"And?"

"And what?"

Sam sighed loudly and sank into what looked like the most comfortable chair in Clarence's living room. It *was* soft, and well broken in; he'd been nestled in its cushions for only a minute when it began to invite him to doze off. A sudden warmth at his knee made him open his eyes. Rufus had rested his head there and was peering benignly at the stranger in his master's seat.

"I think he likes you, Sam," Al commented.

"That's a blessing," Sam murmured. "I thought he was going to tear me to shreds."

"This dog? This is not a mean dog, Sam."

"No kidding."

"And you thought he was gonna . . . ?"

"I Leaped in," Sam said, trying not very successfully to cover his chagrin with impatience, "and this *thing* was on top of me. There were fangs inches away from my

6

face. I overreacted, okay? I'm entitled to overreact once in a while.''

"Well . . .''

"Well what?'' Sam shot back. The Observer was studying him oddly, and it occurred to him that that had probably been going on for several minutes, maybe longer. "What are you looking at? What's the matter?''

"Nothing.''

"Al.''

Al shrugged, then wobbled his head. "You kinda had Ziggy freaked out. Your vital signs shot right off the map. She thought you were gonna have a stroke.'' His gaze drifted around the room several times before returning to Sam. "I guess you're right,'' he said without conviction. "Everybody's entitled to a case of the flaming heebie-jeebies once in a while, especially when they get dumped in the middle of . . .'' He cut himself off, then continued cheerfully, "But look, Sam—I bet this dog loves kids. Don't you, boy? This is a big, happy dog,'' he announced, studying the trail of thick, sticky drool running out of the corner of Rufus's mouth. "This is . . . a *big* dog.''

Sam closed his eyes again. "He's a Newfie.''

"A who?''

"A Newfoundland. Professor LoNigro had two of them. They're very friendly, gentle dogs. Which is about the only plus side to this day so far. He's probably wondering what the hell happened to his master. Which is a question I share with him.''

"We're working on it.''

As if it had been cued, the handlink warbled loudly. Al and Rufus both perked to attention, while Sam chose to go on resting with his arms clamped over his chest. The little device chirped as Al tapped its keys, a tune Rufus answered with a series of soft woofs.

"Okay,'' the Observer announced when the link had fallen silent. "This is a start, I guess.'' He paused, but

7

Sam didn't pick up the ball. "It's November 11, 1983. You're in Edwards Lake, New York. Your name is Clarence Joseph Williams—that's some handle, huh? Must've named him for his grandfather or something. Says here he goes by 'C.J.' Anyway. You're twenty-nine years old, and you work as a caretaker for the houses here. Inherited the job and *this* house from your old man, who moved to a condo in Florida a couple years ago. You're single, you're a free—What?" A thump of the heel of Al's hand against the link brought a screech of protest and more information. "Oh. You're a freelance writer. You pull in a few extra bucks writing mystery stories for magazines. With the emphasis on 'few.' "

"And what am I here to do?" Sam prompted.

"Don't know."

"Now, there's a surprise."

The Observer waggled the handlink at his partner and chided him: "It ain't that easy, Sam. You know how Ziggy is—she's always gotta check the variables to make sure she's not missing anything. Sure, we could pick something right away so I could pop in here and give you an answer, but it might be the wrong thing! You wouldn't want to waste a lot of time working on the wrong thing, would you? That wouldn't accomplish squat. So just take it easy. Relax. This is a nice cozy little house. Take a nap."

"A nap," Sam echoed.

"Yeah. You know. Like the little kids do." Al pressed his hands together, tipped his head against them, and let go of a loud, buzzing snore. "A nap."

"And what if the thing I'm supposed to fix happens while I'm asleep?"

"It won't."

"You know that for sure?"

"Well . . . yeah."

"Why don't I believe you?"

Al buried the link in the right-hand pocket of his red-

8

white-and-blue leather bomber jacket and pretended to be mortally offended. "That hurts, kid," he replied. "What would be the point in you Leaping in here, or anyplace else, if you were cutting Z's instead of doing what you were supposed to do?"

"I don't know," Sam said.

"See?"

"But I do seem to remember several occasions when I woke up to the sound of you screaming in my ear. 'Sam! Sam! You gotta wake up, Sam!!' What was that? Your version of reveille?"

"Okay," Al conceded. "But I woke you up, right?"

"Yes."

"And I'll wake you up again. So don't worry about it. You won't sleep through the important stuff." Al shot another glance around the room, nodding his approval of C.J. Williams's casual furnishings: overstuffed chairs and matching couch, braided rugs topping hardwood floors, brass lamps—everything in shades of green and brown. "Look, he's got the fireplace all ready to go. Why don't you light a fire? You look like you're still cold." Wandering into the kitchen, he continued over his shoulder, "Fix up some soup. A guy like this, I bet he survives on canned soup and sandwiches. Have some lunch and take a nap. Me and Ziggy, we'll work on this and figure out what you have to do." The handlink beeped again, and he hauled it out to investigate. "Ziggy agrees," he said, waving the device at Sam. "She says you should do what C.J. would be doing if he was here."

"Which is?" Sam asked.

"Caretake. You know, rake some leaves or something."

"Rake leaves."

Al bobbed his head enthusiastically. "Yeah! Clean the place up. Nobody's here. These are summer houses. You're supposed to keep things neat and tidy when the owners aren't here. Wash some windows. Looks like the

9

wind really kicked up last night—I saw a couple chairs blown over outside that blue house over there.'' He pointed to a structure barely visible through the window beside the front door. He was about to continue when another beep made him glance at the handlink one more time. ''Ziggy says C.J.'s cranking out a hot mystery novel. Got tired of the short stories, I guess. She says maybe you could do a chapter or two.''

''I'm not a writer, Al,'' Sam protested.

''Yeah, well, neither are a lot of other people. The point is . . . do whatever you want, and we'll get you the details as soon as we can.''

Rufus seconded that with a cheerful bark. Sam had little choice but to cave in to the persuasion of his best friend and C.J.'s; after a minute of trying to maintain the skeptical frown he'd been wearing, he sighed quietly and nodded. ''I'll find something to do,'' he promised Al. ''But tell Ziggy to hurry, would you? It makes me nervous to just sit and wait. I keep thinking I'm missing something important.''

Al nodded readily. ''We'll hurry.''

''Thanks.''

''No problem. I'll be back as soon as we find anything.''

Sam got up then, aiming for the coat closet to find himself a jacket or another sweatshirt to top off the plaid flannel shirt he'd pulled on. Rufus trotted along beside him, apparently reluctant to let Sam out of his sight. ''Okay, Rufe,'' Sam told him. ''We'll go find something to 'caretake.' And hope we don't have to do it for too long.'' The dog concurred by flailing his tail from side to side. Sam smiled at that, then stuck his head into the closet.

He neither saw nor heard the enormous sigh of relief that Al heaved as he left the Imaging Chamber.

CHAPTER
TWO

"Oooohhhhh boy."

Albert Anthony Calavicci, Rear Admiral, United States Navy, leaned against the wall of the narrow passageway that led out of the Imaging Chamber of Project Quantum Leap and rested his face in the palms of his hands. For good measure, he said the words again—the ones he knew Sam had spoken so many times that they had turned into a sort of mantra for each new Leap. Maybe that small habit was a comfort to Sam. Had to be; Al couldn't think of any other explanation for indulging in it. There'd been a lot of Leap-ins that, to Al's mind, called for a long, emotional stream of profanity—but Sam, instead, had greeted them with "Oh boy."

Yeah, maybe that was it. "Oh boy" was like getting up at the same time each morning. Or having the same thing for lunch. Or going to the same office and sitting at the same desk to perform the same monotonous tasks. It was a bit of routine meant to help Sam survive a life in which everything else had stopped being familiar.

Albert Anthony Calavicci, the man in charge of Project Quantum Leap until Sam Beckett came home, doubted that anything as simple as an "oh boy" would help *him* right now.

But it was worth a try.

"Ooohhh . . ."

"Admiral?"

Al opened his eyes. Seven not-happy faces were looking at him, which was exactly what he'd expected, because those same seven faces had been not-happy when he left them twenty minutes ago. Busby Berkeley wasn't running this show, he mused, but it would have been nice, now and then, to come out of the Imaging Chamber into a little singing and dancing. A little cheering and shouting and backslapping. Champagne. Noisemakers. Loud music. Confetti. A little . . . hoopla.

Al hadn't seen any hoopla around here since the day they'd found out Sam Beckett *hadn't* killed himself by stepping into the Accelerator.

He stopped walking at the foot of the ramp that led out of the Chamber. His audience didn't move. He took another step, but none of them twitched a hair.

He couldn't blame them for looking glum; their expressions mirrored his own. Sam's beginning a brand-new Leap hadn't changed a thing. The past was over and done with, whether Sam revised it or not. It was the here and now that had rolled Al's guts into a knot: the here and now had begun to reek big-time. In Al Calavicci's life, that was not exactly a novelty. Life had backed up, flipped down its tailgate and dumped a load of wet, stinking garbage on his doorstep plenty of times. But crap was still crap, Al thought, whether it happened to be your first truckload or your hundred and fifth. Previous experience did not make the event any more tolerable.

For lack of a better option, he painted his features with a gentle, bland, Mona Lisa–ish smile. That ought to be enough to convince the not-happy faces that all was right with the world (and with Sam), so they'd let him walk on out of here without questioning him.

Sure, he thought. *And the sun is gonna pop up in the west tomorrow morning.*

Maybe, at least, one of them would smile back. Experimentally he widened his own smile, as if he were dealing with small children, or monkeys. Not one of the people surrounding him had an IQ less than 150, but geniuses could be swayed.

Geniuses could be fooled.

Geniuses could be . . . a pain in the butt.

None of them smiled.

"Al?" Donna said quietly. Out of the seven not-happys, her face was the most filled with gloom. That happened a lot: every time Ziggy let slip that Sam was in trouble. Would've been nice, Al mused, if any of *his* wives had gotten this percolated when *his* butt was dangling over the fire.

"He's fine," Al told her.

"His vital signs were in the red zone," she reminded him.

"He took an unscheduled dip in the lake. He's p.o.'ed." Al cracked another Mona Lisa that no one matched. "Said 'shit' instead of 'oh boy.' But he'll get over it. He always gets over it, after he peels himself down off the ceiling. He's fine."

"Are you sure?"

Rather than respond to what he had always thought was the world's most useless question, Al took a few more steps and turned the handlink over to Gooshie, the not-happy face currently in charge of Ziggy's main console. The programmer closed his fingers over the link, then opened them again and stared blankly at it, as if he had never seen it before. "Are you going to tell him, Admiral?" he ventured. "Dr. Beckett, I mean? I noticed that your conversation didn't include any mention of our . . . ummm . . . situation."

"Of course I'm not going to tell him!" Al sputtered. "What are you, loopy?"

"Well," Gooshie said, "no."

There was a gap in between Donna and the techie with

13

the red hair—a girl Al had decided could not possibly be more than fourteen years old and who seemed to try to hand him a blue acrylic clipboard stuffed with paperwork about every eight minutes, all day long. She wanted him to sign off on something, he supposed, but he never wanted to autograph her papers, or even find out what they were. (Which was a perfectly justifiable attitude, he told himself—paperwork wasn't his job, it was Donna's.) The only thing he *had* bothered to find out was the redhead's name, which according to her ID badge was Toolie Gibson. That made no sense to him: the name on the badge was supposed to be her legal one, and who in the world would christen a baby girl Toolie?

"Tell him . . . ," he muttered. "Tell him?? Jeez Louise."

"Then we *are* going to take care of this ourselves."

That would be Beeks. Al didn't look at her. He was too busy calculating how many steps would take him through the gap between Donna Alessi-Beckett and Toolie Gibson, out the Control Room door and into the silence and solitude of the corridor.

"Al?" Verbena Beeks prompted.

"You got a better suggestion?" Al shot back.

"Not at the moment."

Al grunted at the psychiatrist, which made Toolie Gibson flinch. Almost everything Al did made Toolie Gibson flinch; she was terrified of him. When he began to barrel through the gap, Toolie jerked herself out of his flight path and barely escaped doing a backward flip over a castered chair.

He made it almost two-thirds of the way to the elevator before he heard high-heeled shoes clattering down the passageway after him. He didn't slow down, but he did listen more carefully. Yup, Donna was following Beeks. In sneakers. She didn't bother with heels much, now that Sam wasn't around.

"This isn't something we ought to treat lightly,"

14

Beeks announced a second before the elevator doors opened.

Al turned around and peered at her. "Who said I was treating it lightly? If I remember right, Beeksie, I'm the one who told *you* there was a problem."

"You keep trying to avoid . . ."

"I keep trying to find a little peace and quiet so I can think!"

Beeks folded her arms over her lab-coated chest and tapped the toe of one high-heeled shoe against the floor. When Al fled into the elevator car, she followed him, with Donna two steps behind. The two women bookended him, and, in complete disregard of elevator etiquette, neither of them took her eyes off him. That made him want to flinch, just like Toolie Gibson.

"We'll figure this out together," Beeks told him. "It isn't something you need to solve on your own. I assume that's why you came to me in the first place."

"And it's really more my problem than yours, Al," Donna put in.

"It's *Sam's* problem," Al blurted.

"Sam's not here," the two women said in unison.

"That's a good trick," Al grumbled. "But I don't think I need an encore. I just want to go to my office for a few minutes and think."

"We need to talk this over," Beeks insisted.

"No," Al said. "We don't need to talk this over. Maybe I'm not saying it plain enough. I'm going to go into my office—I'm going to go into the *can* in my office—and think. Okay?" When the elevator softly chimed their arrival on Level Eight, he moved close to the doors and stepped through the instant they opened. He allowed the women to follow him as far as the locked entrance to his office, then put up a hand, palm out, to halt them. "Listen," he said firmly. "I know between the two of you, you know more fancy stuff than anybody Ed Sullivan ever brought out on a stage. But you can't

15

tell me you know how to help me 'think.' Now, go away, would you? If you want to confer, we'll do it in half an hour.''

Beeks looked down at her watch. "Half an hour."

"Yeah, Beeksie, half an hour. Thirty minutes. In the blue conference room.''

Without any further prompting, Verbena Beeks walked away, aiming for the elevator. Al and Donna watched her retreat; then Donna turned to the Project Observer and said softly, "This came out of nowhere, Al.''

"I know it did, honey,'' he replied. "Don't worry. We'll figure it out.''

"I hope so,'' Donna said.

He kept his promise and sat at the head of the conference table exactly twenty-nine minutes later. He'd spent eight of those minutes "thinking,'' and the rest of them thinking. The former had made him feel a little better. The latter made him feel a lot worse.

Donna came in carrying a plastic bottle of filtered water, half of which she swigged down immediately after she sank into a chair. He remembered himself swilling booze almost that fast and was glad that Donna's beverage of choice was H_2O. After she'd hydrated herself, she finally smiled at him. It was, Al thought, the kind of look you'd give somebody at a funeral.

"Does anybody else know what's happening?'' Beeks asked when she joined them.

"I don't know,'' Al replied. "How many people have you told?''

The door clicked shut, sealing them inside the conference room, as Verbena took a seat opposite Gooshie. "I haven't told anyone,'' she said.

"Nobody else at the Project knows what's going on?''

Three heads shook.

"Everybody in Control knows there's a 'situation,' '' Verbena offered, glancing at Gooshie, "which means that by dinnertime, everybody in the complex will have heard. But if I had a dollar for every time these people have heard there was a 'situation' in progress around here, I could buy my own island. They won't ask. And they won't dig.''

Al dismissed that with a nod. ''Do we have any idea how many people on the outside got a letter?''

''Worst case, anybody who's ever known Sam,'' Donna said softly.

The Observer shut his eyes for a moment. The big oak-veneer table had seats for a dozen people, but only four of its padded swivel chairs were occupied, one on each side, like the points of a compass: himself, Donna, Verbena, Gooshie. People Sam Beckett had handpicked to help him bring his Project to life. People he wanted at his side. Now *they* were here, and Sam wasn't, a situation that hadn't been in any of Sam's blueprints. He was only supposed to be gone for a couple of hours, maybe a day or two. Not . . . years.

In Al's original picture of this Project, Sam wasn't supposed to be gone at all.

Not right . . . dammit, it just ain't right.

His eyes came open again, and landed on 'Bena's black silk dress. It was a pretty thing, liberally shot through with thick gold threads. A shirt like that would look great with his gold jacket. Or a vest . . . *yeah! Black shirt, gold jacket. Tina would love it.*

He desperately wanted to talk about black silk. Or cars. Or the odds on the heavyweight title match coming up in Vegas next week. Hell, he'd even let Donna tell him about quarks.

But that wouldn't get rid of the crap.

It wouldn't even make it stop stinking.

''All right,'' he said finally. ''Let's just lay this out, one piece at a time. Who do we *know* they've contacted?''

Donna ticked the answer off on her fingers. ''Sam's

17

mother. His sister and brother-in-law. His brother and sister-in-law. His friend Sibby in Elk Ridge. Professor LoNigro. Stu Linderman. Paula Burke. Abby Howell. Peter Lin. And the four of us.'' She lost some steam with each name. When she stopped speaking, she put both hands on her plastic water bottle and stared fixedly at it. ''There are more. I'm sure there're more. Those are just the people who got through to me. Thinking that Sam would be with me.''

''He's with you,'' Verbena said.

''You're not that metaphysical, Bee,'' Donna told her. ''Don't say that kind of stuff. Don't . . . don't pat me on the head, all right?''

''Want a hug?'' Verbena offered mildly.

Donna sighed and rolled her eyes. Then she slouched back into the soft cushions of her chair, listening to it squeak as its back flexed under her weight. ''Yes,'' she said. ''From my husband. I want my husband, right here, in this room, to tell us how we ought to deal with this problem.''

''Although,'' Verbena pointed out, ''if Sam were here, we wouldn't have a problem. When someone called looking for Sam, you'd just have to put him on the phone and let *him* answer their questions.''

''But Sam's not here.''

''So what do we do?''

''We could let it blow over,'' Gooshie suggested. ''Like when that reporter from *Time* tried to get in touch with him a couple of years ago. Remember? He wanted to talk about the fifth anniversary of Dr. Beckett's winning the Nobel Prize. He gave up after a while. He said it was Dr. Beckett's loss, not wanting to be featured in *Time* again.'' Although Al didn't say anything, Gooshie's attention was slowly pulled in the admiral's direction. ''This isn't going to blow over, is it?'' he asked.

Al shook his head. ''That's not where my money is.''

''Money . . . ,'' Gooshie ventured, paused, then offered

18

lightly, "Maybe he wants to tell Dr. Beckett that he won a hundred million dollars in one of those big sweepstakes."

"Is that what you think?" Al countered.

"I don't know."

With the others watching him closely, as if they thought he was David Copperfield and was about to make the conference table vanish in a puff of smoke, Gooshie took out of his lab coat pocket and flattened out on the tabletop the letter he'd received that morning—a letter identical to the ones that had been sent to Verbena, to Al and to Donna Alessi-Beckett. It was badly wrinkled, as if he had crumpled it up, intending to throw it away. The letterhead, in dark blue ink, said "LOVETZ AND BOYLE ATTORNEYS AT LAW." At the bottom was the scrawled signature of one Mitchell P. Lovetz, Esq. The space in between read:

Dear Dr. Gushman:

This firm has been attempting to locate Dr. Samuel Beckett in order to discuss a legal matter of some urgency. We understand that you may have knowledge of Dr. Beckett's present whereabouts. If so, please contact this office immediately by phone, fax or mail with that information.

Thank you in advance for your kind cooperation.

Very truly yours,

" 'A legal matter of some urgency,' " Gooshie read. "That always means money. Maybe Dr. Beckett inherited some. Or he never paid back a loan? There's got to be a lot of money involved in this somewhere."

"Doesn't matter," Al said.

Donna earnestly nodded her agreement. "What matters is that all these people Mr. Lovetz has sent letters to are looking for Sam now. Calling. Or writing. None of them have gotten in touch with Lovetz to tell him where they think Sam is—they want Sam to do that. And nobody's really worried about him being in any kind of serious legal trouble—not Sam Beckett." She smiled wryly, an expression that faded after a few seconds. "But they *are* all giving me the same speech. 'How's Sam? Gosh, I haven't heard from him in a long time. Can I talk to him? I just got an idea for a paper I'd like to get his thoughts on. I want to see him. I want him to see my kids.' They all want the same thing. Including Sam's family, who haven't been happy since Day One about his dropping off the face of the earth. Ignoring them for the sake of his work. And I don't blame them. I don't blame them a bit."

"Maybe we ought to just call Mr. Mitchell P. Lovetz E-S-Q and ask him straight out what he wants," Verbena said.

After a long look at the letter Gooshie had put on display, Donna told her, "I did call him. He wasn't there, and his secretary wouldn't tell me anything."

"But you're Sam's wife."

"She said Lovetz would call me back."

"He didn't?"

"Not yet."

"Maybe it's a scam," Gooshie put in. "Maybe he doesn't really want to find Dr. Beckett."

"Yeah?" Al countered. "Then what's he want?"

"Just what he's doing. To make other people curious. And upset. And angry. Maybe he has some grudge against Dr. Beckett."

"If that's true," Verbena said as she placed her letter alongside Gooshie's on the tabletop, "then we need to find out, before he *does* make anybody angry."

The four people Sam Beckett had handpicked to help him turn his dream into a reality—and to share his life— stared at one another for a long while. Small sounds accompanied their lack of action: the drumming of a pencil on the tabletop, the creak of a chair. Throat clearing. The shifting of arms and legs. Outside this room, though, the complex was filled with activity, as it had been during every moment of the last four years. Even during "down-time," those periods when Sam was in between Leaps, hundreds of hours of work was being done, all aimed toward one goal: retrieving the man whose family thought he had abandoned them.

The man whose friends were puzzled by his lack of attention toward them. For four years he had let birthdays go by, and Christmases, the births of new babies, the death of a parent, promotions, awards. There was no criticism in the tone of their voices or their letters, just puzzlement.

Sam had always cared about them, but he did not seem to care any longer.

"I don't know what to tell any of those people," Donna murmured. "I'm tired of making excuses for Sam's absence. I'm tired of lying."

"We'll find out what this bozo wants," Al said firmly. "And put him out of the pen-pal business."

"What if it's not that easy?" Verbena asked.

The admiral's head moved very slightly, turning in the psychiatrist's direction. He smiled for a second, not any more genuinely amused than Donna had been a few minutes ago. "D'you forget who you're talking to?"

"Not for a moment," Beeks replied.

"Gooshie's right," Al said, though admitting that the nervous little programmer could be correct about anything other than the intricacies of artificial intelligence gave him stomach cramps. "There's money mixed up in this somewhere. But I don't think the shyster wants to give it to anybody. I think it's waiting for him at the end of the rainbow." He hadn't finished speaking when he noticed Verbena gazing steadily at him. "What?" he growled.

"Why do you think he's a 'shyster'?" she asked.

"Because they're all shysters."

21

"I was married to an attorney, Admiral Calavicci."

"Yeah," Al said. "But you're not married to him now." He paused, expecting Beeks to press her point and feeling a pinch of annoyance when she didn't. "They're all shysters. If he wanted something legit, he'd say so. Tell me you disagree with me."

She didn't.

"See?" Al went on. "He's fishing around, writing all these love notes to people." His index finger jabbed out, pointing at the twin sheets of paper that lay a few inches beyond his reach. "Those got forwarded here from old addresses, right?" After the others had nodded, he continued, "This guy not only doesn't know where Sam is, he doesn't know where any of *us* is. He wrote to us, and to LoNigro and Stu and Paula, because . . . what? We used to work with Sam." His face began to droop into a scowl. "Gooshie's right," he said again. "This guy Lovetz wants to do just what he's doing. He wants to *tweak* people."

"But what for?" Verbena pressed.

"I don't know."

"Something important."

"Of course, something important!" Al barked. "He's not sending Valentines. He's tweaking. And sooner or later, somebody's gonna sing the song he wants to hear. He's gonna make the wrong person unhappy that they haven't seen Sam's bright and shining face in way too long."

Gooshie grimaced. "Like that reporter from *Time*?"

"Like any reporter from anywhere. The *Podunk News*."

"But how would he get money from . . ."

The Observer pushed his face toward Gooshie's, eyes wide, nostrils flared. He looked very much like a bull about to charge, and he knew Gooshie would realize that. "The money doesn't matter," he said between his teeth.

22

"It. Doesn't. Matter. Do you know what 'top secret' means?"

"Well," Gooshie said, "yes."

"It means," Al told him anyway, "that there is no answer to the question 'Where is Sam Beckett?' Not just for the press. For anybody. There is no answer. None. There's not even supposed to be anybody asking the question."

"I know that."

"You don't get it, do you?"

"I . . . ," Gooshie said, then stopped.

Albert Calavicci had been involved with the military longer than any of the people surrounding him had been alive. He looked at each of them in turn, then stared for a long moment at the letters in the center of the table. "This is a top secret project," he said softly.

"Well, sure, Al."

Al's gaze shot across the table and locked with Gooshie's. Neither of them took a breath for several seconds. Then Al relaxed back into his chair and pulled air in over his lower lip. "You don't want to get it," he murmured. "You don't want to be in that kind of a position."

"We're civilians, Al," Donna said.

Her husband's partner shook his head. "Doesn't make any difference."

"What if he . . . ," Gooshie began.

"What?" Al questioned.

Gooshie shook his head.

"Finish it," Al told him sharply.

"What if he . . . well, what if he already knows about the Project? What if he's trying to find Dr. Beckett as a way of locating the Project?"

"You don't even wanna think that," Al muttered.

"So you're going to call Lovetz and get rid of him," Verbena said quickly, hoping to soothe the tension that was still roiling out of the Observer and threatening to swallow up the people who sat looking at him.

Al's eyebrows shot up toward his hairline. "Judas on a pony, Beeks, haven't I got enough to do?"

"You just said . . ."

"You're the head doctor. *You* call him."

"And tell him what?"

The wheels on Al's chair squealed when he pushed it back. He sprang to his feet like a jack-in-the-box being turned loose, a move that had made a lot of ensigns regret what they'd just said. "What's the secretary's name?" he demanded of Donna.

Donna, who had known Al long enough not to be frightened by anything he did, thought for a moment, then told him, "Vannette."

"Are you sure?"

"I'm sure."

Al vanished. The others watched the pair of letters, stirred up by his departure, settle gently back down to the tabletop; then Gooshie turned to Verbena Beeks. The programmer was trying very hard to smile and was not succeeding. "You knew before you came in here that he was going to handle this, didn't you?" he asked tremulously.

"Of course," Verbena told him. "And he knew it too."

"What did he mean? All that stuff about the Project being top secret, and . . ."

"I don't think we want to know," Verbena replied.

Mitchell P. Lovetz's secretary was indeed named Vannette. Her last name was Tyler, she was thirty-two years old, stood five-foot-three and tipped the scales at 102 pounds. Her nearsightedness was corrected by blue contact lenses, and her naturally brown hair was tinted Sun Kissed Blonde by a product that had been recommended to her (via a TV commercial) by actress Cybill Shepherd. She was unmarried but "semi-seriously involved" with a furniture salesman named Carl.

24

Al had all that information tossed at him within ten minutes after Vannette greeted him with a chipper and slightly nasal "Good aftanoon, law awfices!" Vannette, he could tell, had never been purred at over the phone, which was a fact he had counted on as his right index finger punched out 702-555-8811. A soft laugh (something his fourth wife had referred to as his "give it to me, baby" laugh) coaxed even more information out of the willing Ms. Tyler, at a speed that made him think they were playing a round of "Beat the Clock." She loved living and working in Virginia (had been born in New Jersey), cats, small children, Italian food, romantic movies and the exhibit of the first ladies' gowns at the Smithsonian. She did not love her boss, Mitchell Paul Lovetz, Esquire, who had a bad habit of not showing up at the office.

No, Mitch was not in the office now. No, she had no clue when he would be back. Nor did she have any clue where he was—out of town, she thought. She hadn't seen hide nor hair of him for almost two weeks.

"So you couldn't get a message to him?" Al inquired.

"Welllll . . . no," Vannette confessed. "See, I did make some plane reservations. But that's all. He did the rest himself. Hotels and stuff."

"Oh."

Vannette sighed heavily.

Al paused. When Tina made that noise, it meant someone (thankfully, someone other than himself) had done something wildly stupid. That noise called for a hug. "Whatsamatter?" he asked her gently, carefully omitting the "sweetie pie" he normally added.

"Ohhhhh," she sighed, "it's . . ." Another sigh. "Ya know." And another.

Al began to line up pencils on his desk blotter.

"He's not alone, I don't think," Vannette blurted.

"Oh?"

"I think he's with Joey's girlfriend. Ya know—his

partner, Joey. Boyle.'' An unspoken *There, I said it* came after that. Al waited: she'd say more, now that the dam had been broken. Sure enough, after one last sigh, the words came rushing after one another like cattle in a stampede. ''Joey doesn't know, I don't think. Maybe that's why Mitch made reservations to all those weird places. Boring, you know? Like Boston. If you were gonna go . . . you know . . . with somebody, would you take her to Boston?''

Al answered after a second, ''I never have.''

A moment of silence told him Vannette was organizing the myriad implications of that statement. Finally she giggled nervously, then said, ''And if they were gonna . . . you know, I don't see why they'd have to go to five different places.''

''Variety?'' Al suggested.

''Or they didn't want Joey to figure it out.''

''Maybe.''

''Joey'll kill him.''

After another pause, Al tossed off, ''When they get back from Boston.''

''Oh, no, they went to Boston first.''

''So . . .'' Al kept his tone light and casual, as if he had no vested interest in this conversation. He was enormously grateful that Vannette couldn't see his face. ''Then he'll want to wait till he gets back to talk about the letter he sent me.''

''Yeah,'' Vannette said. ''I would think.''

''You know about the letters.''

Of course she did; she had typed and mailed them. Yes, she remembered speaking to Donna Alessi, and had the message slip in front of her. And yes, Mitch had a file on Dr. Samuel Beckett, accordion-style with an elastic cord. But, jeez, you know, it wasn't on the shelf, so she couldn't look anything up right now. If she had to guess, she'd say it was at Mitch's apartment, where it was doing nobody any good.

26

"I was just wondering," Al crooned.

"He's some guy, huh?" Vannette commented. "This Beckett guy. He won the Pulitzer Prize."

"Nobel."

"Huh?" said Vannette.

"Dr. Beckett won the Nobel Prize for physics. Listen, Vannette?" the Observer said in a voice warm and liquid enough to bathe a newborn infant in. "If you do hear from Mitch? Tell him if he wants to find Sam Beckett, I'm the guy to talk to."

"Sure, I'll tell him," Vannette promised, and sighed one more time. "But to be honest with ya, I don't know when I'm gonna hear from him. If he's off with *her*— well, I'm not holding my breath, if ya know what I mean. But I got your number written down here. Al Calavicci, right?"

"That's right," Al told her.

"Area code two-two-two? Where is that, anyway?"

"It's new," Al said. Which was almost true, though it was only half an answer. Two-two-two was Ziggy's "area code": dialing 1-222-654-2580*4681 routed callers through the supercomputer, then deposited them at Al's desk without a clue as to where that desk was located. It was a system he was very satisfied with, most of the time. "Oh, and by the way—if you and Carl go out to eat this weekend, try a place called Luigi's. They're listed in the book. Tell them I sent you, and that they should treat you right."

"Oh," Vannette said. "Okay."

After he had laid the phone receiver back in its cradle, Al rocked his chair back and said, "Ziggy?"

The voice of Sam Beckett's hybrid supercomputer— every bit as sultry as the tone Al had been using for the last few minutes—answered him after a pause of three or four seconds, Ziggy's way of proving that she was not at anyone's beck and call. "Yes, Admiral."

"Check the airline records for me. Any carrier that

27

flies out of Dulles, Washington National or Baltimore. Go back two . . . no, three weeks. I wanna know exactly where this shyster has been and where he's going. Mitchell P. Lovetz. L-O-V . . .''

"E-T-Z," Ziggy finished for him.

"Yeah," Al grumbled.

Five minutes later he had the information he'd requested, along with a pile of other facts that Ziggy had seen fit to toss in. When the computer finished talking—finishing off her report with a self-satisfied "Will there be anything else, Admiral?"—Al had stopped believing that an "oh boy," no matter how prayerfully issued, would accomplish anything at all.

He found Verbena Beeks in the corridor outside the Waiting Room, conferring with a member of her staff. He waited in silence for her to finish, then waited for the nurse to walk away. "How's what's-his-name?" he asked then. "Clarence."

"Doing well," Verbena replied. "He's very calm. He thinks he's dreaming."

"I wish *I* was," Al said.

"You found Lovetz."

"I found Lovetz."

"And he's . . . ?"

Al clamped his arms over his chest, hands pinned between his biceps and the front of his red-white-and-blue jacket. He and Beeks stared at each other's face for more than a minute, something they both had a lot of practice at doing. "San Diego," Al muttered when he had grown tired of not blinking. "The *putz* is in San Diego."

"Did you warn Tom?"

"Tom," Al said slowly. "No, I didn't warn Tom. Lovetz's plane got in early this morning. He probably turned up Tom's gas hours ago." He paused then, but Beeks didn't say anything to placate him. Not that he'd expected her to. "Dammit," he said sharply. "The letters weren't bad enough. Now he's visiting people. Washington, Boston, Elk Ridge, San Diego. I'm surprised he hasn't headed for Hawaii, to pester Sam's mother. That's all I need is Sam's mother calling up again.''

"She wouldn't call you, would she?" Verbena asked. "She'd call Donna."

Al let out a squawk, as if Beeks had just stepped on his tail. "Is that any better?" he demanded.

"No," Verbena admitted.

"You wanna know what his next stop *is*?"

"Albuquerque?"

"Albuquerque."

"Damn," Verbena said softly. "I thought he didn't know where we were."

"His letters were mailed almost two weeks ago. You can get a lot of answers in two weeks, Beeksie. Even without Ziggy. He's due in at ten o'clock tomorrow morning."

"A hundred miles away."

"That's close enough."

Movement at the end of the corridor caught Al's attention. He turned to look that way: Donna was there, gnawing at her lower lip.

"What's the matter?" Al asked her.

Slowly, she walked the twenty yards that separated her from her husband's best friend. "I just talked to Tom," she explained, with an odd hesitation between her words, as if English were not her native language. "He left a message on my voice mail. Wanted me to get in touch with him ASAP. So I did."

"And?" Al prompted.

"Mitchell Lovetz came to visit him this morning." Donna stopped, and looked around, then returned her gaze to Al. Then moved it to Verbena. Then back to Al. "Lovetz said it was important that he find Sam. No . . . that it was important that his client find Sam."

Al and Verbena exchanged glances. "His client?" Verbena said.

"A red-haired woman. She was there with Lovetz. Attractive, Tom said. Very . . . he said 'classy.' Wearing a dark blue silk suit. Her name is Stephanie Keller." A grin broke through on Donna's face; then she shoved her fingers up through her hair, leaving it in disarray when her hands dropped back to her sides. "She says . . ."

She stopped again. She looked to Al as if she badly wanted to break something.

"She says," Donna announced an instant before Al could suggest that she find a place to sit down, "that she needs to find Sam. Because she's his wife."

CHAPTER THREE

C.J.'s "To Do" list was fastened to the door of his refrigerator. "Call B," it said. And "Buy oil."

Who was "B"? Sam wondered. And did "Buy oil" mean motor oil? Cooking oil? Stock in an oil company? Would Clarence Joseph Williams's life-as-he-knew-it change if either of these things wasn't done today?

"You're still not much help, you know, 'poochie,'" he said to Rufus, who was sitting alongside his feet. "You could at least give me some suggestions. After all, you know this guy, and I don't." The dog opened his mouth in response to that and waggled his tongue at Sam. Shaking his head, Sam reached down to scratch Rufus behind the ears, then sank onto one of C.J.'s green kitchen chairs and groaned.

The short November afternoon was almost over; following Al's instructions, he had spent most of it "caretaking." Even his mother, who had been (and still was, he supposed) a very particular housekeeper, could not have found any fault with the job he'd done. He hadn't ventured inside any of the homes C.J. was responsible for, but the outsides were raked, swept, polished and tidied. Apparently C.J. was fussy too: nothing that had asked for Sam's attention had been neglected for very long, so each task took no longer than a few minutes.

Retreating to Twelve Maple Lane, he washed and put away C.J.'s breakfast and lunch dishes, tossed his discarded set of still-damp clothes into the dryer and wiped up the wet tracks he'd left on the living room floor. Now, at quarter to four, he had no more chores to do.

"Anytime, Al," he sighed. "Where are you?"

"Ooof," Rufus offered, then strolled over to the stainless steel bowl full of Soop'r Dog that Sam had put out for him. With one eye fixed firmly on Sam, he began to scarf down some Tasty Real Beef Chunks.

"Guess you're right," Sam said. "Supper's not a bad idea."

Four years of Leaping into the lives (and homes) of strangers had taught him some important lessons. Near the top of the list was the fact that an alarming number of people had (a) empty cupboards, or (b) bizarre and disgusting favorite foods. C.J., to Sam's relief, didn't fall into either category. As Al had predicted, the cabinet closest to the stove was packed with cans of soup in a dozen different varieties; another with cans and jars of vegetables, fruit, peanut butter and tuna fish, and bags of dried pasta. The refrigerator and freezer were also jammed. C.J. had stored enough food to see himself, and Rufus, safely through a very long, hard, cold winter— one that Sam seriously hoped he would not be here to see any of.

He prepared and ate a hearty dinner with Rufus standing guard nearby. Each small sound he heard made him look up, expecting Al to appear. After he'd finished off a dessert composed of a banana and a couple of Oreo cookies, he washed dishes again. The brass carriage clock on C.J.'s mantelpiece chimed off the hour as he put away the last dish.

Still no Al.

"I hate it when he does this," he told Rufus, who gazed at him sympathetically. "He knows I need information. I'm here to *do* something, see." Rufus trailed him into the living room and sat down when Sam did, thumping his tail against the hardwood floor. "But is it something that happens here? Close to the house? Or am I supposed to go into town? Is it something that happens to me, or to you, or somebody else?"

Who the "somebody else" might be, he didn't know. He'd seen no one other than Al since his arrival here, and had begun to feel as if he were sitting in the middle of a "Twilight Zone" episode. Up until now, he thought, if someone had asked him if he minded solitude, he would have said no. The hours he had spent studying, or reading, or working alone probably numbered in the thousands. He did not mind his own company; in fact, he had grown very accustomed to it during the years before he met . . .

Al. Al? He frowned at his indecisiveness, then banished it. Of course, Al. His best friend.

"Don't know why I picked him," he told Rufus. "He's not easy to be friends with. He's a pain in the butt sometimes. He's not anything like me. But he did me a favor, and I went down to thank him, and there was something . . ."

The words trailed off as he propped his elbows on his knees and rested his chin on his fists. The room around him was painfully quiet except for the steady ticking of the carriage clock.

Yes, there had definitely been something about that angry, drunken man with the ball-peen hammer in his hand. Something that had nothing to do with the two million dollars in seed money for Quantum Leap.

"Sorry you came?" The question had been accusing, nasty. Something thrown in Sam's face.

"No."

"Well, you should be. I don't know why you bothered."

"Because," Sam had said, hauling in a deep breath that didn't do much to counter the coating of permafrost

33

on Admiral Calavicci's expression, "I wanted to meet you. I wanted to thank you for your help."

"You could've sent me a card."

"No. I couldn't."

"I owed him before I even met him," Sam told Rufus softly. "He was the only one who believed in me. You know what I mean? My mom and dad were always behind me, but Al was the first one who really helped me. Without him . . . I suppose there wouldn't be a Quantum Leap."

And I wouldn't be here. I'd be home.

"Maybe I should have listened when he told me to get lost," Sam sighed. "He tried. He did his best to get rid of me, that night when we met the first time. And . . . he really did finally get rid of me, didn't he? But I don't think this was what he planned on. I told him I needed his help. But I never told him how much."

"Ufffff," Rufus said sympathetically.

Sam offered the dog half a smile. So C.J. intended to sit here all winter, with only the dog for company. He'd get his mystery novel finished, maybe. For Sam, a winter's worth of uninterrupted studying could mean another doctorate—number seven. Al had jabbed him a lot over the first six . . . hadn't he? The idea seemed to be true, but the images that backed it up were faint, like the remnants of a dream. One of them was a little clearer than the others: Al had had him paged once, in a hotel in Las Vegas: "Doctor-Doctor-Doctor-Doctor-Doctor-Doctor Beckett." It hadn't been a joke; Al had been seriously pissed. About . . . something. He could see the look on Al's face, but the words that explained it had fallen into a hole in the Swiss cheese of his memory.

"I owe him," Sam murmured.

He slouched back into the chair, letting C.J.'s broken-in cushions surround his shoulders. He could let himself doze off this time, he thought, and rely on Al to wake

34

him if there was a need for it. He could do that, because
Al *would* wake him.

You know *that. He's never let you down. With little
things, yeah . . . showing up late. Not paying attention.
But he's never let you down when it counts. Not like . . .*

"I got myself into this," he announced. "And it's my
responsibility to make sure it's all done right. I can't
blame anything on Al. Because I . . ."

*Because you left him behind, without a word of expla-
nation.*

"I'm not here to take naps," he told the dog.

Rufus's brown eyes stared back at him. He wanted
badly to be annoyed—with waiting, with himself, with
Al's absence, with *something*—but that wasn't going to
happen with Rufus happily chuffing warm breath onto
his hand.

"Thanks, boy," he said quietly. "If I can't get any
answers, it's at least good to have some company."

"SaaaAAAAMMMM!!!"

Sam jerked upright in bed, hands fluttering frantically
through the air around him until one of them collided with
the lamp on the night table. After several seconds of fum-
bling he managed to turn the light on. "What . . . ?" he
sputtered, pushing his legs toward the edge of the bed.
"What is it? I'm . . ."

Al, reflexively backpedaling to get out of Sam's way,
stuck out a hand, palm toward the other man. "No, no,
no. It's okay. Stay there."

"What's the matter?"

"Nothing's the matter."

"Nothing's . . ." Sam's left ear was still ringing from
the decibel level of his wake-up call. "What is the *matter*
with you?" he demanded. "If nothing's wrong, then why
did you . . ."

Al blinked at his partner for a moment, as if he didn't

35

quite understand the question, and did nothing to acknowledge Sam's distress. "It's morning," he said finally.

"Morning? It's not morning." Sam peered at the digital clock on the bedside table. "It's ten minutes to five."

The Observer seemed to take that as a confirmation. "Yeah."

Rufus, who had been startled awake an instant before Sam, shambled over to the bed and watched closely as Sam pulled himself out from under the covers and climbed out of bed. Sam hadn't turned on the heat in C.J.'s little house; the bedroom was uncomfortably cold and the scientist was wearing nothing but boxer shorts. Shivering, he dragged on the flannel shirt he'd tossed aside a couple of hours before. Then, finally noticing the dog's amiable scrutiny, Sam reached down absently to pat him before turning to face the Observer again.

"I grew up on a farm," he said in a tone that fell a little short of being conversational. "We got up early all the time to do chores before school. And you were probably used to getting up early when you were on active duty. But Al"—he gestured at the window, a curtain-framed rectangle of darkness—"it's not morning. It's ten minutes to five. I don't have chores to do, and you don't have to report for . . . whatever it was you used to report for. It's five o'clock. So why are you screaming in my ear?"

The handlink beeped and warbled, but Al said nothing. He studied the readout on the link intently, pressed a series of keys, then smiled brightly at Sam. "I thought you might want to . . . get going."

"On what?"

"Whatever," Al said.

"What time is it there?"

"Ummm . . . early."

"You're not sleeping again? I told you how to do the breathing exercises. And you had Medical give you . . ."

36

The shrug that prompted from the Observer made Sam scowl at him. "You never even talked to Medical, did you? Al, all the studies they've done on the cumulative effects of inadequate REM sleep ... Why can't you sleep? You don't need to hold Ziggy's hand. She's a computer. Ask her the question, and let her spend the night working on it. You're not a computer, you're a human being. *You* need to sleep." Sam sighed and ran a hand through his rumpled hair. "And so do I."

Al stuck the handlink in Sam's direction. "You *were* sleeping."

"I fell asleep about two hours ago."

"Three o'clock? What about the breathing exercises?" Al countered.

"I had too much to think about."

"Huh," Al snorted. "Well, I had ... Tina." The Observer's expression shifted as he straightened his shoulders, tugged down the front of his jacket and reached up to mock smoothing his hair. The routine made him look very much like a teenaged boy about to ring the doorbell of his prom date. "She's got ... desires, Sammy. You can't disappoint a woman like that. What's a little lost shut-eye compared to keeping a woman happy? Last night, she told me she'd read this article in a magazine, and she was going to—"

Sam cut him off. "Why are you here?"

"What?"

"Did you wake me up so you could tell me what Tina read in a magazine? We agreed that you'd wake me up if there was a *problem*. Why are you here?"

"We got some, you know, stuff for you."

" 'Stuff'?" he demanded. "What 'stuff'?"

"Information. Not a lot, but Ziggy's still checking a few possibilities. We'll have more later on." Al tossed a smile at his friend, but that accomplished nothing. "Hey, buddy," he said mildly. " 'If looks could kill ... ' "

37

Sam said tersely, "You enjoy this, don't you? Tormenting me."

"Why would I want to torment you?"

"To get even with me for what I did."

Al frowned. "For what, what you did? What did you do?"

"I Leaped. Without telling you."

"That's got nothing to do with anything," Al replied. "What, have you been stewing ever since yesterday afternoon? I told you I'd come back as soon as I could."

"That was sixteen hours ago."

Al waved the handlink at him. "Do you want this information or not?"

Rufus moved in between the two men and examined first one, then the other: Al in a wonderfully shiny, metallic silver jacket and matching shoes, and Sam in a rumpled shirt that still held traces of the scent of Rufus's master. Neither of them seemed to notice him. "Owff," he said to let them know he was unhappy with being ignored.

"Is it going to help me?" Sam asked.

"Maybe."

"That's all? Just 'maybe'? That's great." Sam grunted loudly, reached up to massage a cramp in the back of his neck and sat down on the edge of the bed. "You woke me up at five o'clock for . . . All right, all right. What is it? Aauuugghhh! Ah, man, Rufus! Jeez."

Rufus, who had garnered himself some attention by licking Sam's bare foot like a Popsicle, grinned and whapped his tail against the rug.

"Jeeeeez," Sam said again.

"What're *you* complaining for?" Al asked him. "He's the one who's got the taste of 'foot' in his mouth now."

"Okay," Sam surrendered. "Okay. I appreciate your effort. I appreciate your keeping me informed. I'm grateful. Thank you. Now, what's the information?"

Al shook his head. "Maybe I'll just come back later

38

on. Say around noon? Or is that too early? You wanna sleep in?''

"Albert," Sam said.

"All right, all right." With one eye on Sam, Al paced back and forth a couple of times, tinkering with the hand-link as he walked. "According to everything we've been able to dig up, nothing important happened to C.J. in November of '83. Or December. Actually, nothing much happened to him in the eighties at all." After a glance at Sam, who was trying his best to hold onto what remained of his patience, he returned his attention to the link. "He finally sold his book in '91. Somebody optioned it for a TV movie but the movie never got made. He moved to Oregon in '98—fell in love with somebody he met up there while he was traveling around promoting his book. They had a baby about two months ago."

Nodding, Sam filled in, "Then I'm not here to do anything for C.J. himself."

"Guess not."

"For who, then?" Sam's gaze drifted down to Rufus, who had settled himself on the rug with his head resting on his big paws. "Nothing happens to the dog, does it?"

"Don't know," Al said, shaking his head. "We're checking, but it's harder to get anything on animals." After a pause, he added, "They don't leave paper trails."

Sam peered at him. "You don't seriously think I'm going to take bait that cheap, do you?"

"Thought it was worth a try."

"I'm sorry, Al."

"You oughta be. I'm only trying to help you."

"I know that."

"Hmmm," Al said.

"Do you have anything else?"

The Observer wobbled his head again, checked the link as an afterthought, then said, "Nope. Ziggy's checking to see if there was a fire around here, or a burglary. Anything that has to do with the houses and not people. Or

39

. . . what is he, again? A Woofie?'' He pointed to Rufus with the link.

"A Newfoundland.''

"Or big dogs. We're trying,'' he promised Sam. "I . . . I gotta get back to Tina now. She promised me a surprise I'd never forget. Said it wouldn't just ring my chimes, it'd make 'em sing the score from *Show Boat*.''

A grimace crossed Sam's face as he looked down at his still-slimy foot, then at Rufus. "Well, don't let me stand between you and your libido,'' he sighed.

"I'll be back,'' Al said.

"Yeah,'' Sam replied quietly. "Yeah, I know.''

This time he didn't even slow down long enough to register who was in the Control Room, let alone allow any of them to speak to him. He barreled on through as if he were aiming for first place in the hundred-yard dash, tossed the handlink in the general direction of the main console, oblivious to whether anyone caught it or not, and actually made it all the way to his office without being intercepted. He was tempted to lock the door behind him, but that would have accomplished nothing; Beeks knew his access code, as did Donna and the three top dogs in Security. They might have respected his privacy, but not for very long. He figured they'd allow him maybe fifteen minutes before they started knocking, whether he locked himself in here or not.

Taking full advantage of his temporary solitude, he went into his private bathroom, switched on the overhead light and stared at his reflection in the mirror over the sink. Stared, specifically, at the effect the last four years and two months had had on him—something Sam did not have the luxury of doing. He would have, he supposed, looked pretty much the same even if Sam hadn't Leaped, because Time was Time was Time, and he was, after all, four days short of being sixty-five years old.

He didn't look *bad* for sixty-five, he thought. Still had

40

all his teeth, and most of his hair, and not much of it was gray. The rest of him had held up well enough to allow him to follow the unpredictable schedule that Sam's Leaps dictated: the catnaps, the meals that were interrupted, or skipped, or wolfed down so that they sat in his belly like half-dried cement. He could make it through this, he told himself, if for no other reason than that he had always made it through before. He had never been conquered by anything, or anyone.

Except once. Almost.

"Breathing exercises," he muttered at the mirror. " 'Just do the breathing exercises.' Jeez Louise."

Four years and two months—that translated into more than fifteen hundred nights. He suspected he hadn't gotten "adequate REM sleep" on any of them. *It ain't as easy as it sounds, pal. Settle in for some serious Z's, and Ziggy sounds the alarm to tell me you Leaped in someplace. And you always want me there prompt-a-mente. Or I try to catch a quickie, and somebody's banging on the door. Sleep?* He sighed at the image in the glass. *I figure I can sleep when I'm dead, and that's about the name of that tune.*

And now this. A wife nobody knew about? D'you forget to mention that, kid? Not worth talking about? Or it hurts too much to talk about it? I guess I could understand that. I never said much about Beth till you met her. But that's me. I never figured you had any secrets. That's the Sixty-four Thousand Dollar Question, ain't it: you got any secrets, Sam?

And I'm supposed to just turn off the lights and conk out. Forget about everything. Eight hours of quality shut-eye every night. What was it Beeksie said? "Not in this reality, boys and girls."

He had finished flinging cold water onto his face and was en route to his desk when the knock finally came.

"Yeah," he said, just loudly enough for whoever was on the other side of the door to hear him.

Beeks came in and sat down in his guest chair. "Was he upset?"

"Yeah," Al replied. "He was upset."

"I told you five o'clock was too early. If you want somebody to share your insomnia with, try me. Sam's under enough pressure. You can't go in there just to—"

"Beeks . . ." He peered at her wearily for a moment, then pointed a finger at the wall alongside his desk. "Sam Beckett was in that office, or wandering someplace around this complex, way earlier than five o'clock every morning for more than a year. He could've been in the Book of Records for surviving on no sleep. Don't tell me you don't remember that."

"Things are different now," Verbena responded.

"Yeah?" Al said. "No shit."

"Will he go back to sleep?"

"Of course he'll go back to sleep. Thinking I'm a fugitive from the state nuthatch. Or that we really have all the answers but I'm jerking him around to get even with him for Leaping out of here without sending out an engraved announcement that he was gonna do it." He fell silent then, watching Beeks watch him. "He's wearing down," he offered after a minute.

"So are you," Verbena replied.

"Nah."

The psychiatrist rolled her eyes at him. "I keep hearing that tale you started that 'Calavicci' means 'screwdriver.' I think 'Calavicci' means 'pigheaded.' "

"And you figure that's an unusual trait around here?"

"No," Verbena said. "I don't."

She was waiting for more. Four years ago, he would have let her wait. But lately it seemed that handing her what she wanted got rid of her a lot quicker than stonewalling her. Which would also have been true, he admitted reluctantly, if the situation had been reversed. "I was on the phone for an hour," he told her, "having my quarterly debate with Tom Beckett over what I can and

42

cannot tell him about his brother. Then half an hour apiece shooting the breeze with Sam's brother-in-law and Abby Howell. Another twenty minutes trying to track down Sebastian LoNigro. A lot of playing footsie, trying to find out whether Lovetz found them without actually asking the question. Then I go play footsie with Sam, whose bowels are in an uproar because he didn't Leap into the middle of Bill and Ted's Excellent Adventure. This ain't an easy job, Beeks. If you keep thinking you're gonna come in here and find me whistling a happy tune, you're wasting brain cells.''

"I'd like to come in here and find you taking a nap once in a while" was Verbena's response.

"*Et tu,* Beeksie?" Al said dryly. "Then get me somebody to do my job for me."

"We've tried to help you, Admiral."

Al's eyes narrowed.

"Tell me that's not the truth," Verbena said.

"I'll take a nap when this is over."

"When what's over, Al? This Leap? The business with Lovetz? Or when Sam comes home?"

He knew her well enough to understand that he wasn't being manipulated. He *had* felt that way almost every time he talked to her, years ago, back in the beginning. Back when she was just someone Sam had hired to fill a post he insisted needed to be filled. Back when she was just another annoying shrink. Now he could look across the desk at someone who cared about him, at least as much as he would allow her to.

"I do what I gotta do," he told her.

"And then some," she said.

"Give out the medals later," he replied wryly. "After we get rid of—"

The phone on Al's desk clicked, then began to warble its announcement of an incoming call. He shifted his eyes to glare at the instrument—he missed the old days, when phones rang instead of chirping. And when they had to

43

be attached to the wall, so that you couldn't carry one around in your pocket. You could get the rest of the world (most notably, Tom Beckett) to leave you alone then. He missed that.

He let the thing trill at him four times, then seized the receiver, stuck it against his ear and said into it, "Calavicci."

"Albert Calavicci?" quizzed the voice on the other end.

So, he thought, the *putz* had finally picked up his messages. He wondered for a moment whether that had made Vannette Tyler happy, then said, "Yes."

"My name is Mitchell Lovetz."

"And you're looking for Sam Beckett."

"That's right, Mr. Calavicci."

"Admiral," Al corrected him.

"Ah," Lovetz replied. "Yes. Admiral."

"Lovetz."

"Yes?"

Al looked across his desk at Verbena Beeks, then sat back in his chair, rocking it gently a couple of times and rubbing the pad of his thumb up and down the back of the phone receiver.

"Let's do lunch," he said.

CHAPTER FOUR

Wife.

Wife????

Al snorted loudly, then shook his head. Gooshie was dead wrong—Lovetz wasn't sniffing around the country trying to locate the Project—instead, as his letters had claimed, he was trying to find *Sam*. His game was one that Al had competed in many times before: Al on one team, a lawyer and a disgruntled woman on the other, and, for the first time in two days, Al was tempted to feel more amused than worried.

She says she's his wife . . .

Now, too, he had a spot to plug in Gooshie's original piece of this puzzle: the piece that had "MONEY" written on it. Nobody could sniff out money like an ex-wife.

If she was his wife. Sam never said Word One about another wife. And he ain't me, he's Sam. No secrets. Right? So it's all baloney.

But she says . . .

The question that had followed him doggedly for the last couple of hours was *Why?* Sam was a good-looking guy—Al had heard people with very disparate tastes say so. Somebody who could really decorate a woman's arm at a party. Somebody she could even have a few X-rated fantasies about, Al supposed. But "good-looking" didn't float enough of the right boats. The guy in question wasn't Elvis, or the President of the United States, or Bill Whatzisname, the computer whiz. Dropping Sam's name wouldn't even steer this babe to a better table at her favorite restaurant.

The last time Al had heard Sam's name being dropped, all it'd gotten in response was a sniff.

"So what do you want out of this?" he asked the air. "Huh? What's the deal?"

No one answered him. No one could; he was the sole passenger in the jeep he'd commandeered from the motor pool, now eleven miles from the front gate of the Project grounds and headed north. The jeep, unlike his own car, wasn't linked to Ziggy. Nor was he, at the moment. He'd left behind all of the gadgets that would allow Sam's supercomputer to kibitz on his conversations. He was finally, blessedly alone, at least until he arrived at Silvio's.

His wife . . .

Hell, he thought, this Keller woman, whoever she was, could get more out of claiming she was *his* wife.

Unless she knew about the stocks . . . ?

No. Impossible.

So maybe she's nuts.

Yeah. A fruit loop. A ding-dong. Half a bubble off plumb. Couple sandwiches short of a picnic. Like the woman who'd kept moving in on that talk show host a few years back. The cops would drag her out; a couple of months later she'd be back, insisting she had a right to be there because she was Mrs. Talk Show Host. But Sam was no famous talk show host. Sam wasn't a public figure of any kind, not anymore. The press, who had started believing back in '92 that Sam's picnic basket was pretty much empty, had dropped him from their A list, their B list and their "we have an inch to fill" list while the Project was still a collection of mostly empty caves underneath the desert. Sam *wasn't* Elvis, even if he could do an okay impersonation of the King when he had a few beers in him. He wasn't famous, he wasn't rich (except for the stocks), the public didn't find him interesting.

He was nobody that anybody would claim to be married to.

Unless she knew him.

Unless . . .

Nah, there was no way. Another wife? From way back, when the kid was still racking up all those doctorates? Somebody to keep him warm and snuggly while he studied his dead languages and his quantum physics and anatomy and math and music and . . .

Somebody to keep him from being alone?

"Nah," Al said.

It wasn't possible. Sam, his best friend, the champion of Truth, would have mentioned it. If a couple of beers made the kid break into loud choruses of "Heartbreak Hotel," a couple more made him unburden his soul, as if he were leaving old, worn-out suitcases by the side of the road. He talked every time frustration made him pass his one-beer limit. He talked until Al's head went numb. About how hard it was to be "different." About not being understood. About trying to make his family proud. About finding Donna, who'd made him stop wondering if anyone would ever really love him.

Okay, Al mused, so Donna was Ms. Right. But what if there'd been Ms. "She's All Right, She'll Do"? What if Sam had made a mistake? Said the "I take thee"s to somebody just because it seemed like a good idea at the time? Al himself had made four mistakes like that. And while Al didn't have Sam's smarts, he certainly had as much common sense as his partner did. Maybe more.

No, definitely more.

What if . . .

Cut this the hell out, he told himself. *You're almost there. And you gotta be in control when you get there. No slips. No fumbles. You're running this show, not this shyster and his ding-dong "client," the little honey*

47

*who's cheating on the other half of Lovetz and Boyle.
Got that? Nobody's married to Sam except Donna. Nobody's ever been married to Sam except Donna. And you
owe it to both of them to establish that right off the bat.
So go in there, find out what their agenda is, handle it
and get out.*

He gripped the steering wheel in both hands, then loos-
ened his hold a little and turned the jeep onto a narrow
road that led off to the northeast. The road wasn't
marked, nor was it on any map of this area he'd ever
looked at. He'd chosen Silvio's place as the site for his
meeting with Mitchell Lovetz and Stephanie Keller
knowing they'd have a bitch of a time finding it—but
also knowing that they *would* find it. And that they'd
reach Silvio's before he did. So they'd have to wait for
him.

So that the man who was coming to meet them, driving
a jeep from the Project motor pool, dressed in Navy
khakis with creases sharp enough to cut grass, spit-shined
shoes and mirrored sunglasses that would prevent them
from seeing his eyes until he was ready—that man would
have home court advantage.

Al had first found Silvio's place five years ago, utterly
by accident. He'd been wasting an afternoon cruising the
two-lane roads near the Project with Tina, happily dem-
onstrating the myriad wonders of his new "experimental
model" orgasm-on-wheels to his almost-as-new girl-
friend, when Tina had been struck by a sudden and ur-
gent need to, as she put it, "find a . . . you know." She
refused to elaborate in words, but the way her jaw began
to clench told Al that a "you know" was a rest room,
and that he had better pray that the Good Lord had seen
fit to furnish one somewhere very nearby.

Of course, the Good Lord hadn't, or it didn't seem that
way. Al, unnerved by the squeaking/wincing noises Tina
had begun to make, was about to suggest stepping behind

a bush when, like a mirage, Silvio's appeared on the horizon.

As mirages went, he considered as Tina disappeared inside, this wasn't much of one. But as watering (or dewatering) holes in the middle of the desert went, it was pretty typical: a low, unpainted, flat-roofed, forty-foot-square cinder-block building with a dented Texaco gas pump stuck off to one side and an even more dented sixties-vintage Coke machine flanking the front door. Out back sat an aging but well kept up and reasonably large mobile home surrounded by a motley collection of aluminum and plastic lawn furniture, knee-high painted plaster statues of Snow White and the Seven Dwarfs, a rusty Honda motorbike, a trio of straggly rosebushes in terra-cotta pots and the Queen Mother of all satellite dishes.

Sitting in one of the lawn chairs, sipping from a long-neck bottle of Dos Equis and watching the intermittent flutter of the frayed American flag that protruded from a bracket on the trailer, was Silvio himself.

"Need help?" he asked when Al got out of the car.

Al nodded, nudging his sunglasses up away from his eyes for an unfiltered view of Silvio's kingdom. "The lady needs to use your rest room."

"Need gas?"

"No, thanks. I've got plenty."

Fortifying himself with a long pull of his beer, Silvio set the bottle down, eased himself out of the lawn chair and strolled over to his visitor with his hands loosely tucked into his armpits. "You're a long way from anyplace."

"Actually," Al said, "I'm not."

"You work with Gooshie?" Silvio asked.

"You know Gooshie?"

"Hell, yes," Silvio said.

"He eats here?"

Al had been sized up before. Somewhere in the range

of ten thousand times, he figured: by teachers, cops, senior officers. Junior officers. A priest or two. Eight or nine dozen nuns. Store owners who had pegged a small, dark-haired boy as a shoplifter and were sometimes right. Women he couldn't even begin to count. Bullies. Tough guys. Guys who thought they were tough and weren't. He was being sized up again now, by a man who stood about six-four, two-ten, salt-and-pepper hair, sharp gray eyes that didn't waver. Hands that didn't waver, either. Thick forearms exposed by the rolled-up sleeves of a white-trimmed black cotton shirt. Strong shoulders. Somebody who took care of business and didn't bother to ask anybody else to do it.

Somebody who could, beyond any shadow of a doubt, beat the living shit out of Al Calavicci, then dust his hands off and sit down quietly to finish his beer.

"Yup," Silvio said.

"Food any good here?" Al asked.

One of those steady hands went up slowly to touch the brim of the dark gray Stetson that shielded Silvio's eyes from the sun. The Stetson slid back a degree or two. There was a crucifix around Silvio's neck, framed by the V the shirt collar made at his throat. A little one, made of hammered silver.

"Yup," Silvio said.

"Didn't know there was a restaurant over here," Al commented.

"Well," Silvio said, "there is."

Silvio had been truthful that day: the food (TACOS BURGERS COLD BEER, as advertised by the stumpy, sandblasted wooden sign on the roof) *was* good, if a little unpredictable in selection, and so was the beer. And the place was a definite change of scene from the government-controlled sterility of the Project grounds. But in spite of that, why most of the Project staff would bother driving the eighteen miles out here at least once a week to spend a couple of hours sitting on a butt-busting picnic bench in a cinder-block building with no air conditioning didn't make sense.

Unless, of course, you considered Monica.

A stranger might have supposed Monica was TACOS BURGERS's lone waitress, or that she was Silvio's wife. Strictly speaking she was neither. How she'd come here, and why she'd stayed, Al had never heard explained. All anyone seemed to care about was that she was here now.

"Hey," she called out when Al cut the engine of the jeep.

She was waiting for him, standing in front of the screened entrance to TACOS BURGERS in faded, frayed-at-the-cuff short-shorts that had once been a full pair of Levi's and a sleeveless white T-shirt sporting a drawing of a baying wolf pack and the legend "SANTA FE, NEW MEXICO" in dark blue. Exposing a wide ribbon of tanned midriff, the shirt was tightly knotted underneath breasts that had always interested Al a lot more than Silvio's tacos.

God, he thought every time he saw her, making love to a woman built like that—full and soft—would feel fabulous. Tina, who had been his one-and-only, more or less, for the last five years, was young and energetic and very cheerfully open to suggestion, but she was . . . well, bony.

And Monica wasn't.

As if she'd just completed a walking tour of his subconscious, Monica chuckled softly and opened the driver's door of the jeep for him. "They're inside," she told him quietly. "I gave 'em each something to drink. They're not real happy."

"Didn't think they would be," Al told her.

"And you're glad they're not?"

Al let his mirrored glasses slide down the bridge of his nose and peered at Monica over the rims. "Yeah," he murmured. "I'm ecstatic."

She smiled at him, making him feel for the first time

today that someone was genuinely on his side. "We'll be out in the trailer," she said. "There's food if you want it. You know where everything is."

"I hope so," Al replied.

"Everything okay?"

He wanted badly to tell her no. Instead, he nodded and pushed his glasses back into place. "Yeah," he said. "It'll be fine."

The rectangle of gravel that was TACOS BURGERS's parking lot could have served as a dress rehearsal for hell. Al stood in the middle of it for a minute, feeling the desert heat scorch the soles of his shoes. *Their* car was a few yards away: a big rental, its white paint job liberally covered with road dirt and the squashed corpses of a wide variety of bugs. Closed up tight. Good move, Al noted: if Lovetz and his dingbat client wanted to make a fast getaway, they'd be climbing into a blast furnace. After they unlocked it.

"Don't know who they think is gonna steal it," Monica observed. "Me, I guess."

"You want it?" Al asked.

"You remember who you're talking to?" Monica chuckled, then stepped back, folded her arms and ran her eyes up and down Al's body. "Nice uniform," she told him. "You're scary when you get serious, Al."

"That's what I'm counting on," Al replied.

He felt more than a little like John Wayne, swaggering in through the swinging doors of an old Western saloon, one hand twitching and ready to grab his shootin' iron. The only things available for him to grab were his cap, his glasses and the jeep keys, but his hand quivered anyway. *Bad guys*, he thought. *Jeez Louise. The Silk Suit Gang.*

Lovetz, who was facing the screen door, stood up slowly.

"Mister . . . ," he began.

Al heard a distant *gong*, like the bell on a pinball machine. Yup, the uniform had scored points. Hundred, maybe a hundred and fifty. Lovetz was licking sweat off his upper lip.

What a geek, Al thought.

Kids like this had made fun of him. Because his parents had left him. Because his clothes were old and worn at the cuffs and didn't fit him well. Because he was short. Because the nuns cut his hair.

He'd knocked a lot of kids like this onto their butts when the nuns weren't looking. They all sniveled, every last one of them. None of them ever punched him back.

Lovetz, who was a sniveler if Al had ever seen one, was melting into his Italian leather shoes. His completely curl-less dark hair, which had probably been blow-dried and moussed to perfection this morning, was now hanging limply over his forehead and the tops of his ears. His suit had passed "limp" a while back; the sweat rings under his arms reached all the way to his waist, and his slouch accentuated the fact that he had no shoulders but did have an odd little potbelly that looked like a four-month pregnancy.

"You're Admiral Calavicci?" he said listlessly.

"I'm not the guy who fixes the fax machine," Al said, and let the screen door bang shut behind him.

Lovetz flinched.

Al took another step, still feeling like the Duke, ready to demolish his adversary. His hand was midway to his glasses when Lovetz did something that startled him.

Lovetz looked him in the eye.

Through the sunglasses.

"Admiral Calavicci," he said. Smoothly. Pleasantly. As if he were sipping a frozen daiquiri and awaiting the arrival of his Crab Louis, sitting in a booth at someplace with *le* in front of its name. Someplace with starched white tablecloths. Someplace climate controlled. Al was too far away to be offered a hand; instead, Lovetz inclined his head slightly and went on, "I'm Mitchell Lovetz. This is my client. Stephanie Keller."

A few months back, Sam had been kidnapped at gunpoint by a woman named Norma Jean Pilcher, who thought she was abducting her favorite soap opera star. The woman who had been sitting with her back to the screen door stood up now, and turned around, and for an instant Al thought he was looking at Norma Jean Pilcher's twin sister.

Then the fog of his expectations drifted away and he realized that Lovetz was not attorney-ing somebody who'd pursue the object of her fantasies dolled up in a quilted blue satin bathrobe. This woman was no raving ding-dong. This woman was not going to scream out, "Don't you call me *crazy*!!!" and hurl a tray full of tea-party paraphernalia at the bedroom wall.

This woman was big trouble.

Because this woman was . . . normal.

Taking initiative that Lovetz did not seem to have, Stephanie Keller moved away from the picnic bench she had been seated on, surreptitiously straightened her skirt and crossed the distance that separated her from Albert Calavicci. When she was near enough she extended her hand.

"Admiral," she said.

From the other side of the room, she looked about thirty. Each step added another year. By the time she held out her hand, Al had put her in her early forties, four or five years younger than Sam. Redheaded, as Tom Beckett had told Donna, hair cut in a little bubble that framed her face. Milk-and-honey complexion. Tall. Slim. Had more sense than Lovetz too, because she wasn't wearing the dark suit that Tom had described; she'd exchanged it for a pale, sleeveless linen dress.

Al closed his hand over hers and was surprised at how cool it felt, until he remembered that she'd been holding onto a glass of ice water.

"You know where Sam is," she said.

"Maybe."

His eyes, behind the glasses, drifted between lawyer and client. Lovetz did TV commercials, he decided: the kind claiming to win million-dollar settlements for people with worker's compensation gripes. Probably drove a Mercedes back home in Virginia. Lived in a town house. The guy had a *manicure,* for crying out loud. He would have been a real pretty-boy if he hadn't been built like Mr. Potato Head.

"Would you like to sit down?" Stephanie Keller offered.

Al glanced at her. If she wasn't a nut case, he thought, then she was a barracuda. But that was wrong too. Unless she was a barracuda who could pretend to be a lamb.

"Yes," Lovetz concurred. "Sit down. Please."

Over near the archway leading into the kitchen was a white molded plastic chair, the only non-picnic-bench seat in the room. Al seized it, deposited it at the end of Lovetz's table and lowered himself into it. The gleam in Lovetz's eyes told him the lawyer expected him to dump the pleasantries now and cut right to the chase. In fact, he would have done exactly that if Monica hadn't emerged from the kitchen balancing three plates of steaming Mexican food.

Lovetz's gleam faded considerably. "What's . . . ," he began.

"Lunch," Al said. "We *did* come here to have lunch." He questioned Monica's presence with a tilt of one eyebrow, struggling to contain a frown as she busied herself arranging three sets of utensils on the picnic table, disappeared and returned one more time with a pitcher of beer and three glasses.

"House special," she announced. "Enjoy."

Then she was gone again.

"What is this?" Lovetz asked, poking at the mound of food on his plate with the tip of a fork.

55

Al smiled amiably at him and poured beer into the three glasses. "Not sure it has a name."

"It's . . . What's in here?" Lovetz continued to plumb with his fork. "Peppers? And . . . what's that, chicken?"

"Probably," Al replied.

He had no intention of saying anything more. Wearing a look of sweet benevolence he thought would have done Mother Teresa proud, he picked up his own fork and dug in. Five years of eating Monica and Silvio's house special had prepared his stomach for what it was about to receive.

"*Pollo,*" Lovetz said to Stephanie. "That's Spanish for 'chicken.' This is *pollo* something. Chicken, and rice, and some peppers. It looks good. Yes. It does look good. Authentic Mexican cuisine."

That said, he loaded up his fork and shoveled the load into his mouth.

His nose began to run almost immediately.

Al had told the truth: the house special had no name you could find in a cookbook. It did, however, have a nickname among the staff members of Quantum Leap, bestowed by one of the Project's security guards after he had finished coughing, blowing his nose and wiping away the last of the tears that had started flowing the moment he swallowed his first bite. "Oh, man," the burly Marine had whimpered. "Meltdown."

"Kinda makes the top of your head sweat, doesn't it?" Al inquired cheerfully.

"You *did* that," Lovetz gasped, jabbing his fork in Al's direction as he seized his beer with his free hand. Several gulps later, he went on, "You did that deliberately. Let me eat that, knowing what she put in there."

"Mr. Lovetz," Al said, "I have no clue on this earth what she puts in there. If you want something milder, ask her if she'll whip you up a tuna sandwich. She's out back. Just go out by the trailer and yell." When Lovetz scowled at him, he amended his instructions to "Or you

56

could go out in the kitchen and fix yourself something. Help yourself. Everybody else does.''

''Everybody else?'' Lovetz shot back.

''Yup.''

''Would that include Dr. Beckett?''

''Sometimes,'' Al said.

''Why didn't you bring him here with you?''

''He's busy.''

''Too busy to see his wife?''

Finally, Al reached up, pulled the mirrored sunglasses into the palm of his hand, folded the bows and tucked them into the pocket of his uniform blouse. ''Dr. Beckett's wife's name is Donna Alessi,'' he told Lovetz. ''I believe you sent her a letter, similar to the one you sent me.''

''I sent a letter to a Donna Alessi, yes.''

''Then you're aware . . .''

''I'm aware that if Samuel Beckett married Donna Alessi, or anyone else, at any time subsequent to June of 1976,'' Lovetz said, daubing at his eyes with the corner of a white monogrammed handkerchief, ''then Dr. Beckett was committing bigamy. Which, I'm sure you know, is illegal in the United States.''

The lawyer, Al thought, expected a quick comeback. An argument. Or at least a sign that he'd startled his opponent. So Al didn't offer any of that. With Lovetz watching him, he sipped at his beer and continued to eat his lunch.

He stopped when Stephanie Keller took a sheet of paper out of the portfolio that was sitting near her feet and laid it on the table at his elbow. Looked at it for a couple of seconds, then resumed eating.

''Are you married, Admiral?'' she asked.

''Nope,'' Al said.

''But you've been married.''

Al shrugged. ''Yeah.''

''I married Sam because I loved him. I still love him.

57

I want to find him so that we can . . . talk."

"Talk."

"Yes."

"Ms. Keller?"

She didn't answer, just looked steadily at him.

"I don't believe you," Al told her.

CHAPTER

FIVE

She stood staring out the window, unmoving, for such a long time that Al's imagination began to wander. His mind's eye saw her turn into a plaster statue, like the Snow White Silvio had stuck into the dirt out by the trailer.

Worse, he saw her face turn into Alia's.

That idea made him seize his glass and drain the beer out of it in one long gulp.

No . . . couldn't be. She couldn't be. Ziggy would know. Wouldn't she? She'd have to know.

He forced himself to calm down, to go on breathing normally as he refilled his glass and took the last few bites of Meltdown from his plate. He'd explained to Sam once, when both of them were half in the bag, that he'd learned how not to let other people see that he was nervous.

"Huh?" Sam had responded.

The way Sam kept blinking at him told him that Sam could see at least two of him, maybe three. He grinned at that.

He let the adrenaline run out the soles of his feet, he said.

Sam squeezed his eyes shut, then opened them again, like window shades snapping up to the rod. "Huh?" he repeated. "You can't do that." Before Al could say anything more, Sam had scrunched down in his side of the booth and peered under the table at Al's shoes. When he straightened up again, he wavered back and forth, then propped his head up with his hands. "You can't do that," he announced.

"Why not?" Al countered.

"Because . . ." Sam's voice trailed off. "Because."

Sam was wrong.

There were people Al would not, could not, allow to see that he was not in control. Cops. Senior officers. The V.C. Weitzman.

Sam.

People to whom he could not say what he wanted to say, because his own anger would have acted against him. People who would have taken his fear and used it to crush him.

So he would simply not be afraid.

He would let the fear and the anger run out of him, like water down a drain, and be left with strength. Lack of negative emotion. Control.

The hand that laid his fork down on the pitted surface of the picnic table didn't tremble. His Navy ring caught the edge of a beam of sunlight as he rested his palm on the tabletop. The flash made Lovetz blink.

Finally, Stephanie Keller turned away from the window. "We met at Cornell," she told Al. "In New York."

"I know where it is," Al replied.

"I fell in love with him."

"That's great," Al said.

She rolled her teeth over her lower lip and cupped her elbows in her palms. "My company sells textbooks. I started out telemarketing part-time—selling books over the phone. I'm vice president of marketing now. I meet a lot of people who are a hard sell. I have lunch with a lot of people who are a hard sell."

"And they end up with a roomful of books."

Silvio and Monica's place wasn't that big; she was only a few yards away, and Al could see every nuance in her expression. She was as calm as the surface of a duck pond. There wasn't a drop of sweat on her. Her gaze and Al's both fell on the sheet of paper she'd left on the picnic table: a photocopy of a marriage license from Tompkins County, New York, dated June 1976 and bearing Sam Beckett's signature.

"Nice up there in the spring," Al commented. "Sam's family enjoy the wedding?"

"They didn't come."

"No? How'd they miss something like that?"

Lovetz shifted on the picnic bench. Al glanced at him, thinking at first that the man's butt was suffering stabs of agony from almost an hour of sitting on a wooden plank. But Lovetz was looking at his client, nodding almost imperceptibly, like a parent urging on a reluctant child.

"They were having problems then," Stephanie went on. "He didn't have much contact with them."

"Oh . . . ?"

"Because he wasn't there, at home, when his father passed away. I think his family—his brother, especially—questioned what his priorities were. So they were . . . estranged." She smiled humorlessly. "That sounds like something out of a magazine article."

"His brother . . ."

"Tom."

"The guy you met yesterday morning."

"Yes," Stephanie nodded.

"The guy who says he doesn't know anything about Sam getting married to anybody except Donna Alessi. He was at *that* wedding."

"Then I assume he and Sam worked out their differences."

"But Sam never told him about you. He never told his

brother that he got married. Sounds a little strange, doesn't it, Ms. Keller?''

''He was twenty-two years old,'' she said after a minute. ''He was lonely and unhappy and he couldn't get anyone to support the work he wanted to do. I listened to him. I cared about him. After a couple of weeks he asked me to marry him and I said yes. I was twenty. I didn't have any family close by either. We were married less than a month. He said he needed to go back to school. He was working on his medical degree. My tuition was already paid at Cornell. My friends were there. I didn't want to leave. And he wasn't interested in transferring to med school at Cornell. Maybe . . . I suppose we both knew subconsciously that what we'd done wouldn't work out. That we were too young. That we didn't have much in common. So he left. He went back to school, and so did I. I've . . . I never saw him again.''

''But you never bothered to get a divorce.''

''No.''

''Kind of a big oversight, isn't it?''

''I loved him, Admiral.''

Al shrugged mildly. ''That doesn't answer the question.''

Stephanie crossed the room and picked her portfolio up off the floor. After she had set it down on the bench, she held out to Al two items she'd pulled from among its contents: a photograph and a stack of letters fastened together with a rubber band. When Al didn't accept them, she laid the letters on top of the marriage license and displayed the picture so that he couldn't avoid looking at it.

The kid looked happy, he thought. Or was trying to be. He was wearing jeans and a T-shirt, with shaggy, sun-streaked hair falling almost to his collar. A younger version of Stephanie had her arms tucked tightly around Sam's middle with one hand stuck in the back pocket of his jeans. Maybe that explained the glimmer of doubt in

Sam's expression: the Sam Beckett that Al had known for thirteen years would definitely not be fond of having his picture taken while somebody else's hand was warming his butt.

Stephanie pressed the photo between his fingers, and he realized then that there were half a dozen of them, not just one. He laid them out in a row on the table and studied them. Bright sunshine, a lake in the background. Other kids smiling and laughing.

"These are all from the same day," he pointed out.

"You said you were married," Stephanie replied. "Did you have someone with a camera follow you and your wife around?"

"No," Al said.

None of these pictures meant anything—not even the one of Sam kissing her, which had undoubtedly been taken without Sam's knowledge and which made the kid look like he was mining for gold. *Insufficient evidence,* he thought. *Doesn't prove squat.* Kids went on dates out by the lake. Kids made out—even Sam. And Stephanie Keller the college student was a pretty girl with a great figure, not much of which was covered by her shorts and tank top. For a second Al was tempted to ask Stephanie Keller the textbook marketing queen if she'd sold Sam a roll in the hay that afternoon.

"Twenty-three years," he said, pulling his eyes away from the photos. "Why now?"

He looked at Lovetz, but all the lawyer did was gaze at him grandly, as if he were posing to be the next face on Mount Rushmore. He expected Stephanie to come up with something that would blow him out of his plastic chair—the coup de grâce, the big finale, the half-pound burger with onions, tomatoes and cheese. "I'm dying," maybe. Or "I want him to meet his son." Yeah, that would do the trick. Sam had been a little haphazard about the birth control and had a grown kid in Alexandria, or

Ithaca, or in the motel over in Socorro, who looked just like him.

Instead, all Stephanie said was "Closure."

"What?"

Lovetz spoke up finally, with his manicured hands folded neatly on the picnic table in front of him. He coughed once, then announced, "Ms. Keller would like to tidy things up. This has gone on for too long. She would like to sit down with Dr. Beckett to discuss what happened between them, and then close the door on that part of her life."

"Should've done that a while ago," Al replied.

The lawyer turned to look at his client, then concluded, "Time gets away from you."

You got that right, Al thought.

"Will you tell me where he is?" Stephanie asked.

"I'll think about it," Al said.

"It's important to me, Admiral."

"I'll think about it."

Al got up from the table, as if he intended to leave. Lovetz got up too, abruptly, nearly tripping himself over the picnic bench. Al imagined the lawyer flinging himself in front of the door to block Al's exit, because they'd been here for an hour and Lovetz hadn't gotten what he came for. They were standing there, the three of them, midway between the table and the door, when Silvio came in from the kitchen carrying a half-empty cellophane package of cheap supermarket cookies. He towered over them, like Snow did over her dwarfs out in the back.

"Gimme your keys," he said to Lovetz, "and I'll go open up your car for you. You get in there now and you'll fry the skin right off your ass."

"Ahhhh," Lovetz murmured, staring at Silvio as if nothing he'd said had been in English.

"Keys." Silvio wiggled his fingers in Lovetz's face.

Lovetz could not have surrendered his key ring any

64

more quickly if Silvio had been a carjacker. He stood watching with his mouth open as Silvio went out the front door, cookies dangling from his hand. Then he swung toward Al, with his index finger pointing at Al's nose.

"You," he announced, "are not taking this seriously."

"I take everything seriously," Al told him.

"You could end up regretting your lack of cooperation, Admiral Calavicci."

"You threatening me, Lovetz?" Al inquired.

"I . . . ahhhh." Lovetz clamped his mouth shut and glared malevolently at Al. A moment later he strode out of TACOS BURGERS; hands clenched together, and muttering something about the fate of his rental car.

After the door had banged shut behind him, Stephanie reached out, picked up her water glass and drank what remained in it. There was still not a drop of sweat on the woman.

"If I wanted something," she said quietly, "don't you think I would have gone after him when he was on the cover of *Time*?"

"You tell me, Ms. Keller."

She put the glass down. Condensation had left a trail along her palm and her wrist. With one eye on Al, she tugged a paper napkin from the chrome box at the end of the picnic table and wiped her hand dry. "Sam made a promise to me," she said. "And then he left. I don't think that's entirely fair, do you?"

Neither one of them answered the question. A moment later Al countered it with another one: "How's Joe?"

Judging by the look that shot across her face, she thought that was the funniest thing she had heard all day. "Joe," she told Al, "handles real estate closings."

"So it's his partner who's the head of the scams department?"

"Mitchell's right. You aren't taking this seriously."

Her gaze dropped onto the marriage license, lying alongside her plate. A second later, so did his.

"You can get one of those done up in a few hours," Al said. "Couple hundred bucks—depending on who you know. And that's a copy. If it was the original, I could get the paper dated. But copies . . . you could've cut-and-pasted the hell out of that and then copied it. You can work a lot of magic with a photocopier."

A muscle in Stephanie's cheek twitched as he spoke that last word, as if she had a tic. That was all the confirmation Al needed.

"Listen," he went on. "Get rid of the hired help. You and I can talk."

The tone in his voice—soft, gentle, musical—always worked. He'd used it to propose to Sharon. To convince Ruthie (temporarily, anyway) that divorce wasn't a good idea. To talk Tina into bed the first time. It always worked. Always. It was pure, awe-inspiring Calavicci magic.

It didn't work.

"No, Admiral," Stephanie replied. "You and I are done talking. I want to talk to Sam now."

"If . . . ," Al began.

She shook her head. "Mitchell and I are staying at El Adobe. I assume you know where that is—you seem to be very familiar with this area." With one last tiny smile, she asked, "Or do you just frequent the places that are off the beaten path?"

"No," Al said, unsure what he was denying.

"You'll tell Sam."

He frowned. "Yeah. I'll tell Sam."

A screech from the parking lot snapped their attention away from each other. They reached the hot, dusty square of dirt and gravel to discover that Lovetz, trembling and terrified, had taken refuge alongside the Coke machine.

"What's the matter?" Al demanded.

His eyes followed Lovetz's, first to Silvio, standing

66

near the rental car, then to Monica, who, coming out from the trailer, had taken up a position at the corner of TA-COS BURGERS. Both of them were armed.

"Ahhhhh," Lovetz moaned.

"There was a snake cooling off under his car," Silvio explained.

Al raised a brow. "Rattler?"

Silvio nodded. "Little one, though."

"You gonna shoot it, or him?"

"It was . . . ," Lovetz gibbered.

"Calm down, Mitchell," Stephanie told him quietly. "These people live out here. I don't think they'd stand by and let the snake attack you."

"It's *his* fault." Lovetz's index finger jabbed in Al's direction.

"Yes, well. I'm going to go to the ladies' room. Then we can leave. Go back to the hotel. And give Admiral Calavicci some time to think."

She had been gone for a minute when Lovetz hauled himself away from the shelter of the Coke machine. It occurred to him then that other specimens of the New Mexico desert fauna might have crept into the shadow of the machine, and, dancing like a puppet, he scrambled away from his hiding place, ending up within arm's reach of Al.

"That's why he wanted my keys!" he blurted, shaking his finger at Silvio. "He was going to let the snake into my car!"

Silvio gazed at him for a second, then shook his head and walked off toward Monica.

"You people are *insane*!" Lovetz howled. "Stephanie? Stephanie, come on, or I'm leaving you out here!" When she failed to appear, his face reddened and he resumed flailing his fist at Al. His mouth was open, as if he intended to regale Al with a string of invective that would leave him stunned and whimpering, but nothing reached his lips except several small sputtering sounds. His gaze remained glued to Al's until Stephanie emerged from TACOS BURGERS; then he issued one final squawk and stalked off to his car.

"Should've let me shoot him," Silvio said to Al as the rental car disappeared in a huge billow of road dust.

"Don't tempt me," Al replied.

CHAPTER
SIX

"I know Sam dated other people before we met," Donna murmured. "*I* dated other people before we met. I was engaged. Of course, it was somebody my mother thought was right for me, but . . ."

Her voice trailed off. She was trying very hard not to look at Al, even more so to avoid the pictures that were spread out on her desk—the pictures Stephanie Keller had deliberately left behind at TACOS BURGERS, along with the photocopied marriage license and her letters, which Al had also taken custody of. The letters were still fastened together with the rubber band. He hadn't taken a closer look at those yet. A glance at the top one told him that that one, at least, had been written by someone who could do a damn fine job of forging Sam Beckett's handwriting. Either that, or it had been written by Sam.

"Did you believe her?" Donna asked pointedly.

Al swung around. She was staring at him. "What?" he said, hiking a brow. "That Sam's a bigamist? He married her and then forgot all about her, like a bunch of shirts he left at the dry cleaner's?"

"No. That . . ."

"It's a crock, honey. The whole thing's a crock." When Donna's expression didn't change, he softened his voice, a gesture he wasn't sure would accomplish anything. "I've been around enough con artists to know one when I see one. Hell, I've *been* a con artist."

"A lot of people would say you still are," Donna replied.

He snickered, as if he thought the remark was cute, but that didn't help either of them. "Lovetz is so full of it, it oozes out all over the table. That E-S-Q isn't after his name because he loves the law. It's there because he loves the loopholes in the law. He's out for a buck. I'm still not sure where he thinks the buck is, but he's definitely got a scam going here."

Donna sighed, wandered back and forth a couple of steps, then reached out to line up a pair of manila file folders that lay across the top of her "In" box. She had already tidied everything else on her desk. "But her? What about her?"

"She was tougher to read," Al confessed.

"But you did read her."

A smile crept across his face. He raised his right hand and rubbed it against his mouth, as if he wanted to wipe the smile away. All he succeeded in doing was turning it a little more wry. "I've done a lot of things to—with—women in my life. Did I read her? Man, I don't know." With Donna still watching him closely, he sank onto the sofa that filled most of the only unbroken wall in her office and closed his eyes for a moment. "I'm not gonna try to hand you anything," he told her when his eyes drifted open again. "You'd hand it right back to me. I know in my bones that this is a scam. But talking to her . . ."

"You thought her story was credible."

"Yeah. I did."

"You believe she married Sam."

There was no rancor in Donna's voice; she spoke as evenly as if she'd asked him the whereabouts of a book she'd loaned him, or if he knew the weather forecast for the rest of the weekend.

70

"I thought what she came up with was 'credible,'"
he said. "I didn't say *I* believed her. I think other people
might. He was a kid. She was a pretty girl. She claims
she was a shoulder to cry on, back when he was having
all that trouble with his family."

"When?"

"'Seventy-six," Al said. "June. She says they got
married in June."

Donna shook her head firmly. "Nancy."

"Hmmm?"

"'Seventy-six was the Year of Nancy. The girl he had
the love affair with in Cambridge. Don't you remember?
He was renting a room from her grandmother." Her expression did change then.

"What?" Al asked.

"July. He didn't meet Nancy till July. This Stephanie
person says they were only together a few weeks . . ."

Al snorted at her. "You think he married somebody
in New York in June, walked out on her in July, and
immediately had a fling with somebody else? We're talking about Sam Beckett here, not Warren Beatty. Listen.
Donna. I shouldn't have said anything. Those pictures
don't prove squat. Any more than that picture I've got
of me with Miss February."

"Then what's it for, Al?"

"I don't know. I went out there figuring I could wrap
this up in a nice neat package with a bow on top, and I
ended up not figuring out a thing except that Mitchell
Lovetz gives me acid indigestion."

"She wants Sam's money? Is that it?"

"She didn't say so."

"Maybe she wouldn't, right off the bat. Besides . . .
there isn't any money."

"Except the stocks."

"Nobody knows about the stocks, except for you and
me and Sam."

"What, then? Give me a suggestion."

71

"I haven't got any."

She turned away from him. Right before she did, her eyes were full; when she looked at him again they were dry. How she'd managed that without smudging her mascara, Al couldn't figure out.

"Unless," she said, "she wants the name I decided not to use."

"Where's that gonna get her?" Al asked.

"I don't know. I don't know." She winced and shifted her gaze around the room as if she couldn't decide what to focus on. "Do you know how badly I want to hold him?" she asked at a point when she seemed to be looking at the knob on the door to the corridor.

Al nodded. "Yeah. I do."

"I want . . . I just want him to *be* here. God, I want him to be here."

"Me too," Al told her. He got up off the sofa then, went to her and wrapped his arms around her. She was trembling, but that stopped after a minute, and she rested her head on his shoulder, holding onto the sleeves of his uniform blouse with both hands. "It's okay," Al murmured into her ear. "It's okay, honey."

She shuddered again. Al drew back from her and cupped her face between his hands. "I feel like . . . ," she muttered.

"I know what you feel like," Al replied.

"It's not . . . I shouldn't get this upset. It's a scam. Nobody who knows Sam would believe her. Tom didn't believe her. Nobody else I talked to even mentioned the 'wife' thing. Unless . . . unless that was why they all wanted Sam to call them. And the rest of what they told me was just an excuse." Her eyes suddenly grew very bright, the rest of her face artificially cheerful.

Al pulled her back in and stroked the back of her hair with the palm of his right hand. "Don't let your imagination go nuts," he told her. "They're lying. That's the bottom line. And none of what they've got"—he waved

72

a dismissive hand at Stephanie's "proof"—"would hold up in court."

"What if . . ." Donna stepped away from him and studied his expression for a moment. "What if it holds up in the Court of Public Opinion?"

Al didn't reply.

"That's what *you're* worried about, isn't it?" Donna pressed.

"Yeah," Al admitted.

"That they'll say something to the wrong person, and that person will turn to another person, and another, and another, and the ripples they make will turn into a tsunami. Their little scam will shut the Project down." Donna's teeth rolled over her lower lip. "And we'll never get Sam back."

"We'll get him back."

"Al . . ."

"We'll get him back," the Observer repeated.

In another reality, one that Al vaguely remembered, he had not liked Donna Alessi. He had found her unfriendly to the point of being brittle—"the Ice Princess," he'd called her. Sam's third Leap had changed her, softened the rough edges, made her far less suspicious of other people's motives. They still had days when all that bound them together was their shared love of Sam, but most of the time . . .

"I understand," he told her, pretending not to notice the way her hands were trembling. "I know how you feel. I understand everything—except why, when you had him back here, you let him go again."

He had posed that question to her only once before, a year ago, at the end of the simo-Leap that had sent Al to 1945 and Sam back home to the Project. Donna offered the same answer to him now that she had then: "It wasn't my decision."

"Yeah," Al said. "That's the trouble. If your husband would let anybody help him make up his mind, instead

73

of . . .'' He stopped, wandered away from Donna and grimaced. ''I wanted to say, 'leaping into things.' You should've gotten a gun from Security and shot his knee-caps off.''

Donna shook her head. ''I don't think that would have stopped him. At best, it might have slowed him down.''

''Slow down 'Sam Beckett, the Irresistible Force'?'' With another grimace, Al sank back down onto the sofa and tipped his head back to stretch the kink that was building in the muscles of his neck. ''Nobody's ever slowed him down, and God knows, nobody's ever stopped him.''

Donna leaned a hip against the edge of her desk and hugged herself, then put her arms down. She seemed to have shaken off her melancholy all of a sudden, the way an animal shakes water off its fur. With an eye on Al, she leaned over and picked up Stephanie Keller's little bundle of letters. She turned them over in her hands several times, then asked Al, ''Should we read these?''

''I guess that's what she wants.''

Sam Beckett's wife gazed solemnly down at the collection of paper in her hands. Then, as if her feelings had abruptly switched gears again, she snapped the rubber bands off the package, rolled them onto her wrist, and began to read.

CHAPTER
SEVEN

The only part of Sam that Al could see was his shoes. C.J. Williams's shoes, actually—white cross-trainers with dark blue stripes on the sides. They were sticking out from under C.J.'s Chrysler, which had been carefully jacked up and blocked. The jack looked like a good solid one, but still, Al didn't think it was the best idea in the world to crawl underneath a couple of tons of steel while you were all by yourself. Any number of accidents could happen. When a minute or two had gone by without a wiggle from C.J.'s shoes, Al began to worry that one of them already had.

"You asleep under there?" he asked.

Nothing. Sam had to have heard him arrive, he thought; the Imaging Chamber door made more noise than Armageddon, and he'd opened it only a few yards away. Maybe Sam was still peeved over being shaken out of a sound sleep and had decided to pull the old silent act for the umpty-umpth time.

Yeah, he was okay. Wasn't he?

"Sam?" Al said, and bent over to peer under the car. That didn't help much. He still couldn't see Sam's face, or any kind of a sign that Sam was alive and kicking. "What're you doing under there? You changing the oil or something?"

"No," Sam said.

Al shuddered. "You wanna come out of there, so I don't have to talk to your feet?"

Another half a minute or so had gone by before Sam crabbed himself out from under the car. The last couple of bars of the silent act, Al supposed. But there wasn't any indication on Sam's face that he was annoyed at Al. He just had that pinched look he always wore when there wasn't enough slack in his leash.

"There's nothing wrong with it that I can find," he said, not particularly to Al.

"Did you think there was gonna be?"

"I don't know." Sam turned away, brushed dirt and bits of leaves off his jeans and sweatshirt, then stared unhappily at the Chrysler, as if it had let him down in some substantial way. "I checked everything I could think of," he murmured. "It could use a new air filter, but . . ."

"Sam," Al said. "I told you nothing happens to C.J. He's not gonna have a car accident. Is that what you're looking for? You wanted somebody to have cut the brake lines or something? I told you—"

"Yeah, I know what you told me."

"Then what are you messing around with the car for?"

"Because . . ." Sam stared at his partner for a moment, then sat down on one of the green Adirondack chairs that filled most of C.J.'s minuscule backyard. "Because what you've told me is pretty much nothing. I'm here for a reason, and I don't like the fact that so much time is going by without my even knowing what I'm supposed to do. There's nobody here, Al. Just me and the dog. According to the notes in his desk"—he nodded toward the house—"nobody's due up here till Easter. So either something happens here, or I need to leave here and find out where it *does* happen. I really need some help! It's been more than twenty-four hours, and all you and Ziggy can tell me is what I'm *not* supposed to do."

"We're working as hard as we can," Al replied. "It's not our fault the guy's life is boring." He ignored the look that got from Sam. "Look—maybe you're looking for something too grand. Maybe it's something simple. You made one Leap where all you were supposed to do was get a cat out of a tree."

"But the cat was right there when I Leaped in," Sam fussed. "Along with that old lady screeching at me and tugging at my sleeve. She told me what to do. There wasn't any question about it." He began to drum his knuckles absently on the flat arm of the chair. "Isn't it sort of counterproductive to have me wander around here, doing nothing? Huh? If I'm supposed to rescue another cat, wouldn't it make more sense to point that out to me so I could do it and go on to the next thing?"

"I guess," Al said.

"Well, then?"

"Well, then, what? I'm not in charge here. And it's not like I can ask for an appointment with Whoever's running this show so I can point out the problems we're having. Jeez, Sam."

"I know," Sam sighed. To Al, he sounded like a kid who wasn't sold on his parents' explanation of why he couldn't have a new bike.

Sam's eyes began to wander, crawling over things one at a time. He'd never had any formal military training, but he was conducting a careful visual sweep of the territory that rivaled anything Al had ever been taught to do. Al watched him do it, impressed by the level of Sam's concentration. They'd covered about ninety percent of Sam's field of view when Al realized that going over C.J.'s car with a fine-toothed comb was more than likely Sam's last chore of the day. He'd probably spent the morning checking the wiring inside Twelve Maple Lane and cleaning oily rags out of the garage.

"Where's the pup?" Al asked, for lack of anything better to say.

77

"Taking a nap in front of the fireplace. And don't tell me that's what I ought to be doing."

"Unless you want to retrofit the house so it's earthquake-proof," Al replied.

"What?"

"Nothing. Nothing."

"This is not a joke, Al."

"Kid . . . ," Al said heavily. He looked around, not wanting to find anything in particular, but taking note of the vividly blue sky, the towering evergreens, the serene Norman Rockwell–painting quality of the lakefront. This was a *nice* place, he thought, except that if he'd been plopped in here instead of Sam, he would have been no more content with the situation than Sam was. He knew a whole collection of people for whom a few days' worth of vegging out at Edwards Lake, with the company of good old Rufus the Woofie, a stack of books and a fridge full of six-packs, would have been sheer paradise. But everybody had a different idea of heaven—Al could vaguely recall someone telling him that, during those years when his clothes had been too big for him and a nun with a mean gleam in her eye had approached him once a month with scissors in her hand.

A different idea of heaven. Verbena Beeks had been kind enough to point out to him that for him and for Sam, heaven was not a place where you couldn't keep moving.

"What if," Sam proposed, as he went on scanning the perimeter, "what if there's somebody up here that I don't know about?"

"Like who?"

"I don't know. It doesn't matter. Just somebody."

Al warmed to the idea. "A guy somebody or a girl somebody?"

"Just listen, would you?"

"I'm listening," Al said. "But you're right, Sam. Man, it's deserted up here. You could make all kinds of noise, and nobody'd hear you. You're right! I should mention this to Tina. Those walls at the Project aren't exactly soundproof, and she gets a little embarrassed sometimes about expressing her feelings." He grinned broadly. "If you catch my drift."

Sam winced at him. "If I didn't, I'm sure you'd explain it to me."

Al crooned softly, just a couple of bars: "Olllllld maaaaan riiiiiiiver . . ." Then stopped and grinned again. "Place like this . . . yeah, Sam, it'd be perfect. Thanks."

The Observer expected his partner to respond with his usual litany of complaints: that Al's sex life mattered to him more than world peace, that Al could never keep his attention focused on the matter at hand, that Al didn't understand how important it was to complete the Leaps as neatly and quickly as possible, and yada, yada, yada. To his surprise, a look of awed fascination had crept into Sam's eyes. *Kinda like I must've looked that time Lily Ann—what was her name? Harriman, Harrison, something like that—told me if I came out back with her, she'd show me her book report.* Part of him wished Sam's awe had something to do with pigtailed girls and straying fingers; the rest of him knew it didn't.

"What if," Sam said urgently, "what if somebody came up here for a, you know, a rendezvous, and something happened? Huh? What if somebody got, oh, trapped, and couldn't get out? There's nobody up here!"

"I noticed that," Al replied.

"Well? What if something like that happened?"

"If somebody came up here for a Fun Ship Cruise?"

Sam's eyes narrowed. "A what?"

"A—"

A brisk wave of Sam's right hand cut Al off at the pass. "You've got more names for it than my cousin Danny had for going to the bathroom. Can't you just call it— Never mind. I don't want to know. Would you pay attention to me? What if somebody did get trapped in

79

one of these houses, and couldn't reach the phone? Couldn't call for help? They could starve to death. Or die of thirst. Or if they're hurt?" Paying no attention to the reaction his rambling provoked from Al, he got up from his chair, shoved his hands through his hair and began to look at the houses around him, one at a time. "Somebody could die up here, Al, and nobody would know till Easter."

"There aren't any cars here," Al pointed out. "Are there? I don't see any."

"Maybe somebody dropped them off."

"Then the somebody would know that this other somebody is here," Al said. "Wouldn't they? Sam, you're being nuts."

"I'm examining all the possibilities."

"Of some mysterious, helpless person being trapped in one of these houses."

"Yes!" Sam insisted.

"Like for instance if they were handcuffed to the bed?"

Sam grimaced, "You *would* think of a scenario like that. All right, yes, if they were handcuffed to the bed."

"Sam," Al said.

"What?"

"That's a Stephen King novel."

"It's what?" Sam sputtered. "What are you talking about?"

"You remember who Stephen King is, don't you? You met him on one of your Leaps." It crossed Al's mind that Sam—and Al himself—would be better off not remembering that particular Leap. He let his gaze drift around, again taking in the brilliant color of the sky, the delicate branches of the trees that had lost their leaves, the disgruntled face of his best friend. Yin and yang, he thought: if there was good, then there was evil. The worst part of Sam's Leaping was that his friend kept uncovering evil that existed in what looked like human form.

80

He remembered thinking of Alia—the woman the Quantum Leap staff had dubbed "the Evil Leaper"—and shuddered, but Sam didn't seem to notice.

"I said," Sam repeated, "I remember."

Al hadn't heard him say it the first time. "That was a book of his," he went on, dragging himself back to the point. "You read it. It's probably floating around in the Swiss cheese somewhere. There's nobody trapped up here, Sam."

"How can you be sure of that?" Sam asked.

"Go look if you want," Al offered.

"I will," Sam said.

"You're not gonna find anybody."

"You might be wrong."

Al took a step back to get himself out of Sam's flight path and asked, "And what do you win if I am?"

"I'll get out of here," Sam replied.

I've forgotten more than you'll ever know.

Sam had never spoken those words to anyone—had never gloated to anyone about his intelligence, which, after all, was not something he could personally take credit for. But whether or not he had ever said them aloud, those words, right now, seemed to be the greatest truth he could imagine.

I don't remember that book, he thought. *If Al says I read it, then I must have read it. But I don't remember. How many books have I read that I don't remember? How many . . . how many people have I met that I don't remember? How many things have I said, and done— things that were important to me? How much of my life is . . . missing?*

He glanced over his shoulder. Al was still standing there, in the middle of the flagstone path that led up to C.J. Williams's front door, puffing on a cigar and keeping an eye on Sam. He was wearing the silver jacket he'd had on last night, on top of a bronze-colored shirt, black pants and a black necktie. A memory nagged at Sam, and with some effort he was able to pull it into focus: his father, standing on the front steps of the Elk Ridge Presbyterian Church, wearing the hideous red-and-orange tie Katie had given him that morning for Father's Day.

If Al had kids, he mused, *they'd have some job finding him a present that's uglier than the stuff he buys for himself.*

Did Al have kids? he wondered.

Slowly, he sorted through the keys on C.J.'s key ring and found the one tabbed "8." Eight Maple Lane stood in front of him, a house half again as large as C.J.'s, with wide bay windows on either side of the front door.

No . . . just the wives. I'm pretty sure he told me that. Five wives. No kids.

He was opening the door when Al popped in beside him. "I feel like a jigsaw puzzle with half the pieces missing," he muttered.

Al shrugged. "It's not that bad."

"It's not?" Sam said. "How much of your life have you forgotten?"

"Not much. There's a bunch I'd like to forget."

Sam pushed the door shut behind him and turned to stand with his back to it. Al simply walked through the wall to join his friend. "I'll trade places with you anytime," Sam went on. "You have no idea what this feels like, not being able to remember things. I've got eidetic memory—I used to be able to remember *everything*."

"What brought all this on?" Al asked warily.

"I don't remember that book."

"Don't worry about it. King hasn't even written it yet."

"I *have* to worry about it." Sam began to move through the house, the third one in his increasingly more frustrated search. He'd expected each one to match his own perception of a lakeside summer home: durable rugs, comfortable furniture that had already seen a lot of wear and wouldn't mind a little sand being ground into the cushions. Dishes and cookware that had been collected from garage sales and relatives clearing out seldom-used extras. Instead of those things he was greeted by wall-to-wall carpeting in pale colors. Furnishings that even his untrained eye could tell were valuable antiques. China too delicate to stand being clattered around.

"There are people sleeping in bus terminals," he groused, "and look at all this stuff."

"All what stuff?" Al asked.

"That. And that. And that." He pointed.

"I thought you were looking for corpses," Al said. "What're you fussing about stereo systems for?"

He didn't answer the question. Instead, he went from room to room, looking. This house had a second floor, so he checked upstairs too, mumbling at the wide-screened color TV he found in one of the bedrooms. When he returned to the ground floor, Al was examining the rows of record albums lined up beneath the stereo.

"This guy's got a nice collection," the Observer told his partner.

"Swell," Sam replied.

"Anybody dead upstairs?"

"Would you stop?!" Sam barked. "If you think this is such an amusing way to spend time, then you do it. Go back out there, go out to Control, and tell Gooshie to Leap you into me. Go on, try it. You spend a couple of months doing this and see how much fun you think it is. Go on!"

Al gazed at him steadily for a moment, then offered quietly, "We tried. It didn't work."

"You . . . you what?"

"We tried. Leaping me into you."

"When?"

Al's shoulders lifted slightly underneath the silver jacket he'd changed back into before returning to the Imaging Chamber. They remained raised for a second or

83

two, then slowly descended again. "A while ago. I didn't Leap out. I didn't go anywhere. Believe me, we've tried everything we can think of. And we've got people at the Project who've thought of some pretty far-out stuff."

"You could have . . . ," Sam began.

"Could have what?"

"You could have been hurt. Going into the Accelerator. You could have gotten killed."

Al gazed at Sam steadily. "Yeah? Tell me about it." But before Sam could respond, Al had walked through the wall again, forcing the younger man to open the front door of Number Eight so that he could join the Observer outside.

"Ziggy says there's seven hundred and some-odd people in town," he said as Sam locked the door. "She's checking all of 'em. She's found a few whose lives have hit a bump here and there, but nothing out of the ordinary. People get divorced, you know. Break a leg. Have a fender bender. You can't mend everything, Sam."

"I never said I wanted to," Sam replied.

"You could go into town. Meet a few of the locals. Maybe you could do a little of the legwork for Ziggy." Al offered a look of encouragement to his friend. "Maybe somebody'll point out that cat you wanted."

"Cat?"

"In the tree."

Sam stuck his hands in the pockets of his jeans and wandered around for a minute, then shook his head firmly. "No. It's not in town. Whatever I'm looking for is here, Al. Right here, in one of these houses."

"Sam . . ."

"No, I'm sure. I've got a feeling. It's here."

"All right," Al sighed. "Do the Hardy Boys junior detective thing, then, and finish your poking around. But don't blame me when you don't find anything."

"I'm going to find it."

"Yeah. Sure."

84

"Want to bet on it?"

Something in Al's expression changed, so completely that for a moment Sam was sure he'd delivered a blow to a sore spot he didn't know Al had. Then the strange grimace disappeared and Al gestured at him with the cigar. "Yeah," the Observer said. "Wouldn't be much of a bet, though, if we did it for money. No way to pay it off. Tell you what: you find your abandoned somebody handcuffed to the bed, and you get to tell me 'I told you so.' "

" 'I told you so'?" Sam said. "That's all?"

Al winced at him. "Trust me, kid. It's enough."

CHAPTER
EIGHT

A long time ago . . . Sam stopped moving, closed his eyes and began to sort through the fragments of his memory. High school. Yes, he knew he was thinking of high school. Senior year? No, maybe junior year. But no, again, it had been Lisa Parsons who'd pulled him out onto the stage, and he hadn't dated Lisa until his senior year.

"I graduated in '70," he said softly. "And they did the spring production in May. So it was in May of '70."

He opened his eyes then and smiled at his small victory. He couldn't call it anything more than small; details of his growing-up years weren't hard to pin down. It was his adult life that had more holes in it than a fishnet.

"May of '70," he repeated.

The Elk Ridge High drama class had chosen *Our Town* as its presentation for 1970, which was not exactly a groundbreaking decision; every other school in the country had probably made the same choice, if not in 1970, then at some other time. Thornton Wilder's work had a lot of mileage on it, Sam had mused. Some good, some mediocre, some downright terrible. He had the feeling that his classmates' attempt would rate somewhere around "painful," but for Lisa, the chance to portray one of the dead townspeople was a high point in her Elk

Ridge High career. A high point she insisted Sam should share.

"Isn't it *wonderful*?" she said exultantly.

He stood in the middle of the stage, looking out at the rows of metal folding chairs that filled the auditorium and, not wanting to hurt Lisa's feelings, conjured up a smile and offered, "Sure."

"Mr. Dulles would let you be one of the townspeople, if you asked. He likes you."

"Yeah," Sam said, though that was more to indicate that he had heard Lisa's observation than anything else.

"Well?" Lisa pressed. "Are you going to ask?"

"No," he told her. "I don't want to. I . . . I don't enjoy pretending to be somebody else."

The room around him was waiting, he thought. The stage, with its minimal set, ready for the opening of Act One, and the rows of chairs out on the main floor that would be filled by the parents and siblings of the performers. The room seemed to hold the echoes of things that had already happened as it anticipated those that were yet to happen. The only living presence in the room was Lisa. For some reason—Sam was unable to decide why—his own presence did not seem to count.

As it didn't count now.

Laid out around him was the living room of Three Maple Lane, an exhibit he responded to with a scowl and a mumble of displeasure. All the houses he'd investigated before this were 3-D advertisements for conspicuous consumption, but at least they'd each felt like someone's home. This one looked like an upscale art gallery, decorated entirely in black and white, filled with sharp edges and odd, rubbery fabrics.

People *did* live here, according to C.J.'s notebook: a Mr. and Mrs. Daniel Parks and their two children. All four, Sam thought, had to be as stiff as department store dummies. The real C.J. was the writer, but Sam figured he himself had a reasonably good imagination, one which failed to conjure up a picture of anyone relaxing on the Parkses' black leather sofa or eating a midnight snack at the glass-topped dining table. Spilling a drink on the white carpet would probably cause more commotion than a three-alarm fire.

Sam wandered from room to room, shaking his head at the ultra-ultra-modern furniture and listening to the silence that accompanied him. He'd thought C.J.'s house was quiet, but C.J.'s place had Rufus, and the soft clucking of the carriage clock. The sounds of the outdoors too seemed to seep through the walls there, and they didn't here. He suspected this house wasn't any livelier when the Parkses were around.

"Having a great time," he muttered. "Glad you're not here."

When he left, instead of moving on to the next house in line, he stood on the path leading away from the Parkses' front door, gazing in the direction of C.J.'s place. Rufus, he supposed, was still snoozing on the hearth rug, his big black head resting on his paws.

"Now, that's who I should've Leaped into," he murmured. "I wouldn't have to worry about accomplishing a thing. Eat and sleep and get your ears scratched. What a life."

The breeze picked up then, ruffling at his hair and his left cheek. It distracted him as thoroughly as his mother's touch always had, something he realized as soon as it happened. His mother had been a master of subtlety, someone who knew instinctively that she could get more results from a raised eyebrow than from a spanking; more from a single quiet word than from a tirade. Simply resting her hand on his shoulder had persuaded him to follow through on dozens of chores he'd been avoiding.

"Yeah," Sam murmured. "I'm going, I'm going."

He searched two more houses as the afternoon wound down, more carefully than he needed to, he supposed, and certainly more carefully than Al would have. As he checked to make sure that the appliances inside Seven Maple Lane were unplugged, he had a mental picture of the Observer poking his head inside each of the houses under C.J.'s care, calling out, "Hey, is anybody home?" and then moving on.

No one *was* home, of course, and each empty room made his enthusiasm wane a little more. He reached the end of the road closest to the lake without finding anyone, dead or alive. At least Al hadn't come back yet; another full day of no answers was bad enough without the Observer chortling at him.

It's here, he thought as he stood at the land end of the dock half-watching the streaks of color that the lowering sun painted across the mountaintops to the west. *I know whatever I'm supposed to change is* here. *Maybe it hasn't happened yet, but it will.*

The rustle of a leaf dropping to the ground drew his attention away from the sunset. The road ended near the foot of the dock, but, he realized, there was a narrow path winding away from the road and heading north among the trees that lined the shore. It might not actually lead to anything—there didn't seem to be any more houses up that way. More likely, it had been pounded out by generations of feet seeking the best place along the shore to swim. With his hands stuffed into his pockets, Sam began to wander along the path, ducking his head several times to avoid low-hanging tree branches.

It was very much like the little trail that ran near Professor LoNigro's cabin in the Berkshires. He'd walked along that one a hundred times back in the early seventies, trying to clear the cobwebs out of his head, hoping that improved blood flow would cause a flash of inspiration. The crunch of dry leaves under his feet sounded the same now as it had then. But this time Sebastian LoNigro wouldn't be waiting for him when he returned. And unless Al had decided to show up with some information, neither would anyone else.

About a hundred yards north of the dock he found the remains of a house: the crumbling hulk of a stone chimney and the corner of a foundation.

"It's haunted, right?" Sam said to the air. "And I'm supposed to set somebody's earthbound spirit free."

There are no such things as ghosts. He'd told Al that, not very long ago, in spite of a Leap that had urged him to change his mind. But longer ago, he *had* believed in earthbound spirits, because his brother had told him he ought to. As he sat down on a big rock near the shore and propped his head in his hands, he remembered the grin on Tom's freckled face. Tom, who'd been about fourteen, was supposed to be "keeping an eye" on his little brother while their parents and grandparents, with Baby Katie, went to visit a friend. Instead of playing a couple of games of checkers (which was what their parents had had in mind), Tom set himself and Sam off on a bike-riding expedition that ended several miles down the road from their grandparents' home.

Almost out of sight of the road was the shell of a farmhouse. "People died here," Tom announced, tromping among the weeds. "Three of 'em. They didn't wake up, and they got burned to death."

Sam followed his brother hesitantly, not at all happy about playing in a place that seemed to him very much like a graveyard. "Uh-huh," he said solemnly.

"And you know what? They're still here."

Sam jerked himself to a halt, as if the game involved here had been "Red Light, Green Light" instead of "Let's Scare the Crap Out of Sam." So this *was* a graveyard. His hazel eyes widened in a mixture of horror and trepidation as he began to look around for the headstones of those three unfortunate people. "They're buried here?" he whispered.

"No, you doofus," Tom said. "Their ghosts are here."

"There's no such things as ghosts," Sam announced in pure, eight-year-old annoyance.

"Is so," Tom replied.

"Dad says there's not."

"He's just saying that so you won't get scared." Tom, the very picture of knowledge and authority, drew himself up to his full five-foot-four and folded his arms over the front of his plaid flannel shirt. "Ask Grandma. People have heard all kinds of noises. And sometimes they see 'em."

Sam pulled his head in a little, trying to look in several directions at once so that nothing could sneak up on him. "What do they look like?"

"White. They're all white."

"Even their clothes?"

"Yup."

"You're making this up."

Tom shook his head firmly. "Am not. Ask Grandma."

"How come they're still here? You're supposed to go to heaven when you die." He didn't bother mentioning That Other Place; it didn't seem possible that any of the people who lived near Grandma and Grandpa could be bad enough to be condemned to spend eternity there.

Still strolling around in a mess that would leave fat brown burrs sticking to the legs of his jeans, Tom said, "'Cause they didn't finish what they were supposed to do. Everybody's got something they're supposed to do in their life, and if you don't get a chance to do it, you can't leave. You have to stay around forever and ever, as a ghost."

This did not quite jibe with the things Sam had been told in church, or by his parents. Indignant, he shrilled at his brother, "You're making this *up*."

"Am not!"

The sound of Tom's voice and the image of his grin, both deeply etched in Sam's memory, hung in the autumn air, overlaid with another picture: Tom as an adult, his

91

eyes surrounded by tiny lines, the border of his sandy hair receded way back from his forehead. The grin was the same, though, and the voice again filled with joy and exultation. With *life*.

"*Hoooooyaaaaahhhh!*"

Sam had gone pounding through the weeds in frantic pursuit of his brother, terrified of being left alone among the remains of that burned-down house. His face was crimson when the chase ended.

"You *lie*!" he'd shrieked.

"Come back at night," Tom offered as he picked up his bike. "You'll see. They'll be here. You're just here too early."

Too early . . . too early . . . too . . .

"Too early," Sam murmured. "Well . . . that's got to be better than being too late again."

The sun had dipped below the mountaintops. It would be dark in another half hour or so, he realized. If he wanted to do any more searching, he ought to do it now, and quickly, so that he could go back and feed Rufus, then let him outside for a run. He'd need to pull on a jacket for that—the wind was blowing more strongly now, coming from the east instead of in over the water.

He'd gone a few steps up Maple Lane when something prickled at his nose, and he stopped to sniff at the chilled air. An odd scent drifted by, stirred up by the wind.

Garbage? One of the cans you haven't checked yet.

A delicate tinkling sound made him whirl around. He was startled, thinking of earthbound spirits, until he remembered the wind chimes hanging outside one of the houses he'd visited.

Then the smell wafted by again, this time strong enough to carry a name with it. Not garbage; it was something that seventeen years on a farm had taught him to identify. *The smell of Death*, his mind suggested to him for the second time on this Leap.

You're spooking yourself. All that nonsense from Al

about looking for corpses . . . and thinking about ghosts. You're alone, and it's getting dark. You're just getting carried away.

But he wasn't.

None of these houses had basements—they had crawl spaces. And he'd been looking *inside* the houses.

"Ahhhh, damn," he hissed. "What if . . . Oh boy."

His heart pounded as hard as it had that sunny day out in the weeds off Hooper Road. The plumbing and electrical wiring for the dozen homes on Maple Lane ran underneath them. What if someone had crawled in, intending to look for a leak or a bad wire? They didn't need to be handcuffed to a bed. They could be lying under the house, in a bed of old leaves and dirt and mouse droppings with floorboards a few inches above them. Muttering "Dammit" over and over to himself, he bolted back to C.J.'s house, seized a flashlight from among the collection of tools in the garage, then followed his nose to the source of the smell.

The crawl space he chose proved to be as inhospitable as he'd thought it would be: it was filled with small, sharp rocks, cobwebs and dust that made him sneeze hard and repeatedly as he shoved his way through on his belly. Several sweeps with the flashlight revealed clumps of debris that might conceal a human form, and he checked them out one by one. The first two were composed of nothing but chunks of leftover lumber and chimney stones. The third one oozed the smell that had brought Sam down here. Very much aware that if a jolt from a bad wire could kill whoever lay behind this heap of leaves, it could do the same to him, he reached out slowly and began to brush aside the debris.

Things crawled up his fingers.

He flailed his hand as much as he could to shake off the invaders. If there were maggots at work, he thought with a heavy rush of despair, then he was far too late—*again*—to help whoever this was. *But maybe*, he thought,

93

I'm just supposed to find them. And get them out from under the house. Then call the family and . . .

But that wasn't the answer either.

He probed forward once more—and slid his fingers into something wet and slimy and undeniably dead.

He washed his hands four times before he fed Rufus. That didn't seem to be enough, although his skin was certainly clean now (in fact, it was red and burning from the assault he'd given it) and there'd been no threat of rabies. The body he'd uncovered had expired of old age, it looked like, not electrocution and not virulent disease.

Rufus looked up at him patiently as he emptied the can of dog food into a big steel bowl. "Guess I could use your nose, huh, boy?" Sam sighed. "Can't tell the difference between dead person and dead raccoon until I stick my hand into it. Tom would laugh his head off at that one." When Rufus raised a brow, Sam heaved another sigh and set the bowl on the floor. He watched Rufus's tail wag for a moment, then returned to the sink to rinse out the empty can.

"It's still possible," he commented as Rufus wolfed down his dinner. "I mean, somebody *could* be under there. But they're not, are they? If somebody was around, they would've left traces. Their car. An unlocked door. Something! Nobody's around, are they? There's nobody here. I could spend half the night crawling under these houses and not find anything at all . . . except a lot of wildlife that's not happy about being disturbed."

Rufus continued to chow down.

"But it's *here,*" Sam insisted, wandering around the kitchen. "I know it is. I've got to trust my instincts . . . even if my instincts told me you were the Creature from the Black Lagoon." He shook his head wryly, but Rufus failed to notice either the gesture or the chagrin that prompted it. "What I need to find is here someplace," he concluded. "Waiting for me."

94

So he resumed his search, with C.J.'s key ring in one hand and the flashlight in the other. The two houses he had not yet investigated lay at the end of a driveway that forked off Maple Lane. He strode into the first one without any of the hesitation that had marked his visits before sundown, and mentally ran through the checklist he'd established for himself as he moved from room to room. No remains of a fire in the fireplace. Appliances unplugged. No gas leaks. No sign that bright sunlight was overheating anything. No sign that a raccoon, a squirrel or a snake had gotten inside and made itself at home. No dripping faucets, no leaking pipes.

Nothing!

One house left to go.

He was running through his checklist again, berating himself for having overlooked some vital clue, when he unlocked the door of that last house. If he had not been so completely preoccupied, he might have noticed the dark blue Mercedes parked in the carport at the far side of Number Four—a car that had not been there an hour ago.

He went to the kitchen first, to check the refrigerator, the microwave, the stove. Then he returned to the living room and checked the television, the VCR and the fireplace.

As he straightened up, moving away from the hearth, he heard a noise. At first, his mind told him he was wrong. The house was silent, like the others, waiting for its occupants to return. Lying unused in between performances, waiting for the curtain to rise.

Then he heard the noise again.

Sam held his breath. He hoped, rather than expected, to hear it one more time. It had been very faint. Not a sign of life; it might have been a tree branch scratching against a windowpane.

There . . .

Whatever it was, it was coming from upstairs. He

95

climbed the stairs slowly, with his back pressed against the wall of the stairwell. Not a tree branch, he thought. Someone was making noise. A person. A person who wasn't supposed to be here. Ideas churned inside his head: that Al had an "I told you so" coming. That someone's life would be saved, because if whoever was upstairs was still making noise, then they were still alive. Which meant he would not find them lying in a pool of blood. He'd arrived too late on half a dozen Leaps, but not this time.

At least, he hoped not.

The top step creaked, and Sam held his breath again. Really, he told himself, there was no reason for him to be so wary. He was going to rescue someone in trouble, not surprise a murderer in the midst of a vicious crime. Really, he ought to be running toward the source of the sound.

Yes, he should.

He nodded as if to confirm that thought, shuddered once, then straightened himself up and moved forward, toward the room at the end of the second floor's short hallway.

Someone was in trouble here. He was going to rescue whoever that was. They'd be eternally grateful (to C.J. Williams, of course, but that didn't matter much), and when Al showed up later on, Sam would hand him that "I told you so."

By the time he reached the threshold, he was grinning.

The person inside grinned back at him.

"Hi, baby," she purred.

Sam stopped moving in the bedroom doorway. His mouth was hanging open—he could tell that, and supposed he ought to close it, then say "excuse me" and get out of this house. Instead, he stood frozen in the doorway with his mouth open and his hands dangling at his sides.

The woman lying in the middle of the king-sized bed

in the master bedroom of Four Maple Lane was naked. As Sam stared at her in what she didn't know was complete astonishment, she got up from the bed, ran her hands languidly through her thick head of auburn curls, then stood considering the man who had walked in on her. She had been reading a magazine; the sound Sam had heard was the rustle of paper as she turned the pages. Her magazine lay abandoned on the bedspread now. He tried mightily to figure out what the title might be. Or how far along she'd gotten in her reading. Anything to avoid looking at her.

"It took you long enough," she said. "I was beginning to wonder."

"Wonder . . . ?" Sam whispered.

"Where you were."

"Where I were." Sam blinked and shifted his gaze rapidly from the magazine to her face. "I had . . . ummm . . . some . . . uh . . . repairs to take care of."

"Are you finished?"

"Umm . . . uh . . . not really. I . . ."

"I think you are."

She took another step toward him and ran her tongue over her lower lip. She was still eight or nine feet away, and if she kept moving at this rate, he'd have more than enough time to reach the bottom of the stairs before she got to the doorway. If she hadn't gotten up from the bed, he might have been able to turn and run. But her movements held him transfixed. He felt like a snake in a basket at the mercy of a snake charmer.

His lips moved, but all that came out was "Uhhhnnn."

"Did you miss me?" she asked him.

God, she was beautiful. *Think!!* he tried to scream at himself, but there was no possibility of obeying that command. If Al was connected to his neurons, he thought, then Al had probably just hit the ceiling back at the Project, because every one of his neurons was wide awake and firing triple-time. *Well,* he thought, *you wanted to find somebody. And . . . you did.*

"How come you look so surprised?" she wanted to know.

"I . . . ummm . . ."

He flinched when she wrapped her arms around his neck. He found some vague relief in the fact that she was too close for him to look at anything other than her face, but that disappeared when she began to run her tongue over *his* lower lip. He willed his hands to remain at his sides, although they were screaming to be allowed to stroke her shoulders, her back, her . . .

In the moment before she kissed him, he hauled in a long, deep breath. A little extra oxygen would help. Or would it? To his surprise, instead of being able to think clearly, his mind began to talk to itself, as if he had suddenly and spontaneously become schizophrenic.

She's not interested in you. She thinks you're C.J.

Yeah, but I'm here and he's not. Al would be dying right now. She's got the most perfect . . .

They're not real. They're implants. You're a doctor. You know nobody's body looks like that naturally.

So what? They're still perfect.

Look at her hand. Look! Right there. She's wearing a wedding ring. And she's not married to you or C.J. She's a married woman, Beckett. You're making out with a married woman.

So wha—

He took a step backward, abruptly, and collided with the door frame. He was thankful that she didn't pursue him; she just stood where she was, staring at him perplexedly.

"What's the matter?" she asked.

"I . . . have to go," Sam told her.

"Why?"

"I have things to do."

"You have things to do." She folded her arms across

her chest, although she didn't seem to be trying to cover herself. Two deep crevices formed in her forehead, which did a lot of damage to how good she looked. "What's the matter?" she demanded. "You're the one who suggested I come up here. I spent an hour and a half in the car."

"I'm sorry," Sam said.

"You're sorry? C.J., what the hell is going on?"

"I need to take care of something." Although he didn't really need to know her name at this point, his photographic memory provided it from a page he'd examined in C.J.'s notebook. "I'm sorry, Patrice. Pat. Patty," he said quickly, hoping one of those was what C.J. normally called her. "I need to go now. Please. I'm sorry you drove all the way up here. Maybe you should get some rest before you go back. I'll . . . ummm . . . talk to you later."

Then he ran.

Rufus looked up at him curiously when he banged the door shut. He was standing with his back to it, hands pressed flat against the wood, shaking as if he had been pursued by a regiment of demons from hell. Slowly, Rufus got up from the rug in front of the fireplace, padded over to Sam, peered up at him and inquired, "Urf?"

"I need to get out of here," he told the dog.

His hands were vibrating so busily that it took him three tries to grasp C.J.'s car keys. Once he and Rufus were loaded into the car, he banged the door locks down, slammed the car into gear and sent it careening down the dirt road away from the lake.

He was seven miles north of Maple Lane when Al popped into the front passenger seat. Rufus, apparently happy to be in the company of someone other than his sweating, agitated substitute master, leaned forward from his position in the back seat and lolled his tongue at the Observer.

"Sam . . . ," Al said, frowning at his partner.

99

"Uh" was Sam's only response.

"Ziggy said your vitals went nuts again. What's the matter?" The Observer studied Sam's profile for a moment, then his eyes widened. "You didn't . . ." The time traveler didn't reply. "Did you find somebody?" Al prompted, the squeak in his voice a reminder to Sam of the Observer's squeamishness about corpses.

"Um," Sam said.

"Where you going, Sam?"

"Town."

"Then you're going the wrong way. Town's south. There's nothing up this way for another"—he checked the handlink—"eighteen miles. No, seventeen. Sixteen point nine. Jeez, Sam, slow down. You're gonna run into something. Pull over, wouldya? Right there, there's a nice wide shoulder. *Sam*. Pull the car over, before you become one with a pine tree. Now, Sam."

The Observer's voice had grown steadily firmer; his final words were issued as a bark that impressed Rufus but did not seem to have gotten through to Sam. Al was about to repeat them when Sam nudged the car into the wide arc of gravel that Al had pointed out, pushed the gearshift into park and turned off the ignition.

"That's better," Al said.

This stretch of road had no streetlights. Dusk had fallen deeply enough that Sam had to squint to examine his surroundings. When he realized that Al was right, that he had reached nothing other than more vacation homes (though one of them was marked by a sign reading LIVE BAIT KNOCK ON SIDE DOOR), he groaned heavily, slumped back in the seat and put his hands over his face.

"You didn't find somebody dead, did you?" Al ventured.

"No."

"Then . . ."

"I found somebody alive," Sam said. "In one of the

100

upstairs bedrooms. I found a naked woman reading a magazine.''

''A who?''

Sam shifted his head slightly to look at the Observer, whose eyes had widened so much that they seemed to fill his entire head. ''I found a naked woman. Reading a magazine. She was waiting for me. So we could have sex.''

''Okay,'' Al said.

''That's it? 'Okay'?''

''She's not in any danger.''

''No,'' Sam replied. ''She's not in any danger. Unless it's possible to die of frustration. I don't believe this.''

''Believe what?''

The scientist grunted loudly and banged his hands against the steering wheel. ''What am I doing here?'' Before Al could offer a guess, he went on angrily, ''I overreacted again. Again! I'm not fifteen years old. A beautiful naked woman walks up to me and gives me a kiss and calls me 'baby' and what do I do? I flee. For crying out loud.'' He turned to peer at Al, who still failed to say anything. ''Well? This doesn't get any kind of a reaction from you?''

Al said mildly, ''I've done a lot of things in response to a woman who wanted to make love. But you're right, Sam. I don't think 'flee' is on the list.''

''And that's it?''

''And what's it?''

Sam lifted his hands off the steering wheel and gestured for Al's benefit. ''She was gorgeous. All that talking you do about 'casabas'—hers would be in the Casaba Hall of Fame. They were pressed up against me. She wanted me, Al. And I ran out of there. Just like I usually do. Worse than I usually do. I panicked and I ran out of there.''

''What do you want me to tell you?''

''I don't know what I want you to tell me. I was just

101

expecting what you usually do tell me. That I passed up a golden opportunity. That I'm a choirboy. That if I had any common sense, every time a woman approaches me, I should drop my pants and go for it. Don't look at me like that. I didn't hallucinate all those times you gave me that lecture. My Swiss-cheesed brain isn't inventing things that didn't happen. What's different about this time? Why aren't you suggesting that I go back there and say, 'Gee, honey, I'm sorry, I'm ready now'?''

"Because you wouldn't do it," Al said and shrugged.

"That's never stopped you before."

Al considered that suggestion for a long moment, then moved out of the front seat of the car. He stood a couple of paces beyond the front bumper for a minute, carefully trimming the tip off a new cigar, lighting it and taking several slow, thoughtful puffs. Finally, he walked over to the driver's door and gestured for Sam to roll down the window.

"You're right," he said cheerfully. "Never say die. There might come a day when you actually take some advice I give you. So this is what you need to do. Go back to C.J.'s place."

Sam nodded absently. Eventually, he *was* going to have to go there.

"Go in the closet and find a blue shirt. He must have one. Everybody does."

"Uhhh," Sam said, unsure where this was leading.

"Put it on. Then go back to her with your hat in your hands. Figuratively, I mean. You look goofy in hats." Ignoring Sam's expression, the Observer went on, "And you tell her, 'Honey, sweetie pie, dollface, sugarplum, I'm sorry I ran out on you. But I *had* to go put on your favorite shirt. I know how much you like to take it off me.' " That was punctuated by a broadly overplayed lascivious look.

"What if it's not her favorite shirt?" Sam groused.

"Who cares?" Al replied, puffing a smoke ring into

the air above C.J.'s car. "All you gotta do is play it the right way. Walk in there with the right attitude, and she won't care if you're wearing the dog's blanket."

"I see," Sam nodded.

"And it's blue," Al reminded his partner. "Women love blue. Never met one that didn't. In fact, my third—fourth?—wife used to mix up a little batch of blue food coloring now and then, and we'd—"

"I don't want to know."

"Fingerpaint," Al said.

"I told you I didn't want to know."

As if he were entirely lost in the memory, Al began to sketch smooth figure eights in the air with the index finger of the hand that held the cigar. "That woman was a brilliant artist," he sighed.

"There's not a doubt in my mind," Sam told him dryly.

Al snapped himself back to the matter at hand. "So you just go into her bedroom . . ."

"And call her sweetie pie."

"Yeah."

"I've never called a woman 'sweetie pie' in my life. Do you know how dumb that sounds?"

"Sure I do."

"Well, then?" Sam prompted.

"Try 'angel' or 'darling' then. I don't care. They all work. It's not like you're going to be in there reciting 'The Battle Hymn of the Republic' after the blood starts to drain out of your head, buddy boy," Al said, chiding his friend. "Hell, I know it sounds dumb. Everybody knows it sounds dumb. If you wrote down all the stuff people say to each other while they're making love, the poison control people could use it to induce vomiting. It's just a little unbridled passion, Sam. Why are you making this harder than it is?"

Sam replied patiently, "Because I'm not going to indulge in any 'unbridled passion' with a woman who's a

103

complete stranger to me. A woman who thinks I'm some-body else.''

"I pretend I'm Evel Knievel sometimes," Al said. "And that I'm preparing to—"

"I'm not C.J. Williams, Al. And I'm certainly not Evel Knievel. I'm not going to go in there and lie to that woman."

"Yeah," Al replied. "I figured that."

"Then why are you trying to—"

"Because you just carried on at me for *not* trying to."

"I didn't 'carry on' at you. And you were acting weird." Reminded of the problem that had puzzled him a couple of minutes ago, Sam peered at the Observer and asked suspiciously, "What's wrong?"

"Nothing."

"You're not acting like yourself."

Al shrugged. "You try doing this job on an hour's sleep. Tina was so fired up last night that we—"

"Don't tell me about Tina. It's not Tina."

"How do you know that?"

"Because I know you. You don't do this"—Sam mimicked the deep furrows in Al's brow, exaggerating them a bit for emphasis—"when you're just worn out from a long night of . . . whatever it is you do with her. And I *don't* want to know what that is," he added firmly. "There's something wrong. What is it?"

The Observer took a step away from the car, turning his back to Sam, and drew deeply on his cigar a couple of times. When he turned back, he shrugged again. "We're putting in a lot of long hours. You're right—we could be missing something important. So we're inves-tigating everything we can. Beeks has been ferreting so much information out of C.J., he thinks we want to do a Movie of the Week about him. We even know how old he was the first time he—"

"Al."

104

"The first time he hit a home run for his Little League team," Al said.

"Which is certainly an essential bit of trivia."

"It is to him."

"Why don't you try asking him if the word 'adultery' means anything to him?"

"He's not married," Al said with a frown.

"No, but she is."

"She . . . ? Oh, her. Your friend with the magazine."

"She is not my friend."

"Right. She's C.J.'s friend."

"And she shouldn't be. She's a married woman, Al. She says C.J. asked her to come up here from . . . I don't know, wherever she lives, and . . ."

"Enjoy the wonders of nature," Al said happily. "Speaking of which," he went on, nodding at the back-seat, where Rufus had stopped nose-painting the windows, "I think the Woofie needs to water the plants. You take him for a walk lately? Jeez, Sam, you got a dog, you need to . . ."

One glance at the earnest look on Rufus's face told Sam that Al was right. He wasted no time letting both himself and the big dog out of the car. Rufus promptly scuffled over to the faded greenery at the edge of the road, sniffed it briefly, then let go of what he'd been holding onto since lunchtime, a process that Al watched so intently that Sam expected him to begin color commentary.

"There, boy," Al crooned when the dog came trotting back to them. "That feel better?"

"I don't have a dog," Sam told him.

"Yeah, but you've got some common sense. Or at least I thought you did."

"I'm sorry. Okay? I'm sorry." With a shake of his own head, Sam crouched down in front of the dog and scratched him behind the ears. "I'm sorry," he said again, glancing over his shoulder at Al. "Stop looking at me like that. The worst that would have happened is he would've ruined C.J.'s backseat. Does this look like a badly mistreated dog to you? Calm down! I just got distracted, that's all. It happens. Tell me that if you'd gotten propositioned by a beautiful naked woman, you wouldn't have forgotten about this dog's dire need to go to the bathroom."

The Observer muttered something under his breath, then said, "You're right."

"Of course I'm right. The thing is . . ." Sam paused as he climbed back to his feet. "The thing is, I over-reacted. Again. I don't like that, Al. I shouldn't . . . I should be thinking these things through. I'm a scientist. And I don't think I'm the kind of person who panics easily. Am I?"

"Not usually," Al told him.

"Am I calm? Would you describe me as calm, most of the time?"

When Al didn't respond right away, Sam leaned toward him, tipping his head and silently demanding an answer. "I don't know if 'calm' is the right word," Al said, peering into the darkness beyond Sam as if there were actually something there worth looking at. "No, you don't panic easily. I don't guess you would've gotten through med school if you did."

"Med school," Sam mused.

"Yeah, you—"

"I remember med school."

"That's terrific," Al said.

Nodding, over and over, which made him look as if his head were attached to his body by a spring instead of his neck, Sam started to walk in circles around the hologram of his friend. "I remember it," he repeated. "I remember my roommate. Steven. Westerman. Steve Westerman, but everybody called him Blackjack. His hair stood straight up from his head, like this"—he gestured with both hands—"and he had a girlfriend named Susan. Always wore black."

"He did."

"No, Susan did."

"Sam . . ."

"She had a Siamese cat named Wheezer because it had a bunch of allergies." As frantically as he had crawled into the nest of dirt and spiderwebs underneath Seven Maple Lane, he rolled back the left sleeve of his sweatshirt, then his flannel shirt. "There." He displayed the inside of his elbow for Al, pointing at a spot just below the crease. "There's a scar there. See? It's not much of one. But I got that from Wheezer. Tried to pick him up when he didn't want to be picked up."

The Observer took a look—one that seemed just long enough to be polite. Then he drew back and puffed solemnly on his cigar. The fact that he didn't like Sam's rambling was written all over his face.

"I know, I know," Sam said. "I shouldn't be worried about a cat that's probably been dead for ten years."

"That's right."

"But I *remember*. It's . . . it's nice to be able to remember, Al."

"Sure it is, kid."

"I'll try to relax," Sam promised, even though his partner hadn't asked him to. "I'll go back to C.J.'s. I'll have some dinner. Somewhere along the line, I'll figure out a way to smooth things over with Patrice. It's not any of my business what she and C.J. are doing. I don't like it, but it's not up to me. Right? That's not what I'm here for. I'll apologize, and make up some kind of a story, and send her back home. Then I'll get a good night's sleep, and in the morning you'll have an answer for me. That gives Ziggy an entire night to work on it. That's more than enough time."

"Ought to be," Al agreed.

"Then that's it. In the morning we'll know what I'm here to do."

"I sure as hell hope so," Al murmured.

Sam, who was ushering Rufus back into the car, didn't hear him. He slid into the driver's seat, pulled his door shut, and again spoke to Al through the open window. "You were right. You were absolutely right. I need to relax, and think this through. The answer is probably right in front of my face. I'm too tense, and I'm not thinking clearly. Right? I don't have a history of over-reacting."

He gazed steadily at Al, again waiting for a reply. After a moment, Al told him quietly, "Just that one time."

"I'm sorry, Al."

"Yeah."

The engine kicked over with a noticeable hesitation when Sam turned the key in the ignition.

"Maybe you oughta check that over some more," Al suggested.

"I will." Sam put his hand on the gearshift, then took it away and resumed looking at his friend. "I don't have a dog," he said.

"No. You don't have a dog."

"Good night, Al."

"G'night, kid."

Al stayed where he was, blowing smoke rings into the night air, watching Sam turn C.J.'s car around, aiming it back toward Maple Lane. Because of the curve in the road, the car was visible for only a few seconds once it had rolled off in the right direction. As soon as it was gone, Al whooshed out a long, wobbling breath. His trick hadn't worked this time; instead of draining away from him, the emotion he had refused to allow Sam to see seemed to have pooled in his shoes. His hands were cold, and he had no desire to leave the Imaging Chamber and confront whoever happened to be standing in Control,

108

especially not if his socks squished with every step he took.

This is a bad road to be on, kid. A real bad road. I know how bad you want to remember . . . but you can't.

I can't let you.

He intended to fulfill Sam's request, though: he *would* have an answer for him in the morning.

Somehow.

CHAPTER NINE

"Calavicci."

"She came back, Al. Thought you might want to know that. Said she left some personal stuff here. Pictures, and some letters."

Al leaned back in his chair, listening to the unruffled sound of Monica's voice, coming from eighteen miles away and routed through Ziggy.

"Told her I hadn't seen it, maybe you had it," she went on. "Seems like she knew that all along. It was just an excuse to show up here—leaving your hat behind so they've gotta let you back in. She asked me could she have something to drink, and she sat down. Wanted to have a chat."

"So you chatted," Al said.

"Yup."

"About Sam?"

"Yup."

"What'd you tell her?"

"Mostly?" Monica inquired, then was silent for a moment. "That he's got the cutest ass in New Mexico, and he's a great kisser. They had an address, you know. Said they talked to somebody at the Alumni Association at MIT."

That made sense. Like Sam, Al had lived in ten or

fifteen different places since he'd left MIT (though, unlike Sam, he never applied the term "home" to any of them) and rarely remembered to file a change of address notice. The Alumni people, as persistent as dogs sniffing out drugs at the airport, had tracked him down every time, and twice a year sent him a newsletter and a request for a contribution to the treasury of his alma mater. Of course they'd know where Sam was. Or, at least, where he was supposed to be.

"And the DMV," Monica added.

That made sense too. A couple of phone calls, or a few minutes with a PC and a modem . . .

"They got a post office box in Stallion Springs," Monica continued, her voice tinged with humor for the first time. "Could tell by the look on her face—thought they were aiming for someplace with a main street and a Wal-Mart, and a little one-room post office tended by somebody with white hair." She paused again. "Think it kinda pissed 'em off to find out there's no such place as Stallion Springs. And that it certainly don't have a post office."

"She go back to the Adobe?" Al asked.

"Said she was. Don't think they'll be there long, though. She said the little nervous guy didn't like the food. Said it gave him gas."

"Monny . . ."

"Sam okay, Al?"

"Yeah."

"That's good. They want to find him really bad."

"I know," Al said.

"She sat there for a while and drank her iced tea, and asked me did I have any idea what it's like to lose a husband when you're just a kid. I told her yeah, I did, and did she have any idea what it's like to have the Army ship him home in a bag. I showed her Davey's picture. That shut her up for a minute. Then she told me she's got unfinished business. Like I'd be impressed. Between

111

me and Sil, I'd hate to tell this babe the shitload of unfinished business we've got. You oughta cut these people
off at the knees, Al.''

Al chuckled softly. ''I will. Soon as I figure out where
their knees are.''

''That little guy must have some kind of a life, if the
worst thing he's worried about is a couple of stray farts.''

''Tell me about it,'' Al replied.

''Al?''

''Yeah.''

''Keep it so when we ask you if Sam's okay, you never
have to say no. And the same for you. I don't want anybody to ever tell us no.''

''I'll do my best,'' Al told her.

He considered the phone for a while after he'd hung
it up, until Donna Alessi appeared in his doorway.

''Where's your Siamese twin?'' he asked.

''Talking to C.J.''

''Walk with me.'' He emerged from behind the desk,
pulled his office door shut and set off at a slow amble
down the corridor with Donna tagging along beside him.
All the doors they passed were closed, including Sam's,
which had been opened only rarely since April of 1995.
''We've got to give him something to do,'' he said as
they reached the elevator. Instead of pressing the call
button, he moved a couple of steps to the side and pushed
open the door to the stairwell. Once he and Donna were
closed inside the well, he leaned against the concrete-
block wall and crossed his arms over his chest. ''He's
remembering too much,'' he said quietly.

''About what?''

''Nothing important. Not yet. Told me about med
school and a cat that ripped up his elbow.''

''Wheezer,'' Donna said.

''Yeah, Wheezer.''

''And you figure it's not many steps from Wheezer to
me?''

"Do you want to find out?"

"No," Donna murmured. She didn't say anything more for a minute. She sat down on the first step leading up to the next level and rested her chin on her fists. "Part of me would give anything in the world if he remembered me," she sighed, without lifting her head. Her gaze was centered on the cuffs of Al's pants and the gleaming shoes beneath them. "It would . . . it would help."

"Did you read the letters?" Al ventured.

"Yes."

"They're on the level?"

She nodded. "Yes. Sam wrote them."

"You're sure."

"I'm sure." Donna's fingers twined together, and she began to study them instead of Al's carefully rolled cuffs. "There's nothing in them that suggests they were married. It's funny, though."

"What is?"

"I've known Sam for fifteen years. I know how he thinks. How he expresses himself. He's written me love letters. They weren't very long. Most of them you could fit on a Post-it Note." Her head tipped a little, and she smiled wryly, then looked down again. "These aren't love letters. If you didn't know Sam, I suppose you'd think there was some intimacy in them. They're very personal. But they're not addressed to anybody specific. Does that make any sense?"

Years ago, Al Calavicci had wondered why the young man who had taken a four-hour plane ride from Boston to the Star Bright Project complex just to say thank you was so eager to relate his feelings to a stranger. As far as Al was concerned, for a long time he and Sam Beckett *were* strangers. He felt that he'd lost his last friend when Chip Furgeson died in 'Nam in '69, and this young man with the mega-brain and the cheesy department store suits was certainly not another Chip. Still, the kid would sit on the other side of a booth with his hands wrapped around a glass of beer and pour out strings of words as if he thought Al Calavicci was Dear Abby in disguise. He would talk and talk and talk, and after a while Al, who was certainly not Dear Abby, understood that the kid didn't want Al to solve his problems for him. He simply wanted to *tell* them. How that was of any use, Al had no clue. But it did seem to help. When each torrent of words ended, and when the beer was gone, the kid would smile at him. A little wearily, as if all that yammering had drained him. And Al supposed it probably did; if nothing else, it had to have given the kid a sore throat.

"He needed to let it out," Al confirmed. "Like venting steam. Didn't matter who was on the receiving end, as long as—"

"The letters don't mean anything."

"They mean he trusted her."

Donna squeezed her eyes shut. She was accepting those words, Al thought, like a little girl wincing over a booster shot. At least nobody was trying to tell her "this won't hurt."

"It was a long time ago, honey," he reminded her.

"Not long enough."

He held out a hand to her, curling his fingers around hers when she took it and holding onto her as they walked down the two flights of stairs to Level Ten. Neither of them reached for the door when they got to the bottom.

"We gotta tell him something to keep him from strolling any farther down memory lane," Al said, trying not to let Donna's look of pained resignation bother him. "Even if it's a fairy tale."

He repeated those words to Verbena as she emerged from the Waiting Room. At this point, she announced, she knew more about C.J. Williams than she did about herself—and not an iota of it was useful.

"We could feed him some of the chapters of C.J.'s

book,'' Donna suggested without any enthusiasm.

Al shook his head roughly. ''That'd go over like a brick. Ziggy!''

''Yes, Admiral,'' the computer cooed.

''Gimme a damned answer.''

''Very well.''

That was not one of the ten possible responses he'd anticipated. His head jerked backward so sharply that the two women heard his neck crack. ''What?'' he demanded, addressing the ceiling, though he might as well have spoken to the floor, one of the walls surrounding him, or any point in midair.

''After a careful examination of the relevant data, as well as the information provided by Mr. Williams concerning his background and the projections regarding his life for the next ten years''—a process which had taken Sam's creation well over twenty-four hours—''I can now postulate a hypothesis concerning Dr. Beckett's presence at Edwards Lake.''

''They built the Pyramids quicker,'' Al announced.

''Perhaps you could have reached a conclusion more rapidly on your own,'' Ziggy offered.

''Talk,'' Al barked.

''There is an eighty-four point three one percent probability that Dr. Beckett is there to repair a broken relationship.''

''Whose?'' Verbena asked.

''Insufficient data.''

''Well, that's a big honking help,'' Al said in disgust. ''You took a whole day to tell us Sam's supposed to mend somebody's broken heart? Do you believe this?'' he demanded of Verbena, then of Donna, both of whom responded with a mild expression and a shrug. ''We spend how many billion bucks building this pile of microchips, and all we get after a whole flaming day is 'He's there to repair a broken relationship'? I could have gotten that for two-ninety-five and a call to the damned Psychic Buddies Hotline!''

After a moment of silence, Ziggy said evenly, ''I see no reason to be abusive, Admiral.''

''You don't,'' Al snorted.

''Perhaps you could explain what purpose is served by insulting my capabilities. As you are well aware, I am able to function only within the parameters of my programming. If you find insufficiencies in that area, perhaps you should take the matter up with Dr. Beckett, since it was he who performed the bulk of my initial programming.''

''Okay,'' Al retorted. ''You get him back here, and I'll take it up with him.'' Turning to Verbena, he began, ''Does this—''

Ziggy interrupted him. ''It would be my pleasure to retrieve Dr. Beckett, Admiral. However, as you are also aware—''

''Yeah, yeah,'' Al said.

''I recall you being a good deal less verbally abusive before Dr. Beckett Leaped. His presence seemed to have a mediating effect on your temper.''

Donna looked at her husband's partner for a moment, offered him a sympathetic smile, then said, ''Dr. Beckett's presence had a mediating effect on a lot of things, Ziggy. We're a little . . . frayed right now. We apologize.'' After pausing to allow Ziggy to mull that over, she continued, ''It would help a great deal if you could tell us whose relationship Sam is supposed to mend.''

''Probably the babe with the magazine,'' Al grumbled.

''Babe . . . ?'' Donna frowned.

''The one who . . .'' Al cut himself off. After a moment of enduring the two women's scrutiny, he grumbled, ''The one who sent his heart rate up into the ozone. Because she wasn't dead. What's-her-name.''

''Her name would probably help,'' Verbena suggested.

''It's . . . ,'' Al said. ''Ah, jeez. I don't remember. He

116

said it." *Yeah, he said it . . . along with all the other details.* The Observer snapped his attention away from the picture that was forming in his mind: "what's-her-name" floating toward Sam, completely naked, with sex on her mind. He suspected the expression that had flashed across his face had lasted a little too long to go unnoticed, though he had no intention of explaining it to Donna. He'd spent four years trying to protect her from information he thought would hurt her, and that effort was not going to stop now, regardless of whether the information would help Ziggy draw a conclusion—and regardless of anything Donna might figure out on her own. "Patricia. Something like that. No . . . Patrice. That's it. Patrice. What about it, you conceited pile of gummy bears?" he tossed off to the ceiling.

"I have insufficient data," Ziggy announced.

"Couldn't you *try*, Ziggy?" Donna coaxed.

"Insufficient data does not become sufficient data when the request is framed more politely."

"That's true."

"I need more data."

"All right, Ziggy," Donna said, with a glance at Al that told him she knew at least part of what he hadn't told her. "We'll get you more data."

Sam's face smiled back at her from the photo that sat alongside his computer terminal—his favorite of the hundreds that had been taken on their wedding day.

"I want to be alone with you," he had murmured into her ear.

The nonstop activity of that day, added to the fact that neither of them had slept very much the night before, had begun to wear them both down. When the photographer took a break to change film, they wandered a few steps into the shade of an old tree.

She turned, inside the circle of his arms, to look into his face. He didn't have anything sexual in mind; he meant exactly what he'd said. He wanted to be alone with her, anywhere they might find some peace and quiet. The ceremony had ended a little before two, and they'd spent the time since then chatting with and accepting congratulations from what seemed like thousands of people. By four o'clock they had both had enough of being the center of attention.

"Look this way, you two!" Thelma Beckett called out. Her hands cradled the little camera her family had given her two Christmases ago. She was beaming as if it were still Christmas.

Sam shifted slightly, so that he was standing behind Donna, his arms tightly wound around her waist, his palms resting just above her hips. She leaned back against him, and in the moment before Thelma snapped the picture, he rested his cheek against her hair. She understood, as she heard the shutter click, that she had never been so entirely loved in her life, and had never felt more secure. That showed in the picture, far more obviously than how tired she was.

She reached out slowly and laid her fingertips on the side of the picture frame.

They had only known each other for a few weeks when she told him about Jim, the medical student she'd been engaged to, the man her mother had insisted would make an excellent husband. Jim was personable, and handsome, and unquestionably intelligent—not Sam's equal, of course, but well into the "genius" category. But Jim was . . .

Not the right one, she'd thought.

Sam didn't seem to want to return the favor. That wasn't surprising, Donna decided; didn't all those magazine articles warn against revealing too much of your romantic past? She doubted Sam spent much time reading *Cosmopolitan,* but he certainly was reluctant.

"You don't have to tell me," she offered. "It's all right."

118

He spent almost ten minutes studying the basketball game that was playing on her TV. He finished the beer she'd given him and set it carefully down on an old magazine so that the condensation coating the outside of the bottle wouldn't drip onto her coffee table.

"I . . . ," he began, and stopped, picked up the beer bottle and moved it to a different spot on the magazine. "There were . . . I mean . . . there were some people. Girls. Women. Girls," he corrected himself. "I've never been married." He lifted his head then and looked her straight in the eye. Stage fright, she thought: he looked like he had a paralyzing case of stage fright.

"I think I knew that," she replied.

"It was . . . I mean, I thought about it. That's what you do, where I come from. You find somebody, and you . . . you know. You get married. Settle down."

"Sam," Donna said gently. "You're from Indiana. I'm from Ohio. There's not a real big difference in philosophy between those two places. And I'm only a year younger than you. Most of the kids I went to high school with got married right out of the box too."

She had never seen him so ill at ease. He was entirely different at work, especially with his hands on a computer keyboard. There, he knew what his goals were, and how to achieve them. Or at least what direction to aim in. Here, sitting on the second-hand couch in her tiny living room, with white paper Chinese take-out boxes scattered around them and his empty beer bottle dripping onto a four-color cigarette ad, he was as out of control as a fourth grader stammering his way through a book report.

"What's wrong?" she asked him quietly.

"Nothing."

Give it up, she thought. *You never should have said anything. You know men don't like to* discuss *things. He said he loved you. Why do you even need to know who he . . .* To distract herself, she got up from the couch,

119

picked up the beer bottle and carried it into the kitchen. When she returned to the living room, Sam was blotting the puddles off the cigarette ad with a paper napkin. He smiled gamely at her when she returned to her place at the end of the couch. Returning the smile, she took the napkin out of his hands and set it aside, then moved closer to him and kissed him warmly. Nothing in the way he responded said he didn't want to be kissed, but she knew her question was still on his mind. When she drew away from him, he stood up and wandered away from the couch.

"There's not . . . There isn't . . . ," he muttered.

"Sam," Donna said. "It's all right. You don't have to tell me anything. I just thought I should mention Jim in case my mother said something. Just so you'd know. So you . . . wouldn't think I'd kept anything from you. That's all."

He turned around and looked at her. The chagrin on his face confused her. "I . . ."

"It's okay."

"I . . . I've always been . . . kind of . . ." He stopped again, took a breath, and finished. "Alone."

She was startled by that one word, more so when she realized how much it had cost him to say it. Nobody at the Lab saw this side of him, she was sure; there, he was the boy wonder, their prize, the brightest man in the country working on *their* team. Some of them seemed not to want to be friendly with him, as if they believed too much camaraderie might tarnish him somehow, might dilute his brilliance. And oddly, it seemed to suit him that most of his colleagues never offered more than an occasional "howyadoin." She had watched him: he returned their greetings with a smile, a nod, a "great, thanks." He didn't try to deepen any of those relationships. Had someone hurt him? she wondered. Someone he'd gotten close to, someone he cared about, so that

120

maintaining his distance from the people around him seemed like a wise thing to do?

When she went to him and slid her arms around him, he relaxed into her embrace and rested his head on her shoulder.

"I love you, Sam," she told him.

I love you, Sam...

"So why are you upset?"

She jerked upright in Sam's chair, certain that someone had spoken the question aloud. No one could have; the office door was closed. Maybe, she suspected, she'd said the words herself. Or Ziggy had said them.

"Ziggy?" she ventured.

"Yes, Dr. Alessi."

"Did you..." Donna cut herself off, and groaned loudly. "Nothing. Thank you." That was good, she thought; she'd just given the computer more fodder on Illogical Human Behavior. With a sigh she settled back into Sam's chair and pulled closer around herself the green cardigan sweater she'd taken out of his closet.

You know he loves you.

And you did *say "for better or for worse."*

She leaned forward then and pressed the keys to boot up his desktop terminal. The machine hummed at her quietly as the warmup information scrolled down its screen.

It should be him sitting here. It should be him trying to...

Dammit.

The terminal, since it was more or less an appendage of Ziggy, had access to all of the Project's library banks—and, with a little finagling, to any computer system in the world that would talk through a modem.

Words continued to waft through Donna's head as she typed.

How can you mend a broken heart...

How can you...

121

Her lips moved along with her thoughts. Her eyes roamed over the computer monitor, watching information pop up, then disappear.

Mend a broken . . .

There.

"Are you sure?" Al asked her.

"I'm positive."

"Does Her Omnipotence agree with you?"

Donna bobbed her head. "You said her name was Patrice. That would be Patrice Frey. Her husband, Michael, is an MVP at one of those three-hundred-lawyer law firms in Manhattan. I found several mentions of him in the *New York Times* in the late eighties, some of them in connection with very high-powered criminal cases. He was hot stuff. Which undoubtedly means he was spending more time at the office, or in court, than at home. They bought the house at Edwards Lake in '82. Out of the almost three hundred credit card charges originating in the area around Edwards Lake between '82 and '90, only eighteen were on his card. The rest were on hers. Which says to me that she spent a lot of time there, and he didn't."

Al reached over to lift Verbena's six-cup coffeepot off its burner and, after peering suspiciously at the liquid inside, emptied some of what was left into his mug. "It says to me, she spent a lot of money there and he didn't."

"The charges were for personal things."

That made Al squint over the lip of his cup. "What kind of personal things?"

"Never mind," Donna said firmly. "The point is, this is a woman who's unhappy because her husband is buried in law books. So she's having an affair with the caretaker. There's your broken relationship: Mr. and Mrs. Michael Frey. Sam needs to send her home to her husband."

"Who isn't *at* home," Verbena put in.

122

Donna sighed softly. After a moment of silence, she went on, "It's just a question of attitude."

"What kind of personal things?" Al asked again.

"Albert," Donna said.

"It's pertinent information," Al told her. "If she's buying a closetful of toys, then that says something about her too."

"That's what Sam's there to do. I'm sure. And Ziggy agrees. Sam is there to put this woman back together with her husband."

"What if she doesn't want—"

"She wants."

Before Al or Verbena could say anything, Donna had pulled herself up off the couch. She smiled cheerfully at her friends, then tugged Verbena's door open and walked steadily out into the corridor. Outside the complex, it was nearly midnight. Inside it, time of day didn't mean much; there were people working in most of the rooms she passed. Instead of returning to her own office, or to Sam's, she continued to walk, with her hands stuffed into the pockets of Sam's sweater. Down one corridor after another, all of which looked the same. Same walls, same floor, same light fixtures. Same little rooms opening off them, all occupied by people in white lab coats.

This isn't what I planned. This isn't what I thought would happen . . .

"My old man had a sweater like that."

She opened her eyes. Time seemed to have burped; she was no longer walking down one of those endless hallways. She was sitting on the floor outside the Waiting Room, her back pressed against the wall, her knees drawn up close to her chest.

"So did mine," she murmured.

"I think you need some sleep, sugar," Al told her.

"Sam said he felt comfortable wearing it. It's warm. Remember the trouble we had with the air conditioning when we first went on-line? He wore it then. I remember

123

him sitting at his desk, and he was . . . wearing this . . .
He said . . .''

"Yeah, I know.''

"He needs to send that woman home to her husband,''
Donna mumbled on. "Even if this Michael puts in a lot
of hours . . . there are ways you can . . . It doesn't
mean . . .''

Al rooted in his jacket pocket for a fresh cigar, considered it for a moment when he found it, then put it
away again. "What if C.J. is supposed to be with her?
Maybe she's supposed to divorce her husband and hook
up with him.''

"No,'' Donna said, waggling her head. "If *that* relationship is broken, Sam broke it.''

"But if—''

She shook her head again, pushed up off the floor and
tapped her security code into the keypad beside the door
to the Waiting Room. Al had no choice but to follow her,
and was close enough to her to hear her breath whoosh
out when C.J. Williams turned to face her. The real C.J.
was shorter than Sam and about twenty pounds heavier,
with thinning blond hair. But he was wearing Sam's
Fermi suit—and Sam's aura.

"Hi there,'' he said in Sam's voice.

Al remained near the door, but Donna moved forward.
"I . . . need to ask you a question,'' she told the Visitor.

"Go right ahead.''

"You have a friend,'' Donna said.

The aura appeared to Al only as a faint silvery glow
surrounding the man in the Fermi suit. For him, that man
was C.J. Williams, age twenty-nine—blond hair, blue
eyes, small white scar on the right side of his jawline, a
voice that was half an octave deeper than Sam's and ac-
cented with a Northeastern twang. That man was watching Donna's eyes. "You have a friend'' could have
meant a dozen different things, but C.J. picked the right
one, and picked it immediately.

124

"Uh-huh," he nodded.

"Do you love her?"

C.J.'s eyebrows lifted and a broad grin rolled across his face. "I don't think I'd call it that."

"Does she love you?"

"Is this a survey?"

"Could you just answer the question?"

C.J. leaned against the examining table in the middle of the room and smiled affably at Donna. He was only a few steps removed from being a good old boy, Al thought—and only a few steps removed from being a teenaged boy. This man with the winning grin, he decided, belonged to the jeans and flannel shirts that Sam had been wearing, and to the dog who'd been keeping Sam company, but not to any human being. He had a distinct mental picture of C.J. sitting in his motorboat with his big black dog carefully perched alongside him, sipping a beer and humming an off-key tune while he waited for a fish to chomp down on his bait. As he watched the man study Donna's face, Al became reasonably sure that if C.J. Williams was in love with anyone, it was himself.

"If you're talking about the stuff they write songs about," C.J. said after a minute, "then the answer's no. We have . . . an excellent physical relationship. No strings. Just a lot of very excellent sex." He paused, then asked, "That the right answer? What do I win?"

"Not much," Al replied.

C.J.'s attention shifted. "You know, I like this dream," he commented. "Hope I remember it when I wake up. There's a lot of very attractive women walking in and out of here." Then he rolled his eyes at Al. "Why I conjured *you* up, I don't know. Bunch of nice-looking women, and you. It doesn't figure."

"No," Al said, "I guess it doesn't."

"I'd think maybe it was a power thing—they call you Admiral, I heard that—but if it was a power thing, you

125

ought to be taller than me, don't you think? And we're the same height, give or take.'' Shaking his head, he strolled out from behind the exam table and stood midway between Donna and Al. ''The woman is taller than me. So's the other one. Doctor . . . what's her name? Beeks? Course, that's with the shoes. But still. What's that mean? That I think the woman is more important? Guess I need to give this some serious thought.''

''Good idea,'' Al said. Without waiting to see if Donna would follow him, he left C.J. Williams's home-away-from-home and sat down on one of the castered chairs in the narrow observation area that lay to the left of the Waiting Room. Donna joined him there a moment later. ''You're right,'' he told her. ''I don't know anything about Patrice Frey, but unless her husband's abusive, he's got to be a better deal than *him*.'' He jabbed a finger in the direction of the Waiting Room.

''I don't know, Al,'' Donna commented mildly. ''I kind of thought he sounded a lot like you.''

''Thanks.''

''At least,'' Donna murmured, ''the you that you pretend to be.''

Al let that go by. ''I told Sam I'd be back in the morning. You want me to go talk to him now? If I wake him up again, he'll go nuts.''

''Do you think he's sleeping?''

''I don't know. Somebody ought to be.''

The trio of video monitors set into the wall between the observation area and the Waiting Room gave them a view of C.J. from three different perspectives. Donna glanced at each of them, then heaved a long sigh and pulled her sneakered feet up to prop them on the work table that ran along the wall underneath the monitors. Her arms lay folded over her stomach. Her eyes closed halfway, and she was silent for a while.

''I try to sleep,'' she said quietly. ''The nightmares come and go.''

126

"I thought . . ."

"I told Verbena they'd stopped."

"Hmmmm," Al said, and let it go at that. He couldn't very well advise her not to lie to Beeks about anything that concerned her mental health, not when he spent a considerable amount of time doing the same thing.

Donna's eyes opened. "There was no way he could build it and not use it."

"No."

"The day we broke ground for the Project, I knew that. I knew that if we built the Accelerator, he was going to use it. Even if there was a possibility that it wouldn't work. Even if there was a chance it would . . . hurt him."

Al smiled at her wryly. "I think they said the same thing about the Bomb."

"Then we can blame *everything* on Einstein, can't we?"

"The guy who loved old sweaters."

A small noise came out of Donna's throat. It might have started out as a laugh, but it didn't end up as one. "Oh, Al," she said, and put her hand over her mouth.

"He'll come back, Donna."

"Right from the day we broke ground . . ."

Al nodded, thinking of another day, long after the Committee, thinking some sort of grand photo-op ceremony was necessary to mark the occasion, had watched Sam stick a shovel into the dry New Mexico soil that now lay more than eight hundred feet above Al's head. They—he, and Sam, and Donna—had thought the construction, wound up in miles of government red tape, would take a decade to complete, but it hadn't. The last connector was snapped into place and the last coat of paint was dry at about the same time that Sam's enthusiasm for his Project began to turn into frustration.

He had looked angry—no, he *was* angry—as he stood in the middle of the gleaming metal disc in the Accelerator Chamber.

127

"One to beam up, Scotty," Al had quipped.

If Sam even heard the joke, he made no sign of it. He began to mutter to himself, shuffling the soles of his socks against the metal pad.

"They're not gonna cut off the funding," Al told him, for at least the tenth time that day. "You know how stupid that would make them look? They're not gonna build something this big and then abandon it." He didn't bother to mention that the complex would probably be diverted to another use; that was probably the truth-and-nothing-but-the-truth, but pointing the truth out to Sam wouldn't have accomplished a thing. "They'd have too much explaining to do, and they *hate* explaining," he offered instead. "So stop worrying."

"I don't think he's worried about *them*," Donna whispered.

Sam didn't seem to hear that, either. His attention was focused entirely on the pad underneath his feet. He paced back and forth across it, then again, then walked the circumference of it. He wasn't trying to figure out how big it was; he knew how big it was, and what lay underneath it, and what it was connected to. This metal circle, as three different members of the Committee had taken great joy in pointing out to anyone who would listen, was where the magic was going to happen.

Magic, Al thought, was one of three possibilities. Magic would happen, nothing would happen . . . or Sam Beckett would turn himself into a charcoal briquette.

Right now, Sam didn't look like somebody who believed in magic. Sam looked like somebody who was mightily, and righteously, pissed. At himself.

"Sibby had a dog," Sam said, all of a sudden, loudly, with a broad wave of one arm, as if he were trying to regain the attention of a bunch of bored first-year students. "My friend Sibby. In Elk Ridge. He had this dog who kept trying to jump the fence in back of their house. It was too tall for him to clear, and he'd crash into it and

128

fall back down. But that never stopped him from trying. Sibby's dad used to say he was the dumbest dog in the world, that if he had any brains, he would've learned after the first couple of tries that he couldn't clear that fence.''

"What's the point, Sam?" Al had asked.

"The point." Sam stopped pacing and shoved his hands through his hair. "The point . . ." He paused, then blurted out what he had in mind. "Maybe I'm just as dumb as Sibby's dog. I'm too dumb to realize that I can't jump that high.''

"Why? Because the retrieval program isn't finished?"

"Maybe the retrieval program can't *be* finished.''

Donna went to him, intending to embrace him, but physical contact wasn't what he was looking for. "Of course it can," she told him as she backed away. "You've almost got it. There's no more than a piece or two missing.''

"A piece or two," Sam repeated. "That's the problem. A piece or two. But the pieces keep changing shape.''

"You'll find the answer.''

Sam turned to look at Al, whose expression mirrored Donna's. That too wasn't what he was looking for. "You know," he said flatly, "there comes a point where all the cheerleading in the world doesn't help. It could be that I can't find the solution to the equation because there is no solution. I could be going down the wrong road. Did anybody think of that? Huh? Did that occur to anybody?''

"Nobody who works here," Al replied.

"Yeah, well, maybe you ought to open your eyes." Sam's voice had turned bitter—something the two people who stood at arm's length from him hadn't heard for a long time. They both tried not to wince: it seemed like every naysayer in the world had come forward to voice an opinion on Sam Beckett's dream. But neither Al nor

129

Donna had honestly thought they would see *Sam* begin to doubt Sam.

"You'll figure it out," Al announced. "There's got to be a workable retrieval program. Dorothy got home, didn't she?"

Sam stared at his partner for a second, then made an ugly noise.

"Maybe that's the trick," Al went on, keeping his voice light. "Just think yourself there, and back. It'd be cheaper."

"Al," Donna warned him softly.

"Is this a joke?" Sam snapped. "What is this, just something to keep you busy in between wives?"

"You know better than that, Sam," Al said.

Sam stared at him for a moment. His expression softened briefly, as if he intended to apologize for the burst of temper, but all he did was shake his head.

"It'll work, Sam," Donna told him gently.

His only reply, still filled with frustration, was "Sure."

Lying in the back of Al's memory was another, slightly fuzzier version of that day, one in which Donna had not been present. For thirteen years, Donna Alessi had been a part of Al's reality, because Sam had put her there. But before Sam's third Leap, Donna Alessi had lived and worked somewhere else. She had not married Sam Beckett. When that day in February of 1995—the one Al thought of as The Big Bump—rolled around the first time, Sam and Al were alone in the Accelerator. And Al's mind had entertained the idea that Sam had not perfected a retrieval program because, deep down inside, Sam did not want to be retrieved.

But in *this* now, he had every reason to come home. The woman he loved, the woman he had stubbornly put back into his life against Al's advice, was sitting in the observation area of the Waiting Room waiting for him.

"You can't let your head work that way," Al told her. "You'll make yourself nuts. Yeah, he could get hurt, but

130

he could get hurt if he was driving a bus for a living. He's made out okay so far."

"What if . . ."

Al pressed a finger to his lips. "No 'what if's.' "

To avoid seeing the look of encouragement he was giving her, Donna returned her gaze to the bank of monitors. C.J. Williams was sitting cross-legged on the floor. He appeared to be daydreaming. He appeared to be Sam. But the body language was wrong. Everything about him was wrong. Tom Stratton had fooled her for a while, four years ago, looking at her through Sam's eyes, speaking to her in Sam's voice. But Tom Stratton—and all the Visitors who had followed him—had not been Sam, any more than the captured images on the old home-movie videotapes that lay neatly arranged on the shelf beside the VCR in her living room were really Sam. Sam, whose entire life had been arranged around a plan to travel back in time, was somewhere else. Somewhere where she could not see him, or touch him, or talk to him.

"Hey, Beckett . . ."

She had smiled, and he'd smiled back.

"Time for a break."

No . . . he would never build it and not use it. Not his dream. The one that had laid out the path his life would follow: where he would go, what he would study, who he would choose to help him. When the moment came when it was possible for him to Leap, he would Leap. There had never been any question of that.

In a wry, black way, she thought it was funny. The man who had told her he would never leave her intended to do exactly that, but not by walking out the front door with a suitcase in his hand.

He had no choice. No choice at all.

Not after he had fought so hard.

"That's the dumbest suggestion I've ever heard. No! I'm not spending forty billion dollars so I can see my father again. That's not what this is for."

With Al. With the people in Washington. With . . . everyone, it seemed like.

"You can't change history. No matter how much we believe it might benefit 'mankind.' It's too dangerous. All we're going to do is observe."

He'd always said "we." But there had never really been a "we" where the Leaping was concerned.

"I lived it once. Why would I want to do it again?"

". . . but the pieces keep changing shape."

"How much is it worth to you to go back? Don't look at me like that, Doctor. Answer the question. How much is it worth . . ."

". . . to observe . . ."

Al was looking at her. When she allowed herself to meet his eyes, they locked on hers, as if he could see into what she was thinking.

"He's not Superman," Donna said.

"Nope," Al agreed.

"There . . . there's going to be a time when he can't do what he's supposed to do."

Al nodded. "I think you're right. He'd never admit it, but it's true. We're gonna hit the end of the line sometime." He paused. "And he'll come home."

Home?

"Hey, Beckett. Come put that aside for a little while and have some dinner."

"Not hungry, honey."

"Then have some of this."

He'd had the sweater on. She could smell the warm wool when he wrapped his arms around her shoulders and accepted the kiss she'd settled into his lap to bestow.

"Love you."

"I love you too."

I love . . .

"He does not belong to that woman," Donna said angrily. Al obviously intended to say something in response, but she waved him into silence. "I have not sat

132

here for four years, waiting, being afraid that something will happen to Sam over which I have absolutely no control, trying not to believe that he'll never finish what Somebody thinks he's supposed to do and he'll never come back to me. I have not done that for four years so that that woman can lay any claim to him at all. It's a lie, every word of it.''

Al nodded again, but this time didn't try to speak.

"It's not fair. None of this. It. Is. Not. Fair.'' She burst up out of the chair then, took a step forward, seemed to decide that that path would lead nowhere she wanted to go and settled for huddling inside Sam's sweater with her arms wrapped tightly around herself. "Goddammit,'' she moaned. "It's all I have. Doesn't anybody understand that? It's all I have.''

She had not had a full night's sleep in almost two weeks—not since the first of the phone calls had come. Those two weeks settled down on her now, and exhaustion erased the last shred of the professional attitude she tried to maintain when she was not alone. With her dignity entirely gone, she began to sob in the arms of her husband's partner, soaking the shoulder of his shiny silver jacket.

A few yards away, the man in the Fermi suit began to tap his bare foot against the tile floor of the Waiting Room as he softly crooned to himself the words of an old Beatles song.

CHAPTER
TEN

Today's new word, boys and girls, was "ploy."

One of the nuns had announced to Al—and a roomful of other disinterested eight-year-olds—that it would be a good thing if he learned a new word every day. And that, no, the colorful Italian he picked up from his father when the old man had a snootful did not count. Little Albert Anthony decided not long after that that his father's ramblings *did* count. Of course they did: the way Sister Margaret failed to react to the word he had announced to her told him that it was interesting, even if it might not be usable in everyday conversation. Most of the people Albert repeated his father's Italian to looked confused, which meant they didn't understand him. But Italian was a lot like Latin, and Sister Margaret knew boatloads of Latin. Sister Margaret knew exactly what he was saying. Sister Margaret was *very* impressed by whatever it was he had called her, which was why she didn't react. Probably didn't get called that very often, Al realized later, when a kid the nuns called "That Frankie" told him what the word translated into in street English.

So the word stayed in Albert's vocabulary. As did several others he had picked up from his old man, and some he heard mumbled by the old derelicts who came into St. Ignatius to keep warm. He learned more from his buddies at North Island, and more still in Vietnam. Just to balance things out, he also learned a few from the intelligent and presumably well-mannered people who surrounded him at MIT. And from newscasters on television. And even a few from Sam Beckett. Though he was still not entirely sure what "ancillary time" might be.

Somewhere along the line, he had learned the word "ploy."

This was a ploy.

A trick. A maneuver. Designed to throw him off guard, to gain advantage.

But Mitchell P. Lovetz, Esq., did not understand that at Project Quantum Leap, the rules the rest of the world accepted did not apply. It had not occurred to him that calling Albert Calavicci at 1:30 A.M. would not throw his intended victim off guard, because he had not been told that there were no "wee hours of the morning" inside the boundaries of the Quantum Leap complex. And none for Albert Calavicci: the man whose buddies had given him a gold-painted toilet seat as an award in 1964 because he had flown to the Philippines and back within forty-eight hours without suffering a minute's worth of jet lag.

"Admiral," Lovetz said into the phone.

"Got that pinned down finally, did you?" Al inquired.

"I'm not in the military," Lovetz told him, as if he did not quite understand the question.

"Movie over?"

"What movie?"

Al smiled, rolled back in his chair and put his feet up on his desk. "Whatever movie you were watching before you called me. The Adobe doesn't get much up-to-date stuff—they still running that one about the housewife and the cable guy?"

"I . . . I have no idea," Lovetz said.

Which meant: "Yes, but I'm not admitting that to you." Al grinned again and flicked a spot off the back of the phone receiver with his thumbnail. "You meet Molly?"

"Who?"

"At the front desk. Her sister installs satellite dishes."

"I . . . No."

"Her name's Kimberlie. With an i-e."

There was a long silence at the other end. Lovetz didn't dare talk, Al knew; the first word he tried to come up with would make him sound as if he'd just started going through puberty.

"So what's new?" Al inquired.

The noise at the other end sounded as if Lovetz had spit on the mouthpiece.

"I hear the food at the 'dobe isn't agreeing with you," Al chatted on. "Too bad. Takes a while to get used to the cooking out here. Spicy. Sometimes they'll put a code on the menu so you know which ones to avoid. Don't think the 'dobe does that, though. You have to ask. And the peppers. Peppers used to get my old man every time."

"Admiral Calavicci," Lovetz said.

"You alone there, Lovetz?" Al asked, as if Lovetz had not said anything.

"Of course I'm alone. Why would I not be alone?"

What Lovetz meant was, he was not sleeping with Stephanie, which was a foregone conclusion if Al had ever heard one. But spoken aloud, the words were a firm indictment against the man with the odd little potbelly.

"Ask Molly to help you out, then," Al said. "She knows the staff out at the Ranch."

"*What* ranch??!" Lovetz squealed.

"You take a left out of the parking lot. Go down, let's see, six miles? Maybe closer to seven. There's an old boarded-up building there—used to be a little store. Go about fifty yards past that, and turn left onto the dirt road. Don't let the potholes bother you, but I'd be careful in that ark you're driving. Most of the people who go up

136

there go in something that's meant for rough roads. Anyway, go about another mile and a half, and keep to your right when the road forks. Go all the way to the end. Park at the bottom of the hill, where there's no cactus. And be careful when you go up. The Dobermans get upset sometimes. Works better if you honk the horn first, and let somebody come down and get you."

Lovetz, whose voice had gone as shrill as a three-year-old girl's, demanded, "Are you telling me there's a bordello out there?"

"Well," Al said, "yeah."

"Good God in heaven," Lovetz whimpered.

"Have a good time," Al told him. "And tell Mitzi I said hi."

He lifted the phone away from his ear slightly but had no intention of hanging it up. He counted silently as he waited for a response from the other end: one-one-thousand, two-one-thousand, three-one-thousand . . .

"Calavicci," Lovetz said.

"Uh-huh?" Al replied.

"I suppose you think you're funny."

"Why would I think that?" Al asked. "I was trying to help you out."

"I did not come to the East Side of Nowhere, New Mexico, to find *hookers*."

"Oh," Al said. "What did you come out here for?"

"To find Sam Beckett!"

"Oh," Al said again, and paused to study the toes of his shoes. "You still haven't told me why."

More silence greeted that comment. Lovetz was having a hard time: the in-room phones at the Adobe Inn were bolted to the small night tables in between the beds. The cord connecting the handset to the base was less than four feet long, stretched out completely. To talk on the phone, Lovetz was forced to either sit or lie on one of the beds, or stand between them. He could not pace. And he probably was not within reach of anything he could throw. The man who had picked up the phone at 1:30 in the morning to put Albert Calavicci off guard now had no way to vent his annoyance. Except one.

A muffled thump reached Al through the phone line, followed by one of the words Sister Margaret had discouraged him from using, which was also muffled.

"I made arrangements," Lovetz said a minute later.

Al didn't answer him.

"Calavicci?"

"How's your foot?" Al asked.

"I made arrangements for Stephanie to appear on television," Lovetz said, with a two-second gap between each word.

And Al thought the same word that Lovetz had used a minute ago. He did not dare voice it; he had already lost far more ground than he wanted to. The word played over and over in his head, like a tape loop, punctuated by "one-one-thousand, two-one-thousand, three-one-thousand."

"Are you familiar with the 'Roberto!' program?" Lovetz asked.

Al's mind began to sing him an unhappy tune, the lyrics of which would have turned Sister Margaret into a pillar of salt. In a tone he hoped sounded disinterested rather than numb, he said, "What about it?"

"Mr. . . . Gutierrez, I think his name is? Roberto. Is going to do a segment on missing persons."

"I didn't think Ms. Keller was missing."

"She's not," Lovetz said. "Sam Beckett is."

"No," Al responded. "He's not."

"Then let me talk to him."

"He's too busy to play this game with you, Lovetz."

Pain seemed to have done wonders for Lovetz's composure. With a lilt that approached the one Al had heard in his voice when he opened this conversation, he asked the Observer, "What are you protecting him from, Calavicci?"

"People who want to waste his time."

"And was it he who decided that Stephanie Keller is a waste of his time? Or you? She's *his* wife, Calavicci. Let her talk to him, and you and I can step out of this."

"Except for your fee, you mean."

"That's between myself and Ms. Keller, Admiral."

"What do you see at the end of this road, Lovetz?" Al asked evenly. "A condo on Maui? Huh? You see the big dough in this for yourself, don't you? That woman isn't married to Sam Beckett. You know that as well as I do. Why don't you just cut through the crap and tell me what's really going on here?"

"Television," Lovetz said.

"What, your fifteen minutes of fame?"

In his room at the Adobe Inn, Lovetz shook his head. "I talked to Mr. 'Roberto!' for quite a while. He's an interesting man. A lot of people think he's a nutcase— he claims he was abducted by aliens a few years ago. Have you heard that story?"

"Not from him," Al said.

"Well. The experience seems to have opened his mind to . . . shall we call them, unusual events. Unusual people. And he's very intrigued by the story of our friend Dr. Samuel Beckett. I brought him a magazine article he was very happy to read. Maybe you've seen it? *People* magazine from a few years back. The title of the article is . . . Let me get it, here. Yes. It's called 'Congressman Takei's Lifesaver Is a Genius of All Trades.' Under the heading of 'Heroes.' Seems he took care of a congressman from Hawaii, who'd had chest pains during a plane flight they were both on. Nice of him. He sounds like a very caring, compassionate man. Raised on a farm . . . nice picture of him playing basketball with his brother. And one with you. Yes, there you are! He says . . . Let me find it. Here it is: 'Beckett earned the interest of the scientific community while still in his early twenties, when, under the stewardship of Professor Sebastian

139

LoNigro of MIT, he produced what he refers to as the String Theory of Universal Structure.' Blah, blah, blah . . . the upshot of it being, Dr. Beckett intended to employ this theory to travel . . . here . . . 'backward and forward within his own lifetime.' Time travel! Mr. Gutierrez loved that. Time travel. Is that where Dr. Beckett is, Admiral? He's not available to talk to Ms. Keller because he's traveling in *time*?''

Lovetz began to giggle softly into the phone. Al, who was gripping the handset so tightly that his forearm had started to throb, said nothing at all.

''I think it ought to do wonders for Mr. Gutierrez's ratings, don't you? The man with the highest IQ on the planet talks about building a time machine, then disappears. Yes, this should really go over well, with those people who like to curl up with a cup of tea and the tabloids. New Mexico is a lovely place to visit this time of year, you know, Admiral. I'm sure those wonderful people will enjoy seeing it. When they come down here to talk to Dr. Beckett about the chance to travel back in time so that they can have a long talk with their dear departed Uncle Fred.''

The man whose voice had jumped up three octaves in response to the mention of a rambling, run-down house full of prostitutes was no longer at the other end of the phone. In his place was a man Albert Calavicci realized he needed to be worried about. Whether Lovetz saw the outcome of this battle as a condominium in Hawaii, a boxcar full of cash or something else, he was determined to win. He was no buffoon.

But neither was Albert Calavicci. Right now, that was the only card Al still held in his hand.

''Where is he?'' Lovetz asked sweetly. ''Back in the thirties, having tea with Albert Einstein? He told *People* that Einstein was his hero.''

''Lovetz . . .''

140

"Put Dr. Beckett in a room with Ms. Keller tomorrow, and I'll cancel the TV show."

"I can't do that," Al said.

"No," Lovetz agreed. "I didn't think you could."

"She can talk to *me*."

"But, Admiral," Lovetz crooned, "you're not the one she wants to talk to."

"I'm the only game in town. Take it or leave it."

"I think we'll leave it."

Al sat in silence for a moment, mauling the phone cord and hoping that repeated deep breaths would prevent the blood vessels in his brain from bursting. "How much do you want?" he said finally.

"How much?"

"Money. *Dinero*. Gold bricks. How much?"

Clicking sounds came through into Al's ear: Lovetz was tapping his manicured nails against the back of his handset. "I know people like you, Calavicci," he said happily. "I know who you think you are, and that you think you're always going to come out on top. Well, not this time, my friend. Not this time."

Then Lovetz hung up the phone.

CHAPTER
ELEVEN

Sam Beckett murmured softly in his sleep, shifted a little farther over onto his left side and nestled into the warmth of the person who lay beside him. His subconscious did not bother to tell him that anything was unfamiliar here, because nothing was: he was sleeping in a comfortable bed, being gently caressed by someone who wanted to make love to him. Someone a deeper level of his subconscious told him was female. Someone his body began to respond to.

Someone . . .

He opened one eye and peeked. The bedroom was dark, but he didn't need floodlights to tell him what was happening here, under the covers.

"Let me, baby," the someone whispered into his ear. "You don't need to do anything. Let me take care of you."

"No!" Sam blurted, propelling himself to the far side of the bed.

It wasn't far enough.

She began to squirm down underneath the covers. He was wearing boxer shorts, but they were no deterrent either. Left without options, Sam pushed himself away once more and ended up in a heap on the floor.

"C.J . . . !"

The bedside lamp snapped on. Patrice, who was again—still?—nude, sat glaring at him from a position near the pillow that had welcomed him a couple of hours ago. If she had been angry before, her outrage was off the scale now. His eyes locked with hers, Sam took firm hold of the quilt that formed the top layer of C.J.'s bedclothes, jerked it off the bed and bunched it up around himself.

"How did you get in here?" he demanded.

Her eyes widened. "I have a key. That you gave me."

"Yeah, well," Sam stammered, "I don't think I intended for you to sneak in in the middle of the night and get into my bed and . . . and . . ." He stopped, distracted by the expression on her face. "I was *asleep*," he insisted.

"I noticed," Patrice told him. "And, unless I've completely lost *my* mind, my waking you up this way never bothered you before."

"It bothers me now."

"I see."

Slowly, Sam hauled himself up off the floor, still holding the quilt securely around him. "Look . . . Patrice . . . ," he said, and averted his eyes. She was covered only to the waist, offering him a view that was no less interesting now than it had been yesterday afternoon. "Could you get up and get dressed? Please? It's really hard for me to talk to you with you sitting there like that."

"It . . ."

"Yeah, I know," Sam sighed. "It never bothered me before." Holding onto the quilt with one hand, he grabbed up his jeans and shirt with the other and, before Patrice could protest, left the bedroom for the relative security of the living room. Rufus was waiting there, looking at him curiously. "Helluva watchdog you are," Sam muttered, glancing over his shoulder, relieved to note that Patrice had not followed him. He climbed

143

quickly into his clothes, switched on a lamp and sat down to wait for her.

She emerged from the bedroom a couple of minutes later, dressed in jeans, a sweater and loafers. She'd fixed her hair too, probably with the brush that lay on top of C.J.'s dresser.

"I think I need an explanation," she told him.

"Yeah, well, I guess you probably do," he admitted. Trying not to be obvious about it, he searched her face, looking for signs that she felt something other than fury. She was hurt, he decided, though she was certainly covering it well. Regardless of whether or not he approved of the situation, she and C.J. were having an affair, and the person she thought was C.J. had rejected her twice within the space of a few hours. Of course she was hurt, and she had every right to be. But he hoped she wouldn't think she also had the right to belt him one.

"It was your idea for me to come up here," she said tersely. "If you changed your mind, you could have called me. You *do* know how to work the telephone."

"I do," Sam agreed.

"Then . . . ?"

"I'm sorry," Sam told her with as much conviction as he could muster.

"There's somebody else."

"No. There's nobody else. I just . . . have things on my mind."

Patrice scowled at him. "You keep saying that. What 'things'?"

"Ummm . . . the book! My book. I told you I'm working on a novel," he said, hoping that was true. "It's . . . I'm kind of stuck with it. Writer's block. And . . . I need a little time to try to sort some things out in my head." Pleased with himself for having come up with what seemed like a plausible explanation, he smiled at her, then at Rufus.

The dog seemed to buy his story, but Patrice did not.

144

"You used to tell me that sex helped spur your imagination."

"Ahhhhh . . ."

Shaking her head, Patrice walked over to the window beside the fireplace and stood staring out into the darkness. "I don't know what's happening, C.J.," she said, her voice tight and completely unforgiving.

"I need a little time," Sam offered.

"To do what?"

"To work on the book."

"C.J., that is such a load of crap." She turned slightly, but the sight of him distressed her enough to make her return to the window. "I really appreciate that you think I'm enough of a bimbo that you don't need to tell me the truth. That you can make up some kind of lame excuse that has nothing to do with anything, and expect me to creep away quietly. Is there somebody else? That's the only thing that makes any sense to me. Unless you've decided you'd really rather be with the dog."

There was a nasty and accusatory note in her voice, one that got through to Rufus, who shambled off into the kitchen to avoid it.

"You're a really fine, upstanding guy," Patrice said, scoffing. "You're going to change your mind with no more serious thought than you use to change your socks, and expect me to go along with it. Well, it's funny, C.J., because I'm not going to go along with it. You've been working on that book for two years. You called me on the phone Friday morning and said you wanted to get laid. That lacks a little class, but since there's never been much class involved in this situation, I didn't mind it. Basically, it's what I wanted too. So, as soon as I can break away, I get in the car and I drive all the way up here, to find out that your libido has suffered an abrupt and inexplicable death and that I'm supposed to turn around and go home. Now tell me: how am I going to react to this?"

145

"By being annoyed?"

"Annoyed?" Patrice repeated. "Annoyed? Yes, I'm annoyed. I want to know what happened to 'I want to feel your hot body next to mine.' "

"I could make it up to you," Sam suggested.

To his surprise, she laughed. There was nothing pleasant in the sound. "You would have to launch me into lunar orbit," she told him.

"Really. I am. I'm sorry about this."

"You're a piece of work, C.J."

"I guess I am."

Instead of reacting to the sheepish look that had crept onto his face, she followed Rufus into the kitchen. Sam heard the refrigerator door open, and the clink of glass as she moved things around inside it. After a minute or two she returned to the living room with an open bottle of beer in her hand. Standing just beyond the doorway, she took a long swig, looking at Sam as if she were daring him to take the drink away from her.

"So what's the bottom line?" she asked when half the bottle was gone. "You're going to drop me, like the others?"

"Others?" Sam muttered.

The word echoed inside his head. *"Others"? What others? There were more? What's this guy fix up here, for crying out loud? Rake the leaves, wash the windows, mend a hole in the carport, sleep with the homeowners? No wonder he likes living up here in the winter by himself. What, does he have a whole parade of women coming up here to . . .* Sam was appalled. Though he didn't really remember it, he too had seen the movie Al had mentioned to Lovetz—one which seemed to be a particular favorite of Al's, and which prompted a recurring line of "handyman" jokes whenever the Observer thought the occasion was ripe for it. *This is great,* Sam thought. *This is juuuuuuust great. Thanks a bunch for dumping me into the middle of* this. *Man. Oh, maaaaan. How long*

146

is the line, huh? Dozens? Hundreds? Are they all *gonna show up here and . . . Ahhhhh, boy.*

"I don't know what I could have given you, other than what I . . ." Patrice sighed.

He called her? Like he was ordering a pizza? And I thought Leaping into Al was a problem.

"Oh boy oh boy oh boy," Sam muttered.

This guy . . . ahhhh, man.

Forgetting for a moment that Patrice was in the room, he pulled himself up from the chair, wandered back and forth a couple of times and buried his face in his hands. "Thanks for this," he muttered. "Thanks a bunch. This is great. This is unbelievably unmanageable."

Patrice snorted at him and took another gulp of her beer. "At least that's familiar. It's almost exactly what Ted said."

Sam peered at her through his fingers. "Who's Ted?"

"At the dry cleaners."

"Here?"

"Yes, here. In town. Ted at the dry cleaners."

"And you told him about me? Us?"

"Why would I tell him anything?" Patrice groaned after she had finished off her beer. "I haven't spoken to him in over a year. Although I must say my clothes are suffering for it. I have to take them into Wiltonburg to get them done now, because of that insufferable idiot."

"What insufferable idiot?" Sam asked, totally confused.

"*Ted.* C.J., do you have Alzheimer's?"

Ted? Ted? Sam moaned inwardly. *You have no idea how much it would help if I knew what I'm supposed to know. Who the hell is Ted, and why does he . . .*

Then the light went on.

"And before Ted was . . . ," Sam ventured.

"I don't think that concerns you," Patrice replied.

"Maybe it does," Sam said.

She thumped the empty bottle down onto a table and

147

wiped her hands off on the hips of her jeans. "No," she said, "it doesn't. I am going to go get into my car now, and drive all the way back to the city. I could say more, and I could *do* more, but I don't think you deserve it. I'm starting to think that there's not a man alive who deserves more than ten seconds of serious thought from me, or from anyone else. You cannot change course like this, C.J. It's intolerable. I am not a figment of your imagination. My life is not a game, and I refuse to let you jerk me around. Here. Take your key back."

She intended to drop the key, which she had fished out of her jeans pocket, into his palm and then walk away. Instead, Sam wrapped his fingers around hers, a move that sharpened her scowl. It took her several seconds to retrieve her hand.

"Maybe you ought to wait till the morning," he told her. "It's not safe to drive while you're upset."

"As if that worries you."

"It does worry me," Sam said.

"Sure," Patrice replied hotly. "Sure."

Whether she believed him or not, she didn't get into the car. Sam walked out onto the road and watched her disappear into her house. She didn't bother to turn a light on. She might spend a little time slamming things around; she might even cry, but he doubted she'd head for New York before morning.

The Imaging Chamber door opened as he turned to retreat into C.J.'s cabin.

Al, in the khakis he'd grabbed up and hauled on in the darkness of his quarters, rumpled, haggard and decorated with beard stubble and dark bags under his eyes, blinked at him blearily and sputtered, "What's going on? Ziggy says . . . What are you freaking out about?"

"I'm not," Sam replied. "No, that's wrong. I am."

"Saaaam. It's *real* late."

"I know why I'm here," Sam said.

The Observer peered at him. "What?"

148

"I know why I'm here," Sam repeated patiently.

"You do. You do? We were gonna tell you in the morning. How come you're up? And dressed? What's going on, Sam? I thought you were sleeping."

Nodding, Sam went into the house, holding the door open long enough for Al to follow him in. He locked it carefully afterward, though he doubted that would accomplish much. "I *was*," he told his partner. "Very soundly. This time nobody screamed in my ear. This time somebody just grabbed me by the . . ."

"By the what?"

Sam didn't supply the rest of the sentence; instead, he glanced down at the crotch of his jeans.

That got Al's attention. "She did?"

Rather than lead the Observer down his favorite path, Sam continued, "She said there were others. At first I thought she meant for me. C.J. But that was wrong. She meant there were others for her. She's been involved with other men. Some guy who works at the dry cleaners. I don't know how many others. The point is, she's having these affairs. Running away from her marriage. I think I'm here to convince her to go back to her husband."

Sam smiled, pulled his head down in one more nod and folded his arms over his chest.

Al said nothing.

"Well?" Sam prompted.

"That's funny," Al mused.

"Why is it funny?"

"Because Ziggy said the same thing. She thinks that's why you're here."

Sam sputtered, "Ziggy figured this out? Why didn't you tell me? Why did you let me flounder around like this? Crawling around underneath these houses? Checking the plugs behind people's TV sets? Jeez, Al! Why didn't you tell me?"

"Because she just figured it out a couple hours ago.

And you said you wanted to sleep. I was going to tell you in the morning.''

Badly tempted to go on fussing, Sam managed to contain his blustering and sat down at one end of C.J.'s couch. "Ziggy agrees? That's why I'm here?"

"Yeah."

"What are the numbers?"

"Eighty..." Al consulted the handlink. "Eighty-nine? I thought it was eighty-four. They've gone up. Eighty-nine point six six percent."

"That's good. That's ... Why are you dressed like that?"

"Huh?"

Sam pointed a finger at Al's no longer creased uniform. "That. You never wear that. What's going on? You've been hedging ever since I Leaped in here. Something's going on back there. At the Project. I want you to tell me what it is."

"I forgot to turn off the burner on my coffeemaker," Al replied. "You know how when there's only a little left in the pot, it scorches? It set fire to the box of filters. That set off the sprinklers. Soaked all my clothes. This was all I had left to wear."

"Why are you lying to me?" Sam asked.

"I'm not lying to you. I got nostalgic and felt like wearing my khakis. Is that a bad thing? I'm not lying to you."

"There's nothing wrong."

"There's always something wrong."

"Al," Sam said.

"There's nothing wrong. Listen, you've got it figured out, Ziggy's got it figured out. Couldn't ask for anything better, right? You have a nice long talk with Runaround Sue and send her back to her hubby. Problem solved. You Leap out. What's wrong with that? Turn on the old Beckett charm and you'll be out of here by sundown tomorrow."

150

"Yeah."

Al, responding to the word and not the tone in which it was spoken, continued eagerly, "The guy you Leaped into is a real *putz*. She doesn't belong around here, fooling around with him. She belongs in the city, with her husband. Plant that in her mind. Tell her to go home and work on it."

"Why are you lying to me, Al?" Sam asked quietly.

"I'm not lying to you. That's why you're here. See?" Al turned the handlink around so that Sam could check the readout for himself, but Sam didn't bother to do that. Al's mind churned frantically, searching for something to tell him. "Tina left me" wouldn't work; he'd tried that one before. And "the funding's in trouble" was a bad avenue to follow—too much tempting of fate. He couldn't even invoke the "my grandmother is dying" tale that had proven so popular among his schoolmates, because all four of his grandparents, his parents and his sister were already gone, and Sam knew that.

Tell him the truth?

The truth.

An easy thing, for most people. For him, an infrequent visitor. He had lost track of how much of what he'd told Sam over the last four years was pure fiction. Born of necessity, he'd always thought: back in the beginning, Ziggy had insisted that he withhold information from Sam, unless it was information that Sam already knew. The grand poo-bah of Catch 22s, Al thought. Go on, hurt the kid. Don't tell him his name. Don't give him anything he can hang onto. Don't *help* him. Make him wander around in a void. No name, no memories, no past. That made no sense to Al, so he'd done the same thing to Ziggy's rule that he did to every other rule he didn't understand: he broke it. Again and again and again.

But there were other times when the truth would not have helped. When Sam had to be led in a different direction. Told a fairy tale.

About the me that I pretend to be, Al thought.

"Kid," he said, "you gotta trust me on this one. We'll handle everything. You do what you're supposed to do, and get out of here. Move on. Okay? Trust me."

Sam looked at him unhappily. "It's my Project," he said after a moment.

"Yeah," Al concurred. "It's yours. But you're there, and we're here. Or . . . you're here, and they're out there . . ." He cut himself off, squinted down at the handlink as if he expected Ziggy to offer him some words of wisdom—which certainly was not likely to happen in his lifetime—then put the thing in his pocket and held his hands out, palms up. "We'll handle it," he promised. "I know we're not megabrained like the guy who hired us, but we can iron out a few wrinkles."

"You could at least tell me what it is."

"No, Sam," Al said, "I can't. And even that's probably saying too much."

"I want to help."

"I know you do. I know it. But, kid . . ."

"I'm not a kid, Al."

"I know that, Sam," Al said gently. "But you can't help. You've got more important stuff to do."

Sam's head drooped, his line of sight drifting down to the rug in front of his bare feet, his hands clasped between his knees. "I wish *I* could make that decision once in a while."

"Yeah. I know."

"I don't know how much longer I can do this, Al."

"As long as you need to," Al told him.

That didn't accomplish much, not that Al had honestly thought it would. Left without anything else to say, the Observer pursed his lips and whistled, then called, "Here, Rufe. C'mere, boy." When Rufus dutifully trotted into the living room, Al pointed to his partner and instructed the dog, "Tell him it's okay."

Rufus puzzled those instructions over for a moment,

152

then leaned up and licked Sam's cheek. Sam grimaced at first, then smiled vaguely and patted the dog's head.

"See?" Al said. "He doesn't think you're C.J. He knows you're you, and he's been buddies with you right from the get-go. Which is not hard to understand, considering that his real master is a nozzle and a half." He paused, then encouraged his friend: "Go on back to bed. You need it, and so do I. We'll figure out the next move in the morning."

"Your next move, or mine?" Sam asked.

"Both."

"I still wish you'd tell me . . ."

"Go back to sleep," Al commanded, making shooing gestures in the direction of the bedroom. "Things'll look clearer in the morning. That's what the nuns always used to tell me."

With enough reluctance to fill a fifty-gallon drum, Sam did as he was told. Rufus followed him to the bedroom doorway and stood sentinel there as Sam crawled into bed, then turned to raise a furry eyebrow at the Observer.

"You too," Al said. "Sleep. Dream about cute girl dogs."

Once Rufus had shuffled into the bedroom, Al tugged the handlink out of his pocket and keyed in the command that opened the Chamber door.

It'll be clearer in the morning . . .

The trouble was, ten levels underground, morning never came.

CHAPTER

TWELVE

The parade arrived a little after ten o'clock.

It rolled onto the grounds of Project Quantum Leap without any noise, except for the crunch of tires on gravel, and stopped a few steps from the entrance to Building One. An outsider would not have been able to reconcile the picture: a long, black limousine, which had repelled the desert dust as efficiently as if it had been surrounded by a force field. Three jeeps and a military staff car. All parked outside what looked like an ordinary Quonset hut. Under the scrutiny of three polished and creased Marine guards—who were viewing this through mirrored sunglasses—the doors of the five vehicles opened and people began to emerge. The occupants of the jeeps and the staff car were in uniform. The occupants of the limousine, other than its driver, were not.

"Good morning, Senator," one of the Marines said.

The man he had addressed ignored him for several seconds as he scanned his surroundings. He had been here before, many times, but something in his expression said that he was not comfortable in this place, surrounded by these people. He was very tall, very lanky, with sharply chiseled features and heavily graying dark hair. The press had compared him to Abraham Lincoln, beginning thirty years ago, when he had first entered political life. He shared Lincoln's gaunt, almost emaciated looks, and was prompt to say that he had come from humble origins, like Mr. Lincoln, and that he shared many of the sainted President's political views.

Several of the press had also compared him to Ichabod Crane. On that subject, he had no comment.

"Where's Calavicci?" the senator asked when he turned to face the Marine.

"Below, sir. Waiting for you."

Solomon Weitzman issued a loud, unpleasant "hmmppf," sounding as if he was trying to cough up a furball. The people who had made this trip with him knew better than to react in any way, shape or form to the furball noise. The three Marines, who were talented at nothing quite so much as concealing their emotions, did not react either. At least, not in any way that Weitzman could see through the mirrored sunglasses.

"I'm going in," Weitzman said.

The Marine who stood eighteen inches from him nodded once. "Senator."

The young man turned then and held open the door of the Quonset hut. Weitzman strode inside, followed by his aide, his secretary and the Navy lieutenant who had been lucky enough to be named the senator's official escort. Then the Marine closed the outer door and, in steps that were exactly the same length, walked across what looked to be an office that had not been in active use for several years. At the rear of the office was a large, nearly empty supply closet, the door of which the Marine opened for Senator Weitzman and his entourage. When the entire group had filed inside, the Marine gently pulled that door closed, then pressed his hand against what looked like an ordinary switchplate cover.

Three seconds later, the supply closet began to descend.

Solomon Weitzman spent his time in the closet wondering whether he ought to display open annoyance at

Albert Calavicci for not greeting him outside Building One, even though Calavicci's presence out there would have served no useful purpose other than as a display of protocol. Senator Weitzman dearly loved protocol. It ensured that things were done well, and properly, and according to schedule. It made him look good. It made his staff look like a well-oiled machine.

What was actually going on "below," he was quite certain, was that Admiral Al Calavicci needed a few extra minutes to be rousted out of bed.

The supply closet stopped moving, and its rear wall slid up out of the way. Beyond it lay a white-walled, rectangular area about thirty feet by twenty, occupied by nothing except a large, curved desk filled with security monitors, manned by two more Marines. Past this area was a short corridor that ended at another elevator.

"Good morning, Senator."

That came, almost in unison, from the two boys on duty at the desk. Weitzman thought of them privately as Tweedledum and Tweedledee: he supposed that he never encountered the same set of men on each new journey to the Project, but they were enough alike that their being different people did not matter to him in the slightest.

"Ummm," Weitzman said.

"You may proceed, Senator."

So Weitzman proceeded. He took a half a dozen steps ahead, stopping in front of the blue glass panel set into the wall eighteen inches beyond the point at which the rectangular area turned into a short chunk of corridor. Blue light cascaded out of the panel, pulsing once, twice, then fading away. When it was gone, Weitzman extended his right hand, bringing it within a couple of centimeters of the glass.

"Good morning, Senator Weitzman," cooed a female voice that seemed to come from everywhere and nowhere at the same time. "Clearance has been granted. Please proceed."

Each member of the senator's entourage went through the same procedure. They had to; anyone who tried to pass this threshold without doing so would set off all the bells and whistles. Weitzman hated bells and whistles nearly as much as he hated delays. But, in spite of the fact that Samuel Beckett's damned computer knew exactly who he was, because he was the same he who had visited this complex forty-eight times and therefore did not need to go through this ridiculous routine—in spite of that, this ridiculous routine was protocol.

The second elevator, whose doors would not open until the proper codes had been entered into the keypad beside it, carried Sol Weitzman and his entourage almost eight hundred feet below the New Mexico desert and deposited him on Level Eight of Project Quantum Leap.

Albert Calavicci, who had undoubtedly been rousted out of bed mere minutes before, was indeed waiting for him.

"Senator," he said.

He did not say "good morning." Weitzman did not expect him to. Calavicci never quite greeted him, not in the normal sense, because Calavicci did not like him and did not welcome his presence here. In fact, Weitzman was reasonably sure that Albert Calavicci despised him as much as he despised Calavicci. The man was a drunk. An ex-drunk, supposedly, but Weitzman had been informed by a collection of very well-qualified experts that there was no such thing as an ex-drunk. So he was still a drunk. And arrogant, and stubborn, and very well accustomed to having his own way, particularly here, buried far underneath the desert, where normal rules did not seem to apply.

"Admiral," Weitzman said.

Calavicci tipped his head in the direction of a room Weitzman knew as Conference Room 8-A. Other people knew it as Weitzman's Den, but that fact, as well as the fact that half the staff of this Project did not give him

157

the proper deference (or any deference at all), did not concern him. Let Calavicci's people ridicule him. He was, and always had been, the man with his right hand poised over the checkbook.

And nothing in this world, Weitzman reassured himself every time he entered this complex, spoke louder than money.

He sat down first, at the head of the table, at a place that had been carefully set with his refreshments: a shallow bowl of finely diced assorted fresh fruit (no grapefruit), two matzos broken into quarters and a twelve-ounce glass of chilled springwater. He was given the same selection each time he visited here, in accordance with instructions that had been issued five years ago. What the kitchen staff thought of that did not concern him. He did not, even once, entertain the idea that the person who diced his fruit into half-inch squares might have spit into it. That would have been a childish trick, and these people—even the kitchen help—were not childish.

Not even Albert Calavicci, who was still an active-duty officer in the United States Navy and who was sitting at this table dressed in a purple silk suit that would have been garish even in Las Vegas.

Calavicci, who was alone on his side of the table (Weitzman's entourage filled the other side), watched the senator eat his diced fruit and matzos without saying a word. Although clean-shaven and tidy, he did look worn around the edges, which Weitzman might have thought was odd if he had not reminded himself that Calavicci would be sixty-five years old the day after tomorrow.

Could have been retired, Weitzman thought as he nibbled on his crackers. *Could be making a nice little living making speeches. The former astronaut. The former prisoner of war. They'd pay him. Those speakers' bureaus— they'll take just about anyone, if they're entertaining.*

His refreshments were eaten, and the dishes cleared

away, before Weitzman began to speak. "Where's Beckett?" he asked.

"Upstate New York," Calavicci replied. "1983."

"Really," said Weitzman.

"Really."

"That's not what my daughter tells me."

Calavicci blinked. "Your . . . daughter?"

"Yes. My daughter. Eleanor. You've met."

He could see the wheels turning inside Calavicci's head. The admiral's mouth was open, very slightly, the tip of his tongue pressed against the inside of his lower lip. "I think it was several years ago," Calavicci said after a moment. "She's . . . in high school."

"She's a freshman at Princeton."

Other people said things like "I'm sure she'll do her family proud" or "Congratulations." Calavicci said, "I see."

"I bought her a computer. Students need computers now; they're not a luxury, they're a necessity. Everywhere. The world is turning to computers." Weitzman glanced up fleetingly. The ceiling above him was an ordinary one, white acoustical tiles peppered with sprinkler heads, but it seemed to him that Beckett's computer was up there, watching him. "When I was a student, I did my research in the library, and wrote my papers in longhand. But writing by hand is a forgotten art."

He knew Calavicci would not prompt him. The man in the purple suit would sit there for a week, unmoving, rather than give Sol Weitzman any sign that he was impatient.

"The telephone is a forgotten thing too, it seems," Weitzman went on, frowning at a hangnail on his right index finger. "I had telephone service installed in Eleanor's room at school, but she never calls anyone except her mother. She . . . 'E-mails' her friends. It seems less personal to me when you can't hear the other person's voice. Don't you think?"

159

"I suppose."

Weitzman nodded, as if Calavicci had genuinely sympathized with him. His entourage kept their silence; one of them was doodling on a steno pad, but he pretended not to notice. "I would have thought that a first-year student at a prestigious university would be primarily concerned with her studies. But it seems that what my daughter chats about with her friends around the country is . . ." He paused. "Hunks."

"Hunks?" Calavicci echoed.

"Men," Weitzman said.

Calavicci smiled.

"Movie stars. Television stars. Singers. Apparently, there is some sort of endless debate taking place over this 'Net' creation. Not about improving the world, or even improving oneself. But about . . ."

Sol Weitzman did not find himself lost for words very often. He considered himself a master of improvisation. Of extemporization. Of . . . winging it. But in this room, in this company, he discovered that he had led himself down the wrong path. He did not want to discuss with Albert Calavicci, in front of his poker-faced, doodling entourage, what he viewed as a serious shortcoming in his only daughter's character. He had thought—in fact, he had been sure—that Elly was a lady. She was not delicate, but neither was she a longshoreman. She was his lovely, bright-eyed child.

He had peeked over her shoulder one evening to discover that she was having a conversation with someone whose name seemed to be Cookie on the subject of "The Bulge." The speed with which his lovely daughter shooed him away told him that the discussion had nothing to do with a battle that had taken place during World War II.

"Hunks," he said softly.

His wife had not been horrified. His wife had said

several things, out of which he recalled one word: "normal."

"I want to see Dr. Beckett," he told Calavicci.

Before Calavicci could object, he had stalked out of the conference room (leaving instructions with his entourage via a jabbing finger to "stay here") and led his adversary down two levels to Control and into the observation area outside the Waiting Room. With Calavicci standing quietly behind him, he peered at the three video monitors, at the image of the man inside the Waiting Room. The man who certainly looked like Sam Beckett.

Verbena Beeks, who had been jotting notes into a spiral-bound notebook, told him, "The Visitor's name is C.J. Williams. Age twenty-nine. He's a caretaker, part-time writer. Edwards Lake, New York."

"Then that's not Sam Beckett."

What she wanted to say (he could see it in her eyes) was "Give me a break." What came out of her mouth was "No, Senator."

"My daughter," Weitzman announced, "in the middle of a conversation with her mother, asked to speak to me. I assumed she wanted some money. For clothes, or new pieces for her computer. She asked me, did I not know a Dr. Sam Beckett. I said yes. She said"—he pitched his voice a little higher, and he began to talk more rapidly, in a bad imitation of Elly's cheerful chatter—"she and her friends had been talking about hunks. That Bradley Pitt person. Whoever. Then someone mentioned young Mr. Kennedy Junior. And someone else mentioned Sam Beckett. Someone who opined that Dr. Beckett was 'a hot stud.' "

The first note of a giggle got past Verbena Beeks's lips. Then she pressed her hand to her mouth.

Weitzman, whose thin neck had reddened noticeably, went on, "And someone *else*, who apparently lives in the viewing area reached by television station KDNM of Destiny, New Mexico, informed all and sundry that Dr.

Beckett would be a guest this coming week on the 'Roberto!' talk show. Now," he said, and sucked in air like a rapidly dying fish, "my question is: if Dr. Samuel Beckett is in upstate New York sixteen years in the past, *how* the hell is he going to be a guest on a tabloid talk show on Tuesday?"

Beeks peered at her colleague. " 'Roberto!'?" she mouthed.

"He's not," Calavicci said.

"He *is*," said the senator.

"No," Calavicci repeated, "he's not." After a glance at Beeks, which Weitzman observed even though it told him nothing, Calavicci sat down on a chair and continued quietly, "The person who's going to be on 'Roberto!' is a woman named Stephanie Keller."

"Who is . . . ?"

"Vice president of a textbook publishing company in Virginia."

"And . . . ?"

"She claims she's married to Sam. Which is not the truth," Calavicci continued quickly. "This Keller woman and her lawyer are running a scam."

Then it was Al's turn to watch the wheels turn inside Weitzman's head. Regardless of his personal opinion of the senator, he knew that Sol Weitzman had not gotten where he was by being stupid, or gullible, or unable to make a rapid (and usually correct) deduction from a very limited number of clues. Less than a minute had gone by when Weitzman reached a conclusion regarding what Al had just told him. It was a conclusion he did not like.

"Those people," he said softly, "are going to compromise the security of this Project."

"Yup," Al replied. "That's what I'm afraid of."

"I won't have it," Weitzman snapped.

The room they ended up in was considerably smaller than Conference Room 8-A. It contained a table too, but this one would have fit into a suburban dining room. Four chairs, one of which did not match the others, were grouped around it. All four chairs were filled: by Sol Weitzman, Albert Calavicci, Verbena Beeks and Donna Alessi.

Half an hour had gone by since Weitzman had spoken the word "Roberto!" outside the Waiting Room. In those thirty minutes, he had grown more and more distressed. As they sat here now, Al began to wonder how difficult it would be for the Project maintenance staff to clean the bits of Weitzman's brain tissue out of the ceiling tiles after the senator's head exploded.

"I ask myself every year," Weitzman said, "how does this Project benefit anything? It's very well and good that Dr. Beckett fixes people's lives. The bleeding hearts would love that bit of news, if we were able to issue a press release. But we're *not*. We are most certainly and assuredly not. The government of these United States, ladies and gentleman, is signing over two point four billion dollars—two point four *billion* dollars!—each and every year to this Project, and for what? For what. This Project is not curing epidemic disease. This Project is not increasing agricultural output so that we may feed the hungry. This Project is not accomplishing squat."

The three people sitting with him had heard this speech before. None of them reacted to it with anything more than a tiny, stifled sigh.

"We need something that I can present to my bosses, doctors. Admiral. To my bosses, the American people. When this is over and done with, when the curtain of secrecy has been lifted, what do I tell them? What do my fellow Committee members tell them about what we have accomplished here, at the cost of so many *billions* of dollars?"

"We've answered that question for you, Senator," Donna replied. "In our initial proposal. And in the updates we've given you every year for the funding hearings."

"I understand that, Dr. Alessi," Weitzman said. "I've read your paperwork. I have all but memorized your paperwork. But this is not a funding hearing. This is me, and this is you. According to your presentations, Dr. Beckett is repairing problems that are selected for him by the Almighty. Or by some other force we don't quite understand, or have a name for. Unfortunately, when Dr. Beckett changes history, that change becomes fact here in the present, and the 'original history' is erased. We have no books saying John Joseph Doe didn't die in a car accident twenty years ago. We have no papers to verify that Susie Smith used to be illiterate. We have no proof of anything. All we have is your"—he stuck a finger in Al's direction—"description of what has supposedly happened, which can only be backed up by a lot of computer mumbo-jumbo that, curiously enough, can only be properly interpreted by people who work at this Project." He gave a steely look to the two women, then to Al. "That gives me a headache," he told them. "And you tell me this morning, during which, if all was right with the world, I ought to be out playing golf and not sitting here, that Dr. Beckett's latest crusade is to 'mend a broken heart.' That's a *song,* ladies and gentleman. You are making my head hurt."

"No worse than ours do, Senator," Verbena told him.

"Hmmmppffff," he snorted. "Well, Doctor, you have my sympathies. But we return to the original question." After a moment of ferreting in the inside breast pocket of his suit jacket, he produced a sheet of paper folded into quarters. "Sam Beckett," he said, "was supposed to fade out of the spotlight. A spotlight he put himself into for almost twenty years, with a lot of jabbering about time travel, which he apparently thought would earn him public sympathy and an endless outpouring of cash. When Quantum Leap became a government project, he

164

was supposed to cease being an object of interest to anyone. Anyone! This country is filled with workaholics. People who bury themselves so deeply in their labor of choice that they see less sunlight than a mushroom. Sam Beckett was supposed to be one of those. And all of those people to whom he connected himself, in his life, and in his continuing quest for money, were supposed to be curious for a minute or two, then annoyed for a minute or two, and then they were supposed to forget about him entirely. That is the only way this Project can continue to operate, given the parameters that have been . . ."

He paused long enough to grimace. "Dumped upon us," he growled. "Dr. Beckett is incommunicado. Period. End of discussion. Not a topic of discussion! Not the focus of anyone's interest. And now. Now! We have *this*. Which I'm told was downloaded by not less than a hundred—a hundred!—ardent women in all parts of the United States." The unfolded paper was thumped down into the center of the table with Weitzman's index finger pressing down one corner. What he had presented to his audience was a slightly fuzzy enlargement of a black-and-white photograph of Sam and his brother Tom playing one-on-one, the original of which had appeared in the *People* magazine article that Mitchell Lovetz had mentioned to Al. Tom wore a dark-colored tank-style sports jersey; Sam was shirtless.

" 'Daddy,' " Weitzman continued, again mimicking his daughter, " 'don't you know Sam Beckett?' 'Why?' 'Oh . . . one of my friends wants to write to him. For his autograph.' 'Why?' I say. 'Because she thinks he's hot.' "

"She's right," Verbena offered.

Weitzman scowled first at her, then at Donna, who seemed to have no problem with the comment. "I will not *have* this!" he barked, banging his fist down on the picture. "I will not have every hormone-laden female on that damned Net thing lusting after Sam Beckett!"

165

"It does get a little out of hand," Verbena said with a shrug.

"What?" Weitzman shrilled. "How do you know? How do you know that?"

"It's one of the ways we get information," Donna replied.

"I see," Weitzman said. "I see. I see." He hauled in several deep breaths, willing himself to be calm, then laid his hands flat on the table as if that would help. "Then perhaps the answer is . . . to tell Dr. Beckett that instead of worrying about broken hearts, he should make the right sort of change in history. One that will allow the world to make *sense*."

Verbena smiled humorlessly at him. "I don't think the world has ever made sense, Senator."

"Maybe it ought to start."

The others waited for him to go on, something they had done for more hours during the last five years than they cared to count—or even to remember. Weitzman took a long look at each of them. Then, when the three members of Sam's team believed that the senator was ready to continue, he got up from his chair and carefully straightened his tie and his jacket.

"I'm leaving," he said coldly.

The other three held back sighs of relief. Amiably, as they followed him to the door, Verbena Beeks asked, "Headed back to Washington for a little golf, Senator?"

Weitzman turned and stared at her once more. "No," he said. "I'm going to Destiny."

Once more, Weitzman led through the corridors of Quantum Leap a parade that consisted only of himself and Albert Calavicci. He might or might not have known exactly where he was headed. In any event, when he stopped walking, he and Calavicci were still alone.

"You've talked to these people?" he said.

"Yes," Calavicci replied.

166

"And they still intend to go ahead with this television appearance?"

"Did you want me to tell them that somebody would find their bones out in the middle of the desert?" Calavicci asked dryly.

"If that's what it takes."

"Senator . . ."

Weitzman shook his head sharply. "You may have your own little world down here, Admiral. But the world up there"—he nodded toward the ceiling—"is the same as it's always been. I should not have to explain that to you."

"You don't," Calavicci replied.

The senator was silent for a while, as he examined Calavicci's purple suit, his black patent-leather shoes, his gold and purple and black necktie. Weitzman's face betrayed nothing of what he was thinking. Finally, he inclined his head in something that was almost a nod. "Go ahead," he told the other man. "Play your games. Be cock o' the walk if you like. I'm going to Destiny."

Sol Weitzman's secretary read a paperback novel. His aide listened to music on a portable CD player with state-of-the-art headphones. Sol Weitzman looked out the window of his limousine, silently watching the New Mexico landscape roll by.

He had, he was very sure, maintained his status as top dog (albeit a disliked top dog) in the eyes of Sam Beckett's people. He had admitted to them that Elly was frittering away valuable time—but then Elly was a young girl, and if anyone was entitled to a little bit of wasted time, it was young people. Admitting that Elly was, well, normal did not damage anything. The only possibility of serious damage that existed this morning seemed to lie in the studios of KDNM Television, and in the lap of Roberto Gutierrez. If Gutierrez said the wrong thing, or implied the wrong thing, or if one of his guests (Keller?

167

Yes, her name was Keller) did, then Project Quantum Leap might . . .

It might *end*. Maybe not this week, or this month. But soon. Too soon.

Before Sam Beckett had a chance to set things right.

Before he had a chance to go back to June of 1969, to a small town outside Chicago, where a small boy named Jeremy had drowned on a sunny afternoon in a backyard swimming pool. His parents had not been very far away: they were standing on the patio at the side of the house, gathered around a barbecue grill, watching hamburger patties cook, sipping cold drinks and laughing with the two men who had funded Sol Weitzman's entry into local politics.

Just a little boy, Weitzman thought, watching another mile of brown-and-gray scenery roll by outside his window. A little boy whose life—and the end of it—had made no difference to anyone except his family. The children who had been his playmates were grown now and did not remember him, nor did the rest of the world. The fact that God had seen fit to take him away at the age of three went completely unnoticed.

But surely, if Sol Weitzman waited long enough, God would see fit to give Jeremy back.

With the help of Sam Beckett.

And his Project.

CHAPTER
THIRTEEN

"Are you all right, Admiral?" Gooshie ventured.

Al squinted at him. He would have shaken his head, but he suspected that would hurt. At Verbena's insistence, he'd gotten almost two hours of sleep before Weitzman's arrival, but it had apparently been with his head tucked into his navel. The back of his neck had screamed at him ceaselessly since Security had hauled him out of bed.

"Do I look all right?" he mumbled.

"No," Gooshie said.

The little programmer had a firm grip on the handlink and seemed afraid to relinquish it. Why, Al couldn't imagine; it wasn't as if he could do any harm to anything or anyone by going into the Chamber in less than tippy-top condition. Flying the Chamber wasn't like flying a plane.

God, he missed flying.

If only Sam would come home, he could tuck them both into a little two-seater and float over to Vegas. A long weekend: some gambling, some shows, some laughs. Couldn't take Donna—Donna was luckier at the tables than both of them put together, which was not fun. Besides, she seemed to think she was descended from

Cinderella. When midnight came, she insisted on hauling Sam off to bed.

Vegas had been more fun without Donna. But on the other hand, Sam had been *less* fun without Donna. So which was better?

God, he missed flying.

"Gimme the damn thing," he said to Gooshie, and waggled his fingers at the other man.

Gooshie demurred. "I don't know, Admiral."

"You don't know what?"

"Dr. Beeks says you need to calm Dr. Beckett down. She says he's had too many instances of extremely high stress on this Leap. And you don't look like you could calm him down."

Al stared at him. "What, does she issue a newsletter every morning? Gimme the handlink, for crying out loud, and let *me* worry about who's stressed and who isn't."

"Admiral . . ."

"Give me the handlink before I rip your arm off!"

Gooshie shook his head and took two steps back, removing himself from Al's reach. He had the link firmly clasped in both hands now, in front of his chest, like a set of rosary beads. The spectators to this little performance, who were all behind Al, had begun to murmur among themselves: "Weitzman . . . Weitzman . . ."

Yeah, Weitzman, Al thought. *Right up there in the list of Top Ten Causes of Dangerous Stress.*

"What am I gonna hurt?" he demanded.

"Al."

He turned around, slowly, so that his head wouldn't swim. His own personal Greek chorus was gathered there, Beeks at their center, with one eye apiece on him, and the other on whatever they were supposed to be doing. They watched him, he figured, for the same reason people flocked to the Indy 500 every year: not to see the race, but in hopes of seeing someone wipe out. And their murmurings now sounded very much to him like the

170

background track of the "You're Losing Credibility Blues."

Well, the hell with *that*.

Narrowing his eyes, he looked at each of them in turn, searching for one face. She *had* to be here—she was always here.

"Gimme that," he said, and beckoned to Toolie Gibson.

Exactly as he thought she might, she glanced first to her right, then her left, then behind her, positive he was addressing someone else. Then she pointed to the middle of her chest and mouthed the word "Me?"

"You. Give."

Al grabbed a pair of chairs and hauled them over side-by-side, sat on one of them and nodded for the tiny technician to take the other. She sat on it gingerly and, with a frozen smile decorating her face, handed Al her blue clipboard.

The board was stuffed with papers, fifty pages or more of them. The top sheet had a space at the bottom:

APPROVED: _____

DATED: _____

"What am I signing?" Al asked her.

Her mouth opened, but nothing came out of it for a very long moment. "Energy consumption report," she sputtered finally.

"You don't need me to sign this."

"No . . . ," she agreed in not much more than a whisper. "But Dr. Morris said you should see it. So you'd know."

"Know?"

She nodded.

"Know what?"

"The numbers. Sir. Admiral."

"The numbers." He glanced at the sheet. "So I'd know we're using up more juice than the entire state of Pennsylvania."

"Ummm . . . yes, sir. I guess that's right. Sir."

"Kid?" Al said.

"Sir?"

"You in the service, Gibson?"

"No, sir."

"Then stop calling me 'sir.' Go tell Morris you showed me the numbers, and I'm impressed as hell. All right? Go on."

She would probably break the latest land speed records leaving Control, he thought. But she didn't. Instead, she stood alongside her chair, refusing to accept her clipboard.

"Now what?" Al groused.

"You need to sign. Admiral."

"Okay, okay, okay." Groaning, Al tugged the ballpoint pen out from under the clamp of the clipboard, scrawled his signature in the APPROVED space, dated it, then thrust the board back at Toolie Gibson. He expected the gesture to satisfy the remaining members of the Greek chorus, but it didn't. Holding back a sigh that would probably have rattled the seismographs at Cal Tech, he stood up, turned to the cluster of onlookers and announced, "I'm gonna go up to Records with Gibson so we can turn this over to Moptop Morris. I'm gonna tell him I'm passionately in love with his numbers and his reports and the fact that Gibson wins this month's Persistence Award for doing something that Morris was too lazy to do himself. Then I'm gonna come back down here, and *somebody* is gonna put that handlink in my hand. Okay?"

Nobody answered him. But then, he hadn't thought they would.

Groaning again, he turned his back on them. "Okay, kid, let's go," he said, and rested a hand on Toolie Gib-

172

son's arm, intending to give her a nudge in the direction of the door.

And watched as she passed out cold.

Samuel John Beckett, owner of six doctoral degrees and what a lot of people insisted was the finest mind in the civilized world, was making his bed. From the look of things, he had been making the bed for three or four hours.

"Hey, Sam," Al said with as much good cheer as he could muster, which was hardly any at all.

Sam turned his head, smiled and went back to tugging at layers of blankets. "You look like hell," he commented. "You look worse than you did last night. I thought you were going to handle whatever it was you needed to handle and I don't need to know about."

"Don't pick on me, Sam," Al sighed.

"Friend of mine used to say," Sam commented over his shoulder, " 'you look like you were rode hard and put away wet.' "

"Nobody put me away at all."

"I'm not asking. See? I'm making the bed. I'm not asking any questions. Not a single one."

"I scared somebody," Al said, and sighed again.

"I'm not asking."

"A kid from up in Records. I autographed a report for her, and said I was gonna walk her back up there, to Records, and she keeled over."

Sam let go of the blanket he had been fussing with and straightened up in the narrow space between C.J.'s bed and the wall. An expression Al had seen often enough to do an oil painting of it crossed Sam's face, then evaporated, replaced by a look of slightly less than patient tolerance. " 'Taking you up to Records' isn't one of your euphemisms?" he inquired. "Like 'Want to see my etchings?' "

"She's a kid, Sam."

"If she's a kid, she's not working at the Project. We don't have anybody under twenty-four. I remember that." It was Sam's turn to sigh. "I don't know *why* I remember that, but I remember it. So what kind of a 'kid' are we talking about here?"

"She looks like a kid."

"And you scared her?" Sam frowned. "That's not on your list, is it? Wouldn't that ruin your image? Frightening women? What in the world did you say?"

"I told you what I said."

Bothered, Sam sidestepped out from beside the bed and stood in the middle of the room, studying the holographic image of his friend. Al avoided his gaze for a minute, then reluctantly lifted his head, straightened his posture and tried furiously to adopt a "business as usual" attitude.

"You're not a good liar," Sam told him, "and I'm not blind. You look like hell. I haven't seen you look this bad since—since the Leap with Beth. You're telling me things that don't tell me anything, and I don't know if I can put up with that. I care about what goes on there. With you. With . . . with everyone. Al . . ." The Observer's eyes had lowered again, and Sam shifted his position again to meet them. "Al. I don't remember very much. But it's enough. It's got to be enough. It's . . . Don't disconnect me from everything back there. Don't cut me off."

"I'm . . ."

"Al," Sam said quietly, "it's all I've got."

That startled Al, something Sam had not anticipated. "I'm not cutting you off," he said after a moment, a little too rapidly for the reassurance to sit well with Sam. "It's . . . the rules. You know: the rules you set up. I can't give you information . . ."

"You've been giving me information all along. Especially when somebody else ordered you not to."

"Yeah," Al said.

Sam nodded slightly, and blandly, as if he intended to accept what he was being told. With Al still half-avoiding his scrutiny, he sat down on a corner of the bed and shuffled his shoes against C.J.'s rag rug in a spot where the morning sunshine brightened the muted green-and-brown pattern. "Al?" he murmured, then waited for Al to look at him. "Is there a Tina?"

The Observer scowled. "Of course there's a Tina. She'd be really happy to hear you say—"

"Don't go into a song-and-dance routine. Just answer the question."

"There *is* a Tina."

"Who works at the Project."

"Who works at the Project," Al parroted. "You know her. You worked with her. She thought you were cute." The Observer bit his lower lip, then corrected himself. "She still thinks you're cute. *I* think you're cute. The whole world thinks you're cute. God, Sam, what do you want me to say?"

Sam replied slowly, "I don't want you to *say* anything. I want you not to exclude me from what used to be my life."

"I . . . I'm sorry, Sam."

"I know you're sorry. The thing is, there are days when that doesn't help." A flash of movement in the living room caught Sam's attention: Rufus, lying in a big square of sunlight and gnawing happily on a leather chew toy. "I made up the rules before I had any idea what would happen." He smiled vaguely, then went on. "It's like writing an instruction manual for white water rafting without ever putting your butt in a boat. I didn't *know,* Al. Maybe some of the rules shouldn't apply. Maybe none of them should."

Al kept his thoughts to himself for a while. The hand-link beeped and trilled at him several times during his silence, but he ignored it. "Thought you were gonna talk to *her.*"

175

"How do you know I didn't?"

"Because you've got that 'I can't deal with it' look on your face."

"I *can't* deal with it," Sam said. "I've been trying to come up with something to say. The right way to approach this. This isn't going to be easy, you know. She's not going to tell me 'oh, okay' when I tell her she ought to patch up her relationship with her husband." Pulling himself up off the bed, he nodded toward the window that faced the lake. Visible through it was the end of the little boat dock. Patrice, in her jeans and sweater, was sitting there cross-legged, staring out across the water. "She's been there all morning," Sam told his partner. "Thinking. Waiting. I don't know."

"Maybe she thinks you'll change your mind," Al offered.

"She's going to be sitting there a long time if that's what she wants."

"Talk to her, Sam. You can do it—you've done it before. Make her see the light." The Observer grinned. "And you can get out of here."

"What do I *say*, Al?"

"You'll think of something." Sam shifted his weight from one leg to the other, but before he could move, Al stuck out his free hand, palm toward Sam in a stop gesture. "Don't pace," the Observer warned. "You're gonna wear the varnish off the floor. Tell her . . . ah, jeez, Sam, I don't know what you should tell her."

Sam nodded, hard, as if Al's words had confirmed every supposition he had ever made in his life. "The way she acts . . ." He paused, waving a hand at the window. "It's contrary to everything I was ever taught. My family taught me that when you make a promise, you keep it. You *keep* it, and not just when it's convenient. How am I supposed to relate to somebody who overlooks her marriage vows this way? Huh? She's like a three-year-old with a short attention span."

176

Al didn't reply, but the way he grimaced at Sam spoke volumes.

"What?" Sam demanded.

"Maybe she just wants somebody to pay attention to her."

"Doesn't she have friends who can do that? Or a family?" Sam jabbed a finger at the handlink. "Ask Ziggy."

Reluctantly, Al keyed the question into the link. "Yeah," he said a few seconds later. "Both her parents are still alive, and she's got a couple of brothers and sisters. Belongs to a bunch of charity groups. No info on 'friends.' It's hard to track something like that, without talking to her and asking for names." Lowering the little device, he asked, "You want me to have Beeks give you a script? 'Marriage Counseling for Amateurs'?"

"This is not a joke."

"Sam," Al said, "you've patched up marriages before. And you've dealt with people you didn't like before. You did okay with those guys from the Klan. Remember?"

"I remember."

"Talk from the heart, Sam. You're good at that."

Sam nodded, but his shoulders, underneath C.J.'s sweatshirt, were still slumped with the weight of the world. He spent a minute gazing out the window, continuing to do so even after Al had noticed that the only living being at Edwards Lake who seemed not to be terminally depressed was Rufus.

"I avoided psych courses like the plague," Sam groaned. "I hated the whole idea of digging around in people's heads like an archaeologist looking for dinosaur bones. Now look. What is this, some kind of cosmic revenge on me because I liked numbers better than obsessions and phobias?" Before Al could reply, he sputtered on, "What do I tell her? I don't know what to tell her! What do I say to somebody whose favorite hobby is wandering from one bed to another?" Then he cut himself off. "Ignore that," he told his partner. "I forgot who I'm talking to."

"A hobby," Al said mildly, "is not a bad thing. *You* could use a hobby."

"I'm going outside," Sam grumbled. "I'm going to talk to that woman. She probably won't listen, but I'll talk." He got as far as the bedroom doorway before he turned, interrupting Al in the process of summoning the Chamber door. "Maybe somewhere along the line I'll figure out what I'm supposed to say to *you*."

"Ahhhh, Sam," Al murmured.

But Sam was already gone.

CHAPTER FOURTEEN

He had ended up feeling sorry for people on entirely too many of these Leaps. He tried to convince himself that people were basically pretty much the same, and basically good—and if they acted contrary to that assumption, it was because circumstance had forced them to. He had also been naive enough to think, back when the Leaping began, that life was what you made of it, and that if the party involved simply tried hard enough, they would without a doubt be successful at love, or business, or whatever was important to them. It had pained him to discover that for a lot of people, the exact opposite was true: that life *was* a bitch, and then you died.

He'd listened to a woman cry at the end of one of his Leaps—a woman who had treated him miserably, so by rights he should not have felt any sympathy for her at all. But hearing her sobs, and feeling her shake against him, turned his heart around. Her name was Norma, and at the end she wanted him to tell her just one thing: "Why can't it be like it is on television?"

All he could say to her was "I don't know."

His own life had certainly been nothing like television. His father hadn't worn suits and worked in an office like Beaver Cleaver's dad. Beaver's dad never seemed to sweat, but John Beckett certainly did. There had been a

July afternoon, one of many with high heat, high humidity and no rain, when John had emerged from hours of wrestling with the engine of the tractor he could not afford to replace and stood at the end of the porch sipping a glass of lemonade Sam's mother had pressed into his hand. Sam, sitting on the porch swing with a book, had seen something his mother had not: that John's face had been the same color as a brick when he left the barn, and that he had stopped to lean against the barn door with his hand pressed to the middle of his chest. He had stood that way for a long time—until he realized Sam was watching him.

"Hot day, son, hmmm?" he said, and smiled, because the spell that had held him was broken.

That evening, with the faintest hint of a breeze pushing its way through the house, helped along by an old, creaking electric fan, John Beckett had danced with his wife in the kitchen while their children watched them and laughed. "The Tennessee Waltz" was playing on the radio.

To be fair, Sam could not remember Ward Cleaver ever dancing with June. But his parents *did* dance, and looked into each other's eyes for a moment like two goofy high school kids, and very obviously loved each other.

That was the lesson he'd been taught, he thought as he walked down to the end of Maple Lane and out onto the little boat dock. *Nothing is ever like it is on television. Sometimes it's better. Sometimes it's worse. Sometimes you have to take the hand you're dealt . . . but you can still work with it.*

"Car trouble?" he said when he was close enough for Patrice to hear him.

"No."

"It's a nice day."

It *was* a nice day. Several degrees colder than the day

180

before, but filled with the same brilliant sunshine. *The best part of fall,* he thought.

"What do you want?" she asked, but the question was flat, betraying nothing of what she might be feeling. And she asked it without turning around, so that he couldn't gather any clues from her face.

"Nothing."

He let half a minute go by, then rested his rump against one of the pilings and folded his arms over his chest. He'd pulled a jacket on over his sweatshirt before leaving the house, and was grateful that he had; it really was cold, a suggestion of what the air would be like here in a month or so. Rufus, who had trailed him down to the dock, sat dutifully at his feet and gazed out over the water as if he were trying to figure out what held Patrice Frey so enthralled. If the circumstances had been different, Sam mused, and if he and Patrice had been different people, this would have made a pleasant scene. He would have asked her if she'd like to go for a boat ride down the length of the lake, share a picnic lunch, enjoy the day.

Nobody here was enjoying much of anything, except possibly for Rufus, and that made him grimace.

"What do you *want*?" Patrice asked again, more sharply this time, and this time she turned around.

"Just to talk," Sam said.

"About what?"

"About . . . that I'm sorry you're upset. That I'm sorry our . . . relationship isn't turning out to be what you wanted. Maybe you need something a little more steady than what I can give you."

"You're a piece of work, C.J.," Patrice groaned.

"You said that last night."

"I meant it last night. And I mean it now. If you treat other women like this, then I'm surprised you're still walking around in one piece. Do you know anything about common consideration? The last time I met someone who was so completely unconcerned with anyone else's feelings, I was in grade school. Even the jocks in high school weren't as arrogant as you are. Come/don't come. I want to be with you/I don't want to be with you. Keep it up, C.J. Not a lot more time is going to go by. Somebody's going to unite your head with something big and blunt and heavy.'' She stood up then and moved as if she intended to walk past him, back to the road. ''I really don't want to talk to you.''

''You're still here,'' Sam pointed out.

''I didn't want to drive all the way down the thruway in the dark.''

''It's been light out for almost four hours.''

Patrice took a long gulp of air. Her lips pressed together for a moment. ''Are you trying to make me angry?''

Sam shook his head. ''I did that already.''

''What, then? What do you want?''

''I want to . . . I want to say I'm sorry that you drove all the way up here for . . . for nothing. But it's not working out. You and me. It's not right.''

''Is there a why?'' she asked.

''No. Not really. No.''

''You changed your mind.''

This was like walking a tightrope, Sam thought. It would be hard enough to have this conversation with someone he had actually lived through a relationship with. Performing scenes in a play would be the other end of the spectrum, and he was caught somewhere in between. He was reading lines of dialogue, but for Patrice, the words and the emotions behind them were completely real.

''I guess that's it,'' he told her. ''I changed my mind. You can forget about me. Wipe me right out of your life. And go home.''

''Home.''

Sam nodded. ''Uh-huh.''

182

"And do what, exactly?"

"Whatever you normally do there. Be with your husband."

"Be with my husband." A broad look of disbelief nestled itself onto Patrice's face. "That's good. Yeah, that's exactly what I'll do. Go and be with my husband. Thanks, C.J. I appreciate the advice. That's so good. If you decide you don't want to write mysteries anymore, you can write an advice column for the newspaper. Be with my husband. Oh, that's fine. That's very well thought out and . . . fine."

Shaking her head, she did walk past Sam then, but not rapidly. Leaning in her direction, Sam reached out and caught her by the arm. It didn't take much effort to bring her to a halt.

"It's my fault," she told him. "I never said anything about Michael. I didn't figure you wanted to hear it. Why would you? So you don't know."

"What don't I know?" Sam asked.

"That there's nothing for me to go back to. Why do you think I'm here? Because I figure he'll find out I cheat on him, and it'll make him miserable? He's not there. He's not home. Ever. His work is his wife. He only married me to have somebody to hold onto at parties. Somebody who looks good in a black dress and heels."

Although he told himself he shouldn't, Sam allowed himself a long look at Patrice Frey. In the daylight, in her soft blue sweater and slim jeans, with her dark curls tumbling over her shoulders, she was terrific looking. No, more than that, he corrected himself. In the right kind of a black dress, she'd be stunning. "I bet you do," he offered.

"Thanks," she said. "Although a compliment from you isn't worth much right now."

"I know."

"I'll take it, though. It's the only one I've gotten in a while."

183

"He never . . . ?"

"No." She was firm about that at first, then grudgingly amended, "He does when he thinks about it. But he never thinks about it. Michael the golden boy. Michael the hotshot lawyer. Michael who's going to be worth a million dollars by the time he's forty."

"Does he love you?" Sam asked.

"No."

"Are you sure?"

Patrice looked down at Sam's hand. His fingers were still curled around her arm, and for a moment she seemed to be considering pulling away from him, but she must have decided not to. "No. I'm not sure. He used to. I have no way to tell."

"Maybe . . . ," Sam began.

"Maybe what?" She stared at him. "What's this for, all of a sudden?"

"Maybe you should give it another try."

"Why?"

"He must have married you for a reason."

"I told you the reason."

"It's . . ."

Her face reddening, she yanked her arm out of his grasp and moved out of his reach, ending up a few inches from the end of the road. "Stop it, C.J. Stop it! I don't know where this came from, all of a sudden, and I don't want to know. You have no idea what my marriage is like—and it's really none of your business. So kindly stop handing out advice that nobody asked you for and that nobody wants. Do you hear me? If it's over between you and me, it's over. You don't need to send me away with . . . with this sappy bullshit. Just . . . shut up. All right? Shut up!"

She stalked away, heading for her car, moving at a good clip at first but slowing steadily the farther she got. By the time she was midway between the dock and her house, Sam was almost certain that she was crying.

When he approached her, she buried her face in her hands and pulled her shoulders in, as if that would prevent him from touching her. "Damn you," she choked out. "Damn you!"

"Pat," he said softly.

"Go away!"

Was it right, he wondered, for somebody to be caught up in a mess this deep when they were this young? C.J. had penciled Patrice's birthday into the margin of his notes near her name: she'd only turned thirty a few months ago. Sam wasn't sure how long she and Michael Frey had been married, but supposed it had to be at least a few years—time for her to become disenchanted. Five or six years, maybe? By that time, his parents had had his brother Tom.

Mom and Dad, he thought ruefully. *You always made giving advice look so easy. Boy, do I wish you were here now.*

He floundered on, pointing to Patrice's Mercedes. "You've got a nice car. And a nice house. Your place in New York must be nice too—that seems like a pretty safe guess. And your clothes are . . ."

"Nice," she spat.

"A lot of people would figure you've got a good deal going."

"Fine," she said. "I'll trade with them."

"Is it that bad?"

She took a step back. Her heel landed on a pinecone that lay in the middle of the road, which disturbed her balance and almost made her stumble. She recovered quickly, though, and stood glaring at Sam with the pine tree shadowing her head and her left shoulder. "I'm not like you, C.J. I don't figure solitary confinement is anything to aim for. I don't *like* being by myself."

"I'm not sure I do, either," Sam murmured.

"Okay, maybe it was partly my fault. Maybe I didn't stop to take a good long look at what I was getting myself

185

into. Michael told me what his goals were—where he wanted to work, what kind of cases he wanted to handle. I should have been bright enough to figure out what that meant. That it didn't allow for him to come home every night at six o'clock and have dinner. That there wasn't any slack in the schedule. That there wasn't any *me* in the schedule. I should have seen that. But I didn't. So here I am. Yes, you're right: I've got expensive clothes and an expensive car and an apartment in Manhattan and a house at the lake. And you know, I don't want to give that up. I'm taking Michael's money, and I'm getting through the rest of it as best I can.'' She stopped briefly, examining his reaction, then asked, ''How's that sound? Does that fit in with the Gospel According to Clarence?''

It did, more than likely, Sam suspected. What it didn't fit in with was the Gospel According to John and Thelma Beckett.

''You took a vow,'' he told Patrice.

''And you,'' she told him, ''have been up here listening to yourself talk for way too long.''

He expected her to walk away again, but she surprised him by stepping toward him. She slid in close to him and leaned her head against his shoulder as if she wanted to be comforted, and he gave in to that, curling an arm around her and patting her gently on the back. But instead of crying on his shoulder, she rested a hand against the small of his back and simply stood nestled up against him.

The warmth of her hand radiated through his jacket and the heavy shirt underneath it, down into his skin. The side of his neck was warm too, from the breath she was exhaling against it. Sam closed his eyes for a moment.

He realized what she was doing about half a second before her hand reached his butt.

''Patrice,'' he groaned, backstepping away from her, ''don't do that.''

The hand she'd been maneuvering, instead of reaching

186

his backside, collided with the left side of his face. He saw the blow coming but did nothing to avoid it. When Patrice stumbled away from him they began to glare at each other, Sam pointedly not touching his throbbing cheek.

"There was no reason for that," he said between his teeth.

"No? I disagree."

"Does Michael hit you?" Sam asked.

"Michael?" Patrice's eyes widened, as if that were the most ridiculous thing she had ever heard. "No, Michael does not hit me. Michael isn't in the same room with me often enough to be upset with me."

Sam frowned, then said, "That's not always a prerequisite."

"Well, aren't we grand," Patrice scoffed. "What have you been reading lately?"

He was badly tempted to walk away: to let Patrice Frey do anything, and go anywhere she damn well pleased.

Leaping was like football, Al had told him once: sometimes the clock simply ran out without the touchdown having been completed. Game over, with no victory for the visiting team. Sam, surprised and intrigued by an analogy coming from the Observer that had nothing to do with sex, had considered the idea for a while and decided that his partner was right. Sometimes the clock did run out.

Other times, the battle was won but not the war. He would prevent an accident from taking a life, only to be told that the life would end a few months farther down the road for some other reason. What he had done was a delaying tactic, Al told him.

He was not fond of delaying tactics. Or expired clocks.

"You can't save the world, Sam," Al would remind him. Sometimes, the Observer seemed to be an inexhaustible source of rusty, unhelpful platitudes, and that particular one was Sam's least favorite. If his existence

187

had been a normal one, then no, he would not have been able to save the world, even working one piece at a time. He readily admitted that, to Al and to himself. But nothing about Leaping was normal. Leaping warped all the rules. By rights, now he should have been able to save the world—even if it was still only one piece at a time.

But he couldn't, which made him wonder sometimes whether God, Time, or Whoever had really figured out the best path for him to follow. Put him into the positions that offered the best chance at success. He *wanted* to succeed, after all. Needed to. Otherwise, what was the point of all this?

He wanted to win.

But once in a while, he wanted to walk away. To give up the ball. To smile at the person in front of him and say, "It's your life. Knock yourself out."

He felt like that right now.

Then his conscience talked him out of it. And so did Rufus, who was standing right behind him, as immovable as a boulder.

Patrice's eyes were still damp with the tears that had welled up in them, and that she had wiped away before he approached her. *Maybe Al was right,* he thought. *Maybe she* is *looking for somebody to pay attention to her. To make her feel important. Maybe that's all it is. And even if it's not . . .*

If he'd decided to stay in medicine, his conscience demanded to know, what kind of doctor would he have made if he allowed himself to say, "No, I won't treat you, because I don't like you"? He would have had that situation thrust upon him—what, once a week? Every day? More than that?

Yeah—what does that make you, Doctor *Beckett? If you can say "I know you need my help, but I don't like you, so get lost"? You can't do that. You* know *you can't do that. Whether you agree with the choices she's made doesn't make any difference. No . . . it does. But it* can't.

"Pat . . ." he began. "Listen. Listen to me, okay?"

He walked back to C.J.'s house three hours later feeling that he had accomplished nothing at all. Which was certainly not unexpected; he was firmly convinced that C.J. Williams was the wrong man for this job. If Patrice needed to be talked into going back to her husband, then why hadn't he been Leaped into Michael? Someone who could get down on bended knee and promise to change? Maybe the real Michael, once the Leap was finished, wouldn't have changed at all, but at least Patrice would be open to giving his lifestyle another chance.

Or not. But it was possible, wasn't it?

Sam stood in front of C.J.'s bathroom sink for several minutes, staring at the younger man's reflection in the medicine cabinet mirror. C.J., it seemed, could talk his lover into only one thing.

"She's right," Sam grumbled. "You *are* a piece of work. And so is she."

They'd had lunch together. She'd gotten into his car with as much reluctance as if she thought he intended to take her to some deserted spot—though a place more deserted than Maple Lane was hard to imagine—then murder her and abandon her body in the woods. He had hoped she would recommend a place to eat, but she refused to do anything more than stare out the car window until he parked outside a café in town whose sign announced that it featured "SALADS 'N' SUCH." She was also uninterested in choosing something to eat from the small laminated menu.

What do I have to do to . . . ? Sam wondered.

But he knew the answer, knew how to get her attention. It wouldn't have been difficult, he thought dejectedly. The body that had been bouncing through time for—was it years? it had to be years now—had certainly been amenable to the lovemaking she was looking for.

She wanted him, even if she thought he was C.J., and his body had wanted her. She *still* wanted him, after a whole day's worth of rejection. If nothing else, he had to give her points for persistence. And he understood, as he watched her push bits of tomato around her plate with the tip of a fork, that she cared for C.J. Williams. Not a lot, and not in any enduring way, but she cared.

Then there had to be a way for him, for C.J., to do this job. To convince her to move in the right direction. If he was as persistent as she was. Said the right things. Pushed the right buttons.

"Rake a few leaves," he said to the mirror. "Take a nap. Sure, Al."

Take care of everything C.J. was supposed to do. C.J.'s face looked back at him from the mirror. He knew it was only his imagination, but the other man seemed to challenge him to take on exactly what Al had suggested. *Yeah, yeah,* Sam thought. *Rake the leaves. Clean up after the windstorm. Call B. Buy oil.*

Call . . .

Call?

C.J.'s notebook was right where it belonged, in the organizer on top of his desk. Tucked into the slot next to it was something Sam hadn't noticed before: a collection of mail fastened together with a big paper clip. His first instinct was to dismiss it as something C.J. could deal with later on; his second instinct told him not to ignore anything on this Leap, so he flipped off the clip and took a closer look: an envelope from *Time* marked in big red letters "YOUR LAST CHANCE!"; a glossy flyer from the supermarket in town; a beige envelope that looked like it contained a greeting card; and something from Duffy's Mufflers that was probably a bill. Each piece was addressed not to C.J., but to one of the Freys. C.J. had been holding onto it until Patrice arrived, Sam supposed. Now she was here . . . but he suspected she wasn't very concerned about a missing stack of junk mail.

Shaking his head, he flipped open C.J.'s notebook. On the top page of the section C.J. had earmarked for Four Maple Lane were Michael Frey's home and office phone numbers. Sam had no idea who "B" was, or whether calling him or her would accomplish anything, but calling "M" . . .

"I can talk to him," he told Rufus, who was sitting beside his big aluminum dish in hopes that Sam's presence in the kitchen meant rewards of the Soop'r Dog variety. "Plant a few seeds in his head. Then, when she goes home, they can start patching things up. Maybe he doesn't even realize that anything's wrong! He's probably trying to get his career going. Get in good with his boss. Make some money. Make a lot of money," he amended. "Sometimes all it takes is a hint. He must be a bright guy. He's probably just caught up in his work."

Nodding to himself, Sam carried the notebook over to the kitchen table, laid it down on the tabletop and dropped into a chair. More information about Michael would help, he thought, and began flipping through the other papers in the book.

Most of the section was composed of photocopied check stubs: C.J.'s paychecks from the Freys, along with payments that had been made to various repairmen, the refuse service and what Sam guessed was a local homeowners' association. He was about to flip back to the cover page when he spotted a sheet of paper that had been tucked in between two of the photocopied sheets. On thick, cream-colored vellum, with "Michael S. Frey" scripted across the top in brown ink, was a note from Patrice's husband.

Tx for your help with the boat—damage wasn't as bad as I thought. No suit, Wilkerson is going to pay the bill & he ought to be glad his kid isn't

191

dead. Trust him to think a 12 year old can handle a jet ski. If Bob's prices go up let me know & I'll send more. Good luck with the book.

Mike

Friendly—yes, he definitely sounded friendly. That jibed with the framed photo that sat in the middle of the Freys' mantelpiece, something Sam had taken note of during his search of the ground level of Number Four. The camera had caught Michael in a good mood, holding back a laugh, it looked like. His right arm was flung around Patrice's shoulders, and she too was close to bubbling over. The picture reminded Sam of the ones newspaper reporters liked to caption "in happier times." The guy in it was no sharp-eyed shyster. A good strategist—maybe that was all he had to be. If he was charming too, that might doubly prompt big-moneyed clients to want him on their side.

This was definitely a guy Sam Beckett could approach. A guy that might be a little bit like "Doc" Crosnoff, Sam's dad's attorney. A guy who liked a cold beer and a piece of homemade pie on a hot summer day—to keep his motor going, "Doc" had told the Beckett kids.

Wearing a broad grin, Sam reached over to pick up the phone and punched out the eleven digits of Michael Frey's home number. He'd try there first; after all, this was Sunday afternoon.

"You've reached the residence of Michael and Patrice Frey," a recording told him. "If you'll leave a message, we'll get back to you." Beep.

So much for it being Sunday.

"Hastings, Whitberg and Bell," a voice said after Sam had dialed the other number.

"I'd like to speak to Michael Frey," he told the voice. "Hold, please."

And a moment later he *was* speaking to Michael Frey. He needed a good reason to be making this call, he'd decided; an ordinary message could have been left on the answering machine. This was a busy man putting in office hours on Sunday. He'd be annoyed by someone calling to chat—particularly someone who was an employee, not a friend.

"Sorry to bother you, Mike," Sam said quickly. "But there's a problem at the house."

"Shit," Frey replied. "I knew it."

"You did?"

"The news had all kinds of reports about storm damage on Friday morning. Gale-force winds. Tree limbs down all over the place. I *knew* it. How bad is it?"

That wasn't part of the story Sam had concocted. Nor did it seem logical that C.J., if he was worth anything as a caretaker, would wait two days to report something serious. But what the heck, he thought. Might as well follow Frey's lead.

"Some of the shingles pulled loose," he explained. "The roofers are coming over this afternoon to take a look at some of the other places. I wanted to get your permission—if they find anything—to go ahead and get the work done. Before the weather gets bad again."

"Fine," Frey said, sounding enormously relieved. "Do it."

"Okay. I'll let you know what they say."

"Do that. Listen, C.J.? Patty's up there, isn't she?"

Sam hadn't anticipated that either. This was a man who was supposed to be oblivious to his wife's day-to-day life? "Ummm . . . yes," he ventured.

"She tell you to ask me about the roof?"

What Sam had already told Michael wasn't a lie, exactly. He *had* spotted several areas of loose shingles on the roofs along Maple Lane, and calling a professional to look at them wouldn't be out of line. With a little luck, he might be able to get someone to show up this afternoon, so that the lie would become nothing more than a prediction of the truth. But Frey's question complicated things. "No" didn't make sense. But if he said "yes" and Frey happened to mention that to his wife . . .

I never used to lie, Sam thought. *At least not like this.*

"Yup," he said.

Frey sighed softly into the phone. "Do whatever needs doing. If it's going to run more than a couple hundred, let me know before you commit to anything."

"Ummm . . . Mike?" Sam said, before Frey could hang up. "She . . . seems kind of upset. Patty. Your wife."

"Is that a news flash?"

"What?"

"Don't worry about it, C.J. She won't be there long— she's probably just tired of all the rain we're getting down here. Let her putter around for a while. She'll probably go up to those antiques shops she likes and buy some piece of ugly junk for the house. Then she'll come home. If she's giving you a hard time, don't take it personally."

"I think . . . ," Sam began.

"Gotta go. I've got three or four more hours of research ahead of me. Thanks for the call, okay? Keep me posted."

Frey hung up.

Sam sat there with the phone receiver in his hand, listening in disbelief to the hum of the dial tone. "Aaauuuugghhh," he said loudly, leaned back in his chair and thumped the back of his head against the wall.

CHAPTER
FIFTEEN

Lovetz was as giddy as a child who had been magically transported to Santa's toy factory. He had been dancing back and forth across the hotel room for several minutes, grinning like Jack Nicholson's version of the Joker and gazing significantly at Stephanie each time he passed her, a gesture that Stephanie did not receive with any pleasure. For her, the patter of his feet against the carpet formed an endless tune: *Jekyll and Hyde, Jekyll and Hyde, Jekyll and Hyde.*

"Mitchell," she said finally, "get a clue."

He stopped pattering and tipped his head quizzically. "What?"

"You are not Charles Bronson. I am not Elizabeth Montgomery. This is not the end of the world, and there is no signpost up ahead. Nothing is going to happen here."

"What?" he said again, completely confused.

Stephanie groaned at him. "Go back to your own room, would you? Order something greasy and fattening from room service and watch one of those astounding plotless porno films on TV. I'm sure they have them here, just the same as at that rathole we stayed in last night."

He folded his short arms across his chest and gave her a wounded look that might have stood a chance of work-

195

ing if it had come from someone else. "I thought we planned to have a nice lunch."

"*You* planned to have a nice lunch. I'm tired. I want to read for a while, then take a nap."

"I don't think you're being properly receptive, Stephanie."

"Well, you know, that's too bad."

Lovetz's arms swept up and out in a huge butterfly stroke. "I expected you to be grateful for this. Look at this room! It's a harbinger of things to come."

"A 'harbinger'?" Stephanie echoed.

"Yes. Yes! Isn't that what we planned? You'll be able to leave that pointless job of yours and enjoy the kind of life you've dreamed about." Lovetz grinned at her again and began to tick a mental list off on his fingers, the elements of which he did not bother to provide for Stephanie. When he was finished, he went on, "It's working perfectly. Things couldn't possibly be any better."

Stephanie scoffed. "Oh, really."

"Really."

"Because of what? The 'Roberto!' show? I hate to break this to you, Mitchell, but I don't think his viewership even reaches into six digits. He's local. Not local New York, or Chicago, or Los Angeles. He's local in Destiny, New Mexico. I didn't even know there *was* a Destiny, New Mexico, until you showed me the map four days ago."

"It's the first step," Lovetz pointed out.

"We've got nothing, Mitchell."

"We've got *this*." He gestured again, noting that Stephanie, who had turned her back on him, was watching him in the mirror that covered a wide swath of wall opposite the windows. He was tickled by what the glass reflected: the thick, soft, obviously high-quality carpet; the subtle Southwestern design of the woven bedspread and drapes; the table and chairs of pale wood; the moody, Native American–themed artwork on the walls.

"This," he said again. "A room in the best hotel in Albuquerque." When he still didn't get the reaction he wanted, he paused. The enthusiasm in his voice had dimmed considerably when he continued. "I'm sorry it's not the best hotel in Paris. Or Vienna. Or Monaco. Give it time, my dear."

"Don't call me 'my dear,' Mitchell. This isn't an old movie."

"Or an old episode of 'The Twilight Zone'?" Lovetz countered.

That surprised her. Grudgingly, she turned to face him again. "All right," she said. "All right: we've made a little progress. But we haven't won anything yet. I think we're a long way from winning anything."

"If it didn't take a little effort, would the results be as sweet?"

"Mitchell . . ."

Lovetz's shoulders straightened, and as she watched, Dr. Jekyll became Mr. Hyde again. "I'll get you what I promised you. I'll get both of us what I promised. There *is* a pot of gold at the end of this rainbow—you know that as well as I do. And it belongs to anybody with enough talent to find it."

"We've got a long way to go."

"Maybe," Lovetz admitted. "But Roberto Gutierrez thinks we're wonderful. That's a good start."

"Roberto Gutierrez," Stephanie pointed out, "thinks he was abducted by aliens."

The lawyer took a long look at his client, then leaned over, broke the seal on the room's mini-bar and carefully selected a drink for himself. As he poured the contents of a tiny bottle of scotch into a highball glass, he announced, "That's to our advantage, don't you think? Have a little faith." Watching Stephanie over the rim of his glass, he settled himself into one of the brown-and-gold cushioned chairs and took a sip. "I told you it was going to take a while."

197

"I've got three weeks, Mitch. Then I have to go back to work. I'm a vice president. A *working* vice president. I can't just wander around the country as if I were Ivana Trump."

"I know." Lovetz put the glass down suddenly and got up from his chair. In response to Stephanie's frown, he explained, "I have to use the bathroom."

"Use your *own* bathroom, Mitchell."

To her relief he obeyed the command, leaving her alone in her Regency Deluxe room. She listened to the silence for a minute—the only sound in the room was the soft hum of the air conditioner—then sank onto the end of the bed. The TV set, concealed inside an elegant cabinet, was within reach, but she avoided even thinking about turning it on. There wouldn't be any talk shows on the channels offered by the hotel's satellite pickup, not on a Sunday afternoon, but she had the distinct feeling that any face on the screen would remind her that *her* face would appear on Tuesday. Forty-eight hours from now. Talking about a part of her life she had tried very hard to forget.

Mom would not *be very happy,* she thought. *Stephanie Louise, on White Trash Television.*

Sitting next to a man who was convinced he'd been taken on board a UFO and interrogated by people Not of This Earth.

No, Mom would not be happy.

And all because of a stupid piece of paper that you got from the copier repairman.

Lovetz, to Stephanie's consternation, came bowling back in with a vague but happy, my-bladder-is-now-empty smile on his face and a copy of the Albuquerque Convention and Visitors' Guide in his hand.

"I do not want you walking in here without knocking," she sputtered.

"Why?" he asked her innocently. "Am I interrupting something?"

"This is *my* room, Mitchell."

"Which I paid for, as you'll recall." Reclaiming his drink, he settled back into his chair and stared at her, as unblinking as a wax dummy. "Besides . . . you get very melancholy when I leave you alone, and I don't like to see that. It's not good for you. Pining over somebody who wouldn't marry you."

"Get out," Stephanie told him.

"I will."

"Get out *now*. I mean it, Mitchell."

"Suit yourself." Drink in hand, Lovetz headed for the door. "But I'm serious. It doesn't do you any good to dwell on what didn't happen. You need to think about the future, dear. The future, and the rewards it's going to bring us."

She wanted to slam the door behind him, but the door was on a hydraulic hinge, hung that way to prevent the very thing she had in mind. So she stayed where she was, feeling her shoulders slump underneath the padded shoulders of her silk blazer. The air conditioner was turned a little too high; her toes, without the protection of the shoes she'd pushed off as soon as she'd dropped her purse onto the bed, had begun to feel chilled. In fact, most of her felt chilled. And frustrated. And alone.

"Dammit," she murmured.

All because of that dumb piece of paper . . .

The phone rang, startling her badly. Her heart thumped madly inside her chest as she picked up the receiver. "Yes?"

Completely unaffected by what she had said to him moments before, Lovetz's voice told her, "Go on and take your nap. Rest—you'll feel better. I know all the traveling we've done is draining. I'll ask the concierge about the best restaurants in the neighborhood. For dinner. I want you to enjoy your dinner."

"I'm not hungry, Mitchell."

"You've got nothing to worry about. We're going to

come out on top. If I didn't think that, I never would have come out here. But you know,'' he mused, ''it's a shame. I would've liked to meet this Sam Beckett. That *People* magazine makes him sound like an interesting guy, even if he was a crackpot.''

''Ummmm,'' Stephanie mumbled.

''Yuh-huh . . . would've liked to meet him.'' Lovetz sighed. ''It's really too bad he's dead.''

CHAPTER
SIXTEEN

When she had that look on her face, he expected lightning bolts to shoot out of her fingertips. He outweighed her by fifty pounds, but speed and agility were on her side. He wasn't getting past her. "Outta my way, Beeks," he told her anyway.

"No," she said.

"I'm going to the cafeteria for some coffee."

"There's coffee in my office."

"Coffee, I said. Not that Swiss cinnamon-mocha-whatever. Get outta my way."

He tried cutting to her left—her weak side, since she was right-handed—but "weak" in Verbena's case didn't mean "easily fooled." A quick half-step to her left blocked him, and she folded her arms over her chest and gave him the evil eye. She must've been one scary mommy, he thought; it was a wonder her son wasn't in twenty-four-hour therapy instead of med school.

"Al," Verbena said patiently, "Gibson is all right. I told you that. Several times."

"I heard you," he grumbled.

"Then will you stop worrying about it? She's going to rest for a couple of hours, then go back to work. But"—she silenced him with a waving forefinger before he could even begin to reply—"going up to Records is the last thing you should think about doing. Moptop has the papers you signed off on. He knows you signed off on them." After a glance at her tiny gold wristwatch, she concluded, "He probably filed them half an hour ago."

Al scowled at her. He knew better than to try to talk.

"She was startled," Verbena told him.

Gooshie, manning his usual position at Ziggy's main console, where he seemed to be attempting to play a concerto on the keyboard, murmured softly, "She's certainly not the first person he's spooked."

"What?" Al barked.

"He's right," Verbena concurred.

"About *what*?"

"That you get a little loud sometimes. And someone who doesn't know you might . . . overreact to that."

"By *fainting*?"

Verbena smiled vaguely. Someone who didn't know *her* might have thought she was concealing her amusement. They would have been wrong. "Not normally," she said and shrugged. "If you checked, you'd probably find bundles dropped off at the laundry within an hour or so of every one of your tirades."

"Are you telling me I make people piss in their drawers?" Al demanded.

"Once or twice," Verbena replied.

"I don't believe that."

Her eyes met Gooshie's, just for a second; then Gooshie pinned his attention to the console that lay underneath his hands. Nodding to herself, Verbena strolled around to stand alongside Al and rested a hand on his shoulder. "Well, you know, the thing is, *Admiral* . . . you not only do believe it, the idea tickles you to death."

"Get away from me, Beeks," the Observer warned her.

She ignored him. "Whitley from the motor pool? I seem to remember you telling him that if he put one more scratch in your hood, you were going to tie his private

202

parts into a knot that would make him have to urinate out his left ear.''

"He went through boot camp. I guarantee you he's heard that before.''

"My point is . . .''

"I know what your point is, Beeksie.''

"Do you?'' she countered.

They faced each other in silence for a minute, until Al began to have the absurd sensation that they were alone in the middle of a dance floor. In fact, they *were* alone, except for Gooshie. The other Control personnel were nearby—Al could hear mechanical clattering and the chatter of voices echoing through the corridors that were the spokes of the Control Center's wheel—but thankfully, for once, none of those people seemed to be eavesdropping. Not that that mattered much; the high points of his conversation with Beeks would still reach the cafeteria by dinnertime. His bickering with the Project psychiatrist wasn't "need to know," a fact that every one of the two hundred and eighteen people employed by Quantum Leap was giddily aware of. Sometimes that annoyed him. This was one of those times.

"You gonna give me another lecture on the delicate dynamics of group interaction?'' he snorted.

"Not right now,'' she replied.

Knowing she would follow him, he strode up the ramp to the door of the Accelerator. Approaching the portal earned him a raised eyebrow from Gooshie—and more than likely, the invisible equivalent of it from Ziggy—but he keyed the door open anyway and went on inside. He kept his back to the door until the click of her shoes told him Verbena had entered. The door closed a moment later.

"You know that story about the guy going back in time and changing everything by stepping on a butterfly?'' he asked finally.

Verbena nodded. "Very well, in fact.''

Al's eyes locked on hers. They were the same shade of brown as his own, a fact she had pointed out to him once and then refused to explain why. "I keep getting the feeling that Lovetz is the guy, and this Project is the butterfly," he told her. "He has no idea how much damage he could cause."

Verbena told him quietly, "Nobody watches 'Roberto!' anymore, Al. The heyday of those shows—all that 'I'm sleeping with my brother-in-law, his nephew *and* his pet ferret' stuff was over years ago. They hit their peak when we first came here. I remember watching them with Tina in the lounge at lunchtime." With a grimace Al wasn't sure how to interpret, she added, "That was a long time ago."

"Somebody watches him, or he wouldn't be on the air."

"Maybe somebody does," Verbena conceded. "But what is Stephanie Keller going to say? What could she possibly tell Roberto's viewing audience about Sam Beckett?"

"Lovetz has her coached to spill every bean in the goddamn pot," Al groused. "Sam told her about the String Theory—it's in his letters. If that little shyster did any research, he knows what Sam was aiming for at the point when he went underground. Sam would've been on every talk show on the planet himself if that guy in Duluth hadn't laughed at him on the air and called him a nutcase. And he was in the papers. He was in the *Post* nine times in three months."

"Which proves . . . ?"

"What, are you on their side?" Al demanded.

"No, Al, I'm not."

The words *Shoot her, Sam!!!* flitted through Verbena's mind. The man in front of her had spoken them, only a few months ago, inside the Imaging Chamber. Part of her had wondered that afternoon what wounded part of Albert Calavicci thought the best way to solve a problem

204

was to pull a trigger. The rest of her knew the answer.

"What do you want to do?" she ventured.

"Christ, Beeks, I don't know." He turned away from her then. When he turned back, he seemed to have buried his doubt, but that image faded quickly. "I'm sixty-five years old," he said, as if he didn't quite believe it.

"Not yet."

"Don't split hairs, Verbena."

"Is this because of Gibson?"

"Gibson," he muttered. "Gibson. No, it's not because of Gibson." He let the sound of his words drift away, then changed his mind. "Maybe it is."

"You startled her, Al. That's all."

"What was she doing down here, anyway? She shouldn't be down here. Some little clerk from Records."

Verbena shrugged. "Well . . . she's not 'some little clerk.' She's Morris's assistant. She's got security clearance."

"She still shouldn't be down here."

"I don't think you need to worry about seeing her down here for a long while. After today, I expect she'll stay safely tucked up in Records."

"Why?" Al demanded.

"Because you unleashed the Calavicci tornado." Verbena sighed loudly and paced off a circle around the Observer, paying far more attention to the off-white wall panels of the Accelerator Chamber than she did to him. She had never been in here before with the door closed. Knowing that it was closed made her shudder, even though she wasn't claustrophobic. "You need some sleep, Al," she told him after a minute. "That's not just idle advice. Look at yourself in the mirror. You need some rest."

He tried to dismiss that with a shooing gesture made with his right hand. "We all . . ."

"No, not 'we all.' You."

"I told you. Later. When there's time."

205

She stopped walking then and turned to face him. "When your kid is safe?" she asked softly.

"What?"

"You heard me."

"Yeah, I heard you."

"And you're not disagreeing with me."

A voice inside him suggested that he ought to be angry with her—or at the very least, pretend to be insulted. It was because he was tired, he decided, that he couldn't manage to be either one. "What good would it do me?" he mumbled.

"It could be a long time, Al. You know that."

"And it could be tomorrow," he told her stubbornly.

"Yes. But more likely not."

"What do you want from me, Beeks?"

"I want you to sleep. You're not helping anybody, wearing yourself out like this. Go on. I promise to call you if anything happens—if anything even looks like it might happen." He didn't move, so she gestured toward the door. "Will you? Not for me. Pretend I never said anything. Do it for any reason that suits you. Just do it."

He let another half a minute go by, for appearance's sake, before he shifted his weight and took a step toward the door. She smiled at him, but he didn't return it.

"Two hours," he said. "That's all."

"Hmmmm."

She shivered when the door opened, as if she were being let out of a haunted house. He saw that and pretended not to.

"Al?" she said when they stepped out onto the ramp. He half-turned. "Huh?"

Gooshie was no longer at the main console. Verbena took note of that before she offered the Observer another smile.

"You haven't lost it," she told him.

Before he could insist that she explain that statement, or the wink that followed it, she had scooted around him

206

and was on her way out of the Control Room, leaving him with the knowledge that he had just had his head shrunk by the eminent Dr. Beeks yet again.

You can run, but you can't hide.
  It's all I've got.
  She's asleep, Al. You can talk to her later.
  She's asleep, Al . . .
His eyes sprang open again. The view was the same as it had been five minutes ago: a collection of the acoustical tiles that made up the ceiling of his bedroom.

Five minutes before that, he'd curled up on his left side and studied his purple silk jacket, slung over the back of a chair.

And five minutes before *that,* he'd watched the door.

The silence in his room lay around him like swamp ooze, completely unbroken. He had wanted quiet, and solitude, and—didn't they warn you to be careful what you wished for?—he'd gotten it. Friday afternoon he had yearned for some time alone, but now, Sunday, the idea of time alone prickled at his nerves, because of what awaited him at the end of it.

They're gonna want answers when you come out. They're gonna expect you to do *something. About Lovetz. About Weitzman. About that woman who wants to boff Sam.*

He could think of only one possible response to that. His lips formed the word, let it escape as not much more than a whisper.

"Shit," he murmured.

What did Weitzman think he was going to accomplish by grilling Roberto Gutierrez? On the other hand, what difference did it make? Weitzman thought he was the big cheese, the guy with the right answers, so let him go to Destiny. Let him terrorize Roberto. Let him terrorize anybody he wanted, as long as they weren't a part of Quantum Leap.

207

But Roberto *was* a part of Quantum Leap. The "aliens" Gutierrez thought he had been kidnapped by lived and worked in this complex. One of them was Al himself. Weitzman knew that. He'd read the file on that Leap, just as he read all the files—as avidly as if they were installments in a serialized novel.

So he knew. But what did he . . .

Al concentrated on his hands, which lay palms down on the blanket on either side of him, and told himself that they were rock steady.

Ah, let him do what he wants. He's gonna do it anyway. Let him! Let somebody else solve the problem for a change.

But not for a moment did Al honestly believe that Weitzman was going to solve a thing.

He pushed himself up from the bed, sitting at the edge of it for a minute then shifting his weight onto his shoeless feet. Sam was probably right, he figured: he probably did look like hell. He certainly felt like hell. The muscles in his shoulders and legs cried out with the peculiar singing pain of exhaustion, and his eyes were dry and irritated. A hot shower might have helped, but he couldn't find the ambition to drag himself into the bathroom and take off the rest of his clothes.

It hadn't been that many years, had it, since he'd been able to outfox a little toad like Lovetz without even breathing hard? Experimentally, he balled his right hand into a fist and swung it through the air. His right had been fast and solid once. It connected with the jaw of an invisible opponent, and in his mind's eye Al saw the man crumple and fall.

But this ain't Golden Gloves anymore. You can't win this with a punch. All that'd get you is sued for assault and battery.

Footwork, though . . .

Al peered down at his feet, covered with purple silk socks the same shade as his suit. That was the only answer. Footwork. Something swift and smooth enough to get past Lovetz's defenses.

Screw that little yutz. You came out on top before. Every last damn time. And you're gonna come out on top this time. No little two-bit, penny-ante shyster is gonna win this game. You just have to find the right spot to stick the knife. He's practically nothing but soft underbelly. You just wait for the right moment. Just wait.

You know how. All those years . . . you know how to wait. And you know how to win.

Except for that one time.

That one . . .

But it wasn't once, was it? It was twice. And neither one of them was a lawyer. They were both doctors. Guys who thought (as if it were part of the United States Constitution) that the framed diploma on their office walls gave them the undeniable privilege of wrecking Albert Calavicci's life. The first one's name was Bill. Dr. Bill.

"You work on 'Sesame Street' before you came here?" Al had asked him dryly.

Dr. Bill had cracked a faint, vague smile. He was wearing aftershave that floated away from him in musky waves, and had a haircut that wasn't quite regulation and had probably cost him fifty bucks. He looked at Al with the mixture of impatience and pity that Al saw a dozen times a day. They made each other want to puke. But Al, whose life at the age of forty had contracted into a hazy gray numbness, would give in to nothing that was inspired by this shrink with the expensive haircut.

Dr. Bill, he knew, looked across his mahogany desk and saw a mess: a Navy commander who had spent six years locked inside a bamboo cage. A hero (he had the medals to prove it) who had fought his way home, only to discover that the love that had kept him alive for six years was nothing more than a fantasy.

A man whose life had decomposed into crap.

"Commander," Dr. Bill said, and Al could see the boom getting ready to drop.

Dr. Bill thought he should Go Somewhere To Rest.

Go somewhere . . .

Not back into active duty. Or any kind of duty, for that matter. Dr. Bill had looked into Al's hollow brown eyes and seen nothing worth saving. His recommendation was "rest." He didn't say the word "hospital," but it was implied plainly enough. He said probably two or three hundred words in the same even, soothing tone of voice—none of which made any particular impression on Al—and then reached over and signed his name on a sheet of paper with a gold fountain pen.

Twelve years later, another doctor peered at Al with eyes that looked a lot like Dr. Bill's. This one didn't wear buckets of aftershave, or write with a gold pen. Or speak in a voice intended to sedate lunatics.

This one said, "Who the hell do you think you are, Calavicci?"

To which Al had replied, "I think I'm in charge of this fucking Project."

That had been the wrong thing to say.

This doctor, whose name was Anastasio, could have taught Sol Weitzman a thing or two about protocol. Theoretically, he and Al stood on the same rung of the ladder at Star Bright—or at least they had until Al's fifth wife left him and Al's life began to crumble back into the gray haze he'd climbed out of twelve years ago. A military liaison who operated out of a gray haze didn't fit into Anastasio's view of Life At Star Bright.

"You think you can get away with pretty much anything, don't you, you arrogant scumbag."

It wasn't a question.

"Yeah," Al said. "That's about right."

Anastasio laughed at him. Someone who happened to walk past his office door at that moment might have thought he was genuinely amused—unless they happened

210

to see the bubbling anger in his eyes. "Go right ahead," he told Al in a remarkably even tone of voice. "Play your game. You've gotten away with it for a long time. But the rules are changing, Calavicci. The world is pretty tolerant of people who merit it, for one reason or another. The thing is, you're not one of them. You seem to think you are, but you're wrong. You're dead wrong, my friend, and I'm going to see you tossed out of here on your sorry drunken ass."

As if they were chatting about something inconsequential, Anastasio got up from his desk and idly straightened the row of textbooks on the wide shelf behind his chair. "I don't give a damn what you've been through," he said without turning around. "What's important to me is the way you perform *here*. And you and I both know that that performance is not . . . up . . . to . . . par."

When Anastasio finally did turn, Al was standing three steps from the door. He smiled at the doctor. Then he told him, in very smooth, soft and liquid Italian, to perform an act he suspected Anastasio was more familiar with than he would ever admit.

Anastasio's recommendation for Al's dismissal from the Star Bright Project was delivered to the funding committee via Federal Express the next morning.

Four days later a corporal named Pierson brought Dr. Sam Beckett into Star Bright's Auxiliary-B lab. Beckett thought he'd made the trip down from Boston just to say thank you to the guy who'd secured him two million dollars in seed money for his time travel project—the project nobody believed in except Sam. Half an hour later, he had a partner. Exactly how (and why) that had happened, Al wasn't sure.

Unless Somebody sent him, Al thought. *To put right what I screwed up.*

The idea that that might have been true threatened to

211

make Al's headache worse. So he forced himself to forget it.

Lying on top of Al's dresser was something that was as valuable as Donna Alessi's wedding ring or the big framed picture Beeks had of her son graduating from Harvard. Nobody but Al would have thought so; they would have thought the object that sat front and center on his dresser was a tool left behind by some workman. Wincing at the ache that had burned in his neck since this morning, Al picked up the only souvenir he had of his first meeting with his best friend: a ball-peen hammer with a scuffed wooden handle. Other than the candy machine in Aux-B, he had never actually hammered anything with it, and suspected that he never would.

Should've let you take a crack at me with it, kid, he thought wryly. *Then I should've taken one at you.*

He no longer remembered what he'd thought that first night of the unforgiving young man in the plain, out of style, off-the-rack wool suit. The booze that had nudged him into trashing the candy machine had still been in his system when he fell asleep; when it finally let go of him, it took a chunk of memory with it. He supposed he would have forgotten that Sam Beckett had ever shown up in Aux-B except for the fact that the kid was still there in the morning, waiting to haul him away from Star Bright and into Quantum Leap.

Ahhhh, Sam . . .

Sam had been like a hyperactive puppy finally taken off its leash. The "puppy" image stayed with him most of the time. When he was happy. When he was hurt. When he wanted to be scratched behind the ears. His earnestness had nauseated Al for a long time—but it had never even come close to driving Al away. If anything, it had the opposite effect.

His fingers tightened around the handle of the ball-peen. *Should've broken your damn kneecaps with this. Then maybe you would've been a little slower about go-*

ing into the Accelerator. Maybe you would've asked for some help.

"We're too much alike, I guess, kid," he murmured to the friend who had not been in this room for more than four years. "Both of us suck at asking for help. And if you can't ask . . . you just have to come out swinging, and do the best you can."

The hammer returned to its resting place on his dresser, then Al shucked his clothes and took his second hot shower of the day. This one felt better than the first. It even killed the shrieking in his neck . . . almost. Hair neatly combed, dressed in white trousers and a lime-green shirt he recalled Sam making a rude remark about, with his Navy ring glittering under the overhead lights, he strode away from his on-site quarters, flipped open the door to the stairwell and trotted down the stairs to Level Ten.

"Not this time, huh?" he announced as he flung open the door that faced the corridor outside Control. "Don't start counting your chickens yet, Lovetz."

CHAPTER
SEVENTEEN

Al Calavicci was still shampooing his hair in the shower when Donna Alessi passed a green sign that told her Albuquerque, New Mexico, was seventeen miles away. A minute later she passed another sign, this one warning her "DON'T STOP FOR HITCHHIKERS CORRECTIONAL FACILITY NEARBY." The idea made her laugh softly.

Don't stop for hitchhikers—one of them could be my husband.

When the giggle stopped, she gave half her attention over to actually looking for movement along the sides of the highway.

Would you know him? she asked herself, eyes roving from one edge of the road to the other. *If he'd Leaped into an escaped prisoner, and was hiding there in a ditch—would you know him? And would he know you? Would he remember anything about you? Would he remember being here fifteen years ago?*

Would he remember anything?

Dinner and drinks at Randy's Beef & Brew had been Micki's idea. As far as Donna had been able to determine, no one at Star Bright actually frequented Randy's—for one thing, it was too far to drive—but according to Micki, her choice of venue for Donna's combination thirtieth birthday and bon voyage party had been quickly and unanimously agreed to by their colleagues.

"Of course they agreed," Donna commented as their waiter set a wicker basket full of saltine crackers near her elbow. "None of them wants to be the one to plan anything. You tell them where to go and when to be there, and they show up."

"Hey," Micki said sharply. "Are you intending to pick apart this entire thing?"

She wasn't. This wasn't the celebration of her dreams, but it *was* a celebration. Seventeen—no, eighteen—of her coworkers gathered to eat, drink and be merry, in her honor. Her birthday wasn't actually till tomorrow (and she wasn't leaving Star Bright for another two weeks), but that was all right, Donna decided. There wasn't any difference between celebrating on the eighth or the ninth. This way everyone, including herself, could enjoy a quiet Saturday. Her mother would phone from Ohio in the morning, and they'd chat for an hour. Then she'd take a long dip in the pool. Read. Do a little more packing for the move to Sunspot. Yes, that would be fine.

She turned to Micki to reassure her that the party was turning out just great, and frowned at the odd expression contorting her friend's face.

"Whooooaaa," Micki breathed. "*Nice* butt."

"What?" Donna asked.

Micki tipped her head toward the archway that separated the dining room from the restaurant's foyer, then swiveled it so that she could track the object of her attention.

"Checking out guys again, Mick?" someone asked from the far end of their table.

"You betcha," Micki chortled.

Two men were moving from the archway toward a table in the corner. One of them wasn't Micki's type

(Donna imagined Micki scoffing: *too old, bad dresser, and he's bowlegged*), but the other one . . . Faded jeans, boots, chambray shirt with the sleeves rolled up to his elbow. Shaggy brown hair. Donna couldn't see his face, but the rear view was definitely a good one.

"Am I right?" Micki hissed into her ear. "Is that the best tush you've seen all summer?"

When the two men reached their destination, the younger one took a seat facing in Micki and Donna's direction. Micki, delighted with this outcome, hoisted her glass and tossed him a big grin that he failed to notice.

"Micki, for heaven's sake," Donna mumbled.

"What?" Micki fussed. "What? That is a darned good-looking man. Tell me I'm wrong."

"You're not wrong."

"What? I didn't hear you."

"I said, you're not wrong."

Her glee renewed, Micki picked up her fork and chimed it against the side of her water glass. When the rest of the party had turned to her, she announced loudly, to Donna's great chagrin, "One for the record books! On the occasion of her thirtieth birthday, the very brainy Dr. Donna Alessi has admitted that—and yes, it is likely to severely affect life as we know it—that, I, Michelle Dane, am actually *right* about the studliness of that man at the table in the corner."

"Ohmigod," Donna whimpered.

Of course the man at the table in the corner had heard Micki; everyone in the dining room had. Strangely, though, he seemed to be convinced that she was talking about someone else.

"Oh baby oh baby oh," Micki crooned.

"Would you stop that?" Donna said through her teeth.

The seventeen people Micki had dragged to Randy's had each known her for at least a couple of years. Nothing Micki could possibly say, or do, would surprise any of them. Dave Hedden and Chris Poole were exchanging

216

murmurs about the only woman on the Star Bright staff who made noisier appraisals of the opposite sex than they did. Linda, Meg and Anneke were checking out the guy in the corner.

None of the people at Donna's birthday celebration was crimson—except for Donna.

"Whatsamatter?" Micki inquired after she had finished requesting that a drink be delivered to "the guy wearing jeans like they were meant to be worn."

"I have never been so embarrassed in my entire life," Donna told her.

She broke that record half an hour later, coming out of the ladies' room with her head down to avoid making eye contact with anyone who might connect her with Micki. She'd gone only a few steps toward the dining room when she collided solidly with someone who'd exited the men's room. To keep her from falling, the someone took hold of her arms and held onto her.

Static, she thought. That explained the tingle. Static electricity.

"Are you okay?" he asked.

It was him. Of course it was him; that was the way the universe operated. Micki had created a scene with this person at its center, and out of the forty or fifty men sitting in the dining room right now, of course he would choose to go to the bathroom at the same time Donna did. And he would leave the bathroom at the same time Donna did. And she would crash right into him. The world worked that way.

But the thing was, Micki was right. This was the best-looking man Donna Alessi had seen in a *long* time. The rear view had been appealing, the front view better. And up close: beautiful hazel-green eyes. Full lips. An attitude that said he had no clue how attractive he was. This was an astoundingly gorgeous man. Donna pulled in a lungful of air through her mouth to prove to herself that this stranger had not taken her breath away, and to her dismay

217

produced a sound that he would certainly think was a sigh.

"I'm fine," she managed to stammer.

He smiled. "Thanks for the beer."

"Well . . . it was, um, my friend who ordered it."

"Oh," he said.

His eyes hadn't left her face. And he hadn't let go of her arms. She could feel the warmth of his palms radiating through the thin sleeves of her blouse. Her legs began to wobble a little, and for a second she was afraid that if he released her, she would fall flat onto her face on the carpet.

"Are you sure you're okay?" he asked.

"Low blood sugar," she blurted.

She didn't anticipate the genuine concern that flooded into his eyes. She'd thought he'd turn her loose, or steer her back to her chair. Or not have a clue what "low blood sugar" might imply. Instead, he began to study her, up and down, from her shoes to the elastic tie that held her hair back from her face.

"I'm a doctor," he said. "You've been eating for a while. Your blood glucose levels ought to be all right, unless . . ." He glanced over his shoulder, focusing on the bank of pay phones at the end of the short hallway that contained the two rest rooms. "Maybe I should call . . . Or there's a hospital a few blocks from here, if you think . . ."

"No," she told him firmly.

"No?"

"I'm all right. Doctor."

"But . . ."

Wanna play Doctor, Doctor? a voice in the back of her mind asked mischievously. Then she thought, *God, you've been around Micki way too long.* "I'd feel a lot better if you'd have dinner with me," she ventured.

"I'm . . . finished with dinner," he frowned.

"I meant tomorrow."

218

"Tomorrow?"

"You know. The day after today."

"Oh," he said. "Okay. Sure."

He opened his hands then and let go of her. To her relief, she didn't stumble, but she did feel an enormous surge of regret. With one eye on her—obviously, he still suspected that "low blood sugar" was her real problem—and offering her a very reassuring, doctor-ish smile, he gestured for her to walk ahead of him back to the dining room. When they reached the archway, she turned toward the group of tables that Micki was still presiding over, and he took a step toward the elderly man he'd come in with. Then they stopped.

"I don't know your name," they both said.

"Sam Beckett," Micki said five minutes later, when Donna returned to her seat. "That's Sam Beckett. Dave recognized him—he was on the 'Today' show a few weeks ago, talking about cosmic strings or something, so Dave says. Biggest IQ in the country. The old guy with him is a Professor Somebody who works at the labs. What were you two doing in the bathroom all that time?"

"Staring," Donna said.

Sam Beckett appeared at her door the next afternoon with a bouquet of roses and baby's breath in his hands. "Do you like them?" he asked, as if it were really possible that she might not.

"I love them," she told him. "They're beautiful."

"I thought . . . for your birthday . . ."

She peered at him over the flowers, puzzled. "How did you know it was my birthday?"

"Your friends sang to you last night. And the waiter brought you a birthday cake. That kind of gave it away."

She waited, but he didn't say anything more. *Well,* she decided, *so much for conversation with the man with the biggest IQ in the country.* "They really are beautiful."

"So are you."

"That's . . . Thank you."

219

Another minute went by, and neither one of them said anything. "I'm not good at this," Sam announced finally.

But he *was* good at dinner, through most of which he gazed into her eyes, wearing a wistful, happy expression that seemed to say being with her had radically improved his life. And dancing, which he suggested after dinner was finished. And kissing, which happened in the parking lot outside her apartment building.

The voice in her head piped up again, telling her that it was lack of oxygen that was making her swoon, and not Sam Beckett's kisses. That she was a grown, intelligent woman and not a schoolgirl, and that she ought to remember this was the eighties and not the sixties. That there were things to worry about. Things she needed to be careful about.

Well, that was fine. She knew how to be careful. She knew what year it was. She also knew that she was not going to let go of this gorgeous, sweet, brilliant, considerate, gentle, thoughtful man with the great ass.

Just as she'd hoped, he was very, *very* good at something else.

She lay in his arms afterward, listening to the soft, rhythmic sound of his breathing. He had hesitated enough times on the way upstairs from the parking lot to let her know that he hadn't gone out with her in hopes of ending up in her bed. He didn't try to leave—after all, he *was* a normal, red-blooded American male—but his eyes asked the question more than once: *Are you sure?*

Yes, she was sure. Yes, yes, yes. It had been a long time since the last time, and he was . . . perfect.

And sound asleep.

Even asleep, he was still holding her carefully, as if she were something he was afraid of breaking. The only thing that could possibly break was this moment, she thought. *Let him sleep. I don't want him to leave now. He can go home in the morning. Right now I just want to . . . I want to crawl inside this man and never come out.*

"Donna?" he whispered.

"Ummmm." Then he wasn't sleeping, after all.

"Will you marry me?"

She frowned at him, in the dark, knowing he couldn't see it. "What?"

"Will you marry me?"

"What, now?"

"Okay."

"Sam . . ."

This was a new one. People said "I love you" in bed all the time: she'd said it, and had had it said to her. But . . . this?

"It's three o'clock in the morning, Sam."

"Oh," he murmured.

"Go to sleep, Sam."

He sighed. She could hear the disappointment in it. *Is he serious? He can't be serious. We never set eyes on each other until yesterday. He can't possibly be serious.*

She waited, but he didn't say anything more.

She woke to the aroma of fresh coffee very close by. Half-formed thoughts rolled around in her head as she drifted closer and closer to the surface. In the moment before she opened her eyes she remembered him, and slid a hand across the bed to find him, encountering nothing but rumpled sheets.

He's gone. I hurt his feelings by turning him down, and he left. Oh, Sam . . .

The coffee smell grew stronger. He wasn't gone, after all—he was standing on the threshold of her bedroom. "I had to work with kind of limited resources," he explained as he approached the bed. "I hope this is all right."

"This" was the plastic turkey tray she had bought at Save A Lot last Thanksgiving. Arranged on top of it were a glass of orange juice, a cup of hot coffee and a plate

221

of palm-sized griddle cakes drizzled with margarine and jam. Breakfast in bed, she mused. The only person who had ever brought her breakfast in bed was her mother, and the person waiting for her approval this morning was definitely not her mother. He'd gotten dressed, she noticed—well, half dressed. He'd combed his hair and pulled on his pants and undershirt. He was clean-shaven, too. She puzzled at that until she remembered the ceramic bowl in the bathroom into which she'd dumped half a dozen blue plastic razors, also a product of Save A Lot.

So he'd investigated her cupboards, and her bathroom. Returning his smile, she hoped he hadn't looked into the cupboard *in* the bathroom.

"Could you," she began slowly, "uhhh . . . right there, on the back of the closet door. There's a T-shirt. I feel kind of funny about sitting here eating breakfast with nothing on, when you're dressed."

He brought her the shirt, waited for her to pull it on, then arranged the tray of food on her blanket-covered lap.

"You're not still worried about my blood sugar, are you?"

"No. You convinced me."

"Did you eat?" she asked him.

"Coffee."

"You should eat. Here."

He shook his head at the griddle cake she offered him, apparently content to sit beside her and watch her enjoy his cooking. "I was serious last night," he ventured after a minute.

"Oh, Sam."

"Really. I was."

"I believe you. But . . . it's too soon, Sam."

No sigh came out this time, but his disappointment filled his eyes. "Can I ask you again?"

He didn't ask again until forty-five minutes later. He had taken away the turkey tray, and washed and dried the dishes while she showered. The outfit she put on, although it was only a pair of shorts and a clean T-shirt, seemed to delight him. Or maybe it was just *her* that delighted him.

Oh, come on, Alessi, the little voice said, scoffing. *Your ego isn't that big. He's just . . . He probably gives the same look to all the women he sleeps with. It's part of his charm. He's like a little boy. Or a puppy.*

And wouldn't Micki get a hoot out of *that.*

"I'd like to do this every morning," he offered. "Wake up with you. Make you breakfast."

"You've only known me one day."

"I don't think that matters," he replied earnestly. "Don't you believe in love at first sight? When I saw you . . . I've never been more sure about anything in my life."

"That sets off all the cliché alarms, Sam."

"You don't believe me."

"It's still too soon."

"You're not saying no." His good mood wasn't shattered, as she'd worried it might be. He glanced around the apartment, as if he wanted to memorize every one of its contents—most of which were packed in cardboard cartons—then back at her. "I'm going to keep asking you. And every time I ask you, I'm going to love you more." To keep her from responding, he pressed a finger to her lips. "My mother told me I'd know when I found the right girl. She was right. I found you, and I know. So I'm going to keep asking until you say yes."

He did. And two months later, she did.

A couple of phone calls had provided Donna with the name of her quarry's hotel in Albuquerque. Intuition took her the last few steps—not to Stephanie Keller's room, where she'd originally intended to go, but instead out to the courtyard that contained the hotel's kidney bean–shaped swimming pool. Two small children and a gray-haired man they addressed in shrieking voices as

"Grampa! Grampa!" were playing at the shallow end. At the other end, stretched out on a white metal-and-plastic chaise longue, Stephanie Keller was soaking up the afternoon sun.

Donna shifted the strap of her purse higher on her shoulder and began to stroll alongside the pool. The children interrupted their splashing long enough to give her an appraising look, as did their grandfather. She paused to smile at the little ones, giving Grampa the chance to offer, "Nice day."

"It could be better," she replied.

Before he could continue, she moved away from the shallow end, stepping around the puddles that the children had tossed up onto the concrete lip of the pool. No wonder the old man was so eager to continue indulging them, Donna thought: twenty years hadn't done a bit of damage to Stephanie Keller's figure. The woman looked as good in her green two-piece bathing suit as she had in the shorts and tank top in the photos she'd given Al.

She'd stopped walking, she realized, and her hand had tightened around the strap of her purse. *Cut it out!* she thought angrily. *Why are you jealous of her? So she looks good in a bathing suit. So what? You have no reason to be jealous. Just say what you came to say and . . .*

"Dr. Alessi."

Stephanie's eyes were open. Lifting a hand to shade them, she smiled at the woman who stood ten feet from her chair. When Donna didn't say anything, she went on, "I thought Admiral Calavicci was assigned to do Sam's dirty work."

"It's time for this to stop," Donna told her.

"For what to stop?"

"This charade."

Their voices were light and pleasant. The old man sitting on the steps at the shallow end of the pool undoubtedly thought they were friends. He had an eye on both of them: on Stephanie's green two-piece swimsuit and on

224

Donna's legs, bare underneath khaki shorts.

"I've had enough sun," Stephanie announced.

Donna followed her upstairs. When Stephanie crossed her room to turn down the air conditioner, Donna remained just inside the closed door.

"You're angry," Stephanie said, turning to face her opponent.

"And you're lying," Donna replied.

"How do you know that?"

"Because Sam has only been married once. To me."

Apparently mulling that over, Stephanie slipped into a terry-cloth robe she'd left lying at the foot of her bed and knotted its belt snugly around her waist. "Did you ask him if that was true?"

"I don't need to ask him."

"Maybe you do."

"Ms. Keller . . ."

"I think you're angry because you're afraid it *is* true," Stephanie said, reaching into the refrigerator at the mini-bar for a bottle of mineral water. She watched Donna over her shoulder as she removed the cap from the bottle and poured some of its contents into a glass. "And that he never told you. Maybe you should ask him. It would put your mind at ease." She took a sip of her water and smiled at Donna once more. "Wouldn't it?" Donna didn't reply. "Well? Wouldn't it?"

"What do you want out of this?" Donna demanded.

"Some time with Sam. To talk. To lay things to rest. That's all."

"And appearing on 'Roberto!' is going to help you do that?"

"No."

"What, then?"

Stephanie sipped at her drink in silence for almost a minute. Then she pointed to the chairs that flanked the little round table in front of the window and offered, "Sit down, Doctor, and I'll tell you a story. Go on." With a

225

wave at the refrigerator, she extended the offer to "Have something to drink if you like."

"No," Donna told her tersely. "Thank you."

"Whatever." Stephanie waited until Donna had taken one of the chairs, then began to stroll back and forth across the room in her bare feet. "Okay, a story. It's the spring of '76. The Bicentennial year. Cornell decides to play host to a symposium. Great advances for the last quarter of the twentieth century. They need volunteers to baby-sit the guests for this fabulous gathering. I'll help, I say. Fine, they tell me. You're the guest liaison for Dr. Sam Beckett. Well—this is certainly an honor. I've never heard of Dr. Sam Beckett. I don't have a clue who he is, or why anybody should be excited about his being a part of this big to-do. Although to be fair, I've never heard of anyone on the guest roster except for Isaac Asimov. This Sam Beckett has not one but two doctorates, they tell me. An IQ so high it can't be measured by any of the standard tests. He's come up with something called 'The String Theory of Universal Structure.' This is fine, I think. 'The String Theory of Universal Structure' ought to be a real conversation opener. Sounds like a real sexy topic. And this Beckett guy is probably fifty years old and hasn't seen the light of day in ten years. Can't I take care of Asimov? I ask them. At least I've read some of his books and have something to talk to him about. No, they tell me—thirty-eight people have already volunteered to take care of Asimov. I get the fabulous Dr. Beckett. Take it or leave it."

Her smile now faded into a vague, wry twist of her mouth, Stephanie went on, "I drive down to the bus station to pick up Dr. Beckett. Ask three different men in ugly shirts if they're him. Somebody taps me on the shoulder. He's not fifty."

"Excuse me. I'm . . . I'm Sam Beckett."

"You're kidding."

"Uhhh . . . no."

226

"He's hot stuff. A boy wonder. That's what I hear from the other guests and their 'liaisons.' They want him to talk about the implications this String Theory will have on the space program. Medical research. Efficient energy production. He tries to tell me what his theory means, but I'm not a physicist. I can't figure out what in the world he's talking about. And it seems like nobody else can, either. He gets up in front of those people like he's a contestant on a game show and goes on and on, scribbling on the blackboard. He even pulls one of his shoelaces out and starts playing with it. Tying knots in it."

Oh, Sam, Donna thought. She knew what was coming long before it arrived.

"When he was finished, there were maybe twenty people left in the room. Out of a couple hundred. And you could tell the twenty weren't very impressed. Seemed like they stayed because they'd been brought up to think it was rude to walk out on somebody who was talking. I thought he was going to cry. He gathered up his things and hauled ass out of there. It took me half an hour to find him.

"You were kinda ... out there, Sam."

"No I wasn't. It makes perfect sense. I tailored my talk to fit the audience! There's no reason for them not to understand. If they'd try to understand ... !"

"Do you want some dinner?"

"What? No."

"Maybe you'd feel better if you had something to eat. I'll go get you something to eat. I'll be back in a few minutes. I'll run over to the Union. Stay here, okay? I'll bring you something."

Something in Stephanie's expression slipped, just for a moment, and for those few seconds Donna Alessi saw what it was about this woman that had made Al come close to believing her.

"He talked to me for a long time," Stephanie went on. "I've never seen anybody—before or since—demolish a hamburger like he did that night. He was furious. He kept saying 'Why don't they understand? I made it perfectly understandable.' I'm not even sure he knew I was still there after a while. He kept talking, and talking, and talking. The sun made him stop.''

''What?'' Donna frowned.

''The sun. He saw this light in the window, and he turned around. I guess he thought . . . I don't know what he thought. It was the sun coming up. He'd spent the whole night talking.''

''It's not a joke! Don't you see? It's not a joke. I don't want to write books, like Asimov. I want . . . This is important work! It's important. *It can . . . ''*

Positively affect the future of mankind. The program for the symposium had said so.

''I can't do it alone!''

''That's what he said. He couldn't do it alone. He sounded like an animal with its leg caught in a trap. I thought . . . it wasn't 'them' who didn't understand. It was him. 'I'm *right,* dammit!' He kept saying that too. 'I'm right. I know I'm right.' ''

Donna dropped her gaze to the carpet, unwilling to go on looking at Stephanie. Everything Stephanie had told her during the last few minutes was true. She had described a Sam Beckett that a lot of people had glimpsed over the past two decades: the man who had spent his entire life doggedly determined to prove that he was right about one small thing. (One large thing, from Sam's perspective.) The dismay and frustration Stephanie had witnessed at Cornell in the spring of 1976 had continued for another nineteen years. In spite of the acclaim he won along with his Nobel Prize, awarded for his work on neurological holograms, he was never able by his own reckoning to convince enough people that his dream of time travel was something that could be made real. Talking about it earned him some indulgent smiles—and just as many unindulgent ones. That lack of acceptance countered his brilliant success with the holograms—and then some. The disappointment Sam carried with him from day to day was not something he reserved for sharing with the people closest to him. More than once, he had dragged it out for anyone who would listen. Apparently, Stephanie Keller had been the first one of those people.

Which meant that Stephanie was no threat at all. She was simply one of a crowd.

"And then . . . ?" Donna prompted.

Stephanie didn't answer immediately. She put her glass down on the countertop of the mini-bar. "He was supposed to stay through the weekend. He stayed. Sunday afternoon I took him to the spring picnic to cheer him up. It didn't work. Monday morning he got on the first Greyhound to Boston."

"And you never saw him again."

"I wrote to him. He wrote back. I think you have the letters."

"So he was your pen pal."

" 'No man is an island,' " Stephanie said. "You know that line? He seemed to be one."

Donna was willing to concede that point. She had certainly seen that side of Sam often enough, even though they had rarely been far apart physically since the night Micki's noisy performance had brought them together. Maybe it was because of his brilliance. Or his conviction that he had failed his father in some terrible and irreversible way. But it had always seemed to Donna that there was some part of Sam that no one could touch, no matter how badly they wanted to.

"It's hard for everyone to communicate sometimes," she told Stephanie, careful to keep emotion out of her voice. "Sam . . . sometimes loses track of the fact that he talks way above people."

"He was hurt. And so was I."

"So you got married?" Donna scoffed.

With one eye on her adversary, Stephanie poured the

229

rest of the mineral water into her glass and drained it in one long gulp. "Why do I threaten you so much, Doctor?" she said as she put the empty glass down again. "This was a long time ago. You've got him now. Why should it matter to you that he cared about someone else twenty-three years ago?"

"Because it's not true," Donna said sharply.

"You want to know something about me, Doctor?" Stephanie asked. When Donna did nothing more than stare at her stonily, she continued, "I'm forty-three years old. I have an eighty-thousand-dollar-a-year job, a home in a very desirable area, a Jaguar, and a closetful of designer clothes. I spend a lot of time and energy and money trying to fit into other people's concept of 'looking good.' I suppose it's worked, because that hairy old man out at the pool spent an hour trying not to let his grandchildren notice that he was staring at me. I go to a lot of parties and seminars and concerts and singles events, because that's what you're supposed to do when you're in your forties and not married. I've gone out with more men than I can count, and have turned down a lot more. I belong to a lot of women's organizations. I've had conversations with enough people to fill the entire city of Albuquerque. And one of the things I've discovered after talking to those people, and having relationships with a fair percentage of them, is that anyone who is jealous is either not very secure, or not very bright. Mitchell Lovetz has given me a lot of information about you, Doctor," she concluded. "You're a bright woman. If you need more answers, then maybe you should ask your husband."

A list of replies burst into Donna's head. *I don't need to sit here while you insult me* was the most polite of the lot, but that was a line out of a bad movie, and not a line Donna would let herself deliver. Stephanie probably expected her to stalk out of this room—she seemed to be making sure not to stray into the path between Donna's chair and the door—which meant that Donna could not leave.

"Is your relationship with him that tenuous?"

Donna's head shot up. "You're a vicious bitch, Keller."

"Maybe."

Pushing herself up out of her chair, Donna dropped her purse onto the table and folded her arms over her chest. "I've belonged to some women's groups too. And had a lot of conversations with people, some of whom were bright and some of whom weren't. My relationship with Sam is none of your business. But right now I have a relationship with *you,* and I'll tell you something I'm reasonably sure about. Somebody's crapped on you in a big way and the only way you've figured out to get rid of that pain is to play out an enormous lie that concerns my husband. As far as I'm concerned, you can tell Roberto Gutierrez anything you like. Maybe that's where you belong, sitting on a stage with a bunch of sad, desperate people who are willing to make fools of themselves in order to earn a couple of hundred dollars in guest fees and their fifteen minutes of fame. Go right ahead, Ms. Keller. Go on television and tell Roberto's viewing audience that you provided a shoulder to cry on for a man who was frustrated and disappointed twenty-three years ago."

"I will," Stephanie said calmly. "Right after I tell them about Project Quantum Leap."

CHAPTER
EIGHTEEN

A billowing cloud of road dust signaled Lovetz's approach. Silvio considered the gray-brown cyclone for a moment, then commented, "Dunno if I need customers like that twice in one weekend. Especially since the fool never paid for what he ate yesterday."

Al's right hand strayed in the direction of his wallet, but Silvio shook his head.

"Not your problem," he told Al firmly.

The lawyer landed in Silvio's parking lot a couple of minutes later. To Al's surprise, Lovetz was no longer driving the big white luxury car of the day before; now he was behind the wheel of a pumpkin-orange Jeep. He chose a parking spot near the roadside edge of the lot, turned off the ignition and hopped out of the Jeep as the vehicle coughed and sputtered a protest.

"What the hell," Silvio murmured. "Who's he think he is, Lawrence of Arabia?"

Lovetz, in yet another imitation of his opponent, had outfitted himself in khaki, but rather than duplicate Al's military uniform, Lovetz was wearing a long tunic, worn untucked over matching pants and belted at the waist. Around his neck, and arranged underneath the collar of the tunic, was a silk scarf also in khaki. Vaguely, and not very happily, Al recalled owning a similar outfit (though in another color), which he had bought at a store called Leisure Sutz at a strip mall outside Baltimore. As he remembered it, the only person who had complimented that suit was a cocktail waitress named Lurlene.

"*Recuerdas, amigo,*" Silvio said softly. "If he pisses you off again, remember I offered to get rid of him for you yesterday."

"Too easy," Al replied.

"And it's your fight?"

"Hmmm," Al said.

"Calavicci!" Lovetz called out.

Al watched the potbellied lawyer strut across the parking lot, aware that Lovetz was trying mightily not to react to the Observer's outfit. Lovetz stopped moving about six paces away from where Al and Silvio stood in the small rectangle of shade thrown by TACOS BURGERS.

"It's time," he announced. "To have a little talk. Man to man."

"Or man to turkeyburger. How's things in the bullshit biz, Lovetz?" Al inquired.

Lovetz's eyes narrowed. "I would think you're as qualified to answer that question as I am, Admiral." He paused. "You *are* still an admiral, aren't you? You're somewhat out of uniform."

"I've got a whole closetful of uniforms, Lovetz. I could give you a fashion show that would last all afternoon. I could've come out here in a uniform that would fry your eyeballs. But it wouldn't change a thing."

"You're right," Lovetz conceded. "It wouldn't."

As if Al and Silvio had stopped being there, Lovetz walked between them to the screen door of TACOS BURGERS, hauled it open and went inside. The door creaked once, then banged shut behind him. He went about a third of the way in—about fifteen feet—before he stopped, still as a mannequin for a minute, then craned his head back to peer up at the room's high ceiling and the lazily turning ceiling fan.

"It's forty-eight hours till the world starts to revolve at a different angle," he commented without turning around. "I think it's time to lay the rest of our cards on the table."

Monica, who had come out of the trailer, entered the restaurant through the back and stood in the kitchen doorway frowning at Lovetz's new outfit. "Talking to yourself?" she asked dryly.

"No, my dear."

"You came out to brighten up my day, huh?"

Lovetz pivoted slowly, giving his attention in turn to the spinner of postcards; the glass case half-filled with coin purses, ashtrays, magnets and plastic Native American dolls, all marked RAFAEL, NEW MEXICO; the row of picnic tables; the rack of snack-sized bags of potato and corn chips; and Monica herself. "Why would you choose to live in a place like this?" he asked.

"Real low asshole population," she told him.

"What's that supposed to mean?" he demanded.

She smiled amiably at him and moved backward into the kitchen, where she began to clatter around the stove. "Dunno," she said loudly enough for him to hear her over the din. "Why don't you dwell on it awhile."

He had barely begun to dwell when the screen door creaked open and Al came in.

"Cards, Lovetz," the Observer said. "This was your idea. You're right: it's time."

"You're right," Lovetz agreed, settling himself at one of the picnic tables. "Bring us each a beer, won't you, Mrs. . . . whatever your name is?" he called to Monica. "On the other hand, maybe a pitcher. The admiral may need it." Then he patted the table, indicating that Al should sit opposite him. After Al had done so, he went on, "You're right. We could tap-dance awhile longer. We could finesse each other. We could play a few more tricks, tell a few more stories, but life is short, isn't it,

234

Admiral? It's far too short. So absolutely. Cards on the table.''

"You first," Al told him.

Lovetz hiked a brow. "That quickly? You don't even want to wait for the beer? Well, all right then. Here we go.''

Smiling the whole time, Lovetz reached into the breast pocket of his tunic, produced a single, folded sheet of paper, unfolded it carefully and laid it on the table in front of Al.

As Monica set down a pitcher of beer, Al's eyes began to move along the paper. It was a photocopy of a memorandum—made on a cheap copier, he decided because the print was fuzzy.

He got as far as the line that began with ''RE:''.

Holy son of a bitch, he thought. Even though he said nothing, his dismay must have crept through onto his face at least a little, because Lovetz saw it.

"Gotcha," Lovetz told him.

CHAPTER
NINETEEN

"I don't know what you're talking about," Donna said softly.

"Of course you do," Stephanie replied. "Quantum Leap. Your husband's time travel project. That's what he was so hell-bent-for-leather about twenty-three years ago: traveling in time. That was the reason for all the work on the 'String Theory of Universal Structure.' He didn't care whether the universe was made up of points or strings or Lego blocks. He wanted to find a way to travel in time."

Donna shook her head firmly. "He was working on faster-than-light communications."

"In connection with Star Bright, yes."

How . . . ? Donna was about to ask, then answered her own question. Star Bright's work had never been secret; the few of its reports that had not been made available to the press and the public immediately had been declassified three or four years ago. Everything that had been accomplished at Star Bright during its eight years of existence was freely available now to whoever cared to look at it.

But Quantum Leap, on the other hand . . .

"You said 'was,'" Stephanie pointed out. "He 'was' working."

"He's . . . writing."

"About what?"

In her head, Donna could hear the harsh, strident sound of a buzzer going off. *Time's up!* it shouted.

What do I say? What . . . what . . . oh, God. What did you come here for? Why didn't you let Al handle this?

"Writing," Stephanie mused. "There are certainly more hospitable places to write. His sister lives in Hawaii, doesn't she? And his brother has a beautiful home in San Diego. A little writing in the morning, a nice long walk along the ocean. Or back east, where he'd have access to the best libraries in the country? Why isn't he there, Doctor? Why is he out in the middle of noplace— a place so isolated that the government picked it to test the first atomic bomb? And why do all the computer records list him as living someplace that doesn't even exist?" She took a couple of steps toward Donna, then asked, "Where *is* your husband, Dr. Alessi?"

Donna wobbled in front of her chair. She couldn't go anywhere; Stephanie was in front of her, and the window barely a yard behind her. "What do you *want*?" she shot back.

"I want to talk to Sam Beckett."

"About *what*?"

"About scams," Stephanie replied.

"Yours?"

To Donna's surprise, Stephanie began to laugh. Happily, as if Donna had told her a joke good enough to win her a spot on next year's "Comic Relief" program. "No, Doctor," she said. "Yours. The scam that's sucking in an annual two point four billion tax dollars. Total take to date: thirty-one billion. Project Quantum Leap. Headed by a man who died four years and two months ago in a catastrophic accident at a secret government location somewhere in central New Mexico. That's good enough for 'Roberto!', isn't it? How does Sam head this remark-

237

able project? He communicates from Beyond The Veil, is that it?''

"I don't know where you got all of that," Donna said. "But it's nonsense."

"It is."

"Yes, it is."

"Then no one should mind if I talk about it. Because it'll only be myself that I make look foolish. In the middle of my segment, you can have Sam walk out onto Roberto's stage and show me up as a liar. Go right ahead. I'll give you the directions to the studio if you like. We go on the air live at two."

Struggling to maintain her composure, Donna skirted around Stephanie, went to the refrigerator and poured herself a glass of juice. She drank most of it before she said anything. "Where does this get you?" she asked. "Why bother pursuing this? It's all nonsense. You're wasting a lot of people's time."

"I cared about Sam Beckett," Stephanie replied. "It was a long time ago, but if I think about it enough, the feeling is still there. He seemed to be the only person around who was more miserable than I was."

"Why would you be miserable?"

"Because the boy I dated all through high school and through my freshman year of college married someone else. We were going to be married after he graduated. That's what he'd always told me. But instead, he said 'I do' with someone else. Do you know what that feels like?"

"I can guess," Donna replied.

"Sam gave me something to care about. He made me forget what had happened."

"But you didn't marry him."

"I loved him."

"You knew him for one weekend."

"I didn't say I was in love with him. I said I loved him. I loved the idea of him, if you like that better. I was

238

sucked in by the thought of someone who believed in something so frantically that having other people—strangers—not believe it could destroy him. I loved him, and it saw me through the worst part of my life.'' She paused. ''I never thought that pursuing his dream would end up killing him.''

''It didn't,'' Donna said.

''You're not very convincing, Dr. Alessi.''

''Sam is not dead.''

''Then why doesn't he solve his own problems?''

''Because he doesn't *need* to.'' Donna paused, then asked sharply, ''Why are you doing this now? You can't have been angry for twenty-three years at this man who dumped you! If that's what's happening . . . I think you need to get a life. Get your head straightened out. And forget all this.''

Instead of replying immediately, Stephanie moved behind the table, pulled the curtains aside and looked out the window. A section of the parking lot lay beyond it, but what she was looking for there, and whether or not she found it, she didn't bother to let on to Donna. ''I let go of it for a long time. They always say 'Time heals all wounds.' It did. The farther away I got, the less I needed to think about what he'd done to me, and how much it hurt. But there was something still there . . . I couldn't forget. Not entirely. Things happen to make you remember. Seeing Sam's name made me remember.''

''Why punish *Sam*?'' Donna demanded. ''He's not the one who hurt you.''

Stephanie shrugged. ''It can't hurt Sam, either way. Sam's dead.'' She ignored the grunt of distress that remark prompted. ''Dr. Alessi,'' she said as she let the curtain drop back into place, ''I'm going to go on live television on Tuesday afternoon. I'm going to tell Roberto Gutierrez, his studio audience and everyone who happens to tune in to his show that something called Project Quantum Leap has used up thirty-one billion dollars

239

of taxpayers' money since sometime in the early nineties. Something that is built on a fraud. No, I am not, nor have I ever been, Samuel Beckett's wife. But I know enough about Sam Beckett to blow the lid off whatever is happening out in the middle of the desert.''

"Don't," Donna said.

"Why? Are you going to make me and Mitchell disappear?''

"Not me," Donna replied. "But if I were you, I wouldn't be so sure that nobody else will.''

CHAPTER
TWENTY

The hills were certainly alive with the sound of music this afternoon. Patrice had opened most of the windows on the ground floor of her house and had turned the volume on her stereo system up into the red zone. The voices of the Rolling Stones, distorted almost to the point of being unrecognizable, flooded down Maple Lane toward the lake, along with an occasional shrill and off-key accompaniment from Patrice.

Rufus, who put up with this cacophony as long as his canine patience would allow, finally attempted to escape it by wedging himself under C.J.'s bed. Unable to fit more than a small part of his bulk into what he seemed to think would be a quiet place, he laid his big head down on his paws and began to issue a counterpoint to the racket coming out of Four Maple Lane.

"AaaaaaaaaoooooooooOOOOOOO!"

This would make an interesting subject for a doctoral thesis, Sam thought, trying to distract himself from the fact that Patrice's concert (and Rufus's) was making his teeth ache. The use of objectionable noise as protest. As revenge. As an incitement for murder. He might even think about writing that paper . . . if he ever happened to be in one place long enough to finish it. Or if, he insisted to himself, he ever developed any interest in clinical psychology.

Any.

At all.

"I never wanted to do this," he muttered. "I wanted to prove that traveling in time was possible. I never wanted to clean up the world's problems. I didn't. You *know* that."

No one answered him. But, of course, no one ever answered him.

"Just because you want to listen to this," he remembered his mother saying to Tom, "doesn't mean everyone else does."

He didn't. And Rufus didn't. He suspected that if anyone else had been at home on Maple Lane, they'd be storming into Patrice's house, aiming to rip the wires out of the back of her stereo. Or rip the tape out of her Stones cassette. Or rip her head off her body.

Sam, who was lying on his belly on C.J.'s bed with C.J.'s pillows clamped against his ears, moaned into the mattress, which prompted another howl from Rufus. Why couldn't she fix C.J. by leaving him? Going back to Manhattan? Never seeing him again? That would be the perfect revenge for his rejection, wouldn't it?

Maybe, he thought. But it wasn't going to happen, not if he stayed in this Leap for a year. A hundred years. Till hell froze over. If Patrice went back to Manhattan, she would be admitting that she had lost control of this situation—of C.J.—and Sam could not find a single way to convince himself that Patrice would ever lose control.

Not when there was a way to make her lover pay for what he'd done to her.

He moaned again, then climbed off the bed, moving carefully to avoid stepping on any of Rufus's quivering body parts. He was going to have to do something he'd been avoiding for almost half an hour, since Michael

242

Frey hung up on him. He was going to have to try to talk to Patrice. Again.

Once more into the . . . unto the? . . . something.

His eye found C.J.'s reflection in the mirror over the dresser. C.J. was looking a little worn out, he noted.

"This is *your* problem, you know," he told the other man. "My parents always said 'Clean up your own mess.' So where are you? Sitting around in the Waiting Room, shoveling down a big bowlful of chili from the cafeteria? Huh? You ought to be here, dealing with *her.*"

But that was wrong. This was his mess. Because he was the one who had made Patrice angry, not C.J.

"All right, all right," he groaned. "I'll go."

Rufus trailed him into the kitchen and watched him stall there. He pulled on his jacket. Wiped a glob of Soop'r Dog up off the linoleum. Had a drink of water.

When he turned away from the sink, Rufus's brown eyes were gazing questioningly at him.

"I'm going," he said.

He stopped at C.J.'s desk, fingered the big blue notebook in which he'd found Michael's phone numbers, picked up the little stack of junk mail and flipped through it. He was still examining the collection when Rufus offered a plainly critical "Oooooofff."

"I'm going," Sam grunted. "I'm taking them their mail, okay?"

"Uhhhfff," Rufus replied.

"Yeah, yeah, yeah." Stuffing the envelopes into his jacket pocket, he crossed the kitchen and stopped again at arm's length from the door. "I just wanted to prove a point," he muttered, then went once more into the breach.

Her front door was unlocked. He turned the knob and pushed it open slowly, taking a small step inside, then another. The noise level inside the house transformed a song Sam had listened to in the sixties into a living, breathing thing. It made the walls and the floor vibrate. It surrounded him, crawling up underneath his skin and making him shudder. Getting rid of it would have been simple enough: the stereo was unguarded, and a few more steps would bring him to a position where he could reach out and switch off the tape. But for a long while he didn't do that. He stood just inside Patrice's front door and let the bass line of the music shake him.

Michael Frey had hung up on him. No one else was at home on Maple Lane. Al hadn't been here since before noon. So for almost twenty minutes, Sam had talked to C.J.'s dog. Thinking out loud. Examining his options.

He took a step, then another, and one more.

When he turned the wide chrome knob on the front of the stereo and clicked it into the Off position, silence settled around him like a layer of mud.

The Stones tape's little plastic box lay at the edge of a shelf near the tape deck. Sam picked it up and looked at the front of it, then the back. His brother Tom had owned this album, back in the sixties—still did, he suspected—and had cranked the volume way up more than once, usually when his parents were miles away from the farmhouse. Once, his mother had been there, standing in the doorway of Tom's bedroom, holding a dishtowel and watching her son dance with his sister. Sam had watched too, from a corner of the room, studying the simple joy that was written all over Tom's face.

"I think that's enough, now," their mother had said when the song was over. "You're going to scare the animals."

Sam pushed the Eject button, took the tape out of the deck and closed it inside the little box. Patrice's tapes were lined up in the slots of a wooden rack. One slot was empty, and Sam dropped the tape into it.

He noticed the smell then. Beer. He half-turned, scanning the room, and saw an open bottle resting on its side on the fieldstone apron of the fireplace. Some of the liq-

244

uid had dribbled out onto the hearth, making a dark splotch on the stone. The remains of another bottle lay in shards inside the fireplace. No, more than one; there was a lot of glass sprinkled in the ash. She'd been sitting in a leather chair facing the fire. Drinking, and then smashing the bottles.

You *hur her,* he thought. *Now fix it.*

He found her in the kitchen, in the only corner that did not contain an appliance. She was sitting with her legs crushed up against her chest, head lying heavily on the arms that were wrapped around her knees.

"Get out of my house," she told him without much enthusiasm.

"Patty . . . ," he began quietly.

"What could you possibly say to me?" she demanded. "You've gone way past the point where anything you could tell me would mean anything, C.J. Now, get out. Leave me alone."

"I don't think you want to be alone," he persisted. "You told me last night that you didn't."

"What do you want to do? Play checkers and chat?"

She was looking straight at him, but instead of meeting her gaze, his eyes fell on her hands. They were trembling the way the walls of her house had, and all of her fury was directed at him. If she had been holding a gun in those hands, he knew, he would be lying dead on her kitchen floor.

But there was no gun.

"Would it change anything?" he asked her. "If we made love. Right here. Right now. Would it change anything?"

She peered at him for a moment, then said, "No."

"Then we *could* just talk."

"No. We couldn't. How does your mind work? Don't you *get* it? You have wrecked this relationship, C.J. There is nothing you could possibly say to me—there is nothing you could *do* to me—that would change that.

245

You fucked it up, C.J. Understand? I want you out of my house. I don't want to see you. I don't want to talk to you. I want you to get out.''

She'd put herself into entirely the wrong position. She couldn't escape from him, couldn't lash out at him, because she'd trapped herself in the corner. Obviously, no one had ever taught her to leave herself a way out—or if they had, she hadn't paid attention. To get away from him, she'd have to scramble, as he had, scuttling away from Rufus's giant, slobbering jaws two days ago. His instincts had told him to find the way out. Hers ought to be doing the same thing. But they didn't seem to be. Maybe nobody had ever taught her . . . maybe . . .

What did *they teach her?* he wondered.

He glanced over his shoulder, wishing Al would pop in so that he could rattle off a list of questions for Ziggy. Who *were* "they"? Where did she come from? What kind of background did she have—this woman who kept trying to get his attention by seducing him? Did she have to do that with Michael? Why did she think no other method would work?

He tried summoning Al, silently but furiously.

Come on . . . come on . . .

But the Imaging Chamber door didn't rattle behind him. He didn't hear the warble of the handlink. Al wasn't going to show up.

Instead of asking questions, he walked across the kitchen and crouched down in front of Patrice. She glared at him, trying to be ferocious, but she was so plainly powerless that the result was almost funny. It would have been funny, except that being close to her showed Sam Beckett the astounding amount of pain in her eyes.

"You don't want me," he told her.

She couldn't answer him. There were words in her head, but they weren't coming out.

"You don't need to be here," Sam went on. "You shouldn't be here. You've got a husband and a family.

246

Friends. A home. What are you doing up here? I can't give you anything, Patty. Not anything that's important. If there's a problem at home, with Michael, then you need to work it out. If things aren't good, make them better! Talk to him. Find an answer. Running away won't accomplish anything.''

He didn't expect her to jump up, exclaim that he was right and run to her car—or even anything close to that. But he did hope to see a glimmer of acceptance of his advice, like a spot of blue in the middle of a cloudy sky. Instead, to his complete dismay, the hurt in her expression seemed to double, and she shrank more tightly up against the walls behind her. She seemed to be trying to will herself to go right on through.

Sam got up from his crouch and backed away a couple of steps. *I want to understand! But how do I understand if she won't talk to me? Al, dammit, I need more information! I need something . . . I can't just blunder my way through this. I'm making it worse. Everything I say makes it worse.*

But Al still wasn't there.

Al . . .

Something flashed in front of Sam. For a moment, he wasn't standing in Patrice Frey's kitchen; he was inside a larger room, with bright fluorescent light flooding down around him. Instead of looking down at a crumpled woman in a blue sweater, he was staring at a man in gray coveralls. A man whose whole self was consumed with pain.

"You don't know anything about my life, Beckett."

"I know the good things."

"You don't know anything. *You probably have no idea what it's like to hate your life."*

Then the image was gone.

You don't know anything . . .

Because he could not meet Patrice Frey's eyes again, he spun on one heel and thrust himself back into the living room, where the walls still seemed to echo with the ghosts of the noise she had created. The photograph of Patrice and Michael stared at him from the mantelpiece, making him look at the other pieces of their lives: the rows of tapes and books that one or both of them had chosen; a smooth piece of acrylic mounted on a rectangle of wood, an award of some kind, but Sam was too far from its tiny brass plaque to read who had won it or for what.

I can't do this! he shouted silently. *They send out notices warning you not to dig around in your backyard, so that you won't run into telephone cable. Am I supposed to dig around in somebody's life, and hope I don't break anything important? I need some* help *here! I need . . .*

When no one answered him—because no one ever did—he sank down onto the leather chair from which Patrice had pitched her beer bottles and pushed his face into the palms of his hands.

He heard her come to stand in the kitchen doorway but he didn't look up.

Al had been no quick fix, either. He'd taken the hand Sam offered him, but had let go of it over and over and over again. Having his decisions (or his opinions) questioned would set him off into fits of rage. He would be dry for a day or two, or even a week, then show up hungover. He would greet a hug as if it were an electric shock. He would not discuss his feelings, would not accept gifts. He ran from affection with the efficiency of someone for whom practice had made perfect. He stored up hurt and anger and disappointment like coins in a piggy bank. And on the Fourth of July, when he and Sam had known each other for five months, he did what he had threatened to do on that night in Aux-B, and Sam found himself lying on his back in the middle of a gravel parking lot, his jaw throbbing hotly because it had connected with Al Calavicci's fist. He lay there for what

248

seemed like an hour, confused and stunned by the man who wanted so badly for someone to care about him but didn't know how to react when someone did.

"Maybe you just don't speak the same language," he murmured.

She didn't answer him, but when he lifted his head, she was still standing in the doorway.

"Have you considered that?" he asked. "Maybe Michael acts the way he does because he doesn't know how to act any other way."

"He doesn't need you to defend him."

"Give him another chance."

"Why?" Patrice demanded.

"Because he's your husband."

She gaped at him, astonished. "You," she said, then began to laugh. "Do you hear what you're saying?"

"Yes."

"You're a pig, C.J."

"Why?" Sam asked.

"Why?" Before she said anything more, she went over to the fireplace, picked up the beer bottle that lay there on its side and juggled it in the palm of her hand for a moment. "Because I'm not up here alone, C.J. I wasn't in that bed alone. I cheated on Michael, but I did it with *you*. You. The guy who called me up and wanted me to skip my anniversary party and come to you because you wanted to get laid." Her fingers closed around the bottle, and for an instant Sam was sure she intended to hit him with it. Instead, she smashed it down into the fireplace. "It was you, and now all of a sudden everything's *my* fault."

"I didn't say that."

"You keep telling me what I should do. What about what you should do?"

"I don't have anyone I need to set things right with," Sam told her.

"Nobody but *me*."

That startled him as much as if she'd clobbered him with the bottle. He'd intended to ask her if she loved Michael—if she had ever loved Michael. The longer she stayed at Edwards Lake, the wider the rift in her marriage would become, but if she honestly loved her husband, it would not be irreparable. If she honestly wanted to undo the damage her affairs had caused, that was still possible. Less and less likely as the hours slid by, but still possible.

But this, now . . .

"Do you love me?" he ventured.

"No," she snapped.

"Is that the truth?"

"Why should I love you?"

Sam pulled in a long breath. "I don't know. I don't think you let anybody get close enough to tell what you really feel about them."

"Don't kid yourself, pal."

You don't know anything. Al's voice echoed through his head. Bitter, and angry, a few more coins added to the collection. *You don't know anyth—*

Stubbornly, he got up from the leather chair, leaned forward and took Patrice's forearm in his hand. The turmoil in her expression rivaled anything Al had ever shown him, and made him more determined to plow his way through the problem he had been dumped into.

I didn't want this job . . . but I'll be damned if I'm going to walk away from it.

"Let go of me," she snarled.

"Patrice . . ."

The last coin dropped into the bank then, just as it had in the parking lot of a bar in Socorro, New Mexico, on a Fourth of July that wouldn't happen for another two years and nine months. Something snapped inside Patrice Frey the way it had snapped inside Al Calavicci—an event that Sam recognized an instant too late. Al had been a Golden Gloves champ, and Patrice was not, so she didn't attempt to regain her freedom by slamming a

250

fist into Sam Beckett's face. Instead, her foot found the back of his ankle and pulled forward.

A second before the back of his head collided with the Freys' living room floor, Sam heard Al's voice again: words that Al always accompanied with a sigh of regret.

You pushed too hard, Sam.

You . . .

Then the world grayed out, and he heard nothing.

CHAPTER
TWENTY-ONE

Everything bad that had ever happened in Al's life seemed to have a distinct starting point—like the dropping of the flag at an auto race. Or the cry of "Ignition!" at a launch.

He remembered very well the jolt when his A-4 was hit. And the thump of Father Reilly's office door closing right before Father told him that he and Trudy were not being sent to the same place.

"I do," five times.

And worst of all, the shrill of Gooshie's voice in his ear: "He's Leaping! Ziggy says no, but Sam's Leaping!"

He blinked hard, twice, but the paper was still there, lying on the picnic table. It still had the same words printed on it. And Lovetz was still standing in front of him wearing an expression Al had seen so many times in his life that the idea of trying to remember them made him want to puke.

"Well?" Lovetz said sweetly. "No comment, Admiral?"

Al turned his back on the lawyer and walked across the floor of TACOS BURGERS to the tiny window that faced Silvio and Monica's trailer. He tried to let his mind drift back to the good times he had had in this place. The ground-breaking party for the Project. Sam's forty-first birthday party and, a few weeks later, Donna's fortieth. New Year's Eve. On all those occasions they'd pumped Sam full of Dos Equis and made him sing. Elvis tunes— the kid was a great Elvis when he was looped. Silvio had brought a guitar in from the trailer, a nice one, judging by the reverent look it got from Sam, and Sam had used it to accompany himself. He'd accompanied himself with laughter too: between songs, and during them, when his fingers slipped on the guitar strings.

"Oops."

He'd ducked his head out of embarrassment. But nobody cared; everybody in the place was as drunk as Sam was, or more.

The idea that Sam Beckett might never sit in TACOS BURGERS again, sucking down Dos Equis and pretending to be Elvis Presley, sent an arrow of pain through his best friend.

Something touched his hand. He looked down: Monica was trying to give him a big paper cup of water.

"You okay, Al?" Her voice wasn't much above a whisper.

He met her eyes for a second, then looked out the window again. "I need you and Sil to leave us alone for a while," he told her.

When he turned around, she was gone. But Lovetz was still there, and so was the memo.

"Are you afraid now, Calavicci?" Lovetz asked softly.

A voice cried out from a buried layer of Al's memory: *Whatsamatter, Calavicci, you SCARED?!* Followed by a shrill burst of taunting laughter. *He's scared, look you guys, the little pansy-ass is SCARED.*

The word rolled around inside his head.

He's SCARED.

He's SCARED.

He's . . .

But he wasn't. Slowly, carefully, he let the fear drain out of him, along with all the other negatives—the emotion that would keep him from doing what he needed to do. What he should have done yesterday, but hadn't, because Lovetz and the woman had caught him off guard. That'd been part of the problem, the woman being here. He loved women. Wanted to treat them well. Wanted them to treat *him* well.

"Do you know where you are?" he asked Lovetz after a minute.

The lawyer shrugged at him, then tipped his head in the direction of the postcard rack. "Somewhere near Rafael, New Mexico, apparently."

"And you know who you're with."

"Is this a trick question?" Lovetz grinned.

Al wandered over to the rack, spun it around and took one of the postcards out of its slot. He peered at it for a moment, as if he were considering sending it to someone, then dropped it back into place. He wasn't trembling, although he knew Lovetz was waiting for him to begin doing exactly that. His hands and feet had been cold, but warmth was oozing back into them. It was an odd sensation: as if all the blood in his veins had drained out and had been replaced with antifreeze. He almost smiled at the thought. And at the memory of a man in uniform who had told him over a pair of stiff, sour-tasting drinks, "When you look at the enemy, you don't see a hyooman bein'. *You* stop bein' a hyoo-man bein'. He's the enemy, you got it? You just forget everything else. You forget."

Forget . . .

Albert Calavicci reached into his pants pocket and pulled out the silver cigarette lighter Donna Alessi had given him for his sixtieth birthday. He flicked its tiny flame into life, then picked up Lovetz's memo from the picnic table and touched the flame to the edge of the paper.

"There are other copies," Lovetz told him as they watched the paper burn.

254

"Where did you get it?" Al asked.

"Does it matter?"

"Yeah," Al said. "It matters."

Lovetz shrugged again. "From the copier repairman."

"I'm listening."

One more shrug, then the lawyer complied. "My office has the same repairman as Senator Ryan. Apparently the senator doesn't use standard photocopy paper; he uses linen-fiber. Some of it got stuck in his machine, and when Dave—the repairman—cleared the jam, he stuck the paper in his tool case instead of throwing it out. He's a conservationist, I suppose. Came to my office to do the quarterly service check and was using the senator's paper to write notes on. One of the sheets wasn't blank. Stephanie was there, visiting my partner. Saw the paper. Saw a name on the paper she recognized: Sam Beckett. The words 'Sam Beckett' and 'Project Quantum Leap' didn't fire off any skyrockets for Dave, but they did for Stephanie. Because she knew Sam Beckett, and she knew that in his mind, 'Quantum Leap' meant 'time travel.' "

"And to you it meant 'I'm going to have money piled up to my ass.' "

"Something like that," Lovetz said.

"Why'd she come to you, and not to Joe Boyle? If Boyle was her honey?"

"Because Joe is . . ."

"Honest?"

"Something like that."

When nothing was left of the memo but fragments of ash, and the last of the fire's embers had died, Al brushed the ash into the palm of his hand, carried it into the kitchen and dumped it into the sink. He brushed his hands off carefully, then returned to stand a couple of paces from Lovetz. He could see his reflection in the small rectangle of a window that Silvio had painted over years ago to keep the sun out.

"Do you know where you are?" he asked again.

"I'm . . . ," Lovetz said, then closed his mouth.

Al took a step toward the lawyer, then another. When he stopped, he was close enough for the other man to feel his breath on his face. "This is not a joke," he told Lovetz. His voice was low, almost without inflection, his gaze steady and unblinking. "I want you to understand that. This is not a joke. This is not your opportunity to be a part of history. This is not Watergate. You are not going to be on the 'Tonight' show. You are not going to be famous."

Lovetz blinked.

He's Leaping! Al's mind screamed. *Ziggy says no, but Sam's Leaping!*

He remembered. The feel of the leather seat of his beautiful new car, the hum of the engine tickling up through his body. The blackness of the desert night, broken only by the twin beams of the car's headlights. He had had a lovely evening—had told someone so—had sipped champagne, had made love to an incredible woman, had another incredible woman in the passenger seat beside him. He was warm, happy. Felt good. Felt *good*.

Then the lights danced over the horizon.

"He's Leaping! Ziggy says no, but Sam's Leaping!"

He'd left the woman up above, at Security, not caring what she thought, or whether she was someplace she shouldn't be. The elevator didn't come fast enough, so he took the stairs. Running, two, three, four steps at a time. Two levels down, three, four. Six. Nine. He was three steps from the bottom when his legs stopped co-operating. Instead of bursting into Control, instead of taking charge, instead of demanding explanations, he crumpled down onto the steps and buried his face in his hands.

He was sure—no, he was beyond sure—that Sam was dead. That Sam's frustration had made him desperate, and that the Accelerator, which had never been tested,

256

had killed him. That if he went into Control, he was going to find his friend's lifeless body.

That he was going to be alone.

"Ziggy says . . . but . . ."

"You're out in the middle of *nothing*, you ignorant little fuck," he told Lovetz. "There's nobody here. *Nobody*. They're not gonna find you out in the desert, because there's not gonna be anything left of you to find." Slowly, with Lovetz's beady eyes pinned on him, he reached out and took hold of the ends of the silk scarf that was looped around the man's neck. He grasped it just tightly enough to make Lovetz gasp. "Do you understand me?" he hissed. "This is *not a joke*. You never saw that memo. You don't need to bother to figure out what it means, because you never saw it. Do you understand?"

"There are people here," Lovetz wheezed.

"They're not going to hear *anything*," Al told him.

"They—"

Al jerked on the scarf. Their faces would have collided if Al had not brought Lovetz up short by pressing his fist against the lawyer's Adam's apple. "You're not *getting* me!" he roared. "I *said* there's no one here. Nobody's going to hear you. And nobody's going to find you. You invited yourself to the wrong party, Lovetz."

Lovetz's hands fluttered in the air. His face was reddening, partly from outrage, Al thought, because he wasn't holding the scarf tightly enough to strangle the little man. He could, though, simply by twisting his wrist, and he knew Lovetz knew that. Lovetz, with his fussy hairdo and his manicured nails, had never been trained to defend himself. Al could see that in his eyes. Lovetz's only defense was his mouth.

"Do you believe me?" Al whispered.

"No," Lovetz gasped.

Al twisted his wrist. The pulse in Lovetz's carotid artery began to bang against the backs of his fingers, and

257

the lawyer's color started to deepen from crimson to purple.

"You," Al murmured into his face, "have done all the damage you're gonna do."

Lovetz's arms shot straight up, flapped a couple more times, then dropped leadenly to his sides. Abruptly, Al released the scarf, dropped his own hand to the middle of Lovetz's chest and shoved him backward. The lawyer stumbled, regained his footing, stumbled again and fell into the white plastic chair Al had occupied yesterday afternoon.

Albert Calavicci, who was not going to be anybody's victim today, took fleeting note of the dark stain on the crotch of Lovetz's khaki-colored pants, then turned his back on the little man and walked over to Silvio and Monica's collection of cheap souvenirs.

"There's a lot of nothing out here," he offered conversationally as he fingered a vinyl coin purse. "Maybe you noticed. You can drive for an hour, couple of hours even, and see nothing. Nobody. Not a house, not a car. No billboards. Just scrub brush and grass. Miles and miles of scrub brush and grass. Kinda spooky at night. You go sit out there and there's *nothing*. You like being by yourself, Lovetz? 'Cause if you do, this is the place to be. You could pick a spot and ten years would go by and you'd never see a soul."

Lovetz didn't respond. Al put the coin purse down, taking care to return it to its original position. "There's a spot . . . nice view of the sky at night. No city lights to interfere. You know anything about astronomy, Lovetz?"

The lawyer jerked his head. Probably wanted to hold his ground but ended up looking like a peevish five-year-old in the middle of an apoplectic fit.

"You'd have a great chance to study the stars. If I broke both your legs and left you out there."

"Huhhnngg," Lovetz wheezed.

Al turned and smiled at him. "You know about me,

don't you, Lovetz? You found my picture in your *People* magazine—the one that said I was Sam's partner—then you went to the library and you did your research. Because that's what you know how to do. Go to the library and read, and then throw what you found into somebody's face. You know about me. But you made a mistake. Because you don't know it all. You missed some pieces. If you hadn't, you wouldn't be here."

Lovetz, who apparently had been winding himself up like a spring, shot out of the plastic chair en route to the screen door. He was almost halfway there when Al reached out, seized the back of Lovetz's collar, snapped him to a halt, then danced him across the floor and slammed him into a wall.

"You know how easy it is to snap somebody's neck, slimeball?" Al crooned into his ear.

"You're out of your *mind*!" Lovetz shrieked.

"Maybe," Al replied.

"You're *insane*!"

"And you," Al said, "are not gonna wreck something that Sam Beckett worked his whole life to build, just so you can be on the goddamn TV. You hear me? You jerked the wrong guy's chain. You did it wrong. You turned this into something serious, and now you're gonna play by the serious rules. Things are ugly, now, pretty boy. You're gonna get your clothes messed up."

"Heeelllllllp meeeEEEEEEEE!" Lovetz screeched.

A moment later he was lying in the middle of Silvio and Monica's black-and-white linoleum floor, crushed into the fetal position, his nose bleeding into the hands that were pressed to his face, weeping in great sucking gulps.

"You sent a letter to the wrong guy, asshole," Al told him.

The screen door creaked when Al pulled it open. His

right hand had started to throb, and he rubbed it gingerly as he leaned against the Coke machine.

"Al?"

He turned. Silvio was a couple of steps away, holding out to him a handful of colored wires, most of them only a few inches long. Al hiked a brow at him. Silvio's only reply was to drop the wires into Al's palm.

"Rent-a-car office is gonna be pissed," Al commented.

"They'll get over it," Silvio shrugged. "Christ, he cries just like a kid."

"That's what I figured."

"Want some ice for the hand?"

Al shook his head. "Later."

A minute went by, fringed with the gradually diminishing sound of Lovetz's sobbing.

"He show you the memo?" Al asked eventually.

"What memo?"

Silvio's gaze shifted and met Al's. Then Al smiled and shook his head. Almost two hundred different people had come to TACOS BURGERS on various occasions over the past five years, in pairs, in small groups, in bigger groups. They didn't come from the area Monica referred to as "town." They certainly hadn't landed in a UFO. Every one of them had been given food and drink and a place to come in out of the sun.

The man who welcomed them wasn't stupid. Neither was the woman who was watching Al from the doorway of the trailer.

"Memo," Al said.

"Don't know what you're talking about," Silvio replied. "That hand's gonna hurt like a bastard. Go let Monny kiss it and make it better. That little dirtbag ain't going anywhere."

"Thanks."

"For what?"

Al pushed the wires into his pocket and began to walk

260

toward the trailer. He hadn't gotten far when Silvio spoke his name again. Holding back a sigh, he turned, then turned again to look in the direction Silvio was pointing out.

"That's a *limo*," Silvio frowned. "Who the hell'd come out here in a limo?"

"Calavicci," Weitzman said. Then, as if he simply liked saying it, he said it again. "Calavicci."

"Yeah," Al groaned.

"Calavicci . . ."

Lovetz was again seated in the white plastic chair, holding a food storage bag full of ice against his bruised and swollen face. His eyes, brimming over with malevolence, had not left Al for almost seven minutes. "He hit me," he announced. "That's assault. Assault!"

No one paid any attention to him. Not that there were many possibilities for attention; Weitzman and Calavicci were focused on each other, and Weitzman's aide, who had provided the bagful of ice, was eating taco chips in the kitchen. The rest of the senator's entourage had remained out in the parking lot.

"You didn't need to assault the man," Weitzman said.

"He *hit* me!" Lovetz squealed.

"Shut up, Mr. Lovetz," Weitzman barked.

"I'm going to sue . . ."

"Shut *up*!"

"In court . . ."

"See?" Al said.

Weitzman scowled at him. "I see. But that doesn't excuse the fact that—"

"Taxpayer!" Lovetz screeched.

Enough was enough. Weitzman stalked out of the restaurant, around the building, and came to rest in the midst of Silvio and Monica's cluster of lawn chairs and potted rosebushes. He waited for Al to join him, then demanded,

"What memo is he rambling on about? He found a memo? What memo?"

"From Jack Ryan," Al replied.

"Shit," Weitzman snapped.

"Addressed to the Committee. Recommending cutting off all the funding to the Project. That he thinks the whole thing is a bunch of happy hoo-ha and nobody's gone back in time or is ever going to go back in time because time travel is something H. G. Wells made up."

"He does those memos every month! Every month! You can tell time by it, just like my wife's PMS. Nobody listens to Ryan. He's like somebody's senile uncle. You know that, Calavicci."

"I know nobody on the Committee listens to him. That doesn't say anything about the rest of the world."

Weitzman shook a finger at the admiral, grunted his dismay at Al's clothing, then sat down on a lawn chair. "Did it occur to you that when I said I was going to Destiny, I meant I was going to handle this situation? The 'Roberto!' booking has been canceled. Mr. Gutierrez is very easily persuaded. Without the need for physical violence, I might add."

"What did you promise him?" Al asked dryly.

"Dinner at the White House."

"During one of the weeks when the President is at Camp David, I suppose."

"That doesn't make any difference," Weitzman fussed. A glance at the ground brought to his attention the amount of dirt that had accumulated on his shoes and pant cuffs, which did nothing to improve his disposition. "I know you find this absolutely beyond imagination, Calavicci, but I am on your side."

"Really?" Al scoffed. "Want to go to the dog races with me next Saturday night, then?"

"I want to have you fired."

"And?"

"Calavicci," Weitzman groaned, "if you would stop

262

defending yourself for five minutes, it might strike you in a blinding flash that we're trying to accomplish the same thing. Sam Beckett's Project is up and running. It's sucking in money like a black hole, but the possibility still exists that it might accomplish something. A strong possibility, I believe. And while that possibility exists, I am willing to help keep Quantum Leap running. Do you hear me? If we closed it down now, today, next week . . . that would negate all the money that's been spent, all the labor that's been expended up to this point.''

"Whose labor? Mine? You hate my guts, Weitzman. Why should you care how hard I work? In fact, if I keeled over right now from overwork, you'd probably buy a round of drinks to celebrate.''

"I'm worried about the money," Weitzman shot back, without responding to Al's question. "All forty-one billion dollars of it. If we stop now . . .''

Al said, "My pop used to call it throwing good money after bad.''

"Is that what you think?''

"You know what I think, Weitzman. I want to bring Sam back home. I'm not all that worried about 'accomplishments.' They're great. I get the warm fuzzies from helping people who need it. But I want my friend back. That's what it boils down to. I want him back.''

Weitzman stared out across the desert for a minute. "I understand that," he replied.

"Do you?''

"More than you know.''

"Maybe if you promised a few more people dinner at the White House.''

"Keep making light of it.''

"I'm not making light of it. I *care,* Weitzman.''

"Calavicci," Weitzman growled, "I was handling this.''

"You going to handle that too?''

"What 'that'?''

Al pointed. Twisting around in his chair, Weitzman squinted at the horizon, unable to see anything but two billowing clouds of dust.

"That," Al said.

"Where's everybody else?" Al demanded. When Donna answered him with a puzzled look, he added, "The rest of the staff. How many other people are we expecting? Somebody oughta tell Beeks she's got a big mouth."

"I don't know what you're talking about," Donna said quietly, then nodded toward Stephanie before she related, in very abbreviated form, what Stephanie had told her. "I followed *her* here. I told her they were getting themselves into something they might not have expected. Something dangerous. I'm not sure what I meant. I was following that 'Top Secret' routine you started. But it worked. I think she decided she and Lovetz ought to circle their wagons . . . but it seems like *we* ought to be circling ours. They know, Al. They know about the Project."

"I know they know."

"He told you?"

"He told me. And I told Weitzman."

"Oh, God," Donna moaned. "The minute they get out of here, they're going to run screaming for the press. What did you hit him for?"

"To make him listen."

Before Donna could respond, Al walked away from her. He stopped briefly alongside his car—the gleaming red miracle he had been riding in when the lights began to dance on the horizon—then went on walking, down the dirt road that led away from TACOS BURGERS. When Donna caught up to him, he hunched his head and shoulders, trying not to let her look at him.

"Al," she said.

He ignored her.

"Al. We can handle this. We don't need to *kill* them.

This isn't going to be Roswell all over again, is it? People disappearing? Threatening people that they're going to disappear if they don't shut up? They just want money. You said that. All right, we'll give them some money. The stocks. There's a lot of money there, Al."

Al jerked himself to a halt. "That money's for you. To take care of you, if he doesn't come back."

"He's coming back, Al."

"That's your money."

"Yes, it's my money. Our money," Donna corrected herself. "Mine and Sam's. I don't think he'd be very upset about our using it to solve this problem. I don't need to be 'taken care of,' Al. I'm perfectly capable of supporting myself. I did it for years before I even met Sam."

"Do you know what blackmail is?" Al demanded.

"Don't talk to me that way!" Donna shot back. "I am not your child, Albert."

Instead of firing another round, Al walked away from her. Angrily, she followed him, talking to his back.

"It was a lark, Al. An experiment. He wanted to see if he could use mathematics—probability and random chance—to figure out the stock market. He never thought it would work. It was just a game. He never thought he was going to end up with that much money. And it didn't mean anything to him. He won't care if we use it to shut these people up."

"Fine," Al said. "Go right ahead. Solve it."

"Albert!"

He didn't answer.

"He doesn't like playing the stock market. He said it was just an accident. Al! It was just that one week; then he stopped."

The Observer turned again. His face was pinched, his eyes crunched nearly shut against the brilliant midday light. Donna didn't need to squint; she was wearing sunglasses. "Like he stopped playing chess?" he shouted. "Like he stopped fishing?"

"What?" Donna said.

"He stopped fishing. Because he couldn't stand sitting there waiting for something to happen."

"What does that have to do with—"

"After he Leaped! I dragged myself down there, and he was *fishing*."

"Al . . ."

He walked back to her. His throat felt ripped and raw and suddenly he had no more energy for shouting. "He was fishing. With the kid—Tom Stratton's kid. He forgot. Everything. Even something as dumb as the fact that he doesn't like to fish. Or play chess. He doesn't like to sit around and wait. Don't you remember? That's still there . . . He's got to keep moving. On to the next thing. 'When do I Leap?' That's always the first thing out of his mouth. When do I move on to the next thing. And the next, and the next. But he doesn't remember. There's so damned much he doesn't remember. I'm rebuilding him from the ground up."

"No you're not," Donna said softly.

"I am. With all the stuff I tell him. With the show I put on. He's not the same."

"When he came home," Donna said. "He remembered."

"But what about the time in between? What about *now*?"

"I . . . I don't know about now."

"If he could see you—if he could have seen into the future. He wouldn't have gone. If he knew how much it would hurt you. If he knew how much he'd lose."

Donna gnawed on her lower lip for a moment. "We all make choices, Al."

"Yeah," Al said. "Yeah."

She followed him back to TACOS BURGERS. The same few people were there, but they seemed to take up

266

as much space as a hundred. The motor of Weitzman's limo was running, apparently to operate the air conditioning for whoever was sitting inside. Weitzman was standing beside the car, talking into a cellular phone. Lovetz had resumed his tirade of selected phrases, most of which contained the words "sue" and "taxpayer." Stephanie Keller was waving a rolled-up newspaper at Weitzman's aide, each swat accompanied by a two- or three-word threat. Oblivious to the turmoil, Silvio was now sitting in one of his lawn chairs, reading a paperback book and listening to the color commentary of a baseball game being broadcast from a portable radio.

"I'm sorry," Donna said to Monica as the two women crossed paths.

Monica offered a smile. "Sorry? This is better than pay-per-view. Don't worry about it, sweetie."

Stephanie, finished with terrorizing Weitzman's aide, strode across the parking lot, raising tiny poofs of dust with each thump of her shoes. "We are not going to go down quietly," she snarled as she passed Al and Donna. "I don't care how many MPs are going to show up here. You can charge us with anything you like, but we're still entitled to a defense. And whoever that is, we're going to send straight to the press."

"I thought you already had an attorney," Donna offered pleasantly.

Weitzman's aide, who had bowled out of the restaurant, snatched the newspaper out of Stephanie's hand and threw it in the direction of the Coke machine. "Lady," he told her, "this is no joke. 'A threat to national security' is not a joke. I suggest you shut your trap before you get yourself into even *more* trouble."

"Are you going to arrest the copier man too?" Stephanie demanded.

"As soon as you tell us his name."

"Hah!"

" 'Hah'?" the aide echoed. "What are you, something

267

out of a cartoon? 'Hah'? You're in deep crap, lady. Your buddy in there knows it. I can tell by looking at the pee-pee he made in his nice pants. Maybe you ought to have him explain the situation to you. And do it quick. The two of you won't have much more chance to chat. The MPs are on their way. I figure maybe five, ten more minutes.''

Enraged by his words, and just as much so by the unruffled way he delivered them, Stephanie pivoted on one heel and stormed back into the restaurant. A moment later she began a litany louder and shriller than Lovetz's.

"If I was married to somebody like that," the aide sighed, "I'd be feeding her happy pills in her tea. God help us. Listen to that woman's voice.''

"She's not married to anybody," Donna said.

The aide peered at her for a second, then shrugged and replied, "Whatever," before he wandered off.

Nobody but Al noticed the way Donna's hands rolled into balls, her neatly trimmed nails biting hard into her palms. Her posture didn't invite any kind of embrace; he suspected even a quiet word of encouragement would be rebuffed. So he didn't offer one. Instead, his attention drifted over to Weitzman, who had put away his cell phone and was walking in their direction.

"It's going to be all right, Dr. Alessi," the senator said when he reached them.

She winced; Weitzman didn't know why. Maybe he didn't even notice. "What are you going to do to them?" she asked, her voice not quite steady.

"What I told you. We're going to bring them up on charges. Creating a threat to national security.''

"And that's going to shut them up?"

Weitzman rolled his teeth over his lower lip. "It may take a little more persuasion. But yes, it's going to shut them up. Eventually.''

"You sound like somebody I don't like very much, Senator." When Weitzman glanced at Al, she shook her

268

head sharply. "I don't mean Al. I mean . . . I mean the threats. You don't have to hurt anyone. There's been enough damage done already."

"There's not going to be any more."

"How?"

"Don't worry about it." Weitzman's expression softened as he reached out to touch Donna lightly, and briefly, on the arm. "No one seems to believe it, but I'm on your side. And I'm going to handle this. There are ways to shut people up that don't involve grievous bodily harm. Each of them"—he nodded toward the restaurant—"has a position in the community. A credit rating. A reputation. I can make those things go away as easily as popping a balloon. They'll shut up, or they'll wish they'd never heard of Sam Beckett."

"Do you?" Donna asked him solemnly.

"Sometimes," Weitzman replied, not quite meeting her eyes. "Sometimes knowing about your Project—being a part of your Project—causes me a great deal of pain. But no. Even though I have a lot less hair, and my nervous system is a lot more frayed than it was five years ago . . . no. Your husband is a good man, and I do not wish I had never heard of him."

He began to walk away, in a direction that didn't look as if it would take him anywhere. He had gone a few yards when he stopped and looked over his shoulder.

"Are you going to let me handle this now?" he asked.

"Al?" Donna prompted.

Rather than answer, Al headed toward his car, fishing his keys out of his pocket as he walked. Weitzman heaved a sigh, but seemed to accept Al's departure as a victory. He offered something to Donna that was not quite a smile, then altered his direction and ambled over to the cluster of lawn chairs.

No one other than the man he was addressing heard him say softly, "Colonel?"

No one other than Weitzman saw Silvio nod.

The engine of Al's dream machine was roaring into life as Donna hurried across the parking lot. "Al!" she called to him.

Her husband's partner touched the button on the console to lower his window a few inches. "I'm going back to the Project," he said. "If Weitzman wants me, he knows how to get there."

Donna frowned at the expression on his face. "What are you going to do?"

"See Sam."

"Why?" Donna asked warily.

"To do what I should have done a long time ago. Break all the rules. I'm gonna fix what's really wrong here. I'm gonna give your husband what he wants. I'm gonna tell him the truth. And let *him* decide what to do next."

CHAPTER
TWENTY-TWO

It wasn't his name, so he had no reason to respond to it. After a minute, though, the sound became so annoying that it got his attention. So did the pain at the back of his head. Opening his eyes seemed like one of the ten most difficult things he had ever accomplished.

"C.J."

He wasn't C.J., but did anybody care? He began to think about the possibility of concussion as he rolled onto his right side and carefully pushed himself up onto his butt. His head felt like a smashed pumpkin.

"Are you all right?"

"No, I'm not all right," he said angrily.

"There's a lot of padding under that carpet. Get up. Come on, get up."

Patrice reached down to take his hand, but he greeted her with a glare and pushed her hand away. "Do you want to not touch me?" he snapped. "Please. Just get away from me."

"That's a funny reaction from somebody who was grabbing *me* a minute ago."

"Yeah, well, it's the only one I can come up with right now." Tossing the same stony expression at her every couple of seconds, he levered himself to his feet, wobbled over to the sofa and sat down. His head swam alarmingly along the way but settled down once he'd stopped moving. ''Give me a minute,'' he instructed Patrice. ''As soon as I can walk without falling on my face, I'll leave. I won't bother you anymore. You can do whatever you damn well please. Stay here. Don't stay here. It doesn't make any difference to me.''

''Good,'' she said.

''Good,'' he echoed.

She turned her back on him and went into the kitchen. At first he believed she'd abandoned him, which was certainly not a problem, but she came back with an ice bag in her hands. She approached him slowly, stopping a step or two away to consider him for a moment, then held the bag out to him.

''Here.''

He took it, applied it to his throbbing head, and quirked the corners of his mouth in the only offer of thanks he was willing to provide.

''I'm sorry.''

Sam peered at her. She was a long way from hand wringing, or tears, but she did seem at least a little chagrined that she'd hurt him, as if she'd never expected that to happen. Maybe, he thought crossly, the real C.J. was better trained to do the ol' tuck and roll when someone tripped him.

''You don't have to hover,'' he announced. ''I told you I'd leave as soon as my head stops spinning.''

''Maybe you ought to see a doctor.''

''I *am* a doctor.''

Exactly as he'd expected, she frowned and said, ''What?''

''Never mind.''

Dr. Beckett had already run down a list of symptoms of serious head injury. He'd eliminated most of them; a couple were still maybes but were of the ''watch and wait'' variety. *Don't fall asleep. As if I could fall asleep*

272

in this crazy *place. I'm starting not to remember what it feels like to sleep without . . .*

"Do you want some aspirin?"

"No, I don't want any aspirin."

That wasn't quite true. He did want aspirin. No, he corrected himself, what he really wanted was enough morphine to knock him out until the crocuses started to bloom. Preferably, until they started to bloom someplace other than Edwards Lake. Still scowling, he peeled himself up off the sofa and took a step toward the front door.

Patrice caught him before he could fall. "C.J.," she said again, and this time there *was* genuine concern in her voice. "Maybe I ought to take you to the emergency room."

"No hospital."

"C.J. . . ."

"Let go of me, all right? Just let go of me."

With visible reluctance, she let go, and this time he didn't wobble. "I'm going home," he grumbled. "With any luck, I'll be dead in the morning."

"C.J., stop that."

"Why? What do you care?"

"I . . ."

"What?"

"Nothing."

"*What?*"

"I'm sorry I hurt you. I . . ." She looked away, then back at him, then away again. "I'm sorry."

Sitting up had been enough of a challenge. Following Patrice up the stairs seemed like climbing Mount Everest. He did it one step at a time, clinging to the handrail. *You can make it,* he challenged himself. *You've been through worse than this.* By the time he reached the top, he had broken into a sweat. *And what comes next time? Being thrown out of a speeding car?*

"Patrice," he said.

She was lying on the bed where he'd first found her,

273

her face buried in one of the pillows. She wasn't making any noise, but he could tell by the shaking of her shoulders that she was crying again. Sam turned for a moment, as if he could actually see his anger going out the window.

"Patrice," he sighed.

She didn't answer him—not that he had expected her to—so he sat on the edge of the bed and rested a hand on her back.

"Patty . . ."

He remembered his sister Katie crying like this: silently, so as not to give her tormentors the satisfaction of knowing they'd broken her. Their mother was usually at fault, Tom usually the one who offered comfort. He would gather her up and let her vibrate furiously against him, while Sam stood in the doorway wondering how it was that Tom knew the right thing to do. How Tom could always make Katie smile again.

He had to shift farther over—Patrice's bed was three times as big as Katie's. She resisted him, but not very strenuously, and when he gathered her up she buried her face in his shoulder and clutched the sides of his jacket in her fists. What had Tom offered his sister, he wondered, to make her weeping stop? A piece of cake and some milk? A ride to town? Maybe it was just the embrace that worked. That seemed likely—for Katie, Tom had a magic touch. Tom had been Katie's hero.

And I'm . . . What am I? Am I supposed to be the hero here? I feel like . . . dammit, I feel like my head hurts. I don't want to be the hero. I want to go to sleep.

Maybe it was his own exhaustion, or maybe it was Patrice's weight pressed against him. One or the other—or both—made him topple onto the bed, wincing when his head met the pillow, with Patrice half on top of him. She nestled in against him as if this position was entirely natural for her (and he supposed it probably was). Her warmth felt good. Gradually, the pain in his head sub-

274

sided into a dull, if persistent, ache. And gradually, he fell asleep.

She woke him up. Again.

"Wha . . . what . . . ?" He fumbled, trying to extricate himself from the hands that were hauling him up into a sitting position. "What are you doing? Wait a minute . . ."

Then he heard the voice, and the sound of footfalls on the stairs. The overhead light exploded on, and the voice that had been calling Patrice's name demanded, "What the hell is *this*?"

One moment she was grappling with him; the next, she was standing upright beside the bed, flapping her arms and projecting distress.

"Michael," she said.

Michael?

"C.J.? What the *hell*."

His eyes finally agreed to let him examine the picture in front of him. Michael Frey, the man from the silver-framed portrait, the man he had talked to about missing shingles, was standing in the bedroom doorway. Michael Frey was pissed. No, Michael Frey was so far beyond pissed that NASA could have used him to launch the space shuttle.

"Michael?" Patrice hissed, sounding like a leaky tire. "He . . . he tried . . ."

Michael Frey's right hand shot out and seized the front of Sam's jacket. An incredible achievement, since Sam was certain Frey was still standing in the doorway. But no, Frey was right there, pressing his face into Sam's and generating enough heat to barbecue a steak. "C.J., what the *fuck*," he howled.

"I can explain," Sam said.

"Explain? No, you don't need to explain. I can see. I can see perfectly well."

"He dragged me up here," Patrice announced.

Suddenly Michael's hand was not there anymore. Sam

stumbled backward and landed on the edge of the bed.

"He dragged you? What do you mean, he 'dragged' you?"

Patrice straightened her rumpled clothes, glanced at her reflection in the mirror over her dresser, then sucked in a long, deep breath. "I was . . . out shopping. I came back, and he was in the house. He must have thought I wouldn't be back for a while. He was looking through the box. My jewelry box." She pointed to a carved wooden box sitting in the middle of the dresser. Michael looked at it, as did Sam; then both of them returned their attention to Patrice. "When I confronted him, he . . . he pushed me down on the bed, and . . ."

"I thought you said he dragged you up here," Michael said, challenging her.

"He . . . Yes. That's right."

With one eye on his wife, Michael crossed the room, picked up the jewelry box and upended it. A collection of bracelets, necklaces and earrings fell onto the dresser top. Michael shoved a hand through them and waved it at Sam. "There's nothing good here. The good pieces are all in the safety deposit box. Did you have a look at these, C.J.?"

"No," Sam told him.

"Then you tried to rape my wife."

"No."

"Michael," Patrice gasped. "Thank God you came. He's . . . I never could have . . . He's so much stronger than I am."

"Why didn't I hear anything?" Michael asked.

"What?"

"When I came into the house. Why didn't I hear anything? The sound of a struggle. I didn't hear anything."

"He had his hand over my mouth."

Sam had watched his sister's cats fight over a field mouse one summer afternoon. The cats had snarled and hissed at each other at first; then their battle shifted, put-

276

ting both of them on the same team and the mouse on the other. No matter what might evolve between the Freys tonight, he thought, *he* was going to come out the loser, like that mouse. With a little luck, he wouldn't get his head bitten off.

"It's not true, Michael," he said, as calmly as he could manage.

"You weren't trying to steal her jewelry."

"No."

"You told me you were going to see about getting the roof fixed," Frey commented. "I drove up here to take a look, see if anything else needed to be done. Thought it'd feel good to get out of the city for a day. And I find you up here in bed with my wife."

"We weren't in bed," Sam protested.

"No, you were *on* the bed. Pardon me."

"It's not—"

Frey cut Sam off with a wave of his jewelry-filled hand. "I deal with crimes of passion all the time. I've defended some people who killed their wives, or husbands, or lovers. Couldn't quite figure out how someone could get so angry that they'd murder somebody, and then disconnect, like it was someone else who pulled the trigger. Have you ever talked to one of those people? They seem a little puzzled, when the anger goes away. And hurt. Some of them cry. And I could never figure that out. It seemed strange. But now . . ." He paused, staring at the collection in his hand. "Tell me why, C.J. Do me that much. Tell me why you'd do something like this."

"I didn't try to rape your wife. And I wasn't trying to steal from you."

"Then my wife is a liar."

Sitting down, Sam felt very much smaller than Michael Frey. The real C.J. *was* smaller: his driver's license said he was five-foot-eight, and Frey was well over six feet tall. To Sam's eye the difference was a lot more significant, mostly due to Frey's bubbling fury. The man was angry enough to kill with his bare hands. And Sam doubted he'd be very puzzled about it afterward.

A picture pushed itself into Sam's mind: his parents, dancing to "The Tennessee Waltz" across the kitchen floor, with the creaking old fan providing counterpoint to the music. The looks on their faces were still vivid in his memory, tender, happy, almost glowing, as if they were each other's favorite thing to see.

Then he looked again at the Freys. "Yes," he said. "Your wife is a liar."

"Michael!" Patrice shrieked.

He could have turned the story around, he supposed. Made Patrice the villain. Somehow. Her overpowering him wasn't plausible, unless Michael was familiar with her ability to trip people. But if he thought long enough, he was sure he could come up with a fairy tale that would put Patrice entirely at fault.

Except that that's a lie too.

"Your wife and I have been having an affair," he said quietly. "For a long time now. More than a year. That's why she comes up here. I don't know if she's honestly got any interest in antiques. She comes up here alone, and we . . . have sex."

"That's not true," Patrice shrilled.

"I see," Michael said.

"She was lonely," Sam went on. "She said you weren't paying enough attention to her."

"I see."

"Michael, don't listen . . . ," Patrice began.

Frey shook his head. "Let the man talk. I want to hear the rest of this. Go on, C.J. So you were comforting my poor little neglected wife while I worked eighteen-hour days to pay for the house that you two rock-and-roll in. That right? You're getting even with that bastard Michael for working instead of 'paying attention' to the poor little wife. The poor little wife who drives a brand-new Mer-

278

cedes and wore a thirteen-thousand-dollar diamond neck-
lace to our anniversary party.''

"Maybe that's not what was important to her," Sam
suggested.

"No? Then why did she make a point of showing it
off to everyone who'd stand still long enough?" Frey
paused again, long enough to drop the jewelry onto the
dresser. "This is what it boils down to, I guess. I'm the
Bank of Michael. The man who writes the checks to
cover the diamonds and the car and the hairstylist and
the theater tickets and the cruise to the Greek islands."
He snickered, then added, "And the boob job. I kind of
thought that was for me, but I guess it was for you. You
enjoying them, C.J.? The doctor did nice work, I thought.
Of course he's the best. The boob king of the Upper East
Side."

"Michael . . ."

Sam and Patrice had spoken simultaneously. Frey
laughed at that, sounding as much pained as angry. "I
suppose," he mused, "you could say it's all my fault.
For marrying the wrong woman. All through college I
was with somebody else. I loved her. Pretty girl. She
had red hair. She made me smile. But my parents didn't
think she was the right choice. They didn't think she
would . . . 'complement me,' they said. I ought to pick
someone whose background was a little more like mine,
they said. Someone who'd understand what my goals
were and would support me. Not financially, but emo-
tionally. Someone who'd wait. Someone who'd be there.
And when I got to the top of the hill, well, then, we could
enjoy the fruits of my labor. Together." Frey laughed
again. "Well, Mom and Dad, I guess you got that one
wrong. And so did I, for listening. Or maybe I'm supposed to ignore this. Figure you were passing the time,
darling heart, like going to the theater and doing a little
shopping. Michael's busy? That's all right. You hop in

279

the car and come up here to the lake and let the caretaker make it all better.''

Michael's anger began to boil over. He shuddered, hard, then swung out the fist that had held Patrice's costume jewelry. It connected with the mirror, shattering the glass into a dozen pieces. When he pulled his hand back, blood was dribbling down his wrist.

''It was for you!'' he shouted at Patrice. ''It was for *us!*''

''Maybe that wasn't enough,'' Sam told him.

Michael stood staring at him, his wounded hand cupped in the palm of the other one. ''Thank you,'' he said after a moment. ''Thank you for being honest. You'll understand when I tell you that there's no way you can go on working for me.''

Sam nodded.

''Now, get out of here before I fucking kill you.''

Sam retreated as far as the hallway outside the bedroom. Leaving the house didn't seem wise; Michael was a lot bigger than Patrice, and there were a lot of heavy, blunt objects in their bedroom. It wasn't going to look good on his résumé, he decided, if he escaped Michael's wrath and left Patrice alone to face it. *I'm supposed to save this relationship?* he thought, leaning against the wall to fight the wooziness that had recaptured his head. *There's nothing here to save. You* must *be able to see that. Ziggy's wrong. Nothing I can say is going to keep these people together.*

''Al?'' he murmured. ''I could really use some help right now. I could really use some alternate choices.''

Of course, Al didn't show up.

''All right, then,'' he sighed. ''Then You do it. Give me a hint, okay? What do You want me to do here? If I go back in there, I'm gonna get my lights punched out.''

Of course, no one answered.

''All right,'' Sam groaned. ''One more time, then.''

He took a step toward the bedroom. He was going to

get pounded, he was absolutely sure. But he'd been pounded before. It came with the territory. Like being pursued by other men's wives. Like being drooled on by other men's dogs.

One more step.

Then he heard Michael Frey begin to weep.

He stopped, resting a hand against the wall to support himself, and listened. Anger had given way to anguish. Sam Beckett had been behind enough closed doors, and listened to enough people's pain, to know that Michael Frey was no danger to anyone . . . if he had ever been in the first place.

"Why is it so wrong? Why? It was what you wanted. It was . . ."

Sam left the house.

CHAPTER
TWENTY-THREE

Donna Alessi had a car phone—she'd used it to cut him
off at the pass before. So it didn't surprise Al at all to
find Verbena Beeks blocking his path.

"No, Al," she told him.

"Get out of my way," he told her.

They faced each other down one more time. In his
peripheral vision he could see Security approaching, one
from his left, one from his right. If he tried to keep moving toward the Imaging Chamber, they'd pick him up
bodily and carry him out of Control.

"He's got a right to know," he said to Beeks.

"Al," she said patiently, "we've talked about this for
hours on end. I know how difficult it is on everyone that
Sam doesn't know what he left behind. But—"

"No buts."

"Yes, Al, there *is* a but. You can't just burst in there
and do this. Have you thought this through at all? You
can't just tell him about Donna, as if you're telling him
he owns a leather-bound set of encyclopedias. Do you
know what this is going to do to him?"

"It's the *truth*."

"I know that, Al."

"He has a right to know he's not alone."

"He *is* alone, Al. I don't like that any more than you do. Sam was . . . is . . . my friend too. You seem to forget that when it's convenient for you. He's my friend too! I remember the look on his face when you took me to Havenwell. It cut through me just like a knife. Albert, I'd do anything in the world to help Sam. You *know* that! But this is wrong. You cannot do this. You'll tear him apart. He won't be able to do what he's meant to do."

Al tossed a look at the Security guards. They retreated a step, but remained in the room, standing at attention, ready to follow the orders they had received barely five minutes ago.

"What about what it does to *her*?" Al said.

"She's a strong woman, Al."

"Yeah? Explain that to me. Explain to me that every day that goes by doesn't wear her down a little more. Like water dripping on a rock."

"She can make it through this."

"Without seeing him. Without talking to him. Without having any contact with him."

"Yes, Al."

"The deal is, Beeks," Al began, and moved away from the Chamber door so that the guards would relax— or would at least think about relaxing. "The deal is, you don't understand what's going on inside her head. You can read all the books and talk to all the master shrinks and go to all the seminars you want, but you're never gonna understand until you've been there. You can tell me how much it hurts to give birth, and I could watch somebody do it, and I could say, 'Yeah, okay, I can see, it hurts a whole helluva lot. Point taken.' But the thing is, you got to have been there. You've got to feel the pain yourself. You remember, Beeks? I've *been* there. I know what she feels like because I've felt it."

Beeks was silent for a minute. She was considering options. "Al," she said finally, "come up to my office,

283

all right? We don't need to talk in front of Security."

"Come away from the Chamber, you mean."

"Please, Al."

"You thought things were gonna turn nasty, didn't you? When we simo-Leaped and Sam came home and she didn't want to let him go back into the Accelerator. She wanted him to stay here with her. Didn't care what happened to me. And you all thought my reaction was gonna be 'What a bitch. My life doesn't mean anything to her.' But you were wrong, weren't you? Because I know why she felt that way. I know why she wanted him to stay! I would have done the same thing, Beeks. If it had been me and Beth, I would have done the same thing. I would have sacrificed anybody who got in the way."

Verbena reached up and smudged the sweat off her upper lip with her thumb, making the gesture as casual as she could. "Al . . . I really don't think there's a quick fix here. I really think we ought to talk this over."

"Don't you think I understand?" Al bellowed.

She shuddered. "Yes. I think you understand . . . a little too well."

"He has a right to know about his life."

"And you have a right to call all the shots."

"Don't hand me that," Al snarled.

"What's more important to you, Al? Sam's right to know, or your right to tell him? Don't do this, I beg you. I'm begging you! You're upset. Don't do this before you calm down. Before you think it through. Before you consider what kind of damage you could cause. Please! Listen to me. You could be the man, Al, and Sam could be the butterfly. You might not be helping him. You could destroy him."

It was Al's turn to be silent. After he had stood stewing for a minute, Verbena turned and gestured the two Security guards away. They retreated again, but only as far as the corridor outside Control.

"I thought about her every minute of every day and

284

every night," Al murmured. "It was all I had. Thinking about how much we loved each other. Thinking about how good it would be when I finally went home and I could hold her in my arms again. I could feel her sometimes. As if she was really there. I could feel her. Smell her skin. It got me through, all those years. It got me through, and it's getting Donna through. But it doesn't have to! They could talk to each other. She could go in there." He jerked his head roughly in the direction of the Chamber door. "She couldn't touch him, but she could be close to him. Talk to him. See him. Don't you get what that would mean? To her. To him. To know somebody loves him."

"He knows you love him."

Al made a face. "Not the same, Beeks."

"It's enough of an anchor for him. That you're there. That you know him, care about him."

"Then why's he keep looking for somebody else?"

"Al . . ."

"You read all the reports. And I told you the stuff I didn't write down. The list gets longer and longer all the time, Beeksie. He keeps looking for somebody to love. Somebody makes nice-nice to him and he goes over like an oak tree. The list is longer than my arm. If I told him the girl he picked first is still here, maybe he'd stop looking. Maybe he'd be . . ."

"Happy?"

"Something."

"Would it be easier for you if Sam was happy?"

"I would lay down and die."

"Al, I really wish you wouldn't be flippant."

"Flippant?" Al shrilled. "Judas Priest, Beeks, what do you think? Of course it'd be easier for me if he was happy! It'd be easier for me if the whole world was something out of a John Denver song! Give me a break, would you? Give me one bleeding iota of credit. I *know* this ain't the quick fix. I *know* nothing I can tell Sam is

285

gonna make him dance off into the sunset. Two people got Sam Beckett into this mess: him and me. No, I'm not sure it's the right thing to do, but I think it's worth a try to tell him, 'Look, this is what you got in your bank account, kid. This is what the situation is.' I get tired of all the fiction, Beeks. I get tired of being Mr. Show Biz. I used to do that to make Trudy stop crying, but I was eight years old then. I'm not eight anymore. I'm sixty-five. I'm tired. You keep telling me that, and all right, I agree with you. I'm wiped out. And I figure it might help a little bit if I didn't have to go on lying all the god-damned time. I want to share the load.''

"Do you?" Verbena asked.

"I'm going in the Chamber now, and you're not gonna stop me."

"I really don't think you should."

"Yeah, well," Al said, "like the book says, 'Duly noted.' But I'm in charge here. See ya."

CHAPTER

TWENTY-FOUR

The night air outside the Freys' house was too cold to be comfortable. So was the concrete stoop outside their front door. Sam sat down anyway, resting his head in his hands, listening to the screaming match that was building up speed in the bedroom. Katie had never pitched a tantrum to rival the Freys', which made him hope that Michael and Patrice would run out of energy sometime before midnight and end up sniffling into their pillows the way Katie always had.

The cacophony of the Imaging Chamber door opening made him lift his head. *Gotta fix that,* he thought. *If I ever get back, definitely gotta fix that thing. It's way too noisy.*

But the noise was welcome.

"Sam?"

"Hi, Al."

"Jeez, Sam, you look terrible. You're pale. What happened?" Al's head tipped back—his eyes had been drawn to the Freys' bedroom window. "What's going on up there, World War III?"

"Pretty much," Sam said.

"What happened?"

With a shrug, Sam replied, "He caught us in bed together. Or on the bed together. Whatever."

"He *what*?"

"You heard me."

"You were . . . Jeez Louise, Sam, I thought you were . . . What'd you do that for?"

Sam smiled vaguely at his partner. "Says the world's chief proponent for free love."

"Yeah, but that's me, not you. Jeez, Sam."

"We weren't doing anything. I fell and hit my head. She got upset and started to cry, and I was comforting her."

"Comforting her?"

"Yes."

"Gee, Sam, aid and comfort to the enemy gets a lot of people into trouble. Man, would you listen to that?" Al shook his head in dismay. "Sounds like me and my fourth . . . no, third . . . It sounds like me and *all* of my wives. They'll start throwing lamps anytime now. I thought you were supposed to fix this, Sam, not turn the two of them into the Battling Manhattanites. This ain't Madison Square Garden. Jeeeeeez, would you listen to that?"

Sam replied softly, "I'm trying not to."

Al paced back and forth, examining his friend from every possible angle. Obviously, he did not like what he saw. With Sam watching him out of the corner of one eye, he punched information into the handlink, waited for Ziggy's response and snorted loudly at what he got. As punishment, he whomped the link with the flat of his hand, which produced a screech of protest from the computer.

"Ziggy still says you're here to mend a broken relationship," he said. "No change. Same percentages, same everything."

They spent a minute listening to the battle taking place upstairs. Neither one of the Freys was crying now; they

288

were hurling accusations at each other with barely enough time to breathe in between. None of what they were shouting was particularly nasty, but the tone in their voices provided venom that the substance of their words did not.

"All you're interested in is what I can *buy* you!"

"And I suppose you'd be happy living in a walk-up over on Eighth Avenue! Huh? You're the one who points out the Monet in the front hall! You! Not me!"

"Help me," Sam murmured.

"What?" Al tore his attention away from the bedroom. "Hey, Sam, I've been trying. Ziggy says—"

"Ziggy's wrong."

"Well . . . I guess you're right."

"You guess? Those people hate each other." Even though it had numbed his backside, the cold had cleared Sam's head. Trying to ignore the ache that still lingered in his neck, he got up from the stoop and began to walk away from the Freys' house. The sound of their voices followed him. It would cut its way into C.J.'s bungalow, he was sure, the same way the Stones tape had that afternoon.

No sleep tonight, he thought mournfully.

"I tried as hard as I could, Al," he told the Observer. "But it got to the point where I couldn't try anymore. I can't perpetuate a lie. What those people have . . . that's not what marriage is supposed to be. That's not what my parents taught me. What they showed me. I saw the way my parents looked at each other. I was only a kid, but it was so obvious, Al. They loved each other. It was right, their being together. They were part of each other. And Patrice and Michael . . . it's not right. There's no love there. I'm sorry. I can't go against what I believe. Don't ask me to do that."

"You okay, Sam?"

Sam turned to look at his partner. "No, I'm not okay.

Not particularly. I've had a lousy day. I accomplished nothing. How 'bout you?''

"Well . . .''

"What?''

"Nothing.''

"It's not nothing. You look like I did the time I had to confess to my mother that I couldn't put Tom's record player back together after I took it apart to see how it worked. You've got 'I'm guilty' written all over your face. What's the matter? You've got something to say. Say it.''

"Did you walk the dog?''

Sam's eyebrows shot up toward his hairline. "Why are you so concerned with that dog's bladder? All right, come on. I'll go get the dog. Come on!'' He hustled— as rapidly as the throb in his neck would allow—along the road to C.J.'s place, opened the front door and stepped aside. Rufus, who had apparently been napping, shambled out, greeted his substitute master with a broad grin and aimed himself in the direction of a big clump of weeds. "All right?'' Sam asked Al, who had lingered behind and was standing a good forty feet away.

A crash of shattering glass echoed down the road. Al turned toward the Freys' and commented, "There goes the first lamp. Right through the window.''

"I ought to call the police.''

"For what?'' Al frowned.

"To stop them from—''

Al shook his head again. "If they're like me and Maxine—and it sure sounds like they are—they're not gonna hurt each other. You throw stuff.'' He demonstrated, pretending to hurl the handlink at an invisible target. "Break dishes. Whatever makes the most noise. Our house used to look like London after the Blitz. Ruthie was big on throwing stuff too. She only hit me once, and that was an accident. Don't worry about it, Sam. They won't hurt

290

each other, and they can afford to fix a few broken windows. It's . . ."

The Observer was interrupted by Patrice, who erupted out her front door, stalked to her car, got in and sent the Mercedes roaring down the road, laying rubber in the process.

"See?" Al said. "Now nobody's gonna hurt anybody."

"But . . ."

"But what?"

"If it's not them, then what am I here to fix, Al? Other than making sure Rufus gets to pee regularly." At the sound of his name, the big dog shuffled over to Sam and pressed his head against Sam's hip. Sighing, Sam reached down and scratched the Newfie between his ears. "There's nobody else here, Al."

"I don't know, kid."

"It seems like I made things *worse*. If I hadn't Leaped in here, C.J. and Patrice would have continued their affair, Michael wouldn't have known anything about it . . . it would've all been status quo. I don't agree with that . . . I mean, you know how I feel about extramarital affairs."

"Loud and clear," Al concurred.

"But . . . instead of fixing a broken relationship, all I've done is break it apart completely."

Al was silent for a while, examining his friend's expression. Finally, he pulled a cigar out of his pocket, nipped off the end, then found his lighter. He studied the silver lighter for what seemed to Sam like a ridiculously long time.

"Maybe," he said, his gaze still on the lighter, "that was the right thing to do. Maybe sometimes you can't fix it. And you need to go with your gut."

"There has to be a time to say 'It's over.' "

"Yup." Al nodded.

"But I don't feel like it's the right thing, Al. I feel

291

bad about this. I made these people miserable.''

Al disagreed. ''They were already miserable. All you did was show 'em they were miserable.''

''That's not 'putting right what once went wrong.' ''

''True enough.''

''Then . . .''

''Look, Sam,'' Al said, still playing with his lighter, ''I know you like to be the golden boy. I know you like to be the one that the team carries around on their shoulders at the end of the game. But we don't win all the time. Remember? Success has nothing to do with Leaping. Sometimes the game's just over, and you move on. Don't beat yourself up. You did the best you could.'' Before Sam could argue the point, Al went on, ''Considering you didn't have much to work with. You can't fix something when there's a big chunk missing out of it. Like Ruthie's grandmother's teapot. She threw it, see, and afterwards we took it down to this guy Max who was a whiz at mending things. 'Max the Miracle Mender,' it said on his window. But he couldn't fix the teapot 'cause there was a big piece missing.''

''Is that supposed to make me feel better?'' Sam moaned.

''No.''

''Then why do you tell me these things?''

Al tossed the lighter into the air. It disappeared for a moment, then reappeared as he caught it deftly in his palm. He used it to light his cigar, took half a dozen rapid puffs, then began to toss the lighter into the air, again, again, again.

''Why are you giving him something like that? You're encouraging him to—''

''He's not going to give up smoking, Sam, you know that.''

''But you don't need to encourage him.''

''Hush.''

He'd been in the next room. It seemed like the movies,

where the characters step away to argue, and assume the person they've left sitting on the sofa can't hear them. He could hear. Every word. And Donna was right: he wasn't going to quit smoking, not on his birthday, not ever.

From Sam's perspective, the lighter was blinking in and out of existence. It caught the scientist's attention because of the magic of that . . . and for no other reason. Sam wasn't going to remember.

Not tonight.

"You're not alone, kid," Al told him.

"Yeah," Sam muttered.

"I mean it."

"Yeah. I know you mean it. But that doesn't help. See? It doesn't help me accomplish—"

"Sam."

"My head hurts," Sam groused. "I want to go to sleep."

"Sam, listen to me."

"No more stories, Al, okay? I really don't want to hear about Ruthie's grandmother's teapot and Max the Miracle Man. I want to . . ." Sam turned around, then did it again, a routine Rufus observed with great interest. Still grinning, the dog mimicked Sam by shuffling around in a circle, then lying down on the asphalt at Sam's feet. "I want to go home," Sam said.

"I know you do, kid."

"I want to sleep in my own bed, and wake up smelling fresh coffee and my mom's griddle cakes. I want to take a hot bath, and get dressed, and have a big breakfast, and do my chores. I want to talk to my dad. I want . . ."

His voice trailed off. He shoved his hands into the pockets of his jacket, found something there he didn't like and sputtered something that Al decided was some strangled profanity.

"What?" the Observer questioned.

Sam's right hand came out clutching a collection of

envelopes. "Their mail. I went over there to give her their mail. That's what did it—the coup de grâce. I was delivering the mail." Mumbling to himself, he stalked back down the road. "And it's nothing. Bills. Advertisements. A greeting card that's been forwarded all over the place."

Without checking to see whether Al was following, he plucked the biggest envelope from the group and flapped it in the air. Al, a few paces behind but catching up quickly, caught a glimpse of yellow labels on the front.

Just like our letters from Lovetz, he thought.

"Slow down, Sam," he cautioned. "You're gonna trip over something and kill yourself."

"At least then I could sleep."

"Sam, slow down."

Grudgingly, Sam obeyed the command. They fell into a little parade: the time traveler, the Observer and the dog who refused to be left behind.

"It's junk," Sam announced, and flapped the mail one more time.

And Al caught another glimpse. The return address on the greeting card that had Sam so bent out of shape said, in bold and distinctive block letters, "S. KELLER."

"Huh?" Al squeaked.

Sam spun around and stared at him. "What?"

"Let me see that. The card. Let me see." Even more grudgingly, Sam held it out. Al leaned in for a closer look, as if he expected the name to change before his eyes. *I imagined it. Yeah, it's on my mind, so I . . . No I didn't.* The lettering was still there. S. KELLER. Al began to laugh, softly at first, then in loud guffaws. "Go," he told Sam, gesturing with his cigar. "Quick. Put it in their mailbox. Hurry! Go on. Quick quick. Will you do it?"

Completely baffled, Sam (with Rufus trailing dutifully along) took his handful of junk mail to the Freys' front door, lifted the lid of their mailbox and dropped the envelopes inside. "Are you happy now?" he demanded of Al when he returned to the Observer's side.

"I hope so," Al told him.

"Would you mind explaining . . ."

"Hah," Al said, and went on laughing until tears began to drip down his face. "After all the . . . Oh, man. Junk mail. The little college girl who wanted to look after Isaac Asimov. Hoo hoo hoo." Unable to support himself on his shaking legs, Al folded down onto the floor of the Imaging Chamber. "Hey, Gooshie?" he said to the air above his head. "What'd we get in the mail? What? Yeah, I know it's Sunday. Gimme a break. Friday. What'd we get in the mail on Friday?" He cocked his head for a moment, listening to Gooshie's response, then turned to beam at Sam. "You fixed it, kid. Hoooo! You fixed it. Remind me never to doubt you. Sam the Miracle Man. You fixed it, and I didn't get a damn thing in the mail on Friday. Not a thing. Hoo hoo hoo."

"You've lost your mind," Sam told him.

"Let me tell you something, buddy," Al replied, trying to pick himself up off the floor and tumbling back down. "I came darn close."

"What did I fix?"

"Me. You fixed me."

"I did?"

"Close enough." Still racked with laughter, Al dropped his cigar, retrieved it, dropped it again, seized it and stuck it into his mouth. The look of disgust that earned from Sam sent him into fresh peals of hysteria. "Floor's clean," he said around the stogie. "Where's my lighter?" The silver lighter, invisible to Sam until Al picked it up, glittered—not in the moonlight shining on Maple Lane, but under the lights of the Imaging Chamber. "You know where I got this?" he asked, suddenly somber—or at least something that approached somber.

"From Tina," Sam replied.

"You sure?"

"Yes." Sam nodded. "You told me that. It was a gift from Tina. For your birthday. Why? Am I not supposed to know that?"

"You could have bought him something else."

"Like what? Hmmm? New clothes? What do I get for a man who wears uniforms all day and sleeps in the nude?"

"How do you know that?"

"He told me."

"Why would he tell you something like that? That's a very personal thing to tell my . . . a book. You could have bought him a book."

"I gave him books for Christmas."

"Why would he tell you he sleeps in the nude?"

"Hush, Sam."

"Don't hush me. I'm not five."

"He can hear you."

"What?"

"Al."

"What?"

"It's over," Sam said. "I'll take your word for it. I fixed it. Now, will you please tell me what was wrong?"

"It's gone. It's fixed."

Groaning, Sam sat down on the asphalt so that he didn't have to look at the top of the Observer's head. For a moment, the thousands of miles and the sixteen years that separated them didn't matter. Then the moment passed and Sam became all too aware that he was sitting on the cold ground at Edwards Lake and that his best friend was someone he could not touch.

"Al," he said, not letting the Observer's teary-eyed grin affect him, "please don't do this to me. It's not fair. I used to have a life. There, *there*, where you are, that used to be my life. We built it together. What happened there mattered to me. It still matters to me."

"I know it does," Al said.

"Then bend the rules. You've always done that, right

from the beginning, when you told me my name. Please. If there's a problem, tell me what's wrong.''

''Weitzman.''

''Weitzman?''

''Yeah. You know. Same old same old. Weitzman was here stirring up trouble. Said the Project doesn't produce any visible results. Lotsa money and nothing to show for it. You know all about it. He sang the same song before you Leaped. It's nothing we can't handle.''

''If it's the same old same old, then why were you so upset?''

''I wasn't.''

''Don't lie to me, Al.''

''You wouldn't have hired us if we couldn't do the job.''

Sam made a face. ''I didn't 'hire' you.''

''No, you're right, you didn't.'' Al puffed furiously on the cigar, prompting another grimace from his partner. ''You adopted me. I told you to get lost, and you didn't listen. That kid, that corporal, told you you ought to get lost too, and you didn't listen to him either. I was the project before the Project. You shoulda adopted one of those starving kids in Ethiopia that they advertise in the magazines. Would've been easier.''

''Maybe,'' Sam agreed. ''At least a starving Ethiopian kid wouldn't stonewall me as much as you do.''

''There's rules, Sam.''

''I know there are rules. I wrote the rules. At least, you keep telling me I did.''

''You did.''

''Who gave you that lighter, Al?''

''What lighter? Tina.''

''No, she didn't. You wouldn't be making a big deal out of flinging it around where I can see it if she had. Somebody else gave it to you, and you want me to figure out who. You're transparent, Al. You're like Saran Wrap. You're like my mother, tearing toaster ads out of the newspaper and leaving them under my dad's coffee cup.''

"Sam . . ."

"It's my *life*, Al.''

"Okay. Okay.'' Al held the lighter between the thumb and forefinger of his right hand. His initials were engraved into it: AAC. He turned that side toward Sam. "It doesn't look familiar?''

"Is it supposed to?''

"You tossed it around. That day. Before I got it. You were mad about it.''

"I was?''

"Yup. Said it encouraged me to keep smoking.''

"That's stupid,'' Sam said. "If you didn't light those stinking cigars with that, you'd light them with matches. Or those cheap plastic lighters. Or a stove burner. You lit one off a welding torch one day.''

"You remember that.''

"Yes.''

"And you don't remember D . . .''

He said the rest of her name to a burst of blue-white light.

CHAPTER
TWENTY-FIVE

"Your timing *sucks*," he told the ceiling.

It was a long way above his head. He knew exactly how far, he supposed; he'd examined the specs enough times. Thirty feet? Thirty-five?

With his lighter in one hand and his cigar and the handlink in the other, he got to his feet and glared at his surroundings. All white. White walls, white floor, white ceiling, thirty feet above his head. Or thirty-five.

Or thirty.

The seven faces in Control were smiling at him when he walked down the ramp. Six of them were, anyway; Toolie Gibson looked as terrified as she always did. Then she too forced something that tried to be a smile but was more like the rictus of a corpse.

"Are you okay, Al?" Donna asked. "You look pretty worn out."

"Huh," Al replied. "Is Weitzman here?"

"What? No. Was he supposed to be?"

"Did you get any mail on Friday?"

"Friday? I'm not sure. A magazine, I think. Oh, and a thank-you note from Sam's niece. Was I supposed to get something else?"

"Phone calls? D'you get phone calls?"

"Al, I don't—"

Another voice crooned at him, seeming to come from everywhere and nowhere at the same time. "May I suggest a brief rest period, Admiral Calavicci? Your vital signs are . . ."

"Stop peeking at my vital signs," Al grunted.

". . . which is not conducive to . . ."

"She's right," Donna said. "I think some sleep would do you a world of good, now that Sam's Leaped. You're . . . acting a little strange. And," she added, trying to flip the situation around, "you haven't even had a chance to look at your package from the book club. It's the new Stephen King book, isn't it?"

"Huh," Al said.

"Al . . ."

"Would you like me to outline the results of Dr. Beckett's Leap?" Ziggy purred. "Just as I predicted—"

Al cut her off with a snort of distress. "You didn't predict anything, you overpriced collection of microchips. You said he was there to mend a broken relationship. He spent three days trying to repair a mess."

"Which was, if you will calm yourself long enough to consider the matter, Admiral, most distinctly not my fault. As you recall, I never specified which relationship Dr. Beckett was intended to repair."

"It might have been nice if you *had*," Al barked.

"I had insufficient data," Ziggy sniffed.

"She's right, Al," Donna said. "You can't make chocolate chip cookies without the chocolate chips."

Al gaped at her. "When did you turn into Rebecca of Sunnybrook Farm?"

"Come on." Still smiling, Donna took the link out of his hand and turned it over to Gooshie, then wrapped an arm around his waist and steered him toward the door to the corridor. When they were far enough down the hall to avoid being overheard by anyone in Control, she stopped him. "I know you were trying to tell Sam about

300

me. Right before he Leaped. Thank you. I think it was a mistake, but thank you.''

He leaned back against the wall to get a better look at her. Nothing in her expression or her posture said she was upset. Resigned, yes. He'd seen that in her a lot. It didn't appeal to him any more now than it had any of the other times. "Do you remember why I was trying to tell him?"

"I . . . No. It seems like I ought to, but no."

"He fixed it. He didn't mend their relationship, he ended it. Then he dropped a letter from Mikey's old girl-friend into the mailbox, and bing-bang-boom. The whole problem went away." *Magic,* he thought wryly. *Mikey divorces Patty, marries Stephanie, Stephanie never dates Joe Boyle, never sees Jack Ryan's memo, never hooks up with Lovetz.* Al squeezed his hand into a fist, then popped it open. "Poof. All gone."

"And you're not going to tell me what it was."

"I don't think that would accomplish anything."

Donna winced. "What you mean is, you think it would upset me. Sometimes I'm not sure whether your protecting me from things actually helps. I'm not sure blissful ignorance is the right answer."

"Do you feel 'blissful'?" Al asked.

"I will."

"When he comes home."

"Yes."

"He loves you, sweetie."

"I know."

Movement at the end of the corridor caught his eye: Gibson, clipboard in hand, peering at him from the door-way. The moment his gaze fell on her, she disappeared.

"Am I scary?" he demanded of Donna.

"Sometimes."

"That kid."

"What kid? Petula?"

"Is that her name?" Al scowled. "She's petrified.

301

What did I do? Tell me. What'd I ever do to her?''

Donna shrugged and leaned against the wall on the opposite side of the corridor. ''I don't think it's so much that she's scared of you, as that she's in awe of you.''

''Me.''

''Umm-hmmm.''

''What the hell for?''

''You really need to ask me that question?''

''If I didn't, I wouldn't ask it. You've been around Beeks way too long.''

''Maybe.'' Her expression turned wistful as she re-wrapped her arm around Al's middle and ushered him the rest of the way down the hall to the elevator. She said nothing more until they had reached his office and she had poured them each a cup of coffee out of his coffeemaker. Who had started the thing running in the first place, Al could only guess; he was sure it hadn't been him. He held tightly onto his mug as she sat him down on the cracked and worn leather sofa he'd had shipped here from Star Bright—the only remnant of his life there worth keeping, he thought, except for the kid who'd come down to bother him in Aux-B.

''I got it out of her one night,'' Donna went on, ''after she'd dropped her clipboard. She kept trying to pick it up, and couldn't manage, like it was a greased pig. So I brought her up to the lounge, and we ate some Rocky Road, and after about an hour she 'fessed up.''

''To what?''

''To everything. Why she came here.''

''She's a spy.''

''She was born on the night you orbited the Moon.''

Al took a big gulp of his coffee and scowled at Donna over the rim of his mug. ''And?''

''And her dad told her about it later. About your mission. About you being a POW and how you'd made it into the space program. It didn't seem fair, he said, that after you'd tried so hard, you were the one left behind.

302

That you had to sit in the command module while the other two got to walk on the Moon. You were a hero, he said, because sometimes the heroes are the ones who get left behind.'' Donna paused long enough to sip at her coffee, blowing on it a couple of times first to cool it off. "There's more to it than that—he was a vet. I think he met you at some point, thought you were a fine officer. Something along those lines. But she spent a lot of years thinking about the man who got left behind. Saw your picture in *People* magazine. Wanted to work with you. That was her dream. Her dad pulled a lot of strings. And now she's here. And in absolute, quaking, shivering awe of you.''

"That's the dumbest thing I ever heard,'' Al snorted, and swigged down more of his coffee.

"Is it?''

"Gimme a break, Alessi. It's bad enough I haven't had a good night's sleep in three hundred years. Now you wanna make me upchuck on top of it.''

"It's the truth.''

Al dropped his nearly empty mug onto his desk with a thump and hauled butt out the door. He knew Donna was behind him, even though her sneakers made almost no sound pattering against the floor in his wake. He barreled into the front office of the Records Department less than a minute later, and collided with a woman he was certain he had never seen before. The double handful of plastic file tags the woman was holding exploded into the air and began to flutter to the floor around her like dead leaves dropping off a tree.

Apparently she had never seen him before, either. Or else she was all too familiar with him, but his rank (and his bluster) didn't impress her. "Now look what you've done,'' she announced with a very noticeable British accent as she bent to gather up her scattered tags. "It took me ten minutes to put these in order.''

An apology got halfway to his lips before he swallowed it. Behind him, Donna coughed, prompting him to turn around. "You're bringing the entire Records Department to its knees, Albert," she murmured.

Al grumbled at her as he skirted around the woman into the nest of inner offices and file rooms. There, finally, he found Toolie Gibson carefully arranging papers into a row of manila folders.

"Kid," Al said.

Toolie wheeled around, lost her footing and crashed into the side of the desk her folders lay on top of, spilling half her papers onto the floor. "Admiral?" she squeaked. "Oh God. I'm sorry. Oh. God."

"Kid. Calm down, would you?"

"Sir. All right, sir."

"Gibson. Jeez Louise. Calm down before the top of your head blows off."

"Sir? Oh. Ohhh, boy. I'm sorry, sir."

"For what? Making a mess?" Waving her away, Al crouched down, gathered up her papers and held them out to her. She took them hesitantly, as if she expected them to be as hot as a branding iron. "Gibson, look," Al said, holding back a sigh. "There's no reason to . . ." He paused, aware of Donna standing in the doorway, watching him destroy yet another piece of the Records Department. He *did* want her to hear what he had to say; on the other hand, his making Gibson vibrate like a tuning fork was not something he needed other eyes to see. "Gibson," he said quietly. "I'm just a guy."

"Sir, oh, no, sir, you're . . . not."

"Don't build stuff up in your mind, Gibson. I'm just a guy. See?" Carefully, he held out his hand to her. She stared at it, as she would at a coiled rattler, he thought, but he pushed it a little farther and curled his fingers around hers. "See?" he repeated.

Her lips moved. She didn't produce any sound, but he could read the words well enough. "Sir. Oh. No. Sir."

304

"Admiral. You can skip the 'sir.' Oh, what the . . . You can call me Al."

Her mouth opened, then closed.

"Gibson . . ." This time the sigh got out. "The thing is, Gibson . . ." He stopped, watching her eyes watch him. She had pretty eyes. Bright blue. What was she doing here, working weird hours buried underneath the New Mexico desert? For *him*? The idea made the hairs on the back of his neck stand on end. A pretty kid like this, who ought to be out somewhere where she could enjoy the daylight. Playing Snow White at Disneyland. Selling ice cream cones. Something like that. Not buried way down here, shaking like a leaf because of *him. I'm no hero, kid,* he thought. But what he said was "It looked pretty good from up above."

She was still speechless, but her right eyebrow lifted a little.

"The Moon. I got the bird's eye view. Man, it was pretty. You know, Gibson, most people'll never get that far. They have to look at it from down here."

"I know," she mumbled.

He glanced around, located her blue clipboard with its collection of energy consumption reports, grabbed it and a ballpoint pen and scribbled his signature at the bottom of the top sheet. "There," he told her.

Then he left the room. In the outer office, the woman he hadn't recognized was still cleaning up the mess he'd created there.

"Sorry," he told her absently.

"Well," she said.

At least this one wasn't terrified of him—that had to be good for something, though what the something might be, he didn't stop to consider. Al locked eyes with her for a moment, until the steadiness of her gaze made him blink. *Davina Pereira,* her nametag said. *Davina? Per . . . what? How the hell do you pronounce that? Bad enough I'm supposed to remember two hundred faces and*

305

two hundred names, he complained to himself, *why do they all have to be complicated? Whatever happened to naming kids things like Cathy? Or Susie? Or . . .* She was standing in front of him again now, arms folded over her chest, watching him. *Or Donna. Easiest name in the world, and the kid forgot it. Ahhh, Sam.*

"Sorry," he told Pereira again, this time a little more genuinely.

He was halfway to the elevator when he heard Toolie Gibson say, very clearly, "Oh, God."

Then heard Pereira respond, just as clearly, "He does have nice eyes, doesn't he? I always thought that. Beautiful eyes."

You've still got it, Calavicci, he thought fleetingly.

The coffee in his mug was cold. He waited for Donna to close the door of his office, then hoisted the mug and drank the last mouthful.

"Ugh," Donna said. "You could have warmed that up."

"I have to swallow crap every day of my life, Alessi," he replied. He watched her freshen her coffee, then sank back down onto the leather sofa, listening to its familiar creak and crackle. "Like this whole 'hero' thing. I'm nobody's hero."

"I think you'd be surprised."

"I've never gotten a job I didn't apply for. I signed up for that second tour to 'Nam. My idea. I wanted to be the one who ran the CM. And I was the one who said 'okay, fine' to Sam Beckett. My fault. Mea culpa. Nobody gets any medals for wading around in a mess that they dropped themselves into. If they do, then somebody oughta rethink *that* process."

"Then who *is* the hero here?"

"Your husband," Al said, but it sounded more like a suggestion than a statement.

"Because he didn't volunteer?"

306

"Because he doesn't give up."

"And you do."

"I'm telling you, Alessi, you've been around Beeks too long. You two oughta take your act on the road: the Incredible Headshrinking Sisters. I'm telling you, I'm doing what gets the job done. No more than that."

"Hah," Donna said.

"What about you?" he countered, slouching back into the sofa cushions. "You could put a hundred different women into this spot you're in, and every last one of 'em would've bagged it out of here a long time ago."

"I love him, Al," Donna murmured. "I can't leave."

"Neither can he."

"What do you mean?"

She sat down at the other end of the sofa, swizzling her coffee around in the mug and deliberately not looking at Al. After a minute he reached out and cupped her cheek in his hand. "I mean," he explained, "that he remembers. Maybe it's walled off somewhere, down inside his head, but he remembers. I used to think it didn't mean anything, that God, Time, or Whoever sent him to Lawrence College by coincidence. But the look on his face . . . I've never seen a look on anybody's face like when he found you. I told him no. 'No, Sam, bad, bad idea, that's the one who dumped you.' But he didn't listen. He forgot all about how much he'd gotten hurt. He wanted you back. Not so he could say, 'There, I won that one. I got the last word.' He loves you. And he looks for you everywhere he goes."

Donna frowned at that. "It's not . . ."

"It's true. All these women he makes the calf eyes at, they remind him of you."

"That's ridiculous."

"You don't see him. I see him. His brain's all magnafoozled, and all he remembers is that he's looking for something. But it's all blocked off inside his head. So he sees somebody that's close, somebody who has your

307

eyes, or your smile, or who fights with him like you do, and he thinks that's it.''

"Albert, you're not helping.''

"Then think about when he came home.''

She did. He could tell she was trying very hard not to cry, but her eyes welled up suddenly. There was nothing nearby she could wipe them with, so she slipped into his bathroom and returned with a fistful of toilet paper.

"Whatever works,'' Al told her wryly.

"I want so badly to hold him, Al. I want him here, close to me.''

"I know you do, kid. Believe me, I know. You make it one day, and one more, and one more. You think, you dream, you remember. You keep them close up here.'' He pointed to his temple. "If you concentrate real hard, it works. You can touch them, and smell them, and taste them. And you go one day at a time. There *is* an end to it. And every minute gets you a little bit closer.''

They were both thinking the same thing: that there had been no victory at the end of Al's road. He hadn't reclaimed the one he loved.

"Don't not be here when he comes home,'' Al told her.

"It hurts, Al.''

"You still want me to tell you everything? That's not gonna make it feel any better.''

"It lets me be there. With him.''

"He told me . . .''

Donna's eyes seized his. "Tell me.''

" 'I saw the way my parents looked at each other. I was only a kid, but it was so obvious, Al. They loved each other. It was right.' '' He watched her cling to each of the words. "He went back and got you, Donna. He went back and made things right. For himself. For you. He wouldn't abandon you now. He'll come back. Just make sure you're here when he gets here.''

"And you.''

"Hmmm?"

"He wants you here too. You're his best friend."

They looked at each other for a long time. A couple of minutes, Al thought, but down here time got bent out of shape. What applied to the rest of the world didn't apply here . . . except for a few basic concepts. Al's gaze drifted across the room and landed on a framed photograph of him and Sam, taken on the Committee's big photo op day. They were leaning on shovels, even though nobody was going to dig anything out here with a shovel. The shovels had enormous red bows on the handles.

"Who thought up all this cornball bullpucky?" he had whispered to Sam.

The kid was wearing one of those off-the-rack suits, beige cotton-and-polyester, with sweat stains the size of hubcaps under the arms. He, Al, was in uniform, complete with fruit salad. "Bullpucky," Al hissed. Sam leaned on his shovel, and *flash! flash! flash!* A week later a manila envelope containing one of the pictures had landed on Al's bunk.

Sam had a funny look in his eyes in the photo. Intent, and stubborn, but more than that. Excited, like a kid on Christmas morning. He would've dug this complex with a shovel if he'd had to, Al thought. Would've dug it with his bare hands.

Might've even taken that cheap suit off to do it.

"He asked us to dance, and we both said yes," Al told Donna. *And I'm not mentioning that we had to. We've both got that "Property of Sam Beckett" stamp on us.* "Listen," he added, hoping to distract her, "Tina's out of town till tomorrow. And I hate to eat alone. Do me a favor and have dinner with me."

"Do *you* a favor?" Donna echoed.

"Ummm-hmmm."

She pretended to consider the request, then nodded. "All right. I guess I can do *you* a favor." He offered her

309

a broad smile that she managed to match. "I need you here too, Al," she told him.

"Huh," Al said. "Well . . . where the hell else would I go?"

STAR WARS
YOUNG JEDI KNIGHTS

SHARDS OF ALDERAAN

Jacen and Jaina set off for the Alderaan system,
determined to salvage a piece of the shattered planet as a
gift for their mother. But amid the ghosts of a dead world,
the twins are in for a lethal surprise: some ghosts still
live. A long-lost enemy of the Solo family is about to
return...

Kevin J. Anderson and Rebecca Moesta

___1-57297-207-6/$5.99

VISIT THE PUTNAM BERKLEY BOOKSTORE CAFÉ ON THE INTERNET:
http://www.berkley.com/berkley

*COMING IN APRIL '97 STAR WARS: YOUNG JEDI KNIGHTS:
DIVERSITY ALLIANCE*

Payable in U.S. funds. No cash accepted. Postage & handling: $1.75 for one book, 75¢ for each
additional. Maximum postage $5.50. Prices, postage and handling charges may change without
notice. Visa, Amex, MasterCard call 1-800-788-6262, ext. 1, or fax 1-201-933-2316; refer to ad #691

Or, check above books and send this order form to:	Bill my: ☐ Visa ☐ MasterCard ☐ Amex _____(expires)
The Berkley Publishing Group	Card#
P.O. Box 12289, Dept. B	Daytime Phone # _____ ($10 minimum)
Newark, NJ 07101-5289	Signature

Please allow 4-6 weeks for delivery. **Or enclosed is my:** ☐ check ☐ money order
Foreign and Canadian delivery 8-12 weeks.

Ship to:

Name _____	Book Total	$_____
Address _____	Applicable Sales Tax (NY, NJ, PA, CA, GST Can.)	$_____
City _____	Postage & Handling	$_____
State/ZIP _____	Total Amount Due	$_____

Bill to: Name _____

Address _____ City _____

State/ZIP _____